John Laband has long been the accepted authority on Anglo-Zulu War studies and his new work, *The Fall of Rorke's Drift*, is proof of his expertise. He has skilfully taken the accepted history of this campaign and woven therein some fascinating questions and concepts to examine the 'what ifs' should events and incidents have turned out differently. It is known that battle plans change when the first shot is fired and the Zulu War is no exception. In a number of crucial incidents during this bitter campaign against the Zulus the results could have been so very different with far reaching results for Africa and the British Empire. Until now, and due to the complexities of this campaign, consideration of these alternatives is an undertaking that has hitherto been avoided by historians. John Laband's *The Fall of Rorke's Drift* is a master class in analysis and highly thought-provoking.

Adrian Greaves
Author of *Isandlwana* and *Rorke's Drift*

⎯⎯⎯⎯⎯

It has been portrayed in a classic movie and written about in numerous history books. Some of these works have provided different perspectives, but the ending is always the same, the British come out on top, and win eleven Victoria Crosses in the process. In considering how the Zulus might have won at Rorke's Drift, and what that victory would have meant for both the British Empire in Southern Africa and the Zulu Nation at the point of its ultimate crisis, John Laband has provided a refreshing new take on a battle that looms large in the popular imagination. This is alternative history at its thought-provoking best, and in painting such a convincing scenario the author reminds us that he is a master of his subject.

Professor Tony Pollard
Centre for Battlefield Archaeology, University of Glasgow

⎯⎯⎯⎯⎯

From his expert knowledge of British and Zulu sources, and with the consummate skill of an established historian, John Laband has fashioned a highly credible alternate history of events that might have followed the fall of Rorke's Drift on 22 January 1879. It is an entertaining and thought-provoking exercise in counter-factual history.

Professor Ian Beckett
Author of *Isandlwana* (Brassey's) and *Rorke's Drift & Isandlwana* (Oxford University Press)

The Fall of Rorke's Drift

AN ALTERNATE HISTORY OF
The Anglo-Zulu War of 1879

John Laband

Foreword by
Ian Knight

Greenhill Books

The Fall of Rorke's Drift
First published in 2019 by
Greenhill Books,
c/o Pen & Sword Books Ltd,
47 Church Street, Barnsley,
S. Yorkshire, S70 2AS

www.greenhillbooks.com
contact@greenhillbooks.com

ISBN: 978–1–78438–373–2

CIP data records for this title are available from the British Library

Printed and bound in England by TJ International, Padstow
Designed and typeset by Donald Sommerville

Typeset in 11.2/14.4 pt Adobe Caslon Pro

Contents

Lists of Maps and Plates   vii

Foreword *by Ian Knight*   ix

Author's Note   xv

PART I   Preparing for War: The British

Chapter 1   Priming the Engine of War   3

Chapter 2   Mustering the Troops   13

Chapter 3   Planning the Invasion   23

PART II   Preparing for War: The AmaZulu

Chapter 4   Resolving to Resist   31

Chapter 5   The Zulu Way of War   37

Chapter 6   Mustering for a Defensive Campaign   44

PART III   Repulsing the British Invasion

Chapter 7   The Enemy Has Taken Our Camp   53

Chapter 8   Camped among the Bodies   61

Chapter 9   We Seemed Very Few   66

Chapter 10   Falling Back to Natal   85

PART IV   Defence of the Natal and Transvaal Borders

Chapter 11   Thrown Open to Zulu Invasion   95

Chapter 12   Securing the Ncome Border against Invasion   104

Chapter 13   Agitation in the Transvaal against British Rule   110

Chapter 14   Securing the Thukela Frontier against Invasion   114

Chapter 15   Stalemate along the Borders   125

PART V   Revolts and Reinforcements

Chapter 16   Fresh Threats to British Security   139
Chapter 17   The Transvaal Rebellion   145
Chapter 18   Anxious to Conclude an Honourable Peace   151

PART VI   Battle and Negotiation

Chapter 19   Planning for the Zulu Offensive   161
Chapter 20   Wood's Fortified Laager   167
Chapter 21   The Battle of Koppie Allein   174
Chapter 22   The Transvaal Regains its Independence   185
Chapter 23   Making Peace with the Zulu Kingdom   193

              Afterword   202

              Notes   207
              Select Bibliography   225
              Acknowledgements   233
              Index   234

Maps and Plates

———◦◦◦———

Maps

South Africa in 1879   pages 4–5
Zulu Campaign 1879   52
Battle of Rorke's Drift, 22 January 1879   74
Chelmsford's withdrawal to Helpmekaar 23–24 January 1879   87
The Transvaal Territory in 1879   146
Wood's Fortified Laager at Koppie Allein   171
Battle of Koppie Allein 20 March 1879   176

Plates

Sir Bartle Frere. *(Collection of Ian Knight)*

Colonel Frederick Stanley. *(Wikimedia Commons)*

Lord Chelmsford. *(Collection of Ian Knight)*

Sir Michael Hicks Beach. *(Collection of Ian Knight)*

British infantry in Pietermaritzburg. *(Collection of Ian Knight)*

Sir Theophilus Shepstone. *(Pietermaritzburg Archives Repository, C. 418)*

Sir Henry Bulwer. *(Collection of Ian Knight)*

Brevet Lt.-Col. John North Crealock. *(Author's collection)*

Lord Chelmsford on campaign in Zululand. *(Author's collection)*

Field Marshal the Duke of Cambridge. *(Author's collection)*

King Cetshwayo kaMpande. *(Collection of Ian Knight)*

Isandlwana Mountain. *(Collection of Ian Knight)*

Lieutenant Gonville Bromhead, 24th Regiment, who died gallantly in the defence of Rorke's Drift.* *(Collection of Ian Knight)*

Lieutenant John Chard, Royal Engineers. *(Collection of Ian Knight)*
Umntwana Dabulamanzi kaMpande, Zulu commander at Rorke's
   Drift, with the hunter-trader John Dunn. *(Collection of Ian Knight)*
Surgeon James Reynolds tending Fred Hitch as the defences of
   Rorke's Drift are finally overwhelmed.* *(Collection of Ian Knight)*
Zulu *amabutho* charging in open order. *(Author's collection)*
Chelmsford's retreat on 23 January 1879.* *(Collection of Ian Knight)*
The British fortified post at Helmekaar. *(Collection of Ian Knight)*
Brevet Major John Chard wearing the Victoria Cross awarded after
   his unsuccessful defence of Rorke's Drift.* *(Collection of Ian Knight)*
Greytown laager and Fort Moore. *(Collection of Ian Knight)*
Colonel Evelyn Wood. *(Author's collection)*
Brevet Lieutenant-Colonel Redvers Buller. *(Collection of Ron Sheeley)*
Colonel Wood's laager at Koppie Allein.* *(Collection of Ian Knight)*
Colonel Charles Pearson. *(Collection of Ian Knight)*
Fort Tenedos and Fort Pearson. *(Collection of Ian Knight)*
The interior of the fort at Utrecht. *(Collection of Ian Knight)*
Paul Kruger, in 1879 a member of the rebel Boers' Triumvirate.*
   (National Archives Repository Pretoria, TAB 36951)
Piet Joubert, *Kommandant-Generaal* of the Boer forces in 1879.*
   (National Archives Repository Pretoria, TAB 18009)
Petrus Lafras Uys and his four sons. *(Collection of Ian Knight)*
Men of Wood's Irregulars. *(Collection of Ian Knight)*
A unit of the Natal Native Horse. *(Collection of Ian Knight)*
Mounted Infantry of Wood's escort. *(Collection of Ian Knight)*
AmaZulu attacking Koppie Allein.* *(Collection of Ian Knight)*
Buller's horsemen at Koppie Allein.* *(Collection of Ian Knight)*
King Cetshwayo berating Mnyamana for his defeat at Koppie Allein
   and threatening his execution.* *(Collection of Ian Knight)*
Cetshwayo's emissaries meeting British officials. *(Author's collection)*.
The Zulu delegation accepting the British terms on 17 April 1879.*
   (Collection of Ian Knight)
Henry Francis Fynn, first British Resident in Zululand.
   (Collection of Ian Knight)

* *Asterisks indicate images whose captions reflect this book's*
alternate history.

Foreword

What if . . . ?

It is, perhaps, the most tempting question in any study of history, particularly when addressed to a turning point in which great stakes hung obviously in the balance. What if King Harold's housecarls had stood their ground at Hastings in 1066 and defeated William of Normandy, as they had defeated Harold's brother Tostig at Stamford Bridge just three weeks before? How would England have developed across the medieval era when retaining a Saxon nobility? How might this have shaped the unfolding balance of power across Europe and Scandinavia? Would the English language, culture and arts have developed along radically different lines? What if, in more modern times, Napoleon had elected not to invade Russia, or if Blücher had been delayed on the road to join Wellington at Waterloo, or if Napoleon's grand cavalry charge at the height of the battle had broken the British infantry squares? Would Napoleon have successfully restored the Empire, would France have reasserted herself at the expense of a hamstrung Britain? And to what long-term effect on Europe? Would the upsurge of British influence around the world which followed in the wake of Napoleon's defeat ever have happened at all? What if Britain had not decided to contest its influence with Russia in Afghanistan in the 1830s, paving the way for nearly two centuries of foreign intervention and conflict which have fuelled the rise of modern terrorist movements? During the American Civil War what if Pickett's charge had broken the Union centre at Gettysburg, and Lee had been able to press further towards Washington? Would the Union have sued for peace, and would the European powers have recognised the Confederacy? What, then, would have become of slavery in the Americas, and would the United States today be two different countries? What if the Tsar had not dismissed the Duma in February 1917, pushing Russia further towards revolution – and what if Kerensky's Provisional Government had decided not to continue the unpopular war with Germany over the next few months, fuelling the rise of the Bolsheviks? How might the history of the twentieth century have been re-written without the rise of communism? What if the Luftwaffe's Eagle Day had succeeded in breaking the RAF, enabling Hitler's projected invasion of Britain – Operation Sealion – to proceed successfully?

Yet there is more to the 'what if?' game than the arcane conversations of history buffs in their cups. It is the reminder that history only appears fixed in retrospect; momentous events accrue a weight of inevitability with time, and – ironically – the more they are studied, analysed and debated, the more significance becomes attached to events that, at the time, might have seemed random or even inconsequential. In searching out the threads that shaped a particular course of action after the event, of tracing an often-complex web of causal links towards a single conclusion, it is possible to fall into the trap in retrospect of assuming that the conclusion was inevitable when in fact it almost never was. This is particularly true of the study of warfare; the line between a bold masterstroke and a foolhardy gamble, between masterly caution and hopeless inactivity, is often a fine one, and all the more so when the bullets start flying. The fate of armies, of nations, of peoples, of ideologies, might seem shaped by the grinding fate of the universe through the prism of hindsight, yet as often as not the road to now was paved with false turnings – any one of which might, at any point, have produced a different outcome.

And thus it certainly was of the Anglo-Zulu War of 1879. While it is perhaps easy now to see a fatal hubris in the bullish forward policies adopted by the British High Commissioner to southern Africa in the late 1870s, Sir Henry Edward Bartle Frere, and a dangerous com-placency in the attitudes of his commander in the field, Lieutenant-General Lord Chelmsford, there were few enough dissenting voices in late 1878. Despite the odd humanitarian voice, like that of William Colenso, Bishop of Natal, calling out in the darkness against the injustice of British intervention in Zululand, most British officials and settlers on the spot considered it to be a good thing – or at least a necessary one. As British influence spread across southern Africa, stimulated by the discovery of mineral wealth, and challenged by determinedly independent Boer republics, the existence of a militarily and economically strong African society like the Zulu was seen as an anachronism. And fearful though the reputation of the Zulu army was, few believed that even a small professional British army, equipped with the latest weapons and led by an experienced commander, could not quickly disperse an enemy which was still largely reliant on close-quarter combat with spears.

And so it might have proved, of course. In some respects the battle of Isandlwana was the most bizarre of true 'what ifs'; what if, against some 1,700 British and African troops, armed with two field guns and the best part of a thousand rifles, the Zulus had actually won? It was an idea that very few pundits thought likely before the event, and indeed, to add weight to their scepticism, it would prove largely unique, the greatest defeat of the British Army during the Victorian era, so extraordinary that the butcher's bill outweighed comparable setbacks across sixty years. Only the disastrous Retreat from Kabul in 1842 – which was not a single action but a week-long catalogue of slaughter, much of it inflicted upon defenceless camp-followers – produced a more melancholy body-count.

Yet Isandlwana did happen, spinning history away in a very different direction from that which the architects of the war had envisioned, and damning Lord Chelmsford's reputation ever since. In hindsight, it is easy to see a folly in his decision to split his forces on the eve of battle, knowing that there were Zulus nearby, yet not knowing of their strength or intentions. But Chelmsford, like most military commanders in the field at some point or another, found himself in a situation which demanded that decision; sitting in his tent at Isandlwana at 2 a.m. on the morning of Wednesday 22 January 1879, reading a note informing him that his reconnaissance parties had blundered into a Zulu force twelve miles from camp, he had to react. From the first, Chelmsford had actively sought a confrontation with the Zulu army, convinced by his recent experience on the Eastern Cape Frontier that the Zulus would be no match for the Martini-

Henry rifle in open battle. Now the Zulus appeared to be coming – but were they coming for him? Were they in fact planning to slip into the rugged country which he knew lay on his right flank, and past him into the largely unprotected colony of Natal? He could stay with all his command at Isandlwana and prepare for a battle at first light – but what if all that greeted him the following dawn was a line of smoke rising from burning civilian farms along the Natal border? In that moment he at least had a sense of where the Zulus might be – and fate had given him a chance to intercept them. Yet there was no chance that he could pack up his camp and advance his entire column quickly towards the Zulus – it would simply take too long, his column would be acutely vulnerable on the march, and in any case they were bound to be gone by the time he got there. Instead, he decided to take a mobile element of his force out to surprise the Zulus, whilst leaving enough men – surely? – to guard the camp.

It was a gamble, and had it paid off Lord Chelmsford might have won a decisive victory in the Mangeni hills that morning, and ended the Anglo-Zulu War a fortnight after it had begun – although ironically it is unlikely that history would have remembered either him, or the Zulu people, quite so much if he had.

He didn't, of course; Lord Chelmsford lost his gamble, his bold masterstroke dissolved into a foolhardy gamble and the garrison at Isandlwana – and a good few of the attackers, too – paid the price with their lives.

But what then if the Zulu reserve, who in the aftermath of Isandlwana went on to attack the British border post at Rorke's Drift, had not been defeated? What if they had over-run the post, laying the whole of the central Natal borders open to a Zulu counter-attack? There is certainly no denying the heroism of the defenders at Rorke's Drift but the fact that the battle was a piece of very good news at the end of a very bad day undoubtedly influenced British and colonial attitudes towards the action. It was widely trumpeted in the press as having saved Natal from Zulu invasion. If it had fallen, would the Zulus have rampaged through the colony, destroying smaller settlements and laying waste even to the colonial capital at Pietermaritzburg? Would the African population of Natal have seized an opportunity to forge a united front with the Zulu and – in a phrase popular at the time, and which reveals more than a touch of the strain under which white settlers had lived in Natal for half a century, and considerably less understanding of the true relationship between the Zulu kingdom and the African chiefdoms of Natal – 'driven the white man into the sea'?

It is those hanging possibilities which 'alternative history' can address, weighing up not only how outcomes might have been different over an hour or two of desperate fighting, but picking out the viable threads of consequence from the fog of dread, wishful thinking and confusion expressed at the time. Professor John Laband is the leading historian of the nineteenth-century Zulu kingdom; in his definitive study, *Rope of Sand: The Rise and Fall of the Zulu Kingdom*, he has looked at the forces which brought the nation together, and the pressures which ultimately shook it apart. He has devoted much of his study to the Anglo-Zulu War itself, and he knows the ground intimately; indeed, his *Illustrated Guide to the Anglo-Zulu War* with Paul Thompson provided the first comprehensive mapping of the sites. He is uniquely qualified to marshal a full range of sources from both sides of the conflict to address that most intriguing 'what if?' of the war, and his conclusions are well-reasoned and perhaps to some might be surprising.

What if the Zulus really had won at Rorke's Drift?

*Ian Knight**

* Author of *Zulu Rising: The Epic Story of iSandlwana and Rorke's Drift*.

Author's Note

'Historical truth is not what took place; it is what
we think took place.' *Jorge Luis Borges*

I was on holiday with a group of old friends, all of us historians, and all of us colleagues before retirement picked us off and scattered us about. Merrily together again, we were discussing over dinner the various projects we were still engaged in despite our years, those scholarly conference papers, articles and books. Over the main course I diffidently let drop that I was busy with a fascinating exercise in 'alternate history'. Suddenly, the jolly clatter of cutlery stilled, and I found myself the object of perplexed, if not pitying, stares. 'I hope', one of my comrades finally exclaimed in distressed tones while the others nodded in earnest support, 'that you will be writing this . . . this work, under a *nom de plume*? After all, you have your professional reputation to consider!'

What a disappointment I shall be to those concerned friends. Disregarding their advice, this alternate history appears under my real name and in the firm belief that it is precisely my reputation as an historian of the Anglo-Zulu War that lends it its piquancy. On the strength of my previous publications, readers who pick up this book will be confident that they can rely on my presentation of historical events. Yet after a number of pages they will realise that they are being presented with a melange of fact and fiction, of events that did take place and those that did not – but might well have.

These 'might-have-beens' are the point of the book. I believe that history is the record of human endeavour, in which the motives and decisions of the actors might be carefully considered, but could just as well be ill-informed, contradictory, self-delusionary, panicked or plain inexplicable. The consequent course of events is therefore more often than not accidental or contingent, and history is certainly not marching inexorably towards some pre-determined destination. Thus the course of the Anglo-Zulu War was not fore-ordained, although its actual outcome was likely if the opposed political, social, economic, technological and military aspects of the two sides are taken into account. Yet, against all the apparent odds the amaZulu gained a great victory at Isandlwana over the British. However, it was swiftly negated on the very same day by the morale boost the British gained from their heroic defence of Rorke's Drift. But that battle was close-run, and what might have been the consequences if the amaZulu had succeeded in capturing the post? These conceivable outcomes are what I explore.

In doing so, I employ my close knowledge of the individual leaders involved, of the societies in which they operated, and of events as they played out in fact. To my mind, one of the shortcomings of the extensive literature on the Anglo-Zulu War is the tendency to treat the campaign in isolation. By situating the war in the wider context of Britain's world-wide imperial commitments, and by bringing Britain's fraught relations with the Boers of the Transvaal Territory and various African polities in southern Africa to the fore, I introduce factors that might well have come into play had Rorke's Drift actually fallen to the amaZulu. In creating this alternate scenario, I rigorously confine myself to playing only with the actual pieces on the board in 1878–9 (no extra-terrestrials here!), and do not permit myself to move them in any direction not strictly constrained by what would have been both conceivable and possible at the time. Even so, whether I have succeeded or failed in presenting a persuasive alternate history of the Anglo-Zulu War is for the reader to decide.

PART I

Preparing for War: The British

Chapter 1

Priming the Engine of War

—————>•⋘—————

Sitting straight as a ramrod in the saddle, trim in the short, snugly fitting blue patrol jacket that set off his lanky frame, his eyes peering out fretfully from his aquiline, heavily bearded face from under the low brim of his domed felt helmet – headgear of a singular design favoured by the British in India where he had served for sixteen years – Lieutenant-General Lord Chelmsford was 'as full of go' as ever.[1] He was not an officer given to delegation and firmly believed that 'A commander must ride about and see the country for himself, or he will never be able to handle his troops properly.'[2] So, on the cloudy morning of 22 January 1879 he was adhering to his own precept as he and his small staff trotted sedately about the broken Zulu countryside east of Hlazakazi Mountain, the grass tall and green from the teeming summer rains. Eleven days before, on 11 January 1879, the British forces he commanded had invaded the Zulu kingdom, and Chelmsford was reconnoitring the country ahead while waiting for those troops of No. 3 Column still in their camp at the foot of Isandlwana Mountain some ten miles to the west to begin moving up to the new campsite he had selected.

Just over a year before, on 1 February 1878, the Hon. Frederic Thesiger (it was not until 5 October 1878 that he succeeded his father as the second Baron Chelmsford) had been selected as General Officer Commanding in South Africa with the local rank of lieutenant-general.[3] His commission was to bring the Ninth Cape Frontier War against the Gcaleka and Ngqika amaXhosa (who for a century had been bitterly resisting the progressive seizure of their land by white colonists) to a successful conclusion. Chelmsford, a product of Eton

- African settlements
(e.g.) **Bapedi** African chiefdoms/kingdoms
Fort

N

B E C H U A

K a l a h a r i   D e s e r t

Batlharo

Dithakong •
Manyeding •

Batlhap

Dikgatlhong •
**GRIQUALAND
WEST** **Griqua**
Griquatown •
(British
Possession)

Kimb

Orange (Garieb)

Prieska
Hopetown

CAPE COLONY
(British Possession)

Cole

Victoria West •

*ATLANTIC
OCEAN*

Graaff-Reinet •

Great Karoo

Oudtshoorn •

Robben Island
Cape Town •
Simon's Town •

Stellenbosch •
Swellendam •

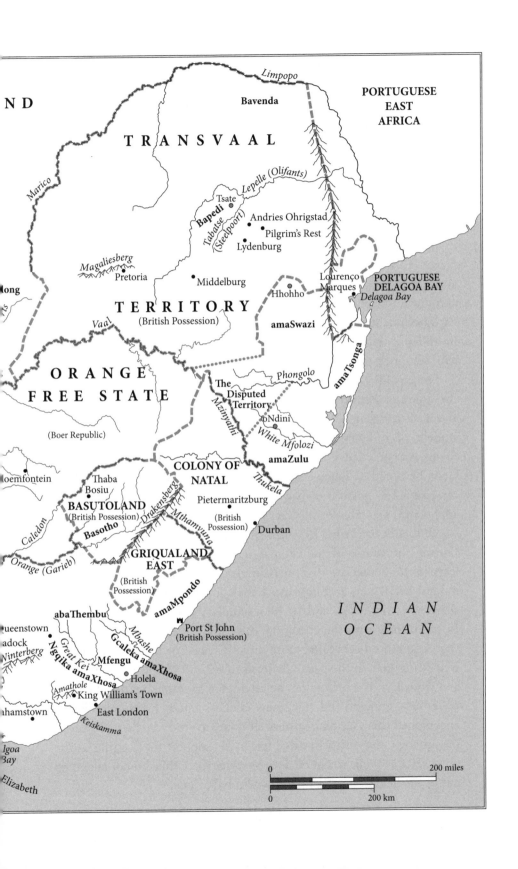

N D

Limpopo

PORTUGUESE
EAST
AFRICA

Bavenda

T R A N S V A A L

Marico

Lepelle (Olifants)

Tsate
Bapedi
Tabatse
(*Steelpoort*)
Andries Ohrigstad
Pilgrim's Rest
Lydenburg

Magaliesberg
Pretoria

long

Middelburg

Lourenço
Marques
PORTUGUESE
DELAGOA BAY
Delagoa Bay

Hhohho

T E R R I T O R Y
(British Possession)

amaSwazi

Vaal

amaTsonga

O R A N G E

FREE STATE

The
Disputed
Territory
Phongolo

Mzinyathi

oNdini

White Mfolozi

(Boer Republic)

oemfontein
Thaba
Bosiu

COLONY OF
NATAL

amaZulu

Thukela

BASUTOLAND
(British Possession)

Drakensberg
Mthamvuna

Pietermaritzburg

(British
Possession)

Durban

Basotho

Caledon

GRIQUALAND
EAST

Orange (Garieb)

(British
Possession)

amaMpondo

abaThembu

Port St John
(British Possession)

I N D I A N

O C E A N

ueenstown
adock
Winterberg

Mbashe

Ngqika amaXhosa

Great Kei

Mfengu

Gcaleka amaXhosa

Holela

Amathole
King William's Town

East London

ahamstown

Keiskamma

lgoa
Bay

Elizabeth

0   200 miles

0   200 km

and the Grenadier Guards, was a well-connected, aristocratic officer who had seen active service in the Crimean War (1855–6), the Indian Mutiny (1858) and the Abyssinian campaign (1868). He had spent the greater part of his military career in India, although since 1874 he had held home commands pending a suitable overseas posting. Although by nature somewhat withdrawn, he was able to adopt a genial manner in company and was an effective public speaker. He was a keen participant in amateur theatricals (so intrinsic to social life in India); nor did he hide his musical accomplishment as a clarinet player. To balance these unmilitary interests, and as befitted his class and upbringing, he remained fond of field sports and outdoor activities and always displayed considerable physical energy. Like many of his background he was compassionate towards animals, and soon after invading Zululand he 'even licked [thrashed] with his own hand a white-bullock-driver . . . for brutality to oxen'.[4]

During his military career Chelmsford had primarily performed the staff and administrative duties at which he excelled, and the Cape was his first independent command in the field. Always a conscientious student of military matters, this was his first opportunity to put theory into practice. Consequently, it was hardly surprising that in the Cape he opted to follow the book, and in his conduct of the Xhosa campaign Chelmsford displayed a certain conservative reluctance to adapt familiar, orthodox military practices to colonial conditions. Even so, he finally succeeded by mid-1878 in breaking all Xhosa resistance. During the course of the campaign the troops under his command learned to appreciate his unfailingly gentlemanly, courteous and modest behaviour, and he earned their loyalty for his willingness to share their hardships and by his exemplary calm resolve under fire. In conformity with the changing attitudes of the late Victorian army that required officers to be more directly concerned about their men's well-being than in the past, Chelmsford set an example of moderation and frugality. As a teetotaller, he attempted to stamp out drunkenness under his command and, to combat idleness among his young officers, encouraged them (as he had himself done) to study further. However, his inherent conservatism came out in his support for flogging as the most suitable punishment on active service since this did not take men out of the field as imprisonment would have done.[5]

Chelmsford's relatively inexpensive victory over the amaXhosa in terms of both casualties and expenditure encouraged Sir Bartle Frere – who since March 1877 had been simultaneously the Governor of the Cape, High Commissioner for South Africa and the Commander-in-Chief of the British forces stationed there – to contemplate further military adventures.

A personal friend of Queen Victoria and of her heir, Edward, Prince of Wales – who like him, was a crack shot – there was no doubting Frere's intellectual powers and forceful personality any more than his ruthless ambition. Nevertheless, to the small number of those determined to be unimpressed, his outstanding qualities were somewhat obscured by his unctuously hypocritical and 'oily, almost old womanly manner and appearance'.[6] A more typical response was that of a susceptible young staff officer in South Africa who wrote of the tall, dapper High Commissioner with his brown eyes, sharp nose and chin, greying hair and thick moustache: 'He had a wonderfully quiet, deliberate manner of speaking, never hesitating and never at a loss for the right word, giving you the idea that whatever might be the subject of the conversation he knew much more about it than any of his audience.'[7]

His multiple offices gave Frere considerable discretion to act as he deemed fit in South Africa because the members of the British government were poorly informed concerning the sub-continent's distant affairs. When these came up in Cabinet they tended to defer to the Colonial Secretary, but he depended in turn on the knowledge of the permanent officials in the Colonial Office, and especially on the advice of the senior administrator on the spot, namely, Frere, the High Commissioner. And Frere was a man in whom the government was inclined to place implicit trust because of his unparalleled experience and vision as a celebrated administrator in British India. Moreover, Frere's responsible posts in India had trained him to act on his own initiative and he never drew back from taking vigorous executive action once he considered it necessary. He saw much scope for such action in South Africa

Frere's mission in South Africa was to consummate the process of creating a confederation of the British-ruled, white settler colonies which the Tories under Benjamin Disraeli, the Earl of Beaconsfield, had set in motion when they came to power in the general election of February 1874. Their reasoning was that it was essential to secure the two sea routes to India, by far Britain's most important imperial possession. One of these was via Cape Colony at the tip of Africa and the other was through the Suez Canal. If South Africa were to fulfil its prime purpose as a stable, unassailable strategic link on the way to India, then it was necessary to ensure that the region was politically and economically integrated. If this were effected South Africa would gain an improved capacity to pay for its own defence, thus relieving the British exchequer of the burden of maintaining the expensive garrisons of British troops there.

However, the presence of British troops would remain necessary until the perceived military threat posed to British-ruled territory by the still independent African polities in southern Africa was eliminated. The Basotho had already apparently been dealt with when in 1868 the rulers of their mountainous kingdom had placed themselves under British protection to prevent the Boers of the neighbouring Republic of the Orange Free State from seizing more of their land. In 1871 the British had passed the administration of Basutoland (as they called it) on to the Cape Colony. The successful Ninth Cape Frontier War was a truly significant step towards ending African resistance; while another was the contemporaneous, but much more minor Northern Border War of April–November 1878 in the region of the British colony of Griqualand West that finally subjugated the Griqua, Batlhaping, Prieska amaXhosa, Korana and Khoesan.[8] The amaMpondo between the Cape's recently pacified eastern frontier and the southern borders of the Colony of Natal were effectively overawed when on 31 August 1878 the British occupied the mouth of the Mzimvubu (St John's) River and built and garrisoned a fort there. Frere was consequently absolutely confident that after only one or two more campaigns the Africans of southern Africa would all be effectively cowed and disarmed. That would allow him to place the capstone on confederation, and the government had intimated that once he had done so that he would be retained as the first Governor-General of the new South African dominion he had created. Simultaneously, as a great architect of empire, he would receive the ultimate official accolade he craved and be raised to the peerage.[9]

To Frere's way of thinking – in which he was enthusiastically abetted by celebrated colonial officials whom white settlers regarded as experts on African affairs – even though the stubbornly independent Bapedi on the eastern borders of the British Transvaal Territory (annexed on 12 April 1877) presented a nagging difficulty that most certainly had to be resolved, it was the Zulu kingdom with its fearsome military reputation that posed the greatest standing threat to the security and stability of the confederation he was building. More than that, Frere developed the obsessively held belief that the Zulu kingdom was the political and military lynchpin of a developing, co-ordinated movement of African resistance to British rule, and that King Cetshwayo kaSenzangakhona was 'the head and moving spirit' of this alarming combination.[10]

Consequently, no sooner had Chelmsford finished off the amaXhosa in the Eastern Cape and Major Charles Warren had all but brought the fighting in Griqualand West to a close, than Frere trained his eyes unblinkingly on the amaZulu. Negotiations and fair words, Frere believed, would never succeed in disarming and neutralising Zululand, and it was therefore essential to 'draw the Monster's teeth and claws' by brute force.[11] But how easily could this be done? Frere was seduced by Chelmsford's successful operations in the Eastern Cape to believe that the amaZulu could similarly be subdued at the price of a minor campaign.[12] Nor was he shaken in this conviction when his Military Secretary, Captain Henry Hallam Parr, relayed the prescient words of an old Gcaleka Xhosa warrior: "You have beaten us well, but there," says he, pointing eastward – "there are the AmaZulu warriors! Can you beat them? They say not! Go and try. Don't trouble any more about us, but beat *them*, and we shall be quiet enough."[13]

Dismissing such warnings, Frere instructed Chelmsford, whom he knew well from their days together in India when from 1862 to 1867 he had held the enormously prestigious post of Governor of Bombay, to begin making military preparations for war against the Zulu kingdom. Basking in the formal thanks of the Cape parliament for winning the Ninth Cape Frontier War, and made a KCB by the grateful British government, Chelmsford duly set up his headquarters on 9 August 1878 in Pietermaritzburg, the scrappy little capital of the Colony of Natal, a British possession since 1843, that abutted the Zulu kingdom on the south.

It must not be supposed, however, that while Frere deliberately continued down the road of military confrontation with the amaZulu, that the government in London was in favour of unnecessary and distracting South African military complications. Frere's immediate superior as Colonial Secretary was Sir Michael Hicks Beach, an aloof but strikingly handsome man – a veritable '*scagliola apollo*'[14] – known as 'Black Michael' for his biting tongue.[15] Hicks Beach was exceedingly mindful of Britain's overstretched global reach, and in particular of Russia's determination to menace the British Empire in India.

Russian victory in the Russo-Turkish War of 1877–8 had not only expanded Russian influence over the entire Balkans, but seemed set to gain control of Constantinople and the Dardanelles. If that ever came to pass, the eastern Mediterranean would be opened to Russia's Black Sea fleet and Britain's vital route to India through the Suez Canal be endangered. True, the urgently convened Berlin Congress of July 1878 had agreed that the Russians must withdraw from the Balkans, but the Russian army refused to comply immediately, and until August 1879 it remained at Adrianople, within a day's march of Constantinople. For as long as it did so, and the 'Eastern Question' remained unresolved, the British Navy took up station in the Dardanelles and relations between Russia and Britain continued dangerously strained to the point of war. To make matters even more perilous, once Russia found itself thwarted in the Balkans, it redoubled its involvement in the 'Great Game', that grand contest of imperial competition, espionage and conquest in Central Asia. A Russian diplomatic ploy for an alliance with the Amir of Afghanistan that would have brought Russian influence right up to North-West Frontier of India provoked an alarmed response by the theatrical Viceroy of India, Lord Lytton, who himself was pursuing an aggressive 'forward policy' in the region. In November 1878 Lytton blundered into the protracted Second Anglo-Afghan War that saw several drastic defeats of British arms before being brought to a conclusion in 1881 in the midst of divisive domestic debate.[16]

Hicks Beach consequently became ever more anxious as it dawned on him that Frere was determined to open yet another military front and force on a war with Cetshwayo. Towards the end of 1878 the Colonial Secretary made it clear in a series of increasingly alarmed messages that Frere must desist.[17] Frere nevertheless encouraged

Chelmsford to continue with his preparations. He knew that he risked his distinguished career, but he was confident that any censure for disobeying explicit instructions would be wiped away by his triumphant clinching of South African confederation. So, even while he continued to prime the engine of war, he used his experience as a seasoned administrator to play the system and coolly exploited the sluggish communications with London to keep the Cabinet off balance and a step or two behind the fast-moving crisis he was orchestrating.

These unsatisfactory international communications would play a significant part in the disastrous Zulu campaign about to unfold, and require a word of explanation. Communication between South Africa and Britain had been entirely by sea until the laying in 1874 of a trans-Atlantic undersea telegraph cable connecting Brazil to Europe by way of São Vicente in the Cape Verde Islands off the west coast of Africa and then via the island of Madeira 1,300 miles to the north.[18] But once a telegraphed message from London reached either Madeira or São Vicente, it languished there awaiting the weekly mail steamer that was to carry it to Cape Town, a slow sea voyage that took about three weeks from the former island and a fortnight from the latter – and longer if the weather were poor. In April 1878 Cape Town was linked overland by copper telegraph cable to Durban, the port of Natal, that since 1864 had been connected thus to Pietermaritzburg. Pietermaritzburg in turn was connected to Pretoria in the Transvaal Territory. Official telegraphic messages were often sent in cypher, and if they were of any length could take secretaries or officials several hours to formulate and decypher, thus delaying their immediate transmission. All this meant that a telegraphed message from Pietermaritzburg (where Frere took up post on 28 September 1878) to London took 15–21 days to reach its destination, or between two and three weeks. Yet this was rapid compared to the time it took despatches too lengthy to telegraph to arrive in London. They went the entire way by sea from Durban, and this would take about five weeks. The upshot was that even the most urgent official business between the High Commissioner in South Africa and the Colonial Office required at least five weeks to turn about and could take ten or more. Consequently, the British government's decisions concerning the distant sub-continent were unavoidably all too often scarcely more than belated responses to events that had already taken place.[19]

By fending off directives from Hicks Beach with slow-moving despatches detailing his objections, Frere kept the pot at a low simmer while he completed his preparations for war with Zululand. The strain told, and Frere began to suffer from neuralgic headaches brought on, Chelmsford believed, by all the 'perpetual worry and annoyance' he was being subjected to.[20] But in the end Frere's machinations paid off. When Chelmsford invaded Zululand on 11 January 1879 on the expiry of the ultimatum served on King Cetshwayo on 11 December, Frere was able (as he always intended) to present his superiors with a *fait accompli*. All that remained was for Chelmsford to ensure a quick victory that would mollify London and transform potential censure into approbation. Unfortunately for Frere, it was to prove easier to humbug his superiors in Whitehall than to defeat the amaZulu.

Chapter 2

Mustering the Troops

———◦——

While planning for the Zululand campaign, Chelmsford rapidly came to appreciate that it would be more difficult to conduct than Frere had imagined. He had no doubt that once his British regular infantry, the main striking force in any of Britain's nineteenth-century imperial expeditions, met the Zulu in a pitched battle that they must prevail. This was a time in the British Army when tactical ideas were being transformed, and the late eighteenth-century lesson in North America was being relearned that fighting a mobile enemy over broken terrain required open deployment. Breech-loading rifles had a further revolutionary effect on the battlefield as it was now possible to fire more rapidly and to do so while kneeling or lying down. Section 49 of the official War Office manual of 1877, *Field Exercise and Evolutions of Infantry*, stipulated that when extending for the attack an interval of three paces should be allowed for each file, and that when skirmishing the interval could be increased 'according to circumstances'.[1] Critically for Chelmsford's future tactics in South Africa, the experience of the recent Ninth Cape Frontier War seemed conclusive. Like the amaXhosa, the amaZulu were expected to make a mass charge. In the Eastern Cape the weight of disciplined fire from the infantry's Martini-Henry rifles – even when in extended skirmishing order – supported by light 7-pounder guns, had proved sufficient to halt the amaXhosa in their tracks. At that critical moment when they began to waver the mounted troops, supported by black auxiliaries, had sallied out and turned the enemy's withdrawal into a rout.[2]

All too many generals seem cursed to fight their current campaign based on the flawed assumption that it will be a repetition of the last, and Chelmsford was no exception. It was not as if Chelmsford and his officers did not understand the Zulu military system, for Chelmsford, who took an intellectual interest in the profession of arms, had made sure to have a booklet prepared describing the Zulu way of war and the best means of responding to it.[3] The problem, even before Chelmsford's army set foot in Zululand, was that neither Chelmsford nor his officers seem to have believed what they read about the fighting qualities of the amaZulu. True, they were assumed to be tougher adversaries than the amaXhosa, but the British underrated them nonetheless. Naturally, their ingrained sense of racial, cultural and technological superiority to 'savages' would have played its usual part, but it must also be acknowledged that recent experiences in the Ninth Cape Frontier War contributed greatly to their over-confidence. As Major Cornelius Clery, Principal Staff Officer to No. 3 Column, later put it, 'the easy promenade' in the Cape made 'all go into this business with light hearts'.[4]

When Chelmsford took up his South African command on 4 March 1878, some 5,000 imperial troops and two batteries of guns (but no regular cavalry) were stationed in British territories there. A battery of six guns was the Royal Artillery's usual tactical unit, but it was often broken up into three divisions of two guns, each worked by two officers and forty-five men. The standard infantry tactical unit was the battalion, on service comprising a headquarters and eight companies, nominally made up of thirty officers and 866 men (although the field establishment could be considerably lower). The standard overseas dress for infantry (and for Royal Engineers) was a single-breasted unlined scarlet frock with five brass buttons (Rifle regiments wore dark green) and different coloured facings for each regiment on cuffs and collar. Trousers were dark blue with a scarlet welt down the outside seam and were tucked into black leather leggings. The Royal Artillery wore dark blue tunics with scarlet collars and blue trousers with a wide red stripe. Officers wore either the scarlet frock or the blue patrol jacket preferred in the field. Highland regiments wore kilts and their officers trews. Headgear was the light cork sun helmet, covered in white canvas normally stained brown on campaign with the shiny brass shako-plate removed.[5]

When contemplating the coming Zulu campaign Chelmsford took stock of the troops at his disposal.[6] In Cape Colony (ruled by the British since 1806) there were two batteries of Royal Artillery (N Battery, 5th Brigade and No. 11, 7th Brigade); the 7th Company, Royal Engineers; and the 1st and 2nd Battalions, 24th (Second Warwickshire) Regiment, and the 88th Regiment (Connaught Rangers). The 2nd Battalion, 3rd Regiment (East Kent, The Buffs), and the 80th Regiment (Staffordshire Volunteers) were stationed in the Colony of Natal. The headquarters and supply and remount centre of the British garrison in Natal was at Fort Napier, established on 31 August 1843 on the low hill overlooking Pietermaritzburg from the west. It consisted of a rectangle of brick-built barracks enclosed by earthworks constructed in 1876 and strengthened by stone redoubts and gun emplacements.[7]

Two more of the precious battalions of infantry were stationed in the Transvaal Territory. (Until the British annexed it in 1877 as an essential brick in the confederation edifice, the Transvaal had been the previously independent but bankrupt Zuid-Afrikaansche Republiek [ZAR] established in the mid-nineteenth century by Boers emigrating from the Cape into the interior of South Africa on what has come to be known as the Great Trek.)[8] The 1st Battalion, 13th Regiment (First Somersetshire), Prince Albert's Light Infantry initially formed the garrison in Pretoria, the capital of the Transvaal Territory, but soon proved insufficient for the task. The major cause of the ZAR's weakness at the time of the British annexation was its defeat in the Boer–Pedi War of 1876–7 by the forces of Sekhukhune woaSekwati, the canny Maroteng paramount of the Bapedi. The Bapedi abutting the eastern Transvaal habitually avoided set-piece battles and stood on the defensive in their fortified hilltop strongholds. In defending them they made excellent use of the firearms at least a third of Pedi warriors had acquired when working as migrant labourers in British-ruled southern Africa. Having determinedly maintained Pedi independence in the face of attacks by the neighbouring Swazi kingdom to the east, and by the Boers to the west, Sekhukhune was in no mind to concede it to the new British administration of the Transvaal either.[9] Sir Theophilus Shepstone, the Administrator of the Transvaal, consequently appealed to Frere for reinforcements. On 12 March 1878 the 90th Regiment (Perthshire Volunteers Light Infantry), which had recently arrived in

Natal from the Cape, accordingly moved up to Utrecht in the southern Transvaal.

Once arrived in Pietermaritzburg, Chelmsford decided that the Pedi question must be settled before he embarked on a campaign in Zululand, especially since the British believed – misguidedly – that Sekhukhune and Cetshwayo were in an alliance of mutual military assistance. He ordered the 80th Regiment stationed in Natal to join the 1/13th and 90th Regiments in the Transvaal, and on 13 August 1878 he placed all the troops in the Transvaal under the command of Colonel Hugh Rowlands. Rowlands was a Welshman whom the general remembered from the Crimean War (where he had been awarded the Victoria Cross at the battle of Inkerman) and from their Indian days,[10] and whom he had previously appointed his Inspector of Colonial Forces. The Natal garrison was maintained by the arrival by sea of the 2/24th Regiment from the Cape, freed up the conclusion of the war with the amaXhosa. The forces in the Transvaal were further reinforced by the Frontier Light Horse (FLH), a colonial mounted unit some 200 strong which had been raised in Cape Colony during the Ninth Cape Frontier War. In September 1878 Rowlands commenced his campaign against the Bapedi, but the First Anglo-Pedi War proved a disaster for the British. Foiled by Pedi guerrilla tactics, their impregnable strongholds and an exceptionally dry season, Rowlands abandoned operations in late October 1878, to the detriment of his reputation, and withdrew his troops to garrisons in the Transvaal, some along the northern borders of Zululand.[11]

Meanwhile, Chelmsford continued to build up his forces for the impending Zululand campaign. The battalions already in Natal and the Transvaal were brought up to full strength, and the two batteries of Royal Artillery were despatched from the Cape. During September and October seven companies of the 1/24th Regiment arrived in Natal from the Cape, leaving behind one company to garrison the recently erected fort guarding the mouth of the Mzimvubu River in Pondoland.

Concerned that the British troops he had at his disposal were too scattered and altogether insufficient for the intended invasion of Zululand, on 14 September 1878 Chelmsford urgently requested Colonel Frederick A. Stanley, the Secretary of State for War, for reinforcements.[12] But, already embroiled in the Second Anglo-Afghan

War, the government was hesitant to comply. As the aristocratic Stanley – who had been commissioned in the Grenadier Guards before becoming a leading Tory politician and who would eventually cap his career as the highly successful sixth governor-general of Canada[13] – later told the House of Commons, 'While it [the Second Anglo-Afghan War] was going on I think I should have been unworthy of the position I hold, if my attention had not been directed to the reinforcements which might be required there.'[14] Indeed, besides the troops of the Indian Army already deployed in Afghanistan, six regiments of British infantry were also fighting there, along with a regiment of cavalry and batteries of the Royal Horse, Field and Garrison Artillery. It was with reluctance, therefore, that on 25 November 1878 the government embarked 1,190 infantry and 240 Royal Engineers for South Africa. Hicks Beach sternly informed Frere that 'It is my duty to impress upon you that in supplying these reinforcements it is the desire of Her Majesty's Government not to furnish means for a campaign of invasion and conquest, but to afford such protection as may be necessary at this juncture to the lives and property of the Colonists.'[15] His warning had no deterrent effect on Frere's plans, and when, in early January, the 99th (Duke of Edinburgh's Lanarkshire) Regiment and the 2nd and 5th Companies, Royal Engineers, disembarked in Natal they were added to Chelmsford's army of invasion. The 2nd Battalion of the 4th (King's Own Royal) Regiment, however, would not arrive in Durban until a few days after the war had already begun to run its disastrous course.[16]

To supplement this small force of regular troops, a Naval Brigade was landed in Durban on 19 November from HMS *Active* consisting of 170 sailors and Royal Marines, with two 12-pounder Armstrong guns, one Gatling gun and two rocket tubes. It was reinforced on 6 January by fifty more men from HMS *Tenedos*.[17] There was nothing unusual in this because Royal Navy crews were routinely trained in the use of small arms and light artillery to serve in coastal areas. Sailors of the Naval Brigade wore blue frock jackets and trousers with tan canvas gaiters. Their officers wore a double-breasted blue frock coat or a single-breasted five-buttoned blue tunic with blue or white trousers and white canvas leggings. Headgear was a broad-brimmed straw sennet for sailors and a peaked blue cap with white cover for officers.

The uniform of the Royal Marine Light Infantry was similar to that worn by regular infantry.[18]

Chelmsford's winning formula in the Ninth Cape Frontier War had required African auxiliaries and mounted troops. The former were invaluable for undertaking garrison and convoy duties instead of the militarily more valuable British troops, and were also useful in scouting and in following up the enemy once they had been broken by the British regulars' disciplined firepower. Accordingly, during November and December 1878, Chelmsford drafted African levies of doubtful morale from the Natal native reserves and formed them under white officers and NCOs into the seven poorly armed and trained battalions of the Natal Native Contingent (NNC), grouped into three regiments with a nominal strength of 7,000 men. In addition, he raised three companies of the Natal Native Pioneer Corps (about 250 men) to construct earthwork fortifications and maintain the rudimentary tracks.[19]

Even more essential to the success of colonial campaigning than auxiliaries were mounted troops. They had proved pivotal in the later stages of the Ninth Cape Frontier War, and would be crucial in Zululand for reconnaissance and raiding purposes and vital in the pursuit of a broken enemy. Yet, as Chelmsford was uncomfortably aware, he had not nearly enough for his purposes,[20] and no regular British cavalry were stationed in South Africa. Instead, Chelmsford would have to rely on two squadrons of some 200 Mounted Infantry raised from his regiments of infantry (the men exchanged their blue trousers for brown cord riding breeches),[21] the 200 men of the Frontier Light Horse, 80 men of the paramilitary Natal Mounted Police, about 300 men of the ten corps of the Natal Mounted Volunteer Corps who had signed up for service outside the borders of the colony, about 400 African volunteers who formed the six troops of the Natal Native Mounted Contingent, and whatever small units of mounted volunteers he could manage to raise from the reluctant white citizens of the Transvaal.

If Chelmsford entertained no doubts that his forces would defeat the amaZulu in any armed encounter, his problem was how he could make sure of bringing them to battle and so avoid the desultory and time-consuming irregular warfare of the later stages of the Ninth Cape Frontier War. But a swift, decisive campaign such as Chelmsford and Frere envisaged depended upon firm logistics. Unfortunately for Chelmsford, since supplies could not be obtained from the theatre of war and had to be carried, his army would have to be turned into an escort for its food and for the fodder for its draught mules and horses (oxen lived off grazing); while garrisoned depots would have to be established along its line of march.[22] For months before the invasion Chelmsford was engrossed in collecting and organising supplies and transport in the form of ox wagons and mule carts. His task was made the more frustrating by the under-staffed Commissariat and Transport Department. Its inexperience in purchasing and in looking after its draft animals in South African conditions provided an unexpected windfall for colonists who shamelessly disposed of their draft animals at well above the going rate, and hired out or sold their wagons and carts at exorbitant prices.[23]

Chelmsford's logistical difficulties might have been considerably eased if he had been able to secure the cooperation of the Natal government. Ever since Natal had become a separate colony on 15 July 1856 it had enjoyed representative government. Twelve of the sixteen member of the Legislative Council were elected by male colonists with sufficient property to qualify for the franchise. The remaining four members were senior officials nominated by the lieutenant-governor and he and they formed the Executive Council. The lieutenant-governor was responsible to the British government and not to the council,[24] and his goodwill was therefore essential. When Chelmsford set up his headquarters in Pietermaritzburg, the Lieutenant-Governor, Sir Henry Bulwer, courteously put him up as his guest at Government House, an unpretentious and rather cramped residence built of shale with a red tiled roof under the lee of Fort Napier. In their personal relations and private conversations Chelmsford and Bulwer managed to maintain 'a most amicable manner',[25] and it was clear that the general appreciated the well-read Bulwer's 'private character as a gentleman' and respected his 'honesty of purpose and earnestness as a governor'.[26] Nevertheless, the two men soon found themselves at loggerheads on any number of issues, and Bulwer's administration did little to help and much to hinder Chelmsford in his preparations.

Bulwer was born of the landed gentry, and after the University of Cambridge he had gained extensive experience in the colonial service.

His last posting before he came to Natal on 28 August 1875 had been as Governor of Labuan, a steamy island off the north coast of Borneo that the British had acquired in 1848 to combat pirates in the South China Sea. With his tufty red hair, bushy moustache and little imperial, and with his pot belly overbalancing his thin legs, Bulwer was not an entirely prepossessing figure, especially when in didactic mode with index finger wagging. Chelmsford and his military associates rapidly came to regard Bulwer as 'a very obstinate and arrogant man in public affairs' with an essentially 'small mind' who looked 'on every question from a small standpoint'.[27] Bulwer was certainly the pedantic bureaucrat through and through, but the real problem was that until Chelmsford's arrival in Pietermaritzburg neither he nor his government had felt any anxiety regarding a Zulu attack, and were concerned only to maintain good relations with King Cetshwayo. Bulwer was consequently wary of the sudden rush to a 'quite unnecessary' war against the amaZulu,[28] was dubious about the justice of forcing one on, and deplored the attendant risks and cost for Natal. As a result, he was indeed suspicious and resentful of Chelmsford's military preparations and tended to drag his feet. This in turn deeply frustrated Chelmsford and his staff who fulminated about his opposing their preparations 'by obstinacy and every other means'.[29] Their exasperation negatively affected how the military handled him, and for his part Bulwer increasingly found them 'not very pleasant to deal with in official matters', complaining that 'when they ask for anything or desire anything to be done, or recommend anything, their official manner is not always an agreeable one'.[30] Indeed, as he later grumbled, the military habitually 'pooh-poohed' his opinions.[31]

The member of Chelmsford's staff whom Bulwer particularly blamed for this breakdown in relations was John North Crealock, Chelmsford's Assistant Military Secretary who excelled at watercolour paintings and sketches executed while on campaign.[32] In 1868 Crealock had passed through Staff College (established at Camberley in 1858) and had held a series of staff appointments. True, Chelmsford was aligned with the conservative military coterie of the Field Marshal Commanding-in-Chief, the Duke of Cambridge and subscribed to their gentlemanly-amateurish suspicion of the professional accumulation and analysis of intelligence as taught at Camberley.[33] But

Crealock possessed the important additional recommendation of being an officer in Chelmsford's own regiment, the 95th, and of having served with him in India. Made brevet lieutenant-colonel in November 1878 in recognition of his services during the Ninth Cape Frontier War,[34] Crealock continued on Chelmsford's personal staff, even though he was not conspicuously efficient, and the spiky penmanship of his despatches was nigh illegible.

Nevertheless, Crealock eclipsed the other members of Chelmsford's small staff in the general's esteem – all, like him, chosen for their easy compatibility rather than for their talents. Captain Ernest Buller, Rifle Brigade, served as Commandant at Headquarters, and Chelmsford's two ADCs were the heavily bearded Brevet Major Matthew Gossett, 54th Regiment (who had in fact passed through Staff College), and the handsome, sleek-haired and beardless Lieutenant Archibald Berkeley Milne, RN, the well-connected son of the First Sea Lord, serving with the naval contingent from HMS *Active*. Crealock realised that Chelmsford's personal staff was 'miserably weak,'[35] and would have liked to have filled the role of the general's chief-of-staff. But Chelmsford, apparently confident in his own organisational abilities and reluctant to delegate, did not even appoint an intelligence officer and persisted in imagining that he 'could do without an immediate staff'.[36]

Crealock was nevertheless the one man constantly at Chelmsford's side and was staunchly loyal to him in public, even if he did criticise his military capabilities in private.[37] The problem seems to have been Crealock's abrasive personality and facetious manner that not only alienated many of his fellow officers, but also helped poison relations between the military and the government of Natal. Bulwer confided to his brother that Crealock 'is a sort of military wasp and, between ourselves, I think he is rather snobbish sometimes'.[38] (At that time a 'snob' did not have the modern meaning of someone who admires or emulates those of higher status, but described someone who was lacking in good breeding and carried himself with a disagreeable air of superiority.) Some observers deplored the undue influence Crealock had apparently obtained over Chelmsford, yet Clery for one did not believe 'that the general really took advice much from anybody, for he certainly seemed . . . to discourage anything in the way of suggestion'. The problem was that even if Crealock superficially possessed 'all the smartness and method' useful as an AMS, he was not considered the 'man of solidity and ability' Chelmsford so required at his elbow.[39] It is no surprise that, as the date of the invasion of Zululand drew closer, the strain inevitably began to tell on Chelmsford. Crealock reported that 'Our general looks sadly fagged and weary, and no wonder; it is worry from morning to night and he never spares himself. However,' he continued more optimistically, 'when we are moving we shall all be very fit.'[40]

Chapter 3

Planning the Invasion

———⟶>●<⟵———

Chelmsford did not entirely share Crealock's optimism about the coming campaign. His dependence on slow-moving and vulnerable supply trains that could average at best only ten miles a day over the broken terrain meant that his manoeuvrability would be compromised. The larger the convoy, the slower it moved, so Chelmsford decided he must adopt the conventional strategy of sending in a number of smaller columns to converge on oNdini (Cetshwayo's capital) to surround the enemy in a pincer movement with the objective of forcing on a pitched battle in which modern armaments would prove decisive.[1] Certainly, reducing their size made each column more vulnerable to attack, but Chelmsford was confident that each would be strong enough to crush any size of Zulu force; while their seeming vulnerability had the advantage of tempting the Zulu to risk the pitched battle he desired. However, old colonists, harking back to their experience in the Voortrekker–Zulu War of 1838–9, urged him to make each column form a defensive wagon laager every time it halted in Zulu territory. But laagering was a time-consuming and complicated procedure and it had not been Chelmsford's practice to laager temporary camps when on the march against the amaXhosa.[2] Chelmsford persisted therefore in supposing that for his well-armed columns laagering would prove an unnecessary delay, and that partial entrenchments would suffice instead.[3]

Chelmsford believed his strategy of converging columns possessed a further great advantage. He knew that when he advanced into Zululand he would leave Natal and the Transvaal to his rear vulnerable to raids not only by the amaZulu, but by the still-undefeated Bapedi as well. Nevertheless, he calculated that invasion by a number of supporting columns would discourage any enemy counter-thrusts, even if the possibility of one could not be discounted. Consequently, when he first set up his headquarters in Pietermaritzburg he was appalled by the insouciance of the Natal government in the face of this real threat. Bulwer's contingency plans were limited to advising settlers to take refuge in the scattered urban and rural government laagers in the process of improvement or construction about Natal and in the southern Transvaal, or in the private laagers being hurriedly thrown up by some local communities of farmers. These permanent fortifications were merely stone and sod enclosures, sometimes with bastions at opposite corners.[4] There was no provision for accommodating the unfortunate black population in them except for a handful of servants and retainers. Faced with the common attitude held by members of the Natal government that the very idea of a Zulu invasion was 'absurd', Chelmsford set about chivvying them out of their 'fool's paradise'. At a crucial meeting of the Natal Executive Council's Defence Committee on 10 September 1878, Chelmsford at last persuaded the Natal authorities to follow all his suggestions and take appropriate action.

On 26 November Natal was divided into seven rural Defensive Districts and two Sub-Districts comprising the main towns of Durban and Pietermaritzburg. Each was placed on 3 December under a Colonial District Commander who had charge of the colonial forces in his district as well as of the public laagers and the government arms and ammunition stored there. However, since many men would be absent serving with the Natal Mounted Volunteers or Natal Mounted Police, it was up to the remaining members of the various Rifle Associations and other volunteers to defend the laagers as best they could. Small garrisons of imperial troops would remain in Durban and Pietermaritzburg, as well as along Chelmsford's lines of communication and supply to Zululand at the villages of Stanger, Greytown, Ladysmith and Newcastle. But who would defend the countryside in between the various strongpoints?

There were available a very small and uncertain number of Mounted Burghers who were liable to turn out for commando duty if called upon by their local field cornet, but at best they would only be of use patrolling and giving warning of Zulu movements. The Africans of the Special Border Police, stationed under white Natal Border Agents along the Thukela and Mzinyathi Rivers, amounted to only 190 men, and their primary task was to gather intelligence and not to deter a Zulu incursion. It was obvious that the Natal government would have to raise African levies for the defence of the countryside. But Natal was a poor colony and its government could not afford to maintain a large standing force. So it devised a system that came into effect on 20 December whereby every chief in the border Defensive Districts (Nos. I, VI, and VII) would furnish a quota of fighting men who would take the field under white levy-leaders when a Zulu raid threatened. Otherwise, they would remain at home busy with their normal occupations. Besides these part-time levies, or Reserve, the government provided for a small standing force of several hundred Border Guards in each Colonial Defensive District. They were to be stationed at strategic drifts (fords) from which they could move to any threatened stretch of the river frontier. The system was in operation by the time Chelmsford placed the entire border region under military control on 11 January 1879.[5]

Nevertheless, Chelmsford knew that these arrangements would not be enough if the amaZulu decided to make a determined incursion, and he had no further alternative but to fall back on the terrain and climate to assist. On account of the summer rains, the rivers between Natal and Zululand were generally unfordable between January and March except at a limited number of defensible drifts, and so formed a natural line of defence. As Bulwer admitted once the invasion had begun, he feared that the border had been 'left a little too weak', so that 'our best friend is the river'.[6] The Transvaal border country was more open than Natal's broken terrain and had no great rivers to cross, but Chelmsford calculated that a Zulu force would on that account be easier to intercept than in Natal.

Understanding Chelmsford's difficulties, Frere arrived in Pietermaritzburg on 28 September 1878 to chivvy Bulwer along, leaving behind in Cape Town the formidable phalanx of his politically acute wife and four unmarried, intellectual daughters (the two eldest, along with Lady Frere, acted as his private secretaries). The unfortunate Lieutenant-Governor, whose salary was unequal to covering the expense, put Frere up at Government House along with Chelmsford.

Frere found Bulwer 'almost fanatically just and loyal' but sadly unknowledgeable of military affairs.[7] So Frere settled down in dreary, hot, provincial Pietermaritzburg to join his voice to Chelmsford's and to push forward on the political front to ensure that the invasion was launched on the ideal summer date of 11 January 1879 when the rivers would be in flood.[8]

All the same, the inadequacies of his arrangements for the defence of Natal and the Transvaal once he invaded Zululand continued to haunt Chelmsford. As a further precaution he decided to send his invading columns into Zululand in precisely those sectors of the border country he believed most vulnerable to Zulu attack. From east to west, No. 1 Column of 4,750 men (2,000 of them African) under Colonel Charles K. Pearson of the Buffs (and previously Commandant of Natal) would protect the Natal coastal plain; the 3,800 African troops of No. 2 Column under Brevet Colonel Anthony W. Durnford, RE, and No. 3 Column of 4,709 men (2,500 of them African) under Colonel Richard T. Glyn of the 1/24th Regiment would shield central Natal; No. 4 Column of 2,278 men (390 of them African) under Brevet Colonel H. Evelyn Wood, VC, CB, of the 90th Light Infantry would guard the Utrecht District of the Transvaal; and No. 5 Column of 1,565 men (340 of them African) under Colonel Rowlands would protect the volatile eastern Transvaal that abutted the unpacified Pedi, Swazi and Zulu kingdoms. The seven battalions of British infantry, the main striking force of each column, were parcelled out as follows: No. 1 Column: the 2/3rd and 99th Regiments; No. 3 Column: the 1/24th and 2/24th Regiment; No. 4 Column: the 1/13th and 90th Regiments; and No. 5 Column: the 80th Regiment.[9]

Yet, as the day of invasion approached, the prospects for successful coordination between the columns, let alone mutual support, seemed ever less likely. A major obstacle was the lack of any accurate map. Those available were out of scale, full of empty, uncharted spaces, and just plain wrong.[10] The commanders of the invading columns would have to rely as best they could on mounted patrols, supplemented by the NNC, to relay information about the terrain to be traversed, and to locate the enemy. But the dire lack of horsemen for intelligence-gathering was a particular concern;[11] while the dearth of properly trained intelligence officers to process it was another handicap (though generally unacknowledged) . The consequence, of course, was that Chelmsford had only the vaguest idea of where his columns were going, and when they were committed in Zululand they would be hard pressed to find each other, let alone communicate.

Encamped at Bemba's Kop, just east of the Ncome River, Wood's Column was thirty-five miles north of Rorke's Drift where Glyn's column – which Chelmsford planned to accompany – was intending to cross into Zululand. Pearson's column at the mouth of the Thukela on the southern bank of the river was well over 100 miles to the east of Glyn's across extremely broken country. Halfway between those two columns, at Middle Drift, were Durnford's NNC units, and at the last moment Chelmsford decided to hold them back on the defensive since the remote and difficult terrain of the middle Thukela invited a surprise Zulu attack. Concerned about the intentions of the unsubdued Bapedi and uneasy that Transvaal Boers unreconciled to British rule might make trouble, Chelmsford concluded that Rowlands's column at Derby sixty miles to the north of Wood must also stay put. Uncertainty about the amaSwazi reinforced this decision. During the mid-nineteenth century King Mswati II had firmly established the Swazi state, which was closely related to the neighbouring Zulu kingdom to its south. However, he and his successors had to cope with the expansive tendencies of the Transvaal Boers, who asserted their sovereignty over Swaziland, but lacked the means to put this into effect.[12] Mbandzeni, the current Swazi king, consequently suspected that the British, as the new rulers of the Transvaal, would make good their claims over his kingdom. Yet the amaSwazi were also long-standing foes of the amaZulu, who had raided them many times in the past. Caught between two potential enemies, Mbandzeni had consequently prevaricated when Norman MacLeod, the Swazi Border Commissioner, made repeated overtures to him in late 1878 to take the field on the side of the British and protect Rowlands's left flank. The long and the short of it was that Mbandzeni did not intend to commit himself until he could be certain of securing his own best interests by backing the indubitably winning side in the coming war.[13]

Once the already widely dispersed No. 1 (Right), 3 (Centre) and 4 (Left) Columns advanced into Zululand it would be challenging, to say the least, to keep communications open between them. Distance, cloudy summer weather, and hilly terrain made flashed Morse code messages by heliograph either impracticable or intermittent.[14] That meant messages had to be sent by mounted couriers or by African runners. These messengers had not only to seek out where to deliver their despatches, but along the way they had to brave hostile terrain, swollen rivers and potential enemy patrols.[15] Before the invasion even began, Wood's Left Column at Bemba's Kop was already some eight hours' ride away from Rorke's Drift, and Pearson's Right Column was at least twenty-four hours away.[16] Chelmsford had consequently to accept that the columns to the left and right of the Centre Column where he had set up his headquarters would be only tenuously in communication with him for much of the time. And that meant that their commanders would have to act on their own authority without reference to him, especially when they had to make rapid tactical decisions when engaging the enemy.

Appreciating all the many difficulties that confronted him, as the day of the invasion drew close Chelmsford began increasingly to obsess about deficient logistical arrangements, unreliable maps, difficult terrain and insufficient mounted troops for effective reconnaissance. Daily, he exhorted his commanders to coordinate operations despite the odds against doing so.[17] Bulwer tried to calm his own disquiet by stoutly affirming that Chelmsford's military arrangements were 'good and sure to succeed', and that the GOC was 'a good general officer, very, very careful, very painstaking, very thorough'.[18] Yet, even then, Bulwer could not suppress his nervous suspicion that Chelmsford's 'easy success in Kaffraria [the Eastern Cape] had turned his head', and that he was 'very much inflated by the idea of his own ability as a general'.[19]

It was only after the disasters that befell Chelmsford's invading army, and with all the perfect prescience of hindsight, that General Wolseley could declare that in Chelmsford Frere had found 'a poor tool in the shape of a General' whose 'ignorance of his trade' had brought all the High Commissioner's plans for confederation crashing down.[20] As it was, when the ultimatum expired on 11 January 1879, Chelmsford could still be confident – despite all his conscientious anxieties – that he would achieve all his military objectives after a short, sharp, conclusive Zululand campaign.

PART II

Preparing for War:
The AmaZulu

Chapter 4

Resolving to Resist

———⊷•⊷———

While Lord Chelmsford gathered ever-growing numbers of British and colonial troops to menace the borders of the Zulu kingdom, and Frere drove the political crisis to the point of no return, King Cetshwayo and his councillors discussed the threatening situation with perplexity and mounting concern.[1] What was it that they had done so amiss to alienate their old ally, the British? And if a diplomatic solution eluded them, should they resort to arms? These grave men, the country's ruling elite, were gathered at oNdini, Cetshwayo's principal *ikhanda*, or military homestead, that he had constructed in 1873 in the thorn-bush country of the Mahlabathini plain on the northern banks of the White Mfolozi River, right in the heart of the Zulu kingdom.

The *ikhanda* was an immense, elliptical assemblage of close to 1,400 beehive-shaped thatched huts enclosing a vast parade ground. A palisade constructed of a double row of stout timbers two and a half metres high enclosed the whole complex which had an outer circumference slightly over 2,000 metres.[2] A further eight, somewhat smaller *amakhanda* were scattered in the plain in the environs of oNdini. Just south-west across the White Mfolozi eight more *amakhanda* were clustered in the emaKhosini valley, or the 'Valley of the Kings'. This was hallowed ground because it was the sacred burial place for the semi-legendary *amakhosi* (chiefs) of the petty Zulu chiefdom who were the ancestors of King Shaka kaSenzangakhona, the famed founder of the Zulu kingdom who had ruled from about 1816 until 1828 when his half-brother, Dingane kaSenzangakhona, assassinated him and usurped his throne. Dingane in turn had been overthrown in battle in 1840 by Mpande kaSenzangakhona, his half-brother and Cetshwayo's father.

The layout of oNdini was identical in almost every particular except its mammoth scale to the other *amakhanda* in the emaKhosini valley and the Mahlabathini plain, as well as to that of a further ten *amakhanda* positioned across the kingdom as regional centres of royal authority and as the mobilisation points for the age-grade regiments of warriors, or *amabutho*. At the top of the *ikhanda*, and directly opposite the main gate across the open parade ground, was the royal enclosure, or *isigodlo*, which was divided into two sections of about fifty huts in all. In the central, 'black' section were the king's private sleeping hut and his large council hut. Exceptionally, Cetshwayo also had a rectangular, four-roomed, thatched colonial-style house of audience built out of sun-dried bricks with verandahs at front and back. Its rooms were wallpapered and contained European furniture, including a large mirror and a washstand. Cetshwayo regularly spent part of the day there consulting his closest senior counsellors. More traditionally, the 'black' enclosure also contained the huts of his wives, or *amakhosikazi*, as well as those of his favoured *umndlunkulu*, or maids of honour, who had been given to him as tribute. They cooked for and waited on him and the *amakhosikazi*, and served him as concubines. The two 'white' sections on either side of the 'black' one accommodated his deceased father King Mpande's widows and other miscellaneous female relations of the royal house, royal children, those *umndlunkulu* who had not drawn his fancy, and the *izigqila*. These last were women who had been captured in war or were the wives or daughters of men the king had executed. Not only were they obliged to be at the sexual disposal of men of the royal house, but they also performed all the menial domestic chores in the *isigodlo*. Their days were filled cultivating the gardens, fetching water, gathering firewood, cooking food and waiting on the women of higher status.[3]

Two enormous *izinhlangothi*, or wings of huts, three or more rows deep, sprung out from either side of the *isigodlo* and swept around the great parade ground. There several thousand *amabutho* (in the sense of warriors or members of age-grade regiments) were quartered when they rotated in and out to serve their king. A number of cattle enclosures were built in the parade ground against the inner palisade of reeds and grasses that fenced off the warriors' huts. Directly in front of the *isigodlo* at the top end of the parade ground was the *isibaya*, the special cattle enclosure sacred to the king. There Cetshwayo and the members of his inner royal council (*umkhandlu*) would discuss matters of state and he would pass judgement on wrong-doers. It was also the place where he would perform the religious rituals required of the monarch, sacrifice cattle to propitiate the royal *amadolozi*, or shades of the ancestors, and where he would officiate over the great national ceremonies.

Cetshwayo was born in about 1832 at Mpande's emLambongwenya homestead in south-eastern Zululand. Even though he was an *umntwana*, or prince, he was raised like any other Zulu boy, herding cattle and practising military arts. In 1850 or 1851, when he was about eighteen years old and Mpande had been on the throne for about ten years, he was recruited into the newly-formed uThulwana *ibutho* along with seven other princes of the same age-grade. The uThulwana fought in the Swazi campaign of 1852, and Cetshwayo was blooded in combat, an essential experience for a future Zulu king and war leader.

Crucially for the future, while serving with the uThulwana, Cetshwayo developed an intimate accord with its *induna* (commander), Mnyamana kaNgqengelele, the *inkosi* (chief) of the Buthelezi people. As an *isikhulu* (great nobleman, plural *izikhulu*) Mnyamana was high in Mpande's favour and rich in cattle. Apparently never photographed, he was described as being tall and of slight build with a dark complexion and a little pointed beard. His deep, resonant voice was always attended to with great respect in the king's council for he was an astute politician of coolly reasoned purpose. He was steadfastly hostile to the white traders and missionaries increasingly operating in Zululand because he correctly gauged the threat they posed to the established Zulu order. Nevertheless, he comprehended the power they potentially wielded, and always advised exercising caution when dealing with either the British or Boer authorities because he was sensibly opposed to risking war with these dangerous neighbours. The young Cetshwayo absorbed his political philosophy and followed it when in due course he became king in 1872 following the death of Mpande (the only one of the first three Zulu kings not to die violently), and appointed Mnyamana his chief *induna*, or officer of state.

At the time of the Swazi campaign of 1852 Cetshwayo was already growing into a handsome, heavily built man with a powerful chest. In his maturity he was the first Zulu king to be photographed, so we have a far better idea of his likeness than that of his royal predecessors. Reputedly, Cetshwayo took after his mother in looks with his broad face and large lustrous eyes that sparkled when he was animated, and he possessed the same pleasant smile and open, good-natured expression. Unlike many other Zulu men he wore a beard and moustache. He was darker in colour than most other Zulu, and flushed deeply when angered or distressed. In later life he would become fat, but his flesh never became flabby and he worked to maintain his fit, hard condition through long, daily walks even when he became king. No amount of exercise, however, could reduce the size of his immense thighs, a characteristic he shared with many others of the house of Senzangakhona. Cetshwayo always held himself very erect in a royally dignified manner with his head thrown slightly back, a habit acquired from long regarding all those about him as his inferiors. Nevertheless, he unfailingly treated others with courtesy and was genial and engaging in his manners. He said what he thought and spoke in a strong, deep voice. Generally, he was convivial, relishing good cheer and witty conversation – even, some thought, being too willing to gossip for hours with his intimates – but he would sometimes lapse into an intimidating taciturnity.[4]

In September 1878, and again in October, in consultation with his *ibandla*, or full council of state, Cetshwayo partially mobilised his *amabutho* in response to repeated border alarms. Cornelius Vijn, a white trader who found himself detained in Zululand during the coming war, noted that bitter resentment of those 'very bad people', the British, began to sweep the country. Rapidly swelling rumour insisted that the Europeans were coming 'to capture all the males, to be sent to England and there kept to work, while the girls would all be married off to (white) soldiers, and their cattle would, of course, all belong to the English government'. Warriors responded by declaring that 'When it came to fighting, they fought not for the King only, but for themselves, since they would rather die than live under the Whites.'[5]

When debating the mounting crisis with the British the *ibandla* was divided. True, all were agreed that the independence of the kingdom must be preserved, but some nevertheless expressed the hope that the British could still be placated by judicious concessions. Predictably, the leader of this faction was Cetshwayo's chief *induna*, Mnyamana, who remained wedded to his long-standing and prudent policy of seeking accommodation with the British. He was joined in opposing the drift to war by two others of the most powerful *izikhulu* whose motives were more selfish than his.

One was the self-indulgent, physically flabby Hamu kaNzibe, Cetshwayo's full brother, a man notorious for his violent and over-bearing manners. He possessed the immense thighs of the house of Senzangakhona, and wore a hard, disdainful expression on his impassive face. He was King Mpande's first-born son, but through the *ukuvuza* custom he was heir to Nzibe kaSenzangakhona, Mpande's beloved younger full brother who in 1828 had died on campaign of fever. Hamu had inherited Nzibe's great kwaMfemfe homestead in north-western Zululand and ruled as *inkosi* over the Ngenetsheni people. But Hamu was a man of enormous, restless ambition who patently resented that on account of his genealogical descent from Nzibe he ranked behind the rest of Mpande's sons. He transparently envied Cetshwayo and harboured designs on his throne, living in royal style at kwaMfemfe as if he were a ruler in his own right, and forging close trading connections with the colonial world.[6]

Through his colonial advisers, Chelmsford was aware of such rivalries and tensions in the Zulu kingdom, and he was determined to exploit them. Hamu did not wait to be approached, however. Believing that the British must win the inevitable war, he decided to play a double game. While advising Cetshwayo against a military confrontation he simultaneously sent emissaries to G. M. Rudolph, the *landdrost* of Utrecht in the Transvaal Territory, and to Colonel Wood of No. 4 Column promising in the case of hostilities to defect with all his people to the British side. To his satisfaction Hamu received Chelmsford's pledge that in return he would be recognised once the war was over as an independent ruler, owing allegiance to the Queen.[7]

The other opponent of war who wished to maintain good relations with Britain was Cetshwayo's powerful cousin, Zibhebhu kaMaphitha, *inkosi* of the Mandlakazi in north-eastern Zululand and of whom it was widely said that he 'practically looked upon himself as his [Cetshwayo's] equal'.[8] A relatively young man at thirty-eight, the coolly intelligent, forceful and ambitious Zibhebhu with his long nails of the Zulu aristocrat already enjoyed a high reputation as a war leader.

Like Hamu, Zibhebhu was also busily forging close contacts with white traders and Natal officials who admired his 'progressive' attitude to European ways. Also, like Hamu, he administered his domain like a quasi-independent ruler and brooked little or no interference from Cetshwayo. Although he did not follow Hamu in negotiating to sell Cetshwayo out, the king had cause to be concerned about his loyalty too.[9]

The hopes of those leaders hoping for a diplomatic accommodation with the British were dealt a terminal blow when the deliberately draconian terms of the British ultimatum of 11 December 1878 were finally digested. Some of its minor stipulations might have been met. But Frere's central requirements that the Zulu military system – through which his people served their king economically and militarily – be abolished, and that Cetshwayo submit himself to the authority of a British Resident were so destructive of the powers of the Zulu monarchy, its military establishment and the future independence of the kingdom, that (as Frere had intended) even those most opposed to war could ultimately see no alternative but to fight. So in early January 1879 the *amabutho* mustered at oNdini where they were 'doctored' for war and readied themselves to affirm their masculinity and prowess through the death of the invaders.

Chapter 5

The Zulu Way of War

⸻⸻⸻

In 1904 Ngidi kaMcikaziswa proudly verified what was probably the central Zulu cultural predilection when he informed James Stuart, a white magistrate recording Zulu oral history, that the amaZulu 'are always talking of war and battles, even at this day'.[1] Indeed, violence defined the Zulu kingdom which rose and fell within the span of a long-lived person's lifetime. Oral traditions tell of constant raiding from earliest times in what would later be the Zulu kingdom to acquire herds by force from neighbours. The warriors who raided each other would have had their fighting skills honed by participation in organised hunting parties. European sailors in the late seventeenth century saw them using long throwing spears and finishing off their victims with short stabbing spears. These would remain the basic Zulu weapons for the next two centuries. By the mid-eighteenth century at the latest hunting parties were developing into large-scale military formations, or 'regiments', known to the amaZulu as *amabutho*. These *amabutho* were based on age-grade units which had developed out of the by then defunct circumcision schools marking the transition from youth to manhood. It is impossible to say which particular grouping in what later became the Zulu kingdom invented the *amabutho*, but it is certain that by the eighteenth century they were increasingly being deployed as the chiefs' instruments of coercion, and that to keep them fed and rewarded necessitated raids against neighbouring chiefdoms.

The most successful of these warring chiefs was Shaka, who in about 1816 violently seized the throne of the little Zulu chieftainship in the valley of the White Mfolozi River from his half-brother, Sigujana. More than any other man, he exemplified the warrior hero as conceived by the amaZulu. It was Shaka's full development of the military potential of the *amabutho* which enabled him to extend and consolidate his rule over the entire region between the Phongolo River to the north and the Thukela River to the south.[2] For him and all his successors the *amabutho* remained the central instrument of royal power holding together the political structure of the Zulu kingdom. All the men as well as the women of the kingdom were grouped into *amabutho* under the king's direct ritual authority rather than remaining under that of their regional *amakhosi*. Girls stayed at home until it was time to marry. But boys between the ages of fourteen and eighteen would gather at the nearest of the various *amakhanda*, the great military homesteads sited at strategic points around the kingdom that functioned as mobilisation points for the *amabutho*. There youths would serve for two to three years as cadets. Once enough boys of the same age group had trained at the various *amakhanda* across the kingdom, the king would form them into an *ibutho* with orders to build themselves a new *ikhanda*. Members of a male *ibutho* could not marry until the king gave them permission to wed women of the female *ibutho* he designated. The king usually withheld permission until men were about the age of thirty-five because, until then, they technically remained youths under the supervision of their elders and were thus more thoroughly under his control. Once a man was allowed to marry, he assumed the *isicoco* (the distinctive married man's polished head-ring of fibres and wax twisted into the hair) and at last established his own *umuzi* (homestead) as a fully fledged adult.

A new *ibutho* would serve continuously at its *ikhanda* for seven to eight months immediately after formation, and thereafter for only a few months a year. For the rest of the year its members lived at home playing their part in the subsistence economy of their *imizi*. After marriage, the men's wives might accompany them during their annual service at their *ikhanda*. While serving, an *ibutho* would make repairs to its *ikhanda*, tend the king's cattle and fields, and take part in the great national ceremonies. The most notable of these was the annual *umKhosi*, or first-fruits festival, when the army was ritually strengthened and the power of the king reaffirmed. During such ceremonies the *amabutho* would don the elaborate ceremonial attire that distinguished them from one another and comprised many fragile and rare skins and feathers. By the 1870s, when hunting had seriously depleted supplies, attire was simpler than it had been in the past. Even if headdresses in particular were becoming less lavish, cow-tails tied above the elbows and below the knees remained standard, as did the loin-cover of a bunch of tails in the front and an oblong of cowhide behind.

Besides commanding their labour, the king also fully controlled the military might of his male *amabutho*. They collected tribute, participated in great hunts, enforced internal control (which included attacking recalcitrant regional *amakhosi*) and served as his army against external enemies. When going on campaign they wore a much-abbreviated version of their precious and constricting festival attire – a choice which differentiated them from the neighbouring amaSwazi who went to war in full be-feathered and be-skinned panoply – although officers might sport some feathers and others conspicuous items as a sign of their rank. All carried a selection of the basic traditional weapon, the spear. The deadliest variety was the short-handled, long-bladed stabbing-spear, or *iklwa*, intended for close fighting. A warrior would also carry several throwing-spears with long shafts. Used primarily for hunting, the *isijula* could find its target up to thirty metres away. Many fighting men might also heft a brutal wooden knobbed stick or *iwisa* to beat out an enemy's brains. Like the amaSwazi, the *amabutho* also carried a great war-shield of cattle-hide, the *isihlangu*. By the 1860s it had generally shrunk to two-thirds of the man-height stipulated by Shaka. Nor did the uniformity of shield colours and patterns any longer differentiate the *amabutho* as they had once done. Only two *izihlangu* could be cut from a single beast, and there were no longer sufficient cattle available in the kingdom with the required markings. Nevertheless, younger *amabutho* carried predominantly black or reddish *izihlangu* and married *amabutho* mainly white ones.

These Zulu warriors enjoyed a fearsome military reputation across southern Africa, but was it entirely deserved? The *amabutho* were a militia, after all, and not the standing British Army with its professional soldiers.[3] When the campaign experience of the *amabutho* mustering in the Mahlabathini plain in January 1879 is examined, what strikes one is the lack of it. The last mobilisation that had resulted in an actual campaign against whites had been in December 1838 during the Voortrekker–Zulu War, forty-one years before. The record against neighbouring African states was little different, and the last time the amaZulu raided the amaSwazi had been in 1852. Ironically, the most recent campaign the amaZulu had waged had been the civil war of 1856 when Cetshwayo and his half-brother Mbuyazi fought for the right to succeed Mpande and Cetshwayo had triumphed at the battle of Ndondakusuka. But that was twenty-three years before, a considerable hiatus in active service, one might say, for such an apparently ferocious warrior nation. Compare that record with that of the men of the 24th Regiment, battle-hardened veterans of the Ninth Cape Frontier War only the previous year.

Naturally, this does not mean that many individuals who had fought in earlier campaigns did not do so again in 1879, and most of the senior commanders in 1879 had taken part in the Swazi wars or had seen action at the battle of Ndondakusuka – but they had done so in a more junior capacity. Four of the *amabutho* that fought in the Anglo-Zulu War were aged between forty-one and forty-seven, namely the iSangqu, uThulwana, iNdlondlo and uDloko, and they had all been present at Ndondakusuka. Other veterans of Ndondakusuka like the iNdabakawombe and uDlambedlu (who were aged fifty-eight and fifty-six respectively) were considered too old for active campaigning and were mainly kept in reserve in 1879 to protect the king. Otherwise, not one of the other twelve *amabutho* who fought in the Anglo-Zulu War had seen the field of battle: this was to be their very first campaign. Even the most prominent *amabutho* in the war – the uMbonambi, uKhandempemvu (or uMcijo), uMxhapho, iNgobamakhosi and uNokhenke – were previously unblooded warriors between their mid-twenties and mid-thirties, while the recently formed uVe were younger still.

None of this is to suggest that the *amabutho* were not desperately eager to face the British in battle and were not confident of their ability to beat them. But that was precisely the problem. Who among them had any experience in facing disciplined soldiers armed with modern rifles, rather than muzzle-loading flintlock or percussion-lock muskets? Could courage and tenacity in traditional hand-to-hand combat hope to prevail against Chelmsford's forces bristling with modern rifles, artillery and even Gatling guns?

Compared to the Bapedi, amaXhosa, Basotho and the various communities in Griqualand West, the amaZulu permitted firearms to play only a very tentative part in their military culture. Unlike a firearm which is used at a distance, the *iklwa* was wielded only at close quarters, when an underarm stab – normally aimed at the abdomen – was followed before withdrawing by a rip. This was the weapon of the hero who cultivated military honour or *udumo* (thunder) and who proved his personal prowess in single combat. Indeed, this particular heroic ethos pervaded male Zulu life.[4] Zulu males lived in public among their peers every day of their lives from the moment they first mustered as teenagers at the *ikhanda* nearest them. From the outset individuals were in strenuous competition with each other, and would select forceful, courageous youths from among their own ranks as the junior officers of the future. So even if *amabutho* spent the bulk of each year at home, their culture was a highly militarised one that was crucial to notions of masculinity and the creation of Zulu identity as a warrior nation.

The warrior ethos was played out most fully in battle. There the tactical intention was to outflank and enclose the enemy in a flexible manoeuvre, evidently developed from the hunt, which could be readily adapted to a pitched battle in the open field or to a surprise attack. The amaZulu did not attack in a solid body, shoulder-to-shoulder, but advanced in open skirmishing order. They only concentrated when upon the enemy, casting a shower of *izijula* to distract the foe as they rushed in to engage in hand-to-hand fighting with their *amaklwa* or *amawisa*. After a few vicious minutes of frenzied stabbing or clubbing they would fall back and regroup before re-engaging as many times as was necessary before the enemy broke. No quarter was given to a defeated foe, who would be pursued to his complete destruction.[5]

In this sort of fighting a man's prowess was under the constant scrutiny of his comrades. After the battle the king would discuss with his officers which *ibutho* had the distinction of being the first to engage the enemy at close quarters. Men who were members of that *ibutho* and who had killed in battle were designated *abaqawe* (heroes or warriors of distinction) and the king ordered them to wear a distinctive necklace made from small blocks of willow wood (known as *iziqu*) which was looped around the neck or slung across the body bandolier-style. If a man distinguished himself in battle again, he would increase the length of his *iziqu*. On the other hand, if a man who wore the *iziqu* subsequently disgraced himself in war, the king might order his *iziqu* to be cut as a public humiliation.[6] Indeed, those who failed to live up to the required ideals of heroic masculinity, and whose courage deserted them in combat, were publicly degraded until they were able to redeem themselves in battle.

Unlike the close-quarters spears of the heroic Zulu warriors, firearms were long-distance weapons. Muskets had first entered Zululand in 1824 with traders and hunters from Cape Colony who settled in Port Natal, but the full potential of firearms only became apparent during the Voortrekker invasion of 1838. Then the amaZulu discovered that because of the heavy musket fire they could not get close enough to the Voortrekkers' laagers to make any use of their bladed weapons in the toe-to-toe fighting to which they were accustomed.[7] Consequently, even though the amaZulu proved remarkably resistant to the new technology and remained essentially wedded to their traditionalist military ethos, they could not but see how firearms were spreading rapidly throughout South Africa and were being increasingly adopted by their African neighbours such as the Bapedi and Basotho.[8] But how were the amaZulu to keep up in this arms race since no man was permitted to leave the kingdom because he had to serve the king in his *ibutho* and could not therefore earn money as a migrant worker and buy a firearm? Cetshwayo decided he must therefore import firearms thorough traders. An enterprising hunter–trader called John Dunn, who gained Cetshwayo's ear as his adviser, cornered the lucrative Zulu arms market, buying from merchants in the Cape and Natal and bringing in the firearms (mainly antiquated muskets) through Portuguese Delagoa Bay to avoid Natal laws against gun trafficking.[9] The Zulu paid mostly in cattle which Dunn then sold in Natal.[10]

If, conservatively, 20,000 guns entered Zululand during Cetshwayo's reign, of which only one in forty was a modern breech-loader,[11] it seems they were not necessarily in the hands of the *amabutho* who would be using them in battle. Mpatshana kaSodondo of the uVe *ibutho* told Stuart in 1912 that when the Zulu army was concentrating at oNdini preparatory to marching off to fight the British invaders in January 1879, 'Cetshwayo came out by the inner gate at 9 a.m. He said, "Is this the whole *impi* [army, plural *izimpi*], then? Lift up your guns." We did so. "So there are no guns?" Each man with a beast from his place must bring it up next day and buy guns of Dunn.'[12]

What this evidence makes clear is that as instruments of power and as a valuable form of largesse Cetshwayo wished to keep the control of firearms in his own hands. They were not necessarily widely dispersed into the hands of ordinary warriors, and many had little (if any) practical training in their use. This being the case, we cannot wonder at the oft-repeated British assertions made during the Anglo-Zulu War about the very poor quality of Zulu marksmanship. Naturally, part of the reason for this doubtless lay with the known ineffectiveness of the many obsolete and inferior firearms in Zulu possession, with the unskilled way in which they were maintained, with the usually poor quality of their gunpowder and shot and with shortages of percussion caps and cartridges. But these mechanical shortcomings were exacerbated by lack of musketry instruction. For example, the amaZulu were accustomed to the curving trajectories of thrown spears, and aimed firearms high with the not unnatural expectation that bullets would behave similarly.[13] Put simply, most amaZulu did not shoot well because they had scant practice.

It was the Zulu elite, rather than ordinary warriors, who all but monopolised the many firearms in the kingdom and valued who them for the mystique of power they conferred upon the possessor. These men of status had the ammunition to improve their marksmanship with practice. So too did a select handful of men recruited and trained in the use of firearms by white hunters such as John Dunn who needed them to procure the tusks, hides and feathers of their lucrative trade.[14] Otherwise, the bulk of *amabutho* who were unfamiliar with firearms continued to regarded them in the same light as throwing spears, and regularly cast both aside before getting down to the real business of fighting hand-to-hand – the only form of combat that would be celebrated down the generations when a man's descendants declaimed his praises.

Chapter 6

Mustering for a Defensive Campaign

The impending war would reveal how successfully this 'savage' Zulu army would contend tactically with the invaders, but before hostilities commenced Cetshwayo and his advisers had to concert their strategy. From the spies he deployed in Natal, the Transvaal and Portuguese Delagoa Bay, Cetshwayo learned the precise strength and intentions of the British columns poised to cross his borders.[1] Zulu kings habitually employed spies to keep them apprised of what was occurring throughout their kingdom, and in time of war the king expected his subjects to report on the enemy's movements and gather intelligence in hostile territory. The British were aware even before they crossed the border that they were under constant Zulu surveillance, but it took them some time before they realised that the deserters and refugees they succoured or even employed as camp servants were actually spies.[2]

Knowledge of the extent of the threat to his kingdom and the limits of his own resources caused Cetshwayo to cast around for allies. If he really had been the prime mover of the 'black conspiracy' so dear to Frere's heart, it should have been no challenge to summon up aid from across southern Africa, but Cetshwayo could not play the role the High Commissioner and his lieutenants had assigned him. Even though African rulers maintained diplomatic relations with each other as a matter of course, sectional advantage continued short-sightedly to be placed before wider, common interests.

Consequently, despite Cetshwayo making some friendly overtures in late 1878, there was never any prospect of aid from Swaziland.[3] To the contrary, the amaSwazi had for too long been the victims of Zulu raids and threatened attacks, and King Mbandzeni looked eagerly forward to the elimination of Zulu military might. Nor was there any likelihood of cooperation with the Mabhudu-Tsonga, the dominant chiefdom across Zululand's trade-routes north to Delagoa Bay. Although they had long paid tribute to the Zulu, relations had been poor since the 1860s when they had clashed with their overlord over control of the lucrative trade routes and smaller chiefdoms of the region. Muhena, the regent of the Mabhudu-Tsonga, consequently welcomed the prospect of the breaking of Zulu power. Farther afield, Cetshwayo had even less chance of raising black polities under British suzerainty against their white overlords. Despite some activity by his emissaries in late 1878, he had absolutely no success with the Basotho who had been under Cape administration since 1871, or with the amaMpondo on the southern borders of Natal.[4] It should perhaps have been different with the Bapedi. After all, the British were convinced that Sekhukhune was being directed and manipulated by Cetshwayo, his puppet-master.[5] There is in fact evidence that the two rulers were considering a common anti-British front but, in the end, no active alliance was ever formed. Sekhukhune seems to have decided that it was too dangerous to allow his unresolved conflict with the British in the Transvaal to be sucked into Cetshwayo's major war against them. In any case, he was aware that Colonel Rowlands's No. 5 Column was strategically positioned between his territory and the Zulu kingdom.

Knowing then that no other African state would rally to their cause, and unsure of being able to wage a successful aggressive campaign over their borders, in January 1879 Cetshwayo and his advisers opted for a defensive strategy. For success, however, this required a delicate combination of military success and diplomatic finesse. The Zulu leadership knew that the coming campaign had to be swiftly decisive since Cetshwayo would not be able to achieve his political goal of negotiating a cessation of hostilities other than from a position of military strength. Yet here was the poser. Cetshwayo was sure that the British were unlikely to enter into any parleys with him that would leave him with his independence if his *izimpi* followed up a victory on their own soil by invading British territory. Consequently, for his political strategy to succeed, Cetshwayo had to convince the British that the amaZulu had absolutely no hostile intentions against their neighbouring colonies. Therefore, it was essential to fight only within the borders of Zululand so that he could present himself as the hapless victim of an unwarranted attack, legitimately defending his own. As he would declare to Cornelius Vijn soon after the Zulu victory at the battle of Isandlwana: 'It is the Whites who have come to fight with me in my own country, and not I that will go to fight with them. My intention, therefore, is only to defend myself in my own country.'[6]

Having decided on this defensive military strategy determined by policy objectives, the next issue was how best to deploy Zulu forces for the coming war. The problem was that the kingdom faced attack from every quarter, and with a total Zulu population of about 300,000 people there were not enough fighting men of military age to go around. The numerical strength of the *amabutho* is difficult to estimate with any certainty. Chelmsford and his staff made their plans with the figure of 41,900 warriors in mind. In fact, the Zulu army probably did have a nominal strength of about 40,000 men, but some of the senior *amabutho* were past active service, and actual effectives – those who were in an age-band between their early twenties and late forties – were unlikely to have numbered more than 29,000.[7] In addition, Cetshwayo could count upon approximately 5,000 irregulars joining the *amabutho* on campaign. These included the people of the Tsonga chiefdoms to the south of the Mabhudu-Tsonga who were in a strong cultural and tributary relationship with the neighbouring Zulu kingdom, and people such as the amaKubheka living in the disputed north-western region of the kingdom who owed Cetshwayo a shadowy allegiance.

In making his dispositions, Cetshwayo correctly decided to discount the possibility of a sea-borne invasion.[8] By January 1879 it was clear the British were not intending to land troops at Portuguese Delagoa Bay or at St Lucia Bay to its south, nor would they be advancing from the north-east picking up Mabhudu-Tsonga auxiliaries as they went. Nor were they going to attempt an amphibious landing further down the Indian Ocean coast despite a serious effort in August 1878 to identify a suitable landing-place along a shoreline frustratingly deficient in natural harbours north of Durban.[9] The king was far less confident in leaving his borders with Swaziland undefended. Nevertheless, he gambled rightly that Mbandzeni would not risk committing his warriors to the conflict allied to the British until he was absolutely certain they would win.[10]

The upshot was that Cetshwayo could safely ignore his northern border and coastline to concentrate on the British forces to the south and west. His spies correctly informed him that the British No. 3 Column operating out of Rorke's Drift was the strongest, and confirmed that Chelmsford himself was accompanying it. This intelligence persuaded Cetshwayo that the Centre Column was the main British force and that the maximum effect would be gained by defeating it. He consequently resolved to direct his main army against it, while a subsidiary army would break away to confront No. 1 Column preparing to advance up the coast across the lower Thukela River. Local irregulars in the Nkandla forest in southern Zululand would oppose No. 2 Column if it crossed the middle Thukela (in the event it moved west and joined the Centre Column). He also sent some reinforcements to support the irregulars in the open grasslands of the north-west who were confronting both No. 4 and No. 5 Columns.[11]

In early January Cetshwayo sent out orders for his *amabutho* to assemble at oNdini to prepare for war. Kumbeka Gwabe recalled: 'The regiments gathered there had so many men in them that they seemed to stretch right from there to the sea. The first thing our king did was to give us cattle and beer to drink.'[12] During the days following the expiry of the British ultimatum on 11 January 1879 the *amabutho* already mustered in the *amakhanda* in the Mahlabathini plain were 'doctored' for war.[13] The amaZulu believed in an overlap that existed between this world and the world of the spirits. This was expressed by a mystical force, *umnyama*, which was darkness or evil influence, and was represented by the colour black. As Mpatshana explained, it could overtake an *impi* in the form of 'paralysis of action caused by fear . . . futility or stupidity of plan when engaging their assailants, being overtaken by a mist when it is clear for their foes, etc.'[14] It could also be contagious in its most virulent forms. Because such pollution was a mystical rather than organic illness, it could be cured only by symbolic medicines. Death by violence, expressed as *umkhoka*, was an especially powerful form of *umnyama*, as the killer himself was polluted. Thus, *amabutho* on campaign were in especial spiritual danger, and needed to be ritually purified of evil influences and strengthened against them.

Before marching out to war, members of an *ibutho* caught and killed bare-handed a black bull from the royal herds upon which all the evil influences in the land had been ritually cast. *Izangoma* (singular *isangoma*) – diviners possessed by the spirits of the ancestors (*amadlozi*), which made them a link between this and the spirit world – cut strips of meat from the bull, and treated them with black medicines to strengthen the warriors and bind them together in loyalty to their king. The strips of meat were then roasted on a fire of wood collected by the warriors the previous day. The *izangoma* threw the strips up into the air and the warriors, who were drawn up in a great circle, caught and sucked them. Meanwhile the *izangoma* burned more medicines and the warriors breathed in the smoke and were sprinkled with the cinders. Weapons too were incorporated into the ceremonies of ritual purification and strengthening, and with firearms mystical forces were expected to compensate for lack of practical skill in hitting a target, just as they would protect a man from wounds and death.[15]

Finally, in order to expel all evil influences, each warrior drank a pot of medicine, and a few at a time took turns to vomit into a great pit. The ritual vomiting was also intended to bind the warriors in their loyalty to their king. Some of the vomit was added to the great *inkatha* of the Zulu nation, the sacred grass coil which was the symbol of the nation's unity and strength. The following day the warriors went down to any running stream to wash, but not to rub off the medicines with which they had been sprinkled. With the completion of these rituals the warriors (who had undergone a symbolic death) could no longer sleep at home nor have anything to do with girls or women since they themselves had now taken on a dangerous state of *umnyama*.

While the warriors were thus setting themselves apart from ordinary life and dedicating themselves to war, Cetshwayo called up pair after pair of the *amabutho* into the royal cattle enclosure to boast of their courage and to issue ritual challenges to outdo one another in the coming campaign. Mpatshana described the ritual encounter between the uKhandempemvu and iNgobamakhosi which lasted until sunset: 'A man from the iNgobamakhosi got up and shouted, "I shall surpass you, son of So-and-so. If you stab a white man before mine has fallen, you may take the kraal of our people at such-and-such a place; you may take my sister, So-and-so."' Having made his challenge, he then commenced to *giya*, or to perform a leaping war dance with his dancing shield and stick, while his companions loudly called out his praises. The member of the uKhandempemvu thus addressed answered in like kind while Cetshwayo held out his arm towards him, approvingly shaking two extended fingers at him.[16]

For the Zulu, good fortune in a military enterprise depended on the approval of the *amadlozi* who lived under the ground and were interested in every aspect of their descendants' lives. Because the spirits maintained the status they had enjoyed while alive, it was particularly necessary before proceeding on campaign to secure the favour of the *amadlozi* of the king's royal forebears since they were necessarily concerned with the welfare of the entire Zulu nation. The way the living propitiated the *amadlozi* was through cattle sacrifice when the spirits partook of the burnt offerings and 'licked' the meat set aside for them. So, before the *impi* marched away to war, Cetshwayo ensured that the royal *amadlozi* were satisfied with a generous sacrifice from the royal herd. Now the *amadlozi* would accompany the warriors and deploy their powers against the enemy.

Before he despatched his ritually prepared armies to the frontiers, Cetshwayo issued his generals with careful tactical instructions.[17] The king was enough of a soldier to understand the dangers involved in trying to storm prepared positions similar to the Boer wagon laagers in 1838. He therefore categorically forbade his commanders from attacking any form of entrenchment where they would be pitilessly exposed to concentrated fire-power. Rather, he cautioned them to bypass defensive works and to threaten the British lines of supply and the territory to their rear. That would force the enemy out to protect them. Then, Cetshwayo instructed, 'If you see him out in the open you can attack him because you will be able to eat him up.'[18] After all, it was in a pitched battle in the open field that the heroic virtues of the *amabutho* were most likely to prevail.

On the other hand, if the British could not be brought swiftly to battle, the Zulu armies would founder for lack of logistical support. When a Zulu *impi* marched off to war, boys older than fourteen (*izindibi*) accompanied it as carriers of sleeping-mats and other equipment, and also as drovers of the cattle which would be slaughtered for consumption on the march. Daughters and sisters of the *amabutho* bearing supplies kept up with the *impi* for a few days until their stocks were exhausted. The warriors themselves carried iron rations in a skin sack. But these varied sources of food soon began to give out. The hungry *amabutho* tried to spare their own civilian population along the line of march as far as possible, and camped whenever they could at *amakhanda* where stores of food had been amassed. Nevertheless, the *amabutho* could not afford to be squeamish about pillaging their own people when out of supplies, and Zulu civilians took the same precautions against them as against an enemy, removing their grain which was vital as seed for the next season's planting, driving off their cattle and taking refuge themselves out of the *impi*'s path. Cetshwayo knew such disruptions to the lives of his people could not long be borne, and that a war waged on Zulu soil must of necessity be short.[19]

Nzuzi of the uVe *ibutho* recalled that before the *impi* finally marched out to war, the king addressed it as it stood around him in a great circle:

> I have not gone over the seas to look for the white men, yet they have come into my country and I would not be surprised if they took away our wives and cattle and crops and land. What shall I do?' . . . 'Give the matter to us,' we replied. 'We shall go and eat up the white men and finish them off. They are not going to take you while we are here. They must take us first.'[20]

PART III

Repulsing the British Invasion

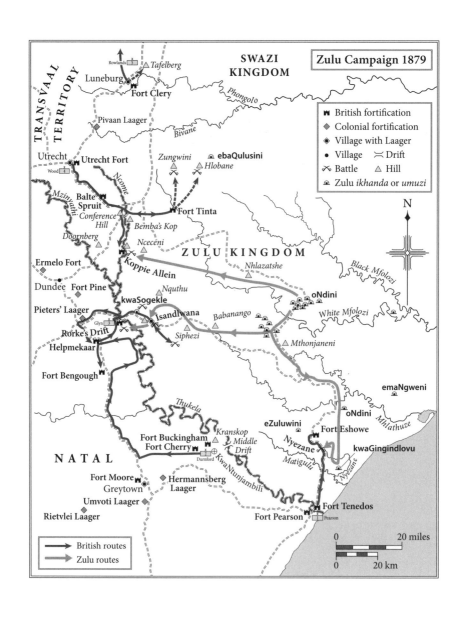

SWAZI KINGDOM

Zulu Campaign 1879

TRANSVAAL TERRITORY

Rowlands
Tafelberg
Luneburg
Fort Clery
Pivaan Laager
Phongolo
Bivane
Utrecht
Utrecht Fort
Wood
Zungwini
ebaQulusini
Hlobane
Ncome
Balte Spruit
Mzinyathi
Conference Hill
Bemba's Kop
Fort Tinta
Doornberg
Nceceni
ZULU KINGDOM
Nhlazatshe
Black Mfolozi
Ermelo Fort
Koppie Allein
Dundee
Fort Pine
Nquthu
kwaSogekle
oNdini
White Mfolozi
Pieters' Laager
Isandlwana
Babanango
Glyn
Rorke's Drift
Siphezi
Helpmekaar
Mthonjaneni
Fort Bengough
Thukela
emaNgweni
Kranskop
eZuluwini
Fort Buckingham
Middle Drift
oNdini
Fort Cherry
Durnford
Fort Eshowe
Mhlathuze
NATAL
kwaNtunjambili
Nyezane
kwaGingindlovu
Matigulu
Nyezane
Fort Moore
Greytown
Hermannsberg Laager
Umvoti Laager
Rietvlei Laager
Fort Pearson
Fort Tenedos
Pearson

N

Legend:
- British fortification
- Colonial fortification
- Village with Laager
- Village — Drift
- Battle △ Hill
- Zulu *ikhanda* or *umuzi*

→ British routes
→ Zulu routes

0   20 miles
0   20 km

Chapter 7

The Enemy Has Taken Our Camp

With the expiry of the ultimatum on 11 January 1879, the British Centre Column already concentrated at Rorke's Drift on the Mzinyathi River began its laborious advance into Zululand.[1] The Zulu did not seem appropriately awed by the spectacle of military might, and, as Captain Hallam Parr recorded, taunted the British, calling out "'What were we doing riding along there?" "We had better try and come up;" "Were we looking for a place to build our kraals?" etc., etc.'[2]

Chelmsford and his small staff accompanied the column. The general inevitably overshadowed Colonel Glyn, a veteran of the Ninth Cape Frontier War and the column's nominal commander, and assumed active control of its direction. His forces scored an immediate and easy success on 12 January in a skirmish at kwaSogekle, the *umuzi* of Sihayo kaXongo, the Qungebe *inkosi*, who was a member of the king's *umkhandlu* and a particular favourite of Cetshwayo.[3] KwaSogekle was built at the foot of the northern end of Ngedla Mountain with its defensible caves and gullies. Even so, the amaZulu failed to make a determined stand, which seemed to confirm British expectations that they would not prove to be any more formidable than had the amaXhosa.[4]

When during the skirmish Major Clery wished to send in some mounted men 'rather widely to flank', Lt.-Col. Crealock, Chelmsford's AMS, checked him: "Do not do that as it will cause what actually happened in the last war – the enemy to take flight and bolt before we can get at them."' Crealock's admonition conformed to Chelmsford's own thinking for, as Clery noted, 'the general issued an order that the artillery was never to open fire until the enemy were within 600 metres of them for fear of frightening them, and so deterring them from coming on, or making them bolt.'[5]

To his annoyance, Chelmsford found that the rain-sodden, muddy ground rendered a rapid advance impossible. On 20 January he halted and set up camp at the eastern base of the sphinx-shaped Isandlwana Mountain while he prepared to reconnoitre the way forward. The position was potentially difficult to defend because it was overlooked by a spur of the Nyoni hills to the north, and the layout of the camp was overly extended. But since Chelmsford regarded the camp as temporary, and considered a Zulu attack most unlikely, no attempt was made to entrench it. Nor were the wagons laagered because they were required to bring up supplies from the advanced supply depot at Rorke's Drift. In any case, until he learned better, Chelmsford regarded a laager more as protection for oxen than as a redoubt for soldiers.[6]

At oNdini, Cetshwayo's response to word that the British had begun their invasion was rapid. After parading past the graves of his royal ancestors to secure the blessings of the *amadlozi*, the main Zulu *impi* of 24,000 men began its march on 17 January. Morale was high, for the *amabutho* believed in their cause and were exuberantly confident that they would scatter the red soldiers.[7] Two commanders strode out in front on foot, rather than riding horses as many other men of status did, thus associating themselves closely with the men they led, as well as setting a comfortable pace that did not exhaust the army.

The senior of these two generals was Ntshingwayo kaMahole, the *inkosi* of the Khoza people in central Zululand, of a lineage long associated with the Zulu kings, and regarded by Cetshwayo as his commander-in-chief. He was a stocky, powerful man of seventy with greying hair and a considerable paunch. As a member of the uDlambedlu *ibutho* he had doubtless fought in the Voortrekker–Zulu War as well as in King Mpande's Swazi campaigns. Mpande had recognised his charismatic leadership qualities, oratorical skills and soldierly flair and had raised him up to be the *induna* of the emLambongwenya *ikhanda*. Cetshwayo also put his trust in him, and on his succession made him *induna* of the kwaGqikazi *ikhanda* and of the *ibutho* quartered there. Ntshingwayo was a close friend and associate of Mnyamana, and with him served on Cetshwayo's *umkhandlu*, second only to him in rank. There, precisely because of his astute military knowledge, he was one of those who had counselled strongly against war with the British. But once the conflict became inevitable, he threw himself and all his considerable energy into planning the campaign.[8]

Ntshingwayo's associate commander and junior in age and status was Mavumengwana kaNdlela, the *inkosi* of a section of the Ntuli people in south-eastern Zululand between the Thukela and Matigulu rivers. His father, Ndlela kaSomipisi, had been King Dingane's chief *induna*. Still in his late forties, Mavumengwana had been enrolled with Cetshwayo in the uThulwana *ibutho*, had served with him in the Swazi campaign of 1852, and remained his close friend. Mavumengwana was one of the greatest men in the kingdom, the principal *induna* of the uThulwana *ibutho* and (as was Ntshingwayo) a member of the *umkhandlu*. Like his fellow commander, Mavumengwana had been a leading member of the peace party who now committed himself wholeheartedly to winning the war once it became inevitable. It seems that his appointment to the joint command with Ntshingwayo reflected the king's desire to have a royal favourite and a man of his own generation in a leading position at the head of his army.[9]

The day after the Zulu *impi* marched out on 17 January, a force of about 4,000 men detached itself from the main body and headed off south-east to confront Colonel Pearson's No. 1 Column. Its commander, Godide kaNdlela Ntuli, tall, thin and with a dark complexion, was nearly seventy years old and had been enrolled in the iziNyosi *ibutho*. Most likely he had fought the Voortrekkers in 1838. He was Mavumengwana's elder brother, hereditary *inkosi* of the Ntuli along the middle Thukela, and already a leading *isikhulu* under King Mpande and member of the *umkhandlu*. He had continued in Cetshwayo's favour and was the senior *induna* of the uMxhapho *ibutho*.[10]

On 20 January the main *impi* bivouacked by Siphezi Hill, only just over twelve miles east of Isandlwana, and its scouts made contact with the British. Chelmsford, however, had no inkling of the close proximity of the enemy army. Instead, he was concerned that the local Sithole *inkosi*, Matshana kaMondisa, might be gathering a force in the broken country to the south-east of Isandlwana in order to interrupt his column's line of supply once it advanced further into Zululand. Accordingly, on 21 January, Chelmsford sent out a reconnaissance-in-force to scout the area south-east of Isandlwana. It consisted of most of the Natal Mounted Police and half the Natal Mounted Volunteers under Major John Dartnell (150 troopers), as well as the bulk of the two battalions of the 3rd Regiment, NNC, under Commandant Rupert Lonsdale (1,600 men). Lonsdale, a retired officer who had settled in the eastern Cape, had earned a formidable reputation during the Ninth Cape Frontier war as a dynamic and inspiring commander of African levies. However, a fall from his horse just before the invasion began had left him with bad concussion, and he was still suffering from the after-effects.[11] As this joint force advanced, some 2,000 amaZulu under Matshana skilfully retired eastwards before it, and by evening were massed on the Magogo heights to its front. To forestall an advance by Matshana's force on Isandlwana, Dartnell and Lonsdale bivouacked nervously for the night on the Hlazakazi heights, westwards across the valley from Magogo and the Zulu watch fires.[12]

Meanwhile, the joint Zulu commanders, who had indeed been considering a flank march to Chelmsford's east to join with Matshana and cut the British column off from Natal, decided instead to take advantage of the general's rash and poorly conceived division of his forces. They detached some men to reinforce Matshana, but on the same evening of 21 January and during the next morning they transferred the main army north-west across the British front from Siphezi Hill to the deep shelter of the Ngwebeni valley. The *amabutho* moved rapidly in small units, mainly concealed from the Isandlwana camp nine miles away by the Nyoni heights. The British mounted patrols that sighted some of the apparently isolated Zulu units had no inkling an entire army was on the move. This was indeed a masterful manoeuvre, facilitated by the local topographical knowledge of Sihayo, the Qungebe *inkosi* and of his spirited senior son, Mehlokazulu. The young man was a favoured *inceku* (personal attendant) of Cetshwayo, one of the royal 'eyes' – those entrusted with keeping an eye on developments along the border – and a junior *induna* of the iNgobamakhosi *ibutho*.[13]

During the moonless night of 21–22 January there was a false alarm and needless panic among the NNC encamped in a hollow square on Hlazakazi.[14] Unharmed but rattled, Dartnell sent Chelmsford a note, which the general received at 01.30, urgently requesting support. This communication confirmed for Chelmsford that enemy movements in the area indicated that the main Zulu army was pushing down the Mangeni valley to the east, and so he decided he must move out immediately to intercept with about half the force still encamped at Isandlwana.

Colonel Glyn, accompanied by Chelmsford, accordingly advanced at 04.30 with four out of the six guns of N/5 Battery, RA, six companies of the 2/24th Regiment, a detachment of No. 1 Squadron, Mounted Infantry, and men of No. 1 Company, Natal Native Pioneers. Chelmsford left the camp with a garrison consisting of a division of two 7-pounder guns, five companies of the 1/24th and one of the 2/24th, the balance of mounted troops not already deployed, two companies each from the 1/3rd NNC and the 2/3rd NNC, and small details from other units. Before he left, Chelmsford ordered up Colonel Durnford from Rorke's Drift with the available men of No. 2 Column to reinforce the camp. This detachment consisted of 11/7th Brigade, RA (a rocket battery of three 9-pounders), five troops of the Natal Native Mounted Contingent, and two companies of the 1/1st NNC. Until he arrived, when the troops in camp would amount to 67 officers and 1,707 men (approximately half of whom were Africans), Brevet Lieutenant-Colonel Henry Pulleine (another veteran of the Ninth Cape Frontier War but who had never commanded in battle) would be the senior officer left in camp.

As Clery later admitted, 'Nobody from the general downwards had the least suspicion that there was a chance of the camp being attacked.'[15] Indeed, as Lieutenant Henry Harford (a regular officer seconded to the NNC as Commandant Lonsdale's staff officer) later noted in his journal, some officers 'were terribly disappointed at the thought of being left behind in Camp and lose [*sic*] the chance of a fight, and begged hard to be allowed to find substitutes'.[16] Even when later that morning a thousand or more Zulus appeared fleetingly on the hills to the east of the camp, no officer was disconcerted. For, as Lieutenant Henry Curling, RA (one of the few officers to survive the battle) later wrote to his mother: 'We none of us had the least idea that the Zulu contemplated attacking the camp and, having in the last war [the Ninth Cape Frontier War] often seen equally large bodies of the enemy, never dreamed they would come on.'[17]

When Chelmsford's badly strung-out relief force reached Hlazakazi at about 06.00, bringing the troops operating in the area to about

2,500, the Zulu on Magogo had broken away. Some had withdrawn south-east onto the Phindo heights and others north onto Silutshana Hill, both with the intention of ultimately pulling back north-east to Siphezi and drawing the British after them, away from the camp. Dartnell took the bait, and became involved in a heavy skirmish on Phindo. Unaware of falling into a trap, Chelmsford decided to let Dartnell get on with taking Phindo while the relief column cleared the area around Silutshana and the valley of the Nondweni River between Magogo and Phindo. While his troops skirmished, Chelmsford used the opportunity to scout about personally, as was his wont, and to select a suitable new campsite for the column when it advanced.

At 09.30, while breakfasting below the northern slopes of Magogo, Chelmsford received a message sent at 08.05 by Pulleine that cryptically reported that amaZulu were advancing on the camp. No one suspected this could be the main Zulu army, and there seemed no sense of urgency in the brief note. Chelmsford himself, when Clery asked him what should be done, nonchalantly replied, 'There is nothing to be done on that.' His staff did not pursue the matter because he had become 'particularly touchy about suggestions being made to him'.[18] Chelmsford nevertheless sent Lt. Berkeley Milne of his staff up the slopes of Magogo to study the camp twelve miles away through his naval telescope. Milne kept watch for upwards of an hour, but saw nothing untoward – which was unavoidable from his perch since the southern shoulder of Silutshana cut off his view of the plain to the east of Isandlwana where the Zulu army was deploying. So, with nothing apparently amiss, between 10.00 and 11.00 Chelmsford sent Captain Alan Gardner of the 14th Hussars, attached as a special service officer to No. 3 Column, with orders to Pulleine to strike camp and move up. Meanwhile, between 10.30 and 12.30 Chelmsford rode off with a small mounted escort to scout further. His movements were consequently unpredictable, and subsequent messages concerning the evolving battle at Isandlwana failed for hours to find him or his staff.

Insouciantly unaware, therefore, of the disaster even then unfolding, Chelmsford hit on a suitable new campsite seven miles to the south-east of Isandlwana, just east of Hlazakazi on the Mangeni River above its spectacular horseshoe falls. Satisfied, he ordered the relief column under Glyn to concentrate there. As its weary units straggled in during the early afternoon, intermittent artillery fire was clearly heard from the direction of Isandlwana, and messages from the camp's beleaguered garrison at last found Chelmsford. Clery afterwards wrote that he heard Crealock superciliously exclaim of one: 'How very amusing! Actually attacking our camp! Most amusing!'[19] Shortly after 13.15 Chelmsford went up Mdutshana hill just north of the new Mangeni campsite with some of his staff to examine the Isandlwana camp through their field glasses. All seemed quiet, and the tents had not been struck as regulations dictated during an engagement. Chelmsford therefore concluded that if there had been a Zulu attack, it had been successfully repulsed.

Nevertheless, Chelmsford was prey to nagging disquiet, and at 14.45 decided he must return to Isandlwana with a small escort to investigate, albeit setting off at a leisurely pace. About five miles from the camp he was encountered by a shattered Commandant Lonsdale who had nonchalantly ridden back to Isandlwana to arrange for supplies to be brought up, and had barely escaped the triumphant amaZulu who were in possession of the camp. Chelmsford was appalled, exclaiming in disbelief: 'But I left over a thousand men to guard the camp.'[20] Clery later described 'the look of gloom and pain' on Chelmsford's 'expressive' countenance which clearly mirrored his inner turmoil.[21] Indeed, a soldier wrote home that he was 'very near crying'.[22] But Chelmsford never 'flunked' his duty and saw there was nothing for it but to attack the Isandlwana camp and, if the Zulu held it, to fight his way through to the river and his base at Rorke's Drift. He immediately ordered the already exhausted forces converging on the Mangeni campsite to prepare for action, but they were so scattered that it took them until 18.30, only half an hour before sunset, to concentrate within three miles of Isandlwana.

Anticipating Zulu resistance, Chelmsford addressed his dismayed troops with determination:

> Men, the enemy has taken our camp. Many of our friends must have lost their lives defending it. There is nothing left for us now but to fight our way through – and mind, we must fight hard, for we will have to fight for our lives. I know you, and I know I can depend on you.[23]

The men cheered lustily in response. Then Chelmsford, always one to follow the book, advanced in the gathering darkness of a moonless night with his force in regulation fighting formation.[24] Brevet Lieutenant-Colonel Arthur Harness, RA, who had fought in the Ninth Cape Frontier War and whose four guns of N/5 Battery had accompanied Chelmsford out of camp, left a graphic description of the march back in a letter to his younger sister, Caroline, or 'Co':

> . . . about eight p.m. we got near the old place, pitch-dark, and we were told we were to fight our way back to Rorke's Drift. We formed up a sort of line of battle in the dark: ourselves [his guns] on the road or track in column, with room to form line for action to our front; infantry on either side next us, then mounted men; then native contingent on each flank. About a quarter of a mile from the neck we halted and I fired about a dozen shells as well as we could in the dark and the infantry on our left went forward to take one of the little hills, which they did without resistance. We then all advanced and found the enemy had gone, but could see in the dark the complete wreck and slaughter which had taken place.[25]

For the loss of about a thousand men, the Zulu had killed 52 of the British officers left to defend the camp, including Pulleine and Durnford, along with 739 white troops (almost all of those in the camp), 67 white NCOs of the NNC and 471 black troops. This was a 75 per cent casualty rate, an utter rout which was the rarest of rare occurrences in a colonial campaign, and all the more shocking for that. How had the amaZulu achieved their stunning victory?

Chapter 8

Camped among the Bodies

———⊰●⊱———

Late on the dull, cloudy morning of the battle the Zulu *impi* was still bivouacked in the valley of the Ngwebeni stream while small parties were out foraging and scouting. Its commanders were in conclave, discussing their next move. It was not their intention to fight that fateful Sunday because, as Mpatshana explained, 'That day the moon had waned. It was not customary to fight at such a time . . . a young woman does not dance that day . . . a garden is not reaped, a hunting party is not sent out.'[1] But, as a 'Zulu Deserter' of the uNokhenke *ibutho* related, while the *impi* was 'sitting resting', a party of mounted British scouts in pursuit of Zulu foragers driving along a small herd of cattle suddenly came over the Mabaso heights overlooking the valley, just above the mettlesome uKhandempemvu *ibutho*. The uKhandempemvu 'at once jumped up and charged', and their fierce if ill-disciplined example was taken up by the other younger *amabutho*.[2] There was considerable disarray in this impromptu advance, and the Zulu commanders were hard-pressed to restore some order. They did succeed in keeping back four of the more experienced *amabutho* in reserve and putting them through the final ritual preparations for battle which their younger comrades had forgone – although (according to Mpatshana) many had taken the precaution of 'carrying drugs in their medicine-bags' with which to 'doctor' themselves.[3]

As it drove on towards the British camp the *impi* deployed into its time-hallowed chest and horns formation with the intention of enveloping the British position. Pulleine made his initial dispositions without any true idea of the size of the Zulu forces bearing down on him and unaware that they were intent on outflanking him. So, in copy-book fashion he pushed forward an extended firing line in an arc on either side of his two 7-pounder guns. Their position was nearly half-a-mile north-east of the camp in order to support outlying units falling back, and to command the dead ground to their front. Colonel Durnford – who earlier that morning had rashly ridden off for several miles to the east with his mounted men to protect Chelmsford (so he believed) from a Zulu rear attack – conducted a fighting retreat to a deep donga on Pulleine's right flank.

When the Zulu centre spilled over the Nyoni heights where the Zulu commanders halted to take up their stations, it was pinned down by the British fire. Even though the troops were in skirmishing order, it was quite heavy enough to stall the daunted *amabutho* who had never, ever experienced the like. The Zulu commanders sent officers running down the hill to rally the *amabutho*, pointedly reminding them of their ritual challenges before the campaign. Sikizane kaNomageji shouted to the iNgobamakhosi, 'Why are you lying down? What was it you said to the uKhandempemvu?'[4] Another exhorted them: 'Never did his Majesty the King give you this command, to wit, "Lie down upon the ground!" His words were: "Go! And toss them into Maritzburg!"'[5] Then, as a 'Warrior of the uMbonambi' recalled, 'they all shouted "uSuthu!" [the national battle-cry] and waving their shields charged upon the soldiers with great fury.'[6]

The Zulu chest's determined charge coincided with an attempt by the British to fall back from their exposed forward positions and concentrate on their camp because they realised they were being outflanked by the rapidly deploying Zulu horns. With scarcely a month's training behind them, the two companies of the 1/3rd NNC in the centre of the British line were not up to a disciplined withdrawal. They broke and ran, and the exultant *amabutho* of the Zulu chest poured through the gap. The Court of Inquiry Chelmsford later set up to investigate the 'loss of the camp' blamed the collapse of the British line on the NNC's poor performance, and Chelmsford gratefully seized on this convenient African scapegoat for the bad judgment of the British commanders on the spot.[7]

The amaZulu allowed the withdrawing British no opportunity to rally. Mehlokazulu kaSihayo remembered that 'When the soldiers retired on the camp, they did so running, and the Zulus were then intermixed with them, and entered the camp at the same time . . . Things were then getting very mixed and confused . . . what with the smoke, dust, and intermingling of men, footmen, Zulus and natives [NNC].'[8] The *amabutho* finally had what they so ardently desired, a brutal hand-to-hand struggle as they drove the British through the camp. The Zulu horns almost succeeded in encircling the camp and entered it from the rear. Some of the British mounted men, pursued and harried the entire way by the amaZulu, succeeded in getting away down the treacherous 'Fugitives' Path' to the Mzinyathi River which was lethally swollen by the summer rains. Small units of British infantry attempted to rally and fight their way out, or at the very least to make a gallant last stand. Nzuzi grimly recalled that as the amaZulu fell upon the white men, 'many . . . said to us in our own tongue: ". . . Spare our lives. What wrong have we done to Cetshwayo?" "How can we give you mercy," we replied, "when you have come to us and want to take our country and eat us up? . . . uSuthu!"' And with their eyes 'dark' in battle fury the warriors 'stabbed everything we came across'.[9]

During battle a ritual many Zulu warriors followed was to *hlomula*, or to stab an enemy who had already died fighting courageously. This practice was connected with the hunt, and was observed only when a fierce and dangerous animal like a lion had been overcome. But killing in battle or participating in the *hlomula* ritual severely contaminated the warrior with an especially virulent form of *umnyama*. A notable warrior might be praised for being 'wet with yesterday's blood',[10] but when he pushed his *iklwa* into the victim's yielding flesh, or battered out his brains with an *iwisa*, the victim's blood which spurted over him and his clothing formed a fearsome bridge between the living and the world of the dead. All sorts of special ritual precautions then became necessary to gain ascendancy over the vengeful spirits of the slain.[11] One essential ritual was to slit open the belly of a slain foe, to *qaqa*, so that *umnyama* would not affect the killer and make him swell up like the dead. The killer would also put on items of the dead man's apparel in place of his own – which would have been contaminated by the harmful influences of the victim's blood – in order that he might *zila*, or observe the customary abstentions after a death until ritually cleansed.[12] The British, when they later came upon the disembowelled bodies of their comrades, naturally saw their mutilation in a very different light. To them it was a horror and abomination which changed the whole nature of the war.

Once the fighting at Isandlwana had died down somewhere after 14.00, the exultant *amabutho* set about comprehensively looting the camp in the sickly light of a partial solar eclipse.[13] Firearms and ammunition were the most highly prized booty, especially the modern Martini-Henry rifles. About 800 fell into Zulu hands, although only a few Zulu marksmen familiar through hunting with modern firearms would be able to make effective use of them. Pillaging continued until, towards evening, the *amabutho* saw the dilatory Chelmsford at last approaching. Sated, they pulled back with their booty to their bivouac at the Ngwebeni. They did not bury the fallen, but as Mpatshana recalled, the bodies 'were here and there covered over with their shields – it is put over by a relative or friend'.[14]

The victorious Zulu had already withdrawn except for a few stragglers when Chelmsford reoccupied the camp at about 20.30 without encountering any resistance. What then followed was what Clery described with quintessentially British understatement as 'not a pleasant night',[15] bivouacked, as Chelmsford laconically informed Frere, 'among the bodies from dead soldiers and of the enemy'.[16]

Charles Norris-Newman (known to his messmates as 'Noggs'), the special correspondent for the London *Standard* and stringer for the *Times of Natal* and the *Cape Standard and Mail*, was with Chelmsford on the fateful day and described the awful night the column spent on the 'field of slaughter'. Fearing a surprise Zulu attack during the night, the general ordered the three companies of the 2/24th to remain on the koppie they had occupied to the south of Isandlwana Mountain during their advance on the camp, and the rest of the force to bivouac on the nek in between where they formed a hollow square and posted guards. They were to move forward only at daylight the next morning.[17] 'How that terrible night passed with us', wrote Norris-Newman, 'few would care to tell.' He was one of those who could not resist doing so, however, and he rose an hour before daylight to report more accurately on the 'melancholy scene of horror' which he described in horrific detail.[18] The traumatised troops encamped that pitch dark night among the heaped bodies of slaughtered men, oxen, horses and mules in a foul miasma of blood, excrement, spilled guts and chemicals from the shattered contents of the Royal Army Medical Corps wagon, had not eaten for hours. Sergeant W. E. Warren wrote home: 'You could not move a foot either way without treading on dead bodies. Oh, father . . . I could not help crying to see how the poor fellows were massacred.'[19] Lieutenant Harford joined one of the small parties of officers sent out to forage in the wrecked commissariat wagons, among the burned, shredded tents, and in the hospital lines for what food the Zulu had not carried off or deliberately spoiled, 'stabbing or smashing up all the tinned articles'.[20] Enough was found for a rough meal for most of the troops (even if some of the more selfish officers kept the more desirable items like unbroken bottles of port and packages of tobacco for themselves).[21]

Harford recorded that no sooner had the bivouac settled apprehensively down on the rocky ground (many sitting up because they were too crowded to stretch out) than the amaZulu began 'to light fires that could be seen moving about on the ridge just across the valley, barring our line of retreat to Rorke's Drift.' During that awful night there were several false alarms and shots were fired at phantom assailants. Men of the 2/3rd NNC tried to creep away and had to be driven back into their position in the square.[22] Making his rounds, Chelmsford approached Harford and asked whether he thought the Zulu would attack or not. The young officer responded that he 'felt pretty certain that they would as soon as it was daylight'.[23] To make matter worse, throughout the night the sleepless troops could see the intermittent flash of firing from Rorke's Drift, some three or four miles off in a straight line, although twelve miles by road. All feared for the safety of the little garrison, but knew they could not march to its relief until daylight came. The swashbuckling military adventurer Commandant George Hamilton-Browne of the 2/3rd NNC – who held his black troops in the utmost racist disdain,[24] and later penned melodramatic and unreliable memoirs – was aghast when he saw great fires break out on the Natal side of the Mzinyathi as dwellings went up in flames. His companion exclaimed, 'By God, the Zulus are in Natal! Lord help the women and children.' Hamilton-Browne expressed it in his characteristic style: 'We had not been very joyful before, but now we felt very sick indeed. If the Zulus chose to raid Natal there was nothing to stop their doing so. Our retreat, also, would be cut off. What was to become of me did not bother me . . . I expected to be killed but hoped to have a good fight first.'[25]

Chapter 9

We Seemed Very Few

———⊷●⊷———

The situation at Rorke's Drift was every bit as disastrous as the anxious British encamped among the dead at Isandlwana feared. When the Centre Column had advanced across the Mzinyathi on 11 January, it had left behind a small, mixed garrison to secure its supply depot at Rorke's Drift, once a trading store and subsequently the station of a Swedish missionary, Otto Witt, until the military took it over. The most important component of the garrison was B Company of the 2/24th Regiment, under Lieutenant Gonville 'Gunny' Bromhead. He came of a distinguished military family and had served in the Ninth Cape Frontier War. He was a popular 'capital fellow . . . a great favourite in his regiment', although his superior officers confidentially considered him to be afflicted by 'unconquerable indolence'.[1] He suffered from deafness, and this may have affected the performance of his military duties.[2] Also holding Rorke's Drift were a company of the 2/3rd NNC (abaThembu from the Klip River Division of Natal) under Captain William Stephenson,[3] and various detached personnel. Thirty-five wagons at Isandlwana were due to return on the morning of 22 January to be refilled with supplies, so there was a large stock-pile of stores at Rorke's Drift under the eye of Assistant Commissary Walter Dunne, a tall young man of considerable determination who had served both in the Ninth Cape Frontier War and in the First Anglo-Pedi War.[4] The garrison had turned an old thatched building (measuring 24.5 by 6.4 metres) – which Witt had used as a church – into a commissariat store to accommodate the supplies. They had transformed the missionary's own eleven-room, single-storied thatch-roofed house into a hospital. This measured 17.4 by 5.5 metres; it was a curious warren of unconnected rooms with the partitions made of soft, sun-dried bricks, and had a verandah facing outwards to the west. It was under the Irish-born Surgeon James Reynolds of the Army Medical Department who had seen service in India and in the Ninth Cape Frontier War.[5] Lieutenant John R. M. Chard, 5th Company, RE, had been superintending the operation of two ponts at the drift across the Mzinyathi. These were simple flat-bottomed ferries, one supported on big barrels, the other on boats, moved by hawsers secured to either bank. Each pont was large enough to transport a wagon and its team of oxen or a company of infantry.[6] Chard, a thirty-one-year-old passionate pipe-smoker, was an amiable, easy-going and rather plodding officer who had not previously seen action. He was considered to lack dash and initiative, and his superior officer described him as 'so hopelessly slow and slack'.[7]

Helpmekaar, a farmstead on the high escarpment of the Biggarsberg (a great spur of the Drakensberg) 425 metres above the open valley of the Mzinyathi and ten miles to the south-west of Rorke's Drift up an alarmingly steep and winding track, was the Centre Column's main depot. Three large stores, constructed of wood and roofed with galvanised iron, along with five 'wildebeest huts' held the bulk of its supplies. The depot was garrisoned by colonial mounted troops and two companies of the 1/24th Regiment. D Company was supposed to have marched down on 20 January to reinforce Rorke's Drift. When it did not arrive, Brevet Major Henry Spalding, who served as the column's Deputy Assistant Quartermaster-General in charge of its line of communications and supply through Helpmekaar, Greytown, Ladysmith and Durban, set off from Rorke's Drift for Helpmekaar on the early afternoon of Wednesday 22 January to fetch it down. He left Chard, whom he verified by consulting the Army List was the senior officer present, in command at Rorke's Drift. Spalding's nonchalant parting words to Chard were to assure him that 'of course nothing will happen' while he was away.[8] Indeed, with no Zulu attack even remotely anticipated, not the slightest attempt had been made to fortify the depot left under Chard's command.[9]

Shortly after 15.00 a few traumatised, fugitive horsemen from Isandlwana began coming up to the drift below the post with the alarming and initially unbelievable intelligence that the Zulu army had overrun the British camp, that the rest of the column with

Chelmsford had probably shared the same fate, and that a large Zulu force was even then rapidly approaching Rorke's Drift.[10] The bedraggled horsemen (one of whom was described as being 'without boots, tunic, or arms')[11] did not pause, but hurried on as best they could to sanctuary at Helpmekaar. Chard might have been an unimaginative officer, but he was staunch. In consultation with Bromhead he resolved that the garrison had no option if it were to survive but to stand and defend itself until it could be relieved. A possibility would have been to attempt to retreat to Helpmekaar, but it was clear the garrison would stand less of a chance if overtaken in the open by the amaZulu than if they fought from a prepared position.[12]

The post was accordingly hastily fortified. Chard's eye as a military engineer played its part, but the basic form of the defences undoubtedly followed the lines suggested by the heavily bearded Acting Assistant Commissary James Dalton, an experienced and energetic career soldier who had served in both the Eighth Cape Frontier War (1851–3) and in the Ninth.[13] It is more than likely that Dalton's advice was based on the part he had played in the battle of Ibeka on 29 September 1878 in the last-mentioned campaign. On that day Colonel Charles Griffith, holding the small but fortified trading store at Ibeka, had comprehensively repulsed a numerically far superior Gcaleka Xhosa army.[14]

The garrison turned the officers' horses, draught oxen and mules loose and set about erecting a breast-high defensive barricade of anything that would stop a bullet. It was made up of large, 200 lb mealie-bags, big square wooden biscuit boxes 'weighing about a hundredweight each', smaller but very heavy boxes of tinned meat, and even barrels of rum and lime-juice.[15] Two wagons were also pressed into service with the gaps between their wheels filled up. The southern side of this improvised perimeter connected the barricaded and loopholed store with the similarly prepared hospital about thirty metres away. On the opposite, northern side, the metre-high breastwork ran from the hospital along the top of a two-metre-high rocky ledge to a neatly built cattle kraal next to the store with walls of stone 1.2 metres high.[16] Since the Zulu had no artillery and few firearms the defenders hoped these improvised defences would be enough to protect them from Zulu projectiles, while the all-round defensive perimeter would work like a wagon laager in foiling Zulu envelopment tactics. It would force the amaZulu into deploying on a narrow front where their numbers would be negated and their numerous reserves unengaged, and it would allow the defenders to concentrate their deadly Martini-Henry rifle fire on the front ranks of the amaZulu pushed on by those behind. Although sighted up to 1,700 yards (1,550 metres), at close range (100–300 metres) the Martini-Henry was effective against a mass attack; while a point-blank range (100 metres or less) it could set up a wall of impenetrable fire if the riflemen were sufficiently concentrated. And if an assailant survived the cordon of rifle fire, then he had to face the 55-centimetre-long triangular bayonet, the so-called 'lunger', which could punch a hole through an ox-hide shield. A bayonet-tipped rifle had a formidable two-metre reach which outdistanced the Zulu *iklwa* and gave the veterans of the Ninth Cape Frontier War the advantage in hand-to-hand combat.[17]

While the garrison was straining every muscle to erect their defences, Hlubi's Troop and some other survivors of the Natal Native Mounted Contingent (about a hundred in number) that had formed part of Durnford's ill-fated No. 2 Column drew rein at the drift. They were driving some cattle with them and were accompanied by a panicky crowd of camp followers who had escaped Isandlwana. Chard ordered their commander, Lieutenant Alfred F. Henderson, to post his weary and rattled men along the river to give advance warning of the Zulu advance, and to retard it if at all possible.[18]

The advancing Zulu force consisted of the uThulwana, iNdlondlo and uDloko *amabutho*, all men in their early-to-mid forties, and the iNdluyengwe, whose 33-year-old men were incorporated with the uThulwana. They were the disciplined reserve of between 3,000 and 4,000 men that had not been engaged with the rest of the Zulu army at Isandlwana, but had advanced in its wake north of the British camp to form up on the high ground above it. They had not joined in the attack on the camp, but being unwearied by fighting had led the pursuit of the British fugitives. The younger, fitter men of the iNdluyengwe moved in open order in advance of the three other *amabutho* of the reserve around the rear of Isandlwana Mountain, pursuing fugitives making for Sothondose's (or Fugitives') Drift six miles downstream of Rorke's Drift, 'firing heavily all the while' as they '"drove" every mealie garden' in search of British fugitives.[19] The other three *amabutho* divided into two contingents and moved off in open order sweeping the country in the direction of the drifts upstream of Sothondose's.[20]

The Zulu reserve's effective commander was *umntwana* Dabulamanzi kaMpande, Cetshwayo's well-muscled half-brother with his high forehead and steady, open gaze, his handsome face adorned by a neat moustache and pointed beard. He was an undoubtedly intelligent (if unscrupulous) man of considerable sophistication who was socially at ease with whites. He delighted to wear European clothing, had developed a taste for gin, and had become a magnificent shot with the rifle and a secure horseman. Vigorous, aggressive and self-confident, even impulsive, but still only forty years of age, he was not a commander of proven ability and Cetshwayo had shied away from appointing him one of his generals. Nevertheless, Dabulamanzi's royal status and domineering personality gave him natural precedence over the other officers of the reserve and they were all happy to follow his dynamic lead.[21]

The iNdluyengwe forded the Mzinyathi a mile or two up from Sothondose's Drift where the waters of the flooded river were calmer, firing at every possible cave or crevice that might have sheltered a refugee, and sat down on a small, green hill on the Natal side to take snuff (or, quite likely, *Cannabis sativa* which the Zulu habitually took before battle). The other three *amabutho* of the reserve crossed upstream where the Batshe runs into the Mzinyathi, some one-and-a-half miles downstream of Rorke's Drift and where the river was shallower and wider and the current less strong. After spending a long time in the water (which came up to their waists) to wash and cool down, they contemptuously brushed aside the brave but ineffectual attempt by some members of the Natal Native Mounted Contingent to oppose their crossing. Then, like the iNdluyengwe, they too sat down to take 'snuff'.[22]

Here, then, were four *amabutho* taking their ease in British territory. In doing so, they were compromising Cetshwayo's policy of fighting only in defence of Zulu soil, and he would subsequently be extremely angry that his explicit orders not to invade Natal had been disobeyed. Perhaps that is why Zibhebhu, the *induna* of the uDloko and one of the best commanders the amaZulu had, turned back when his *ibutho* reached the Mzinyathi, citing a wound he had received; and why other influential commanders, who were privy to their king's intentions, dissuaded the iNgobamakhosi and uMbonambi from maintaining their pursuit of the British fugitives over the river into Natal. These *amabutho*, who had already fought hard and valorously that day, were in any case only too happy to turn back and tend to their wounded. But Dabulamanzi, who was deeply disappointed at missing the fighting at Isandlwana, 'wanted to wash the spears of his boys'.[23] They were of the same mind as their commander, for warrior honour demanded that they could not return without having played their part in the day's fighting.[24] So, for fear of being made laughing-stocks, tired and hungry as they were, they took their 'snuff' and prepared to show their mettle against the British base at Rorke's Drift, shouting out with off-hand bravado: 'O! Let's go and have a fight at Jim's' (KwaJim, was the Zulu name for Rorke's Drift after James [Jim] Rorke, the original settler there).[25]

Doubtless, the astute Dabulamanzi must have seen the strategic significance of capturing the Centre Column's base, for by doing so the amaZulu would cut off Chelmsford's obvious route of retreat to Natal and so consummate their victory at Isandlwana. He would have known from Zulu spies and scouts that the post was weakly held, and that it presented an apparently easy target. Nevertheless, despite the bluster of his men and their brag that they were setting off to sleep with the white men's women in Pietermaritzburg, Dabulamanzi would have grasped that his force was too small and his men too wearied to attempt more than an essentially localised raid into British territory – during the course of which Rorke's Drift offered the most obvious prize. To attempt more was certainly not militarily sensible since the rest of the Zulu army had turned back at the border and would not come to his support if he tried to penetrate deeper into Natal.[26]

While the three older *amabutho* rested near the confluence of the Batshe and Mzinyathi, an advance guard of about ten men of the iNdluyengwe scouted up the valley between Rorke's Drift and the Macombe and kwaSingindi hills to its south. The main body of the iNdluyengwe followed them at an easy pace while detached sections ravaged the plain at the foot of the Helpmekaar heights, setting fire to a deserted farmhouse neighbouring Rorke's Drift and twenty or so *imizi* abandoned by their panic-stricken African inhabitants. Not all got away, and the marauding amaZulu killed twenty women and four boys and took several others captive.[27] A short while later the first of the two contingents of older *amabutho* set off in support towards the southern flank of Shiyane Mountain (Oskarsberg) that overlooked Rorke's Drift 400 metres away from the south-east. The second contingent sent a number of scouts running up the bank of the Mzinyathi towards the drift and the ponts, and then followed in their wake, startled rietbok and duiker bounding ahead of them. Two stout chiefs on horseback led the way, one of whom was Dabulamanzi.[28]

At about 16.20 the British garrison heard firing coming from behind Shiyane where the dispirited men of the Natal Native Mounted Contingent deployed along the river were desultorily skirmishing with the advancing amaZulu. Having only just escaped with their lives from the bloodbath at Isandlwana, and being short of ammunition, they had no intention of sacrificing themselves now. Lt. Henderson of Hlubi's troop dutifully reported the proximity of the amaZulu to Chard, and then galloped off with his men towards the sanctuary of the British post at Helpmekaar. Seeing them go, the company of the 2/3rd NNC finally lost their already wavering nerve and cravenly ran off in their wake to a distant hill where they cowered 'like a flock of sheep'.[29] Infuriated by this betrayal, some of the remaining members of the garrison fired after them. A white NNC corporal, W. Anderson, fell dead among the trees of the orchard, shot in the back: the first casualty of the day.[30]

Chard later ruefully reflected that, with the horsemen of the Natal Native Mounted Contingent and the NNC gone, 'we seemed very few'.[31] Indeed the loss in total of some 200 or more defenders was a serious blow because the perimeter of the fortified post was now too long for the remaining 8 officers and 131 men (about 35 of whom were sick) to hold.[32] Chard accordingly ordered the defensive perimeter to be halved by building a four-foot high barricade (or inner entrenchment) of the heavy, wooden biscuit boxes piled two high across the post from the north-western corner of the storehouse to the mealie-bags along the stony ledge. That meant abandoning the hospital and moving the sick out of it to the reduced perimeter. But the barricade was still incomplete when the advance parties of the amaZulu came into sight, and the sick had not yet been evacuated from the hospital.

Consequently, the depleted garrison were left with no option but to attempt to hold the original perimeter as best they could. At least the amaZulu held no advantage of surprise and the garrison was ready for them. In the mid-afternoon Bromhead had ordered Private Fred Hitch, a sturdy, strong-jawed blond Londoner of twenty-two years who had taken part in the final stages of the Ninth Cape Frontier War, to take up position as a look-out on the roof of the storehouse. At about 16.30 the iNdluyengwe came in sight around the southern side of Shiyane with scouts leading the way. They 'took a pot-shot' at Hitch in his exposed position but missed. He fired three shots back at them and then scrambled down off the roof to give the alarm to his comrades and take up position alongside them.[33]

The advancing iNdluyengwe were between 500 and 600 in number and in perfect silence they rapidly formed a classic bull's horns fighting line which extended from Shiyane towards kwaSingindi to its south-west. Then, yelling their war-cry and keeping up a heavy if ineffective fire from their mainly obsolete firearms, they came at a run against the southern line of defences between the hospital and storehouse. Crouching low with their shields before their faces to avoid the defenders' fire that opened up when they were about 600 metres away, they took advantage of the cover afforded by anthills, dongas and the steep banks of ditches and streams. Undeterred by their losses, and still hoping to overrun the post in their first rush, the amaZulu dashed to within fifty metres of the barricade of mealie bags and two wagons. There they were caught in such a heavy cross-fire from the hospital and storehouse that they could go no further and some threw themselves down or took cover in a low drainage ditch. Most swerved away to their left seeking a less well-defended sector, while some of those pinned down by the British fire occupied the outlying cookhouse and ovens only thirty metres from the barricade and opened a desultory fire on the defenders.[34]

Those iNdluyengwe still free to manoeuvre surged around the western side of the hospital and made a rush at it and the north-western line of mealie-bags. There was desperate hand-to-hand fighting before they were repulsed and took cover among the luxuriant bushes behind

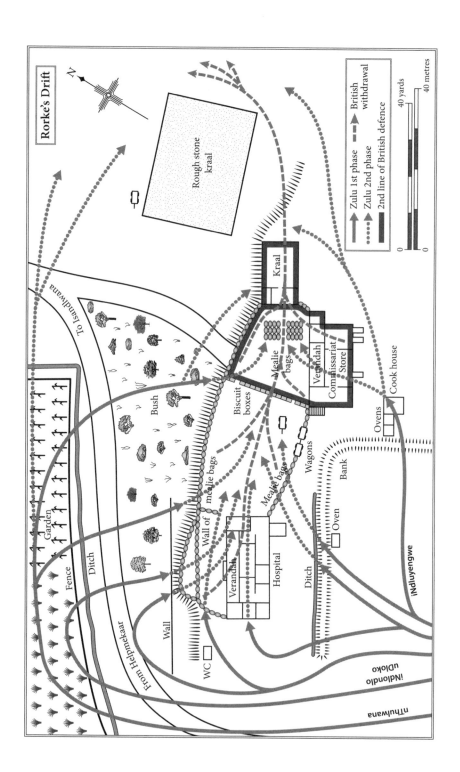

Rorke's Drift

N

Rough stone kraal

To Isandlwana

Bush

Garden

Fence

Ditch

From Helpmekaar

Wall

Wall of mealie bags

WC

Verandah

Hospital

Mealie bags

Oven

Ditch

Wagons

Bank

iNdlondlo uDloko

iNdluyengwe

nThulwana

Biscuit boxes

Mealie bags

Kraal

Verandah

Commissariat Store

Ovens

Cook house

Zulu 1st phase
Zulu 2nd phase
2nd line of British defence
British withdrawal

0 40 yards

0 40 metres

the stone wall below the terrace, behind a grove of Cape poplars and large gum trees, and in the garden of mealies, peach and other types of fruit trees that the defenders had not had time to clear or cut down.[35] Despite their initial repulse, the iNdluyengwe realised that this was a far better sector to attack than the southern perimeter because there was less chance of being caught in a cross-fire, and because of the amount of cover available. Moreover, they saw that the verandah front of the hospital was only flimsily barricaded. They were further encouraged when the two contingents of older *amabutho* that had joined up to the east of Shiyane came up in support around the southern shoulder of the mountain. Some of these took up position along Shiyane's ledges of rocks and in its caves overlooking the fortified post, and from there kept up a constant harassing fire on the defenders, joined by the iNdluyengwe already firing from the captured cookhouse and ovens below.

The bulk of the uThulwana, iNdlondlo and uDloko moved on around to the north-west of the post, carefully keeping out of range of the defenders' fire until they reached the cover of the sunken road, garden and bush.[36] While performing this manoeuvre the two Zulu commanders leading them on horseback were caught momentarily in the open and came into clear range of a pair of privates of the 2/24th stationed side-by-side, J. Dunbar and George Edwards (whose real name was George Orchard). Fortunately for one mounted chief, the other, wearing a distinctive shawl, caught the attention of both soldiers and they aimed at him, firing simultaneously. One, if not both, of their well-aimed shots 'dropped' him, but his mounted companion rode on unscathed into cover.[37] He was none other than Dabulamanzi. Local tradition has it that he took up position on the lower slopes of Shiyane, but this was a location far too exposed to British fire; nor could he have exerted meaningful control over the pattern of the battle from this perch.[38] As Dabulamanzi later recounted, he dismounted once he reached the relative safety of the bush facing the hospital and from there encouraged the efforts of his men during their repeated onslaughts on the defences.[39]

The considerable Zulu reinforcements greatly heartened the iNdluyengwe who joined them in a fresh series of assaults on the northern perimeter extending from the hospital as far as where the incomplete line of biscuit-boxes began. Because of the heavy cover that extended up to the junction with the biscuit-boxes, the new arrivals were able to advance with relative impunity right up to the British defences. They correctly identified the verandah front of the hospital as the weakest point in the British line of defences and attacked it unrelentingly. Intense fighting across the barriers ensued as the amaZulu determinedly charged again and again. As a Zulu combatant put it: 'They fought, they yelled, they shouted, "It dies at the entrance! It dies in the doorway!" They stabbed the sacks; they dug with their assegais.'[40] Some threw spears at the defenders, but most held on to them for the honourable hand-to-hand fighting they prized. Every time they were repulsed they fell back and regrouped in the thick cover, keeping up their fire on the defenders and performing war-dances to re-energise their resolve. Then, on the orders of Dabulamanzi and his commanders, they rushed once more at the defences.[41] Chard was astonished that, despite their losses, they attacked 'over and over'.[42]

Meanwhile, the snipers on Shiyane were taking the British, as Chard put it, 'completely in reverse, and although very badly directed, many shots came in among us'.[43] The range was between 300 and 400 metres, too far for accurate fire from mainly inferior firearms (even when the marksmen were experienced), and effective British counter-sniping kept the amaZulu at a further disadvantage. But the British post was now increasingly under Zulu fire from every side, and the British officers and NCOs in particular, who were constantly exposed to this heavy but inaccurate fire as they led gallantly from the front, began to be shot down. Zulu pressure, especially along the northern barricade and in front of the hospital was unrelenting. Aware of his mounting casualties, Chard was shaken when the tall Dalton, who was fearlessly exposing himself above the barricade while cheering on the men and firing at the enemy, was shot 'through the body' above the right shoulder while standing near him. Dalton coolly handed his rifle over to Chard and quietly let him take the unspent cartridges out of his pocket, but his wound was fatal.[44] Casualties aside, Chard had good reason to be increasingly anxious. He knew only too well that, if the amaZulu broke through his line of defences, even at one point, he and his men would be doomed.[45]

It was now about 18.00, an hour before sunset and the shadows of evening began to draw in. Taking advantage of the fading light, the amaZulu began to extend their attack further to their left from the sheltering bush to the more exposed stretch of the northern perimeter beyond the line of biscuit-boxes where the left-hand fork of the road came to a stop below the rocky ledge. Despite the strength of that part of the defences, Chard 'feared seriously' that in their determination the amaZulu 'would get over in over our wall behind the biscuit boxes' and fatally breach his position.[46] So he took the desperate decision to withdraw his men to the shorter interior defensive line at the biscuit-boxes. This meant abandoning the entire defensive perimeter beyond and evacuating the hospital. Whether this could be successfully effected while under Zulu attack was quite another matter. The likely danger existed that the heartened amaZulu would clamber over the forsaken defences and rush in among the defenders as they fell back (just as, unbeknown to Chard, they had earlier that day when the British line attempted to retire at Isandlwana) and so turn a withdrawal into a catastrophic rout.

Leaving the unfortunate, isolated defenders of the hospital to make their escape as best they could, the men holding the original perimeter beyond the barrier of biscuit-boxes made a sudden dash for it under the heavy covering fire of the men lined along it. The amaZulu were taken by surprise by this unexpected withdrawal and failed to intercept them. Nevertheless, they immediately took up position on the other side of the deserted defences between the hospital and line of biscuit-boxes and exchanged fire with the British behind their reduced perimeter. Sensing that they had at last gained the initiative, the amaZulu renewed their assault on the now isolated hospital with redoubled determination. Meanwhile, those iNdluyengwe previously pinned down outside the southern perimeter began to creep up along the deserted line of defences to within striking range of the interior barricade where it joined the storehouse.

A desperate fight commenced in the hospital where the amaZulu succeeded in setting the thatched roof alight at its western end while they burst into the building. The hospital garrison retired room by room, disputing every step in vicious, claustrophobic hand-to-hand encounters while they valiantly attempted to carry out those sick and wounded who could not walk. A number, but by no means all, succeeded in making it to the line of biscuit-boxes thirty metres away under the covering fire of the defenders.[47] However, it was in another sector of the defences that the fate of the post would be decided.

Gaining 'great confidence' thanks to their success in taking the hospital, the amaZulu embarked on what Chard recognised as their 'most formidable . . . onslaught of the day'.[48] In the gathering gloom of evening the amaZulu began to concentrate right up under the rocky ridge where they were sheltered from British fire, and gathered in the road just to the east of the junction of the interior barricade and the perimeter. Discerning that this vulnerable corner was under immediate threat, Bromhead – who throughout the battle had led his men conspicuously from the front, taking up a rifle when required to fire over the barricades (both he and Chard would have carried a revolver, but no sword)[49] – took up position there with seven other men with the intention of dislodging the attackers who were only a metre or two away.

Chard, who meanwhile was directing fire from further down the internal barricade, grasped with alarm that the situation along the stretch of perimeter being defended by Bromhead was becoming increasingly perilous and that the amaZulu were on the verge of breaking through. If they did so it would be impossible to continue the defence of the post. It was essential therefore to form a contingency plan, and he urgently conferred with a number of the surviving senior defenders as to what they should do. Those he consulted were Assistant Commissary Dunne; the Revd George Smith (the vicar of Estcourt in Natal and Army Chaplain who had stayed on to fight with the garrison); and the scrawny, diminutive 25-year-old Colour Sergeant Frank Bourne of the 2/24th ('the kid') who had been responsible with Bromhead for posting the defenders before the battle began, and who had fought alongside him defending the verandah of the hospital.[50]

The sun was going down, and the four men agreed that should the perimeter be breached (as seemed imminently likely) the only hope for the garrison's survival was for as many defenders as possible to fall back first as fast as they could manage to the stoutly built cattle kraal which formed the eastern extremity of the perimeter, and which was currently manned by about ten men. Once there, the garrison would regroup. Since the amaZulu were not yet deployed in any force to the east of Rorke's Drift, Chard and his three advisers reckoned that in the coming twilight the defenders must attempt to break out in the direction of the river. There was no point at all in trying to make for distant Helpmekaar since the amaZulu were between them and the heights. In any case, the garrison's horses had strayed or been killed and only mounted men could have made the attempt. If those who survived their desperate sally then split up and did their best to conceal themselves during the coming night, there was a chance that those who remained undetected by Zulu patrols would live to tell the tale, either because the amaZulu would have withdrawn, or because British troops would have entered the area. Chard and the others he consulted conceded to each other that their contingency plan was little short of a despairing gamble, but that it was the best option open to them.[51]

The hasty agreement on how the garrison should withdraw was reached only just in time. Only a few minutes later the amaZulu succeeding in breaking though the sector defended by Bromhead and his seven companions. To fire on the amaZulu below the rocky ledge Bromhead and the others had to lean over the barricade, thereby exposing themselves to a dangerous return cross-fire. They began to fall wounded or dead, and all were spattered with blood and brains.[52] It was then that a hardy number of amaZulu made a determined dash on the outer barricade behind the retrenchment. They succeeded in scrambling over it to take Bromhead's diminished band on their right flank while one triumphant warrior remained gesticulating jubilantly on the barricade as he urged those behind to follow.

Bromhead and the one or two men still capable of defending themselves made a frantic fight of it, but all but one perished. One of the Zulu warriors managed to run Bromhead through the right side of his breast with his *iklwa*, close to the armpit. Bromhead fell dying to his knees, and the other *amabutho* now surrounding him all joined in driving their spears into his quivering body. This (as we have seen) was a Zulu ritual known as *hlomula*, and was related to the hunt when all the participants stabbed the carcass of a particularly formidable kill, like a lion or a buffalo. To do the same to a human foe was to acknowledge that he had fought with the ferocity of a dangerous wild animal.[53] The sole survivor of Bromhead's gallant band was Private

Fred Hitch who had previously taken part in the fierce bayonet fighting in front of the hospital after he came down from the storehouse roof. Luckily for him, he was shot through the right shoulder before the amaZulu could overrun Bromhead's position. At first, he continued to fight with Bromhead's revolver held in his left hand, but overcome by pain and faint through loss of blood, he crept to the rear and so lived to tell the tale.[54]

With Bromhead and his brave comrades eliminated, the amaZulu poured in ever-increasing numbers over the barricade to take the British along the northern perimeter and internal barricade in the rear. Chard understood that the time had come to put the planned withdrawal into motion without a further moment's delay. As the glare of the flames from the burning hospital roof mingled surreally with the last, low rays of the setting sun and the flash of musketry fire, Chard shouted out his urgent order to fall back on the cattle kraal. The defenders along the northern perimeter were able to disengage and retire unharmed, but the amaZulu were already between the kraal and most of the British (including Chard) holding the line of biscuit-boxes. There was nothing for it but to fire a volley and make a dash through the amaZulu pouring into the space, parrying spear with bayonet. To add to their peril, as the defenders along the retrenchment turned their backs and ceased firing in the direction of the hospital, the amaZulu they had been pinning down leapt up and made a rush on the barricade.

The twenty or so men who were holding the commissariat store were facing outwards, away from the amaZulu now breaking through the reduced defensive perimeter to their rear. They were consequently slow to assess the perilous situation. Once they did, however, they ceased fire and made a dash for the two doors to the verandah facing the interior of the post. Wounded comrades had been laid out there under its shelter under the care of Surgeon Reynolds. Throughout the engagement Reynolds had courageously attended to them under constant fire with his Jack Russell terrier at his side, once breaking off to carry ammunition to the beleaguered hospital, during which gallant foray a musket ball passed harmlessly through the top of his helmet.[55] The retiring soldiers from the commissariat store paused only to help up the wounded still capable of movement before joining up with the men retreating from the barricade. It was fortunate for them that two great rectangular, steeply pitched heaps of mealie bags were piled between the store and the kraal. They provided cover, and the narrow gaps between them were well suited for defence. Members of the garrison were therefore able to hold the amaZulu back with rifle fire and at bayonet point while the rest made it over the wall into the cattle kraal.

As soon as the British stopped firing from the storehouse, the amaZulu made a dash for the abandoned building and occupied it, opening fire in their turn from its windows and the verandah on the British holding the gap between it and the southernmost of the two heaps of mealies, forcing the defenders back into the kraal. Chard had been superficially wounded in the upper left arm by a Zulu spear-thrust in the retreat to the kraal, but although bleeding and in pain, he was still in command of the situation. Clearly, the kraal could not long be held now that the amaZulu occupied the store and their fire from only thirty metres away would take the densely packed defenders in reverse with deadly effect. If the British were to break out, the moment could not long be delayed since the amaZulu were even then extending their lines eastwards to surround the kraal.

How many men did Chard still have with him at this anxious moment? Only a scattering of the inmates or defenders of the hospital had made it to the kraal, about ten in number. It would later turn out that Private J. Waters of the 1/24th and Gunner Arthur Howard, RA, as well as a patient, Private John Connolly whose left knee was dislocated, managed to escape from the burning hospital and lie undetected by the amaZulu in the grass among the corpses of men and animals.[56] About another thirty defenders holding the perimeter had been killed or, if wounded, finished off by the amaZulu. Besides Bromhead and Dalton, their number included Acting Storekeeper L. A. Byrne, Corporals W. Allen and J. Lyons of the 2/24th, and Corporal C. Scammell of the NNC.[57] That left about ninety men, a number of whom (including Chard) were wounded, and Zulu fire was beginning to take an additional toll of the men crowed into the kraal.

At the very moment when Chard was about to issue the order for the desperate breakout few believed could have much hope of success, a quite unanticipated intervention on the opposite side of the battlefield crucially turned the attention of the attacking amaZulu and their commanders towards the heights of Helpmekaar.[58]

During the late afternoon the mounted straggle of terrified and exhausted fugitives from Isandlwana fleeing by way of Rorke's Drift had begun to come into Helpmekaar. Brevet Major R. Upcher, the senior officer at the depot, decided he must move down to the river with the two companies of the 1/24th stationed at the depot to reinforce the garrison at Rorke's Drift and to help prevent the amaZulu from invading Natal. It was already early evening when he led his two companies down the escarpment. Near the bottom, he met Major Spalding picking his leisurely way towards Helpmekaar, still blissfully ignorant of the disaster at Isandlwana and the dire fate about to engulf Rorke's Drift. Shocked into action by what he learned, Spalding wheeled his horse about and, accompanied by Trooper Dickson of the Buffalo Border Guard, cantered back toward Rorke's Drift to reconnoitre.

Three miles from the post the two horsemen came across a distraught clutch of mounted fugitives who refused to stand and pressed on towards Helpmekaar, insisting fervently that Rorke's Drift had already fallen to the amaZulu. Spalding reported back, but Upcher was undeterred and pressed on with his two companies until they were opposed by a body of amaZulu who threw out their horns in battle array.[59] Following infantry regulations, Upcher immediately deployed his rear company to the right of the leading one and extended them both into a firing line.[60] The amaZulu started to come on but, before they could close, Upcher's men let them have a volley. It was quite enough to deter them, and the Zulu force melted away into the gathering dark, leaving several dead and writhing wounded on the ground behind them.

Despite his sharp, successful brush with the enemy, Upcher decided to proceed no further. The British soldiers could now clearly make out from the summit of a hill nearby that the post at Rorke's Drift was in flames. This disheartening sight confirmed the intelligence Spalding had earlier received from the fugitives. Convinced that Rorke's Drift had fallen and that the garrison must have been overwhelmed, Upcher decided that it was too late to assist. Besides, he and his men now felt alarmingly isolated, caught in the open between Helpmekaar and Rorke's Drift, and in danger of being overrun by a major Zulu attack. So Upcher turned his jittery men smartly around and marched them as fast as he could back up the heights to Helpmekaar.[61]

Upcher's two companies regained Helpmekaar after 21.00, and found that the motley collection of thirty or so fugitives from Isandlwana had begun forming a poorly entrenched wagon laager around the stores and were building barricades of mealie-bags and biscuit-boxes. Besides these survivors, there were now also about 180 officers and men of the 1/24th available to hold the position and they set about strengthening the rudimentary defences. Aware that their numbers were nevertheless small, and their defences inadequate, the garrison at Helpmekaar spent a dismal, sleepless night in nervous expectation that the victorious amaZulu would soon be upon them. To make matters even more alarming, a dense mist settled over the heights as it does so often in the summer months. In fearful suspense, blanketed by the concealing, distorting mist, the garrison stood fretfully to arms until the sun finally rose at 05.15.[62]

Back at Rorke's Drift, Upcher's brief encounter with the detached Zulu force was Chard's salvation. Dabulamanzi and his lieutenants, believing their forces were under serious, unanticipated attack from Helpmekaar, sent out urgent orders to their men to meet the threat.[63] As a consequence, the amaZulu surging around the beleaguered cattle kraal suddenly thinned out as they turned away to repel the British force they believed was advancing on their rear. With commendable alacrity, Chard seized the brief respite to hustle most of his men under the direction of Colour Sergeant Bourne as fast as they could go over the far wall of the small, well-built cattle kraal while he took command of a small rearguard of some dozen men who maintained a sharp fire from the kraal to hold the amaZulu at bay. The rearguard then fell back across the small kraal to join the rest of the shaken men whom Bourne had loosely formed up to the south of the large, roughly built kraal beyond the defensive perimeter. Chard ordered his reunited force to fire two brisk volleys at the amaZulu clambering into the abandoned cattle kraal and over its near wall in pursuit. Then, at the double, and losing formation as they went, the retreating garrison rounded the far, eastern side of the low kraal to their left, and taking advantage of the cover it provided, headed north towards the river. Beyond the low kraal, Chard halted the men of the rearguard to turn and fire another volley after their pursuers, but already individuals were peeling off the main body into the dark. Others, wounded and with their strength failing, or hit by stray Zulu bullets, began to fall behind to be remorselessly despatched by the amaZulu.[64]

About sixty men – some, like Hitch, seriously wounded – were still with Chard, and he knew that if they stuck together and put up a last stand they would all be massacred. So, with the river in sight, Chard ordered those who were able to do so to fire one last salvo at their pursuers, and then to scatter. Divesting themselves of their red coats, helmets and any other accoutrements that would attract Zulu attention or impede their flight, they needed no urging to make as much distance as they were able from Rorke's Drift before finding as secure a place as they could among the bushes and the rocks to conceal themselves from the victorious amaZulu and to wait out events.[65] They were fortunate that the amaZulu were distracted from a determined pursuit by fear of a potential attack from Helpmekaar, and by the overwhelming urge to stop where they were and loot the captured post. Besides, all the amaZulu were suffering from sheer physical and nervous exhaustion after the day's draining events. Many too were daunted by the knowledge that they had already suffered an inordinate number of casualties, and that helped suppress any further desire to carry on the fight.[66]

Even so, not all the pursuers were deterred, and it was inevitable that Chard's men melted into the night with varying degrees of success. Some were run down by still resolute and fleet-footed pursuers, singly, or in small groups, and put to the spear. Others collapsed from loss of blood or exhaustion, and if they fell still close to the concentration of Zulu forces they were located and killed. But many others succeeded in putting a good distance between themselves and their diminishing number of pursuers, and in holing up for the night to await the perils of the new day.[67]

Chapter 10

Falling Back to Natal

———>•<———

More than an hour before sunrise, at 05.15 on 23 January 1879, Chelmsford ordered his men bivouacked on the dread field of Isandlwana to fall in. His intention was to get them away in the grey light of the pre-dawn and so spare them a clear view of the horrible devastation that surrounded them, leaving the British dead unburied – a decision that would cause an indignant storm back in Britain. The head of the column, remembered Lieutenant John Maxwell, was on the road to Rorke's Drift 'before objects could be clearly seen'.[1] Nevertheless, the men of the NNC who were the last to quit the ground, followed by the rearguard of Mounted Infantry and Natal Mounted Police, had all too clear a sight of the abundant horrors in the clear light of early morning.[2]

Chelmsford ordered the column 'to push on with all haste to Rorke's Drift',[3] because he and his staff fully expected that the Zulu army that had overrun the camp the previous day 'would be on our backs' if they did not get away. 'Moreover', as Major Clery explained, 'we had no food or ammunition, except what the men carried of the latter, so we fully expected to fight our way to the river.'[4] Despite their exhaustion, his men, traumatised by what they had seen (if only partially) and filled with a surging desire to take their revenge upon the amaZulu, were not daunted by the prospect. But Chelmsford, who was only too conscious of his lack of ammunition, hoped to cross into Natal without an encounter. He and his staff were relieved, therefore, when the column passed through the valley of the Batshe River without opposition. They could now see Shiyane in the distance a few miles away across the Mzinyathi, and could entertain some hope that the garrison still held Rorke's Drift and the ponts across the river, even though they were troubled by the thick pall of smoke they discerned clinging ominously to the side of the hill. With apprehension mounting, as he later reported to the Secretary of State for War, Colonel Stanley, Chelmsford prudently halted and sent the men of the Natal Mounted Volunteers ahead to reconnoitre and scan the opposite bank through their field glasses.[5]

What they saw filled them with dismay. The two ponts were half-burned and semi-submerged. The post itself was partially burned, the thatched roofs, not only of the hospital but of the storehouse which the amaZulu had set alight soon after capturing them, were still sulkily smoking. Everywhere bodies of men and animals were scattered about and the ground was strewn with pillaged stores: in other words, it was a ghastly repetition of the Isandlwana battleground they had quit a few hours before. But, worst of all, as Trooper Fred Symons of the Natal Carbineers recalled with a shudder, there, all around the wrecked and pillaged post and along the river bank were great masses of amaZulu who 'looked just like a ten-acre mealie field in blossom turned black'.[6] On the other hand, no living redcoat could be discerned.

The colonial troopers galloped back to Chelmsford with the unwelcome news. The General immediately called his chief officers to him to sound out their opinions about how best to proceed. Crealock, once so cocky and disdainful of Zulu military prowess, found himself at a loss. But Colonel Glyn, true to his tough, no-nonsense nature, and aware of the vengeful sentiment among his six companies of the 2/24th, advised forcing a crossing at the drift about 800 metres downstream of the ponts. Lt.-Col. Harness assured Chelmsford that he could give Glyn effective covering fire with the four guns of his battery of 7-pounders; and Major Dartnell undertook to secure the 2/24th's flanks with his 150 or so mounted men. However, Chelmsford was concerned by the column's limited supply of ammunition. Moreover, he was aware that the morale of the men of the sixteen companies of the two battalions of the 3rd Regiment NNC was badly, if not fatally, compromised, and that these 1,600 men would be little help in an assault and would likely prove a liability. And if the amaZulu succeeded in repulsing the attempt to cross the river where Glyn suggested, such a failure would entirely

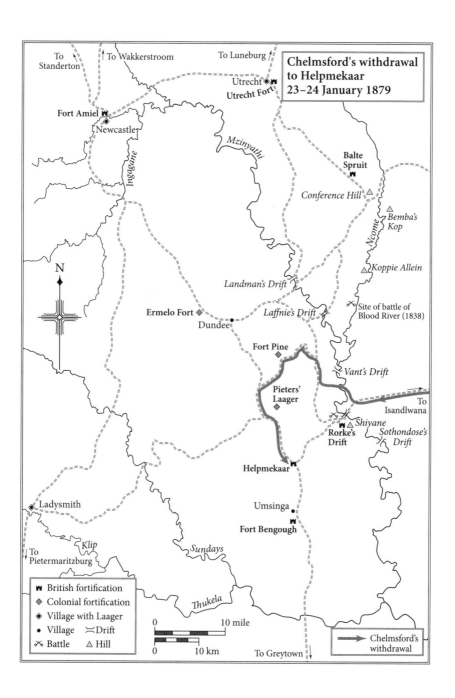

To Standerton

To Wakkerstroom

To Luneburg

Utrecht
Utrecht Fort

Fort Amiel
Newcastle

Mzinyathi

Balte Spruit

Conference Hill

Bemba's Kop

Ingagane

N

Koppie Allein

Landman's Drift

Ermelo Fort
Dundee

Laffnie's Drift

Site of battle of Blood River (1838)

Fort Pine

Vant's Drift

Pieters' Laager

To Isandlwana

Shiyane
Rorke's Drift
Sothondose's Drift

Helpmekaar

Umsinga

Fort Bengough

Ladysmith

Klip

To Pietermaritzburg

Sundays

Chelmsford's withdrawal to Helpmekaar 23–24 January 1879

Thukela

British fortification
Colonial fortification
Village with Laager
Village ⚔ **Drift**
Battle △ **Hill**

0   10 mile
0   10 km

To Greytown

Chelmsford's withdrawal

open up Natal to Zulu invasion and probably destroy the remnant of No. 3 Column as well. Chelmsford believed he simply could not afford the risk. So, ever his own man, he turned Glyn's plan down.

But what then was he to do instead? The whereabouts of the Zulu army that had been victorious at Isandlwana was uncertain. Unaware that it had dispersed home to undergo its post-combat purification rituals and to tend to the wounded, Chelmsford believed it most certainly threatened his rear and he dared not tarry. Since the amaZulu seemed disposed to contest his crossing at Rorke's Drift itself, he concluded that his only remaining option was to manoeuvre and march his men some miles along the river before attempting to cross back into Natal. To do so would be to gamble that the amaZulu currently barring his passage in the environs of Rorke's Drift would not have the stomach to attempt to oppose him at another crossing place. He was encouraged in this throw of the dice by the report brought in by mounted troopers that the amaZulu on the opposite bank were mainly sitting or lying about, clearly too staggered by fatigue and drained by the previous day's battle to be in an aggressive mood.[7]

Indeed, as Dabulamanzi subsequently confirmed, he and his surviving *amabutho* were stunned by the heavy casualties they had sustained in taking Rorke's Drift – somewhere in the region of 500 men. Now that they had achieved their objective and proved their valour, their only thought was to disengage, make their way home with as many of their wounded as possible, report to the king and undergo the usual post-combat purification rituals. Dabulamanzi's own scouts reported that the British force hovering out of sight on the north bank of the Mzinyathi was dauntingly large. He reluctantly concluded that he was honour-bound to resist the British if they attempted to cross at Rorke's Drift, but that he would not be obliged to engage them if they moved off elsewhere.[8]

Unaware that Dabulamanzi's response was as he had staked it would be, but acting nevertheless on that premise, Chelmsford had now to decide where he should attempt to cross the Mzinyathi if not at Rorke's Drift. He rejected the possibility of following the river downstream towards Sothondose's Drift. Not only was the country on the Zulu side impossibly broken and rugged, but it was equally so on the Natal bank, and going in that direction took him away from his established lines of communication and the centres of colonial settlement threatened by Zulu attack.

On the other hand, if he proceeded upstream towards Vant's Drift about twelve miles away, just below the confluence of the Mzinyathi and with the Ncome (Blood) River, the going was altogether more level and less demanding, and there was an established river crossing and a reasonable track back into Natal. Crucially, when consulted, some of Dartnell's colonial troopers were able to inform Chelmsford that less than five miles away and much closer than Vant's Drift, at a place where the river swung west in a tight ox-bow and then turned again steeply to the south (a reverse S), a couple of islands and sandbanks slowed the river's flow just below the second bend and made it shallow enough to ford. That meant that Chelmsford would be able to cross into Natal much sooner, and his column would almost immediately be able to join the steep but passable track that led north-west up the escarpment.[9] Once they reached the high ground, a network of wagon tracks would facilitate movement in several possible directions. If they turned right they could make for Fort Pine. This fortification was an open, rectangular enclosure of loopholed stone walls about four metres high with two rectangular flanking bastions at opposing corners, and had been completed by the Natal government in late 1878 as a proposed post for the Natal Mounted Police. It was also intended as a place of refuge in times of trouble for primarily English-speaking settlers.[10] Alternatively, if they turned left, Chelmsford's men could advance along the top of the Biggarsberg heights to Helpmekaar via Pieters' Laager. This was a square enclosure with two small bastions completed in the course of 1878 on the initiative of local Boer farmers who intended to shelter there if the region were attacked. Its loopholed walls were 2.5 metres high and were constructed of stones and clay.[11]

To Chelmsford's mind there was no dilemma. If he and his column succeeded in regaining the heights across the river and thereby out-flanking the amaZulu at Rorke's Drift from the north, they must make as fast they could for Helpmekaar to reinforce the garrison there, secure No. 3 Column's remaining stores and block the invasion route into the Natal interior. Yet, there were stupendous obstacles to overcome. Even if the amaZulu did not dispute their passage, Chelmsford's exhausted, sleep-deprived and very hungry troops, who had already that morning marched the ten miles from Isandlwana, were facing a testing river crossing and a further march of thirty miles or more, much of it over open country with a considerable stretch steeply uphill. Nor could Zulu resistance be ruled out. Still, the attempt had to be made.

At about 08.15 Chelmsford commenced his march upstream. A company of the 2/24th led the way followed by the four guns and the remaining companies of British infantry. Once more the men of the NNC came at the end of the column. Chelmsford would have liked to have deployed several of their companies on the column's flanks, but their morale was now so low that he feared they would abscond if not kept together at the rear. Instead, he had to rely on his mounted men to scout about and, most importantly of all, to keep an eye on the movements of the amaZulu at Rorke's Drift. The reports they brought back to the painfully anxious general were better than he could have dared hope. At first, the amaZulu to their rear made no forward movement. Then, after about quarter of an hour, they began slowly to cross the river in disorganised groups. Once most had reached the Zulu bank, their commanders managed to form them up into a column with scouts on either flank. For the watching British horsemen this was a moment of excruciating suspense: would the amaZulu wheel left in pursuit of the British column, or would they make for Isandlwana and home? To the watchers' jubilation Dabulamanzi's drained *amabutho* set off at a steady pace to the north, their scouts keeping a careful eye on the British horsemen. It was apparent to the latter that the amaZulu were concerned that the British might attack them, and that they were as chary of an armed encounter as were the British. So, the two battered columns went their separate ways to the unheroic relief of all involved.[12]

And what of Chard and the other survivors who had broken out of Rorke's Drift the night before? As Sergeant Edward Daly wrote home on 5 February 1879, 'We arrived . . . only just in time to save the few left who had made a very gallant resistance.'[13] Scattered along the river bank, infinitely grateful that the amaZulu had creased hunting them down, but in a horrible plight nevertheless, the remnant of the garrison could scarcely credit it when they spotted British horsemen patrolling along the opposite bank. A few sent up a frantic cheer, desperately waving to attract attention. The astonished horsemen reported back to

Chelmsford who detached fifty mounted men to swim and scramble as best they could across the river to rally the survivors and escort them to the place where the column was to cross. With the wounded riding pillion, the haggard, deeply traumatised survivors staggered along as best they could to the rendezvous. Of the sixty or so men who had broken out with Chard, only forty-three had survived the night, and of them eight (including Chard) were wounded.[14]

The column reached the crossing-point at about 10.00. Files of horsemen forded first, followed by a company of infantry, linking arms in the strong current to cross over safely. With the bridgehead established, the four guns went next, soldiers helping the exhausted horses drag them across. The remaining companies of the 2/24th followed, but the demoralised NNC began to panic and break ranks. It was only with the greatest difficulty that their officers succeeded in herding them through the river to the opposite bank, and in the confusion a number were swept away and drowned.[15]

Once the column had re-formed on the Natal bank preparatory to beginning its march up to the heights in the distance, Chelmsford came to a drastic decision about the 3rd Regiment NNC. Doubting their military value, regarding them as nothing more than a drain on his resources and concerned that their demoralisation would spread to other units and that they would slow down the march, he called upon Commandant Lonsdale to dismiss them. The NNC were more relieved than otherwise, and tamely handed over their firearms. The white NNC officers and NCOs also took in the red puggarees that had identified them as members of the NNC, and relieved them of their blankets as well. The men bounded off cheerfully enough for home in separate groups, resembling swarms of ants going up the hillside.[16]

It was now about 11.30 and a further twelve miles or so to the top of the Biggarsberg escarpment. Exhausted and famished as they were, it took the remaining troops of No. 3 Column until nearly 17.00 to make the ascent. Frequent halts were made, and some food and several wagons were commandeered from sympathetic and mightily alarmed local farmers to carry the NNC's surrendered firearms and the sick and wounded. At the end of the climb it was another fifteen miles or more over the relatively level ground to Helpmekaar, and Chelmsford decided his troops could go no further that day and must bivouac where they stood. He had sent mounted troops ahead of him, and they had ascertained that at Fort Pine, about five miles distant to the west, several settler families, learning of the disaster that had befallen his column, had already come in with their wagons to seek sanctuary. Captain William Smith, the commander of the Buffalo Border Guard,[17] was able to requisition both supplies and a few fresh horses from them.

While wagons of food made their slow way to the bivouac, Chelmsford set off with Crealock at his side and a small escort of Mounted Infantry for Helpmekaar, leaving Glyn in command of No. 3 Column. He could not dally for a moment, despite his overwhelming mental and physical fatigue, in setting in train arrangements for the defence of Natal.[18]

PART IV

Defence of the Natal and Transvaal Borders

Chapter 11

Thrown Open to Zulu Invasion

—————

The blond Captain Alan Gardner of the 14th Hussars, staff officer to No. 3 Column, with his heavy cavalry moustache and pert, upturned nose, had made the best of his skill as a horseman to escape from the debacle at Isandlwana across Sothondose's Drift. He had ridden into the laager at Helpmekaar at about 17.00 and was still recuperating when at 21.00 Major Upcher's two companies returned from their foray down the escarpment with the dread news that Rorke's Drift had fallen to the amaZulu. A trained staff officer (he had passed out of Staff College in 1872), Gardner saw at once that Chelmsford's force would likely be cut off in Zululand, and that Colonel Wood should be notified as soon as possible so that No. 4 Column could march to his assistance. Since no one else was willing to take on the responsibility or to attempt the perilous night-time ride, Gardner heaved himself back into the saddle. Riding hard through the moonless dark by way of Dundee, with one companion, he reached Utrecht in the Transvaal Territory an hour before sunrise on the morning of 23 January. He was utterly spent, and was grateful to find a messenger prepared to go the rest of the way to Wood, who was operating more than fifty miles away in north-western Zululand beyond the White Mfolozi River.[1] Chelmsford later applauded Gardner's gallantry and his good judgement in warning Wood – thus anticipating any action on his part – but Major Clery and other jealous members of Glyn's staff spread the nasty libel that Gardner had actually been riding off to save his own life. For a long time afterwards they amused themselves singing a mean ditty in the mess at Helpmekaar that went as follows: 'I very much fear / That the Zulus are near / So, hang it, I'm off to Dundee.'[2]

Chelmsford was mightily relieved to find Helpmekaar safe and to learn that Wood was being apprised of the disaster that had befallen him. But he could not rest, not even for a moment, until he had sent off messengers far and wide to alert the inhabitants of Natal to the likelihood of a Zulu invasion, and had set in motion preparations for the defence of the colony. He then slumped down to compose a letter to Sir Bartle Frere that must have been the most difficult and deeply humiliating he had ever been called upon to write, a despatch that signalled to the High Commissioner that his vaunting, risky schemes to consummate the confederation of South Africa had all been tumbled into the dust, and that his own career lay in ruins alongside them. Chelmsford's calamitous letter began: 'I regret deeply to inform you that No. 3 column has maintained [*sic*] a terrible disaster.'[3]

After snatching barely any sleep, Chelmsford was on the road the next morning bound for Pietermaritzburg to confer in person with Frere and to coordinate defensive arrangements. Before leaving Helpmekaar, however, he sent to Colonel Glyn to bring in the remnants of No. 3 Column and to take up position there with the existing garrison in order to keep guard over the valley of the Mzinyathi and deter any Zulu incursions by way of Rorke's Drift.[4] He then convened a Court of Inquiry that sat from 27 to 29 January to enquire into the loss of camp at Isandlwana and the post at Rorke's Drift. Chelmsford clearly intended that the court would not probe too deeply into his responsibility for the two disasters, and it was soon apparent that his staff and close associates were rallying around their chief to protect his reputation, whatever their private reservations about the calibre of his generalship. In its findings the court duly upheld the honour of both Chelmsford and the regular British troops and threw the blame on a handful of suspect officers (notably Durnford), colonials and Africans. It is this sanitised version that passed into the official account.[5]

Also, before departing for Pietermaritzburg, Chelmsford turned his attention to whether any awards for gallantry should be recommended for the survivors of Rorke's Drift. Their defence of the post had ultimately failed, but their bravery in attempting to hold it against extreme odds had been exemplary. Such outstanding valour not only deserved recognition in its own right, but (as Chelmsford instinctively grasped) would serve to salvage some much-needed honour from defeat and reassure the public about the fighting qualities of the British Army.

Before the Crimean War there had been no medal that recognised individual acts of gallantry in the British armed forces. Then, in December 1854 the Distinguished Conduct Medal (DCM) was instituted for 'distinguished, gallant and good conduct in the field' by all ranks below commissioned officer. Officers remained eligible instead for brevet promotion, a mention in despatches or, if of field rank, an award of one of the lesser grades of the Order of the Bath. The inauguration of the DCM was followed on Queen Victoria's initiative by a new medal for gallantry that was unconnected to rank or length of service: the Victoria Cross (VC). Clause 5 of the original royal warrant of 29 January 1856 laid down that the Victoria Cross 'shall only be awarded to those officers and men who have served Us in the presence of the enemy, and shall have then performed some signal act of valour or devotion to their country'. On 10 August 1858 the warrant was amended to include 'acts of conspicuous courage and bravery under circumstances of extreme danger . . . in which, through the courage and devotion displayed, life or public property may be saved', even if not in the face of the enemy.[6]

Certainly, the actions of many of the defenders of Rorke's Drift met these criteria, and Chelmsford was eager to support the recommendations for the VCs and DCMs that were passed up to him from regimental officers. He forwarded these reports to the Duke of Cambridge who in due course would submit the names of those individuals he deemed worthy to Colonel Stanley, the Secretary of State for War. Stanley in turn would lay those he approved before the Queen, and the awards of the VC – along with the official statement of the 'Acts of Courage' for which they were recommended – would be promulgated in the *London Gazette*.[7]

In the event, while both Cambridge and Stanley concurred that the bravery of the defenders of Rorke's Drift should receive public recognition in the interests of morale, they were nevertheless reluctant to approve too many awards for an action that had ended in defeat. Such was the case with those who had been present during the British defeat at Isandlwana, earlier on the same day as Rorke's Drift. Private Samuel Wassall of the 80th Regiment, was the sole recipient of a decoration for gallantry, and was awarded his VC for rescuing a fellow fugitive from the swirling waters of the Mzinyathi River despite the close presence of the enemy.[8]

In the case of Rorke's Drift, however, the surviving officers all received promotion dated from the day after the battle. Lieutenant Chard was promoted to captain and brevet major; Surgeon Reynolds to surgeon major; and Assistant Commissary Dunne to deputy commissary. Colour Sergeant Bourne was offered a commission but refused it because he believed he did not have the private income to support it.[9] However, he received the DCM for his prominent and exemplary role in the defence and breakout. So too did Privates Henry Hook, Robert Jones, William Jones and John Williams, all of the 2/24th and all distinguished for their resolute conduct in attempting to evacuate the sick from the hospital.

When it came to nominations for the Victoria Cross, both Reynolds and Dunne were deemed to have done no more than their rank required (even if they had performed their duty exceptionally well), and to have been sufficiently honoured by promotion and mention in despatches. Both Bromhead and Dalton were obvious candidates for the award of a Victoria Cross. However, even though the royal warrant contained no specific clause regarding posthumous awards, official policy at the time did not permit them, and no recommendation could be made. Likewise, if they had survived, Lieutenants Melvill and Coghill of the 1/24th would, according to the War Office, have received VCs for attempting to save their battalion's Queen's Colour from the field of Isandlwana and for endeavouring to save a fellow-officer's life.[10]

Consequently, of those whose names had been put forward for the defence of Rorke's Drift, only Chard and Hitch received the Victoria Cross, gazetted on 2 May 1879. Chard was cited for his 'fine example and excellent behaviour', and for his 'intelligence and tenacity' in exercising his command. Hitch was commended for his 'courageous conduct' throughout and for continuing to serve even when incapacitated by his wounds.[11]

With the Court of Inquiry established and awards for gallantry considered, Chelmsford also dealt with Major H. M. Bengough, commander of the 2/1st NNC (about 1,100 men). On the day of the two battles Bengough had been leading his men of No. 2 Column from the middle border towards Rorke's Drift in support of Colonel Durnford, but had arrived on the scene too late to take part in the fighting. A terrified night at Helpmekaar waiting for a Zulu attack had been more than enough for his men and, fearing that they would desert, Bengough had been on the point of disbanding them – just as the two battalions of the 3rd NNC had been sent packing on the previous day. Chelmsford was not having that. He needed the 2/1st NNC to protect the magistracy at Umsinga, where the road from Greytown began its steep ascent up the Biggarsberg to Helpmekaar, in order to deter a Zulu incursion further downstream along the Mzinyathi. Acting firmly and expeditiously, Chelmsford formed the demoralised 2/1st NNC into three sides of a square while British troops of the 2/24th took up position on the fourth side. He then bluntly informed them that the men of the 2/24th would shoot them down if they attempted to desert. Thus persuaded, the 2/1st NNC marched down the escarpment to Umsinga where, over the following weeks they erected the strong, stone-built Fort Bengough and recovered their morale.[12]

These dispositions settled, Chelmsford, with Crealock supportively by his side, made all haste for Pietermaritzburg by way of Ladysmith (thus avoiding the route through Greytown which was closer to the Zulu border), arriving in the colonial capital on the evening of Sunday 26 January. The dire news of Isandlwana and Rorke's Drift had preceded him, brought in on 24 January by two officers of the NNC who had escaped the slaughter. Confirmation (if it were required) had come late the next day when the war correspondent, 'Noggs' Norris-Newman, arrived ill and exhausted in the post-cart from Greytown. He brought official despatches to Frere and other officials, and related his own lurid, first-hand description of events to the anxious crowd pressing about him. The Colonial Secretary, Lieutenant-Colonel C. B. H. Mitchell, in command of the Colonial Sub-District of Pietermaritzburg, had immediate set about constructing a laager in the city to be defended by the volunteer City Guard. The City Laager consisted of a number of substantial public buildings – the magistracy, Presbyterian church and Native High Court – prepared for defence through the loopholing of walls and the fitting of reinforced and loopholed doors and shutters. These strongpoints were then connected by barricades of sandbags and boxes filled with earth to form a continuous (if jagged) perimeter. Each white family taking refuge in the laager was permitted to bring in one reliable African servant. Officials from Government House were to repair to the nearby high-walled gaol in case of emergency, while Fort Napier and its small British garrison offered a final refuge.[13]

Indeed, with Natal now apparently thrown open to Zulu invasion, colonists flocked in panic to the existing government and private laagers and to hastily improvised strongpoints – in total, there were eventually forty-four fortified places of refuge, big and small – and some settlers even trekked west out of Natal and the Transvaal bordering Zululand to the safety of the Orange Free State. Defensive arrangements were put in place as far away from Zululand as the southern borders of Natal with Griqualand East and Pondoland. Yet not even the general state of alarm could overcome the old animosities in the settler community. In the countryside in particular, English-, Dutch-, and German-speaking colonists preferred to take refuge with their own kind in their own laagers, repeating throughout Natal the situation already noted at the 'English' Fort Pine and the 'Boer' Pieters' Laager.[14]

In the crucial port of Durban through which supplies and reinforcements flowed, the Colonial Commandant, Major J. W. Huskisson, refused as impracticable and unnecessary the hastily convened Defence Committee's frantic clamour for the entire town to be encircled by a ring of fortifications. Instead, he assigned volunteer units to a network of key buildings unconnected by barricades to be held in case of attack in accordance with the principles for the defence of an open town. A high wooden stockade was erected across the Point (a spit of land on the north side of the bay and harbour) behind which settler women and children, indentured Indian labourers and 'loyal' Africans were to retire if Durban were attacked. Just north of the town, the Durban Redoubt, a rectangular earthwork fort begun in 1842, was held by a company of British regulars and (like Fort Napier in Pietermaritzburg) was seen as providing an ultimate bastion if the amaZulu overran the port.[15]

The invasion panic reached fever pitch when on 2 February, at 02.00 in the dead of night, a message reached Greytown from the Zululand border that the amaZulu had crossed the middle Thukela. The church bell set up in the stone-built town laager (which dated from 1854) was tolled in alarm, and within a few minutes the whole population had flocked within its walls and anxiously stood to arms all night. In fact, the Border Guard stationed at the drifts across the Thukela, disorientated by a heavy mist lying over the river and undone by their stretched nerves, had mistaken a very minor, localised Zulu foray in search of easy plunder for a full-scale invasion. Consequently, when dawn broke, not a Zulu was to be seen, and the people of Greytown trooped off home again, elated by their safe adventure.[16] But the following evening, when the Greytown post-cart (unapprised of the true situation) brought the terrifying tidings to Pietermaritzburg that the amaZulu had crossed the Thukela, the cry went up: 'The Zulus are coming!' and many of the townspeople fled to the shelter of the laager. The volunteers took up their posts and patrols were sent out. Sir Henry Bulwer and his staff had their bedding and government records moved to the fortified gaol as a precaution, and it was said that Lord Chelmsford stayed up all night, his horse saddled for any eventuality.[17]

Thereafter, barring the occasional nervous flurry, fear of a Zulu invasion began to subside. Chelmsford's return to the capital enabled the civil and military authorities to co-ordinate their defensive policies, although this did not amount to much more than trying to cobble together some means of holding the open countryside between the various settler laagers and British forts. Since the settlers clearly could not be relied upon to hold the frontier line, the burden of defence would have to fall on the African population of Natal. That in any case made perfect sense since, as the Natal government had made absolutely clear, the laagers and posts were primarily for the use of the estimated 22,000 white settlers, and that meant that the African population of 290,000 people (except for a few 'reliable' servants taken into laager with their masters) were left in the open countryside to take their chances as best they could with potential Zulu invaders.[18]

Accordingly, over the next weeks the existing Border Guard and its Reserve along the border with Zululand were augmented by additional levies that the colonial authorities brought up, primarily from the unthreatened Colonial Defensive Districts to the south. In addition, a River Guard of part-time levies was recruited specifically to watch the strategic drifts across the middle Thukela. Nevertheless, despite these efforts, neither the military nor the colonial authorities were willing to place much faith in the effectiveness of these levies if confronted by a serious Zulu incursion.[19] For the moment, only the rivers flooded by the summer rains seemed to be preserving Natal from invasion. As Lt.-Col. Crealock expressed it: 'With the river high, Natal breathes. How she shakes – and no wonder. What a fool's paradise they have been in all this time.'[20]

With the colonial forces, whether black or white, largely untested and untrained, Chelmsford understood only too well that the major burden of defence would have to fall on the British troops under his command. But after the inconceivable causalities at Isandlwana and Rorke's Drift he believed they were no longer sufficient for the task. Therefore, he steeled himself on 27 January to telegraph Colonel Stanley at the War Office reporting that the effects of his recent defeats were dire, that two NNC regiments had deserted and that more were expected to follow, that a panic was 'spreading broadcast over the Colony which is difficult to allay', and (the main burden of the telegram) that 'additional reinforcements must be sent out. At least three Infantry Regiments and two Cavalry Regiments with horses are required and one more company of Engineers.'[21] Chelmsford followed this telegram up a few days later with a grovelling despatch to the Horse Guards addressed to his patron, the Duke of Cambridge. In it he acknowledged that the twofold 'sad disaster' was bound to 'distress your Royal Highness extremely', and ruefully conceded that it had 'thrown back the subjugation of Zululand to an indefinite period & must necessarily entail sacrifice of men & money in far larger proportions than was originally expected.' Chelmsford closed his mortifying despatch with a request destined to cause Cambridge and the government considerable dismay and alarm. 'Might I suggest', wrote Chelmsford in his distinctive large, round hand, 'the advisability of sending out a Major General who will be competent to succeed me not only as Commanding the Forces, but also as Lt Governor & High Commissioner should anything happen to Sir B. Frere.'[22]

The matter was now officially in the open: were Chelmsford and Frere no longer personally capable of containing and resolving the disaster they had unleashed? Chelmsford later regretted he had allowed his shame and raw emotions to run away with him when reporting to his superiors. In particular, he wished that on 9 February he had not reiterated to Colonel Stanley the need to send out a senior officer 'without delay' to replace him if necessary, and that he had then (most damningly) gone on to add 'that the strain of prolonged anxiety & exertion, physical and mental' that he had felt in June 1878 during the Ninth Cape Frontier War 'was even then telling on me', and that what he 'felt then' he felt 'still more now'.[23] Indeed, there was no doubt among his staff and senior officers that for a week or so following the twin disasters of 22 January that 'the poor general' was 'awfully cut up' and clearly on the verge of a nervous breakdown, although his mental equilibrium and mental health begin to recover by mid-February.[24] Frere, however, proved he was made of sterner stuff. Although equally crushed and looking 'ill', he possessed (as Crealock noted) 'the pluck untarnished of his Indian days' and bore up better in the crisis.[25] Chelmsford undoubtedly leaned heavily upon him for support in the days following his disaster, openly admitting that 'It is fortunate that there is one with so cool a head and so stout a heart at the head of affairs at this present juncture.'[26]

Nevertheless, Frere's and Chelmsford's peace of mind was hardly soothed by the outpourings of grief in settler circles at the nearly 200 casualties suffered by the Natal Mounted Police, the Natal Mounted Volunteers, NNC officers and NCOs, and civilian transport riders,[27] by the widespread anguish that their bodies lay unburied, by the abuse increasingly heaped on the pair by the colonial newspapers for their joint responsibility for the debacle, and by the dismay and resentment of Sir Henry Bulwer and the colonial officials for bringing the disaster down upon them.[28] Bulwer was perfectly aware of the likely consequences of Isandlwana and Rorke's Drift, and privately admitted to his brother: 'Our prestige has received a great blow which I fear will take much to recover it. The effect upon the native mind in South Africa will be deplorable.' He went on: 'The general has come back to Pietermaritzburg to reorganize his plans. We are getting everything into a defensive condition. It is altogether deplorable.'[29]

Chapter 12

Securing the Ncome Border against Invasion

—⟶⟶◆⟵⟵—

Chelmsford, Frere, Bulwer and the colonial public at large all understood that there had now to be a drastically revised plan of campaign, but what was it to be? The general told Crealock that he did not wish to risk anything until the reinforcements he had requested from the British government had come out, but, meanwhile, with 'such a vast frontier' and his concentrations of troops being so 'far apart', it 'was a fair puzzle to know what is best to do'.[1] Indeed, 'puzzled' seems to have been Chelmsford favourite word at the time when contemplating future operations, and he repeated it to the one officer on whose advice he felt confident he could rely, the man he believed was 'going to pull me out of my difficulties'.[2]

Chelmsford's designated military saviour was Colonel Evelyn Wood, commander of No. 4 Column, popular, energetic and very deaf, with a tendency towards hypochondria, and so notoriously vain that it was said that he wore his many decorations to bed. He was the most experienced senior officer in Chelmsford's army, and as a commander was dynamic and self-confident, eager to act on his own initiative. He had begun his career in the Royal Navy in 1852 before joining the Army in 1855. Thereafter he proved a gallant soldier, serving with distinction in the Crimean War before earning the Victoria Cross in 1859 when fighting in the last stages of the Indian Mutiny. He was also an intellectual soldier, passing very successfully through Staff College in 1862–4. Service in the Third Asante (Ashanti) War of 1873–4 had brought him Wolseley's patronage and the membership of his 'ring', which suited Wood well since he was an intuitively political soldier. His excellent service in the Ninth Cape Frontier War had very much commended him to Chelmsford.[3] Wood's trusted associate was Brevet Lieutenant-Colonel Redvers Buller, commander of the Frontier Light Horse, and the two made for a formidable, dynamic team. Gaunt-featured with piercing eyes and an aggressive, brush-like beard, Buller was a tough, brusque, fearless, energetic and proven commander of irregular horse and a veteran of many colonial conflicts, including the Third Asante War (bringing with it acceptance into Wolseley's 'ring'). During the Ninth Cape Frontier War, when he had served with Wood, he had formed the FLH into a tough and efficient unit, and had subsequently led it in the First Anglo-Pedi War before joining No. 4 Column. Very much his own man, Buller preferred on campaign to wear a civilian Norfolk jacket and wide-brimmed 'wideawake' hat with a red puggaree that accorded with his men's lack of specific uniform, although they generally adopted yellow or buff corduroy with black trimmings and the same headgear as their commander.[4]

Wood's invasion of Zululand, in stark contrast to Chelmsford's, had proved successful from the outset. True, unlike the General he had not had to face the full force of the main Zulu army and if he had there is no saying that the fate of No. 4 Column would have been much different from that of No. 3 Column. But as it was Wood had to contend only with local forces. The dominant group in north-western Zululand where Wood was operating were the abaQulusi people. They were attached to the ebaQulusini *ikhanda* which King Shaka had established on the northern flank of Mashongololo Mountain, five miles east of the huge, flat-topped Hlobane Mountain with its coronet of cliffs and freshwater springs, which the abaQulusi used as a place of refuge for themselves and their herds. They fell under the direct rule of the royal house and the men formed a distinct *ibutho* drawn only from males in the surrounding locality. Further to the north, just across the Phongolo River from Luneburg – a tiny settlement which King Mpande had permitted a community of German settlers of the Hermannsburg Missionary to establish in 1869 – was the territory of Mbilini waMswati. He was a Swazi prince who had lost a succession conflict and had put himself under Cetshwayo's protection, building up a strong personal following and forging close relations with the abaQulusi and with the nearby Kubheka people of the Ntombe River valley close by Luneburg. The *inkosi* of the amaKubheka was Manyonyoba kaMaqondo, who also owed allegiance to Cetshwayo and the obligation to assist him in war.[5]

Luneburg was an inconvenient thorn in the sides of both Wood and Colonel Rowlands, the commander of No. 5 Column based at Derby fifty miles to the north-east across the Assegai River. Derby lay between their commands in the ill-defined border-lands between the amaZulu, amaSwazi and the Boers of the Transvaal, the so-called Disputed Territory north of the Phongolo River and east of the Ncome River. The Boers had been claiming the Disputed Territory as theirs since 1861, even going so far as to allot farms to settlers and unilaterally proclaiming in 1875 that Cetshwayo had ceded it to them – an assertion the Zulu king strenuously rejected.[6] Knowing that their situation was precarious, and fearing in particular that Cetshwayo would attack them, the Luneburg settlers had built a stone-walled laager around their little church. After a scare of a Zulu attack in late 1878 that actually came to nothing, on 19 October 1878 Wood had detached two companies of the 90th Regiment to strengthen the Luneburg Laager and to build an earthwork – Fort Clery – close by. Two companies of the 1/13th Regiment and the Kaffrarian Rifles of Wood's command – tough volunteers of mainly German stock whom Commandant Frederick Xavier Schermbrucker had raised in the eastern Cape and dressed in smart black corduroy uniforms with a white puggaree around their wideawake hats[7] – relieved them in December 1878 so that the two companies of the 90th were able to re-join No. 4 Column for the invasion of Zululand.[8]

It was to Wood's advantage that his advance was into a region of open grassland between deeply incised river valleys and granite, flat-topped mountains, country ideal for the effective operation of Buller's Frontier Light Horse. During early January 1879 Wood had assembled his column near Balte Spruit in the Utrecht District of the Transvaal, drawing his supplies from Utrecht and Newcastle. On 6 January the column advanced east across the Ncome to encamp at Bemba's Kop. This place was in the Disputed Territory, and therefore did not technically constitute an invasion of Zulu territory – although the amaZulu would strenuously have disagreed. With the official opening of hostilities on

11 January, patrols from Bemba's Kop engaged local Zulu irregulars in a number of skirmishes. On 18 January Wood resumed his advance, and on 20 January his column halted at Tinta's Kraal on the eastern banks of the White Mfolozi River. On that day a mounted patrol led by Buller was forced to retire from Zungwini Mountain, about four miles west of Hlobane, when it skirmished unsuccessfully with the abaQulusi under their *induna*, Msebe kaMadaka, and with some of Mbilini's adherents. In retaliation, Wood led out the column on 22 January and dispersed the enemy on Zungwini, capturing much of their precious livestock, and forcing them to take refuge on Hlobane. Two days later, on 24 January, Wood's troops broke up another Zulu concentration between Ntendeka Mountain and Hlobane just to its east, once again forcing the amaZulu to seek sanctuary on the latter mountain's defensible heights.[9]

Satisfied that the campaign was going well and that his troops were gaining the ascendancy in the neighbourhood, Wood was about to disengage for the day and make his way back to his camp – where on 21 January his men had erected a square stone fortification (called Fort Tinta) on which to anchor the column's defensive wagon laager – when Captain Gardner's doughty messenger from Utrecht finally caught up with him.[10] Wood could scarcely credit that such a stupendous double disaster could have overtaken No. 3 Column, but he understood instantly that it entirely altered the complexion of the campaign. It was now up to him to secure the Ncome border of the Transvaal, and to move south in support of No. 3 Column at Helpmekaar.

To do so would leave the British borders with Zululand further north exposed, but Frere assured Chelmsford that so pressing was the current threat to Natal that he was of the opinion that the Transvaal and the amaSwazi 'must be left to look after themselves'.[11] So, retaining Utrecht as his base, and where an earthwork fort erected in December 1877 by men of the 80th Regiment protected his supply depot,[12] Wood withdrew west to Bemba's Kop and crossed back over the Ncome. The decision then was whether to halt at Conference Hill on the road back to Utrecht, or to move another fifteen miles down the west bank of the Ncome River to take up position closer to Helpmekaar. Wood and his Principal Staff Officer, the gallant and handsome second son of the Earl of Cawdor, Captain the Hon. Ronald Campbell, Coldstream

Guards, pored over their rather inadequate (if not misleading) *Military Map of Zululand*. They concluded that if they marched southwards down the Old Hunting Road and encamped close by Koppie Allein, an isolated hill like a decayed rocky cone with a bulbous crown that reared up abruptly in the level, grassy valley of the Ncome River, they would remain in good communication via this track with Utrecht. From Koppie Allein, the best route to Helpmekaar some forty miles away was to pick up the road that skirted the eastern flanks of the thickly wooded Doornberg (from where Wood intended to collect his fuel) and to follow it west across the Mzinyathi River at either Landman's Drift or Laffnie's Drift to Dundee, and then south along the Biggarsberg.

With the decision taken, No. 4 Column duly turned south. By the late afternoon of 26 January it was encamped close by Koppie Allein on the western bank of the Ncome, some five miles upstream from the site of the battle of Blood River where on 16 December 1838 the Voortrekkers had famously routed King Dingane's army. As was the case with No. 3 Column at Helpmekaar,[13] Wood's orders were to remain on the defensive at Koppie Allein until reinforced. At Koppie Allein Wood immediately set about constructing an entrenched wagon laager on sloping ground just over a mile south of the singular hill itself. The site possessed the desired advantages of being well drained and with good grazing and a supply of water from the river in range of covering rifle fire.[14] This was an excellent defensible position with good command of ground all round. The open country to Wood's front gave Buller and his mounted men abundant scope to undertake damaging raids into the Zulu territory, and allowed their patrols to give ample warning of any Zulu advance in the direction of Koppie Allein.[15]

Believing that Wood was 'the only person who really understands the situation', Chelmsford authorised him to guide the movements of Colonel Rowlands and No. 5 Column from Derby.[16] Even though there was the danger that the amaSwazi – who thus far had continued uncommitted either to the British or Cetshwayo – might be persuaded to support the amaZulu following their great victories over the invaders; and even though the Bapedi – who had remained quiescent – might likewise be encouraged to take up arms, Wood decided that No. 5 Column must close up south in support of his column. Moreover,

Luneburg remained vulnerable to raids by Mbilini, Manyonyoba and the abaQulusi and required greater protection. Wood accordingly instructed Rowlands to leave Derby and move his column south-west to Luneburg where (as did No. 4 Column) it would draw its supplies through Utrecht. By 31 January No. 5 Column was duly encamped there under the shelter of Fort Clery. Rowlands, who had understood he exercised an independent command, did not take cheerfully to being ordered about by Wood, even if the latter had Chelmsford's sanction to do this. However, the uneasy relationship between the two commanders would finally be resolved when, on 26 February, Rowlands and his staff left for Pretoria (the capital of the Transvaal Territory) to take defensive measure against the Transvaal Boers whose 'attitude' had become 'extremely unsatisfactory' and who were reported to be on the brink of open revolt against the British administration.[17] (As we shall see, events had already overtaken that intelligence.) With Rowlands's removal, all the troops of No. 5 column were attached to Wood's command, 'absolutely', as Chelmsford put it, at his 'disposal'.[18]

Chapter 13

Agitation in the Transvaal against British Rule

Rowlands's departure for Pretoria may have been welcomed by Wood, but it signalled another dire threat to the teetering edifice of British power in southern Africa. No proper census was ever taken of the Transvaal under British rule, but the general assumption was that the Dutch population was at least 36,000 strong and made up over three-quarters of the rural white population. They expressed themselves in their colloquial language, a form of Low Dutch full of loan words and expressions from German, French, English and African tongues which was already in the process of transforming itself from High Dutch into Afrikaans. The majority of the 'Non-Dutch' Europeans, or 'Outsiders', who numbered somewhere around 5,000 and lived mainly in the small towns, were of British stock. The African population was estimated at between 700,000 and 800,000 and so constituted some 95 per cent of the Transvaal's population, thus outnumbering the settlers even more heavily than in Natal where colonists accounted for 7 per cent of the inhabitants.[1]

Fundamentalist religion was the great cement of Boer society, and Calvinist ministers of religion the most influential individuals in the community. Typically of many another self-reliant and independently minded frontier folk, the Boers had no great respect for authority and were certainly politically aware. They were not cut out to be docile and uncritical subjects to British authority; nor were they inclined to submit to paying taxes which symbolised more than anything else their submission to alien rule. In this negative context it was unfortunate that the English-speaking officials who increasingly dominated the Transvaal administration made little effort to fathom the reasons for swelling Boer antagonism towards their government. Nor did they attempt to disguise their contempt for the Boers themselves, whom they characterised as ugly, uneducated, slovenly, xenophobic, unruly and obscurantist with an overweening sense of religiously justified racial superiority over Africans.[2]

Indeed, after some initial optimism Sir Theophilus Shepstone's administration of the Transvaal had rapidly lost any support in the Boer community.[3] Only three months after British annexation, in July 1877, a delegation of disaffected Transvalers mandated by the defunct Boer *Volksraad* – the previously sovereign parliament of their disestablished republic – met the colonial secretary in London to request a plebiscite to test the popularity of British sovereignty. Lord Carnarvon received them graciously but turned them down flat, and the delegation reported back on 7 January 1878 to an indignant mass gathering in Pretoria. Since Carnarvon had refused to allow a plebiscite on Transvaal independence, the decision was taken at a second meeting on 28 January 1878 at Naauwpoort near Potchefstroom to appoint a committee to collect signatures against annexation.

The Signatures Committee, or *Volkskomitee* (People's Committee) as it became known, collected 6,591 signatures against annexation and only 587 in favour. At the stormy report-back meeting held on 4 April 1878 at Doornfontein farm near Pretoria, it was agreed to send a second delegation to London to present the figures to the colonial secretary. Among the delegates the man who emerged as the dominant figure was S. J. Paulus (Paul) Kruger. Born in the Eastern Cape in 1825, he had taken part in the Great Trek as a boy and grew up a true frontiersman, gaining a considerable reputation as a dauntless hunter and a brave and resourceful military commander in the ZAR's wars against its African neighbours. In 1877, on the eve of the British annexation, Kruger had been elected vice-president of the ZAR and had become an unfaltering activist against British rule. He was a *Dopper*, as the extremely conservative members of his fundamentalist Calvinist sect were known, and took the Bible literally. He believed that he possessed a special understanding of God's purpose and undertook always to do His will as revealed to him.[4] His most trusted colleague among the Boer delegates was the heavily bearded, courteous and essentially moderate Petrus (Piet) Joubert who – like him – had taken part as a child in the Great Trek and who had entered politics at an early age to become one of the ZAR's most prominent leaders, acting as its president in 1875–6.[5]

This second delegation found Hicks Beach, who had recently replaced Carnarvon as colonial secretary, as unbending as his predecessor concerning Transvaal independence, and as insistent on the new colony's place within the confederation. The delegation expressed its deep disappointment and reported back to a heavily attended public meeting held on 10, 11 and 13 January 1879 (the 12th was a Sunday, the Sabbath when no business could be conducted) at Rietvallei farm in the Potchefstroom district of the south-western Transvaal. The meeting vented its deep collective anger with British oppression and essentially demanded that British annexation be reversed. It authorised the *Volkskomitee* to remain in being with sub-committees to assist in politicisation, to step up anti-British agitation and to establish what amounted to a shadow administration. In conclusion, it made future provision for 'an assembly of the people' to decide on what further action should be taken.[6]

The meeting appointed Joubert as its delegate to travel to Pietermaritzburg to lay the minutes of the proceedings at Rietvallei before Frere, the highest British official in South Africa.[7] On the afternoon of 4 February the two men met in Frere's office. The tone of their encounter was restrained and gentlemanly, although Joubert made it clear that 'It was the unanimous feeling of the people that they would have their independence and that they would be satisfied by no concession.' On his way to Pietermaritzburg Joubert had learned of the disaster to British arms on 22 January. Although sympathetic at a personal level, he refused to allow it to change his official stance, even though Frere uncharacteristically went so far as to beg him to reconsider, calling on him to put white solidarity in the face of the dangerous 'black conspiracy' first. The meeting terminated indecisively and rather tamely with Frere agreeing to come up to the Transvaal at some future date to hold further talks with the *Volkskomitee*.

However, Frere was left spooked by two considerations. Firstly, rumours were circulating widely that the 'remonstrant Boers' – despite

Sir Bartle Frere, Governor of the Cape and
High Commissioner for South Africa, 1877–9.

Colonel Frederick Stanley, Secretary of State
for War, 1878–80.

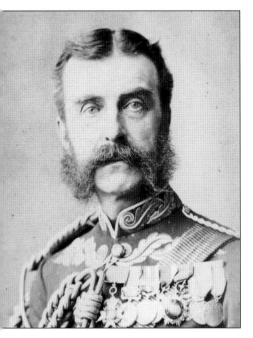

Sir Frederic Thesiger, second Baron
Chelmsford, General Officer Commanding
British Forces in South Africa, 1878–9.

Sir Michael Hicks Beach, Secretary of State
for the Colonies, 1878–80.

A battalion of British infantry on parade in Pietermaritzburg.

Sir Theophilus Shepstone,
KCMG, Administrator of
the Transvaal Territory,
1877–9.

Sir Henry Bulwer, KCMG,
Lieutenant-Governor of
the Colony of Natal,
1875–80.

Brevet Lt.-Col. John North
Crealock, Lord Chelmsford's
Assistant Military Secretary,
1878–9.

Above: Lord Chelmsford on campaign in Zululand as seen in an engraving from the *Graphic.*

Left: H.R.H. Prince George, Duke of Cambridge, Field Marshal Commanding-in-Chief, 1856–95 by 'Atń' (Alfred Thompson), from *Vanity Fair,* 23 April 1870.

Left: King Cetshwayo kaMpande.

Right: Lieutenant Gonville Bromhead, 24th Regiment, who died gallantly in the defence of Rorke's Drift on 22 January 1879.

Far right: Lieutenant John Chard, Royal Engineers, the officer in command at Rorke's Drift.

Bottom right: Umntwana Dabulamanzi kaMpande, the Zulu commander at Rorke's Drift, photographed in 1873 in conversation with the hunter-trader John Dunn who supplied firearms to the Zulu kingdom.

Below: A contemporary photograph of Isandlwana Mountain taken from where the extended British firing line was deployed during the battle of 22 January 1879.

Top: Surgeon James Reynolds tending the wounded Fred Hitch as the defences of Rorke's Drift are finally overwhelmed by the amaZulu.

Above: Zulu *amabutho* charging in open order as they did in the opening phase of the battle of Rorke's Drift. Note their assortment of weapons, including firearms, and the mounted commander

Top: Lord Chelmsford's column retiring across the Mzinyathi River upstream of Rorke's Drift on 23 January 1879. Note Isandlwana Mountain in the distance to the right.

Above: The British fortified post at Helmekaar on the edge of the heights overlooking the valley of the Mzinyathi River.

Awarded the Victoria Cross after his heroic, if unsuccessful, defence of Rorke's Drift and promoted brevet major, the bearded John Chard is seated right wearing his decoration.

The stone-walled Greytown laager dating from 1854 and the adjoining Fort Moore earthwork built by the military in January 1879, from the *Graphic*, 26 April 1879.

Brevet Colonel Evelyn Wood, VC, CB, commander of No. 4 Column by 'Spy' (Leslie Ward), from *Vanity Fair*.

Brevet Lieutenant-Colonel Redvers Buller, CB, commander of the mounted troops of Wood's No. 4 Column.

Colonel Wood's entrenched wagon laager at Koppie Allein under construction in late January 1879.

Above left: Colonel Charles Pearson, CB, commander of No. 1 Column.

Above right: Fort Tenedos in the foreground with a view south across the Thukela River to Fort Pearson on the heights beyond.

Right: The interior of the earthwork fort at Utrecht built in December 1877 adjoining the Utrecht laager. Note the corrugated iron commissariat shed and the tents and stores littering the cramped space.

Above: Men of Wood's Irregulars in full Swazi war panoply.

Above, far left: Paul Kruger, former Vice-President of the South African Republic and in 1879 a member of the rebel Boers' Triumvirate.

Above, left: Piet Joubert, former Acting President of the South African Republic, and in 1879 a member of the rebel Boers' Triumvirate and *Kommandant-Generaal* of the Boer forces.

Above: A unit of the Natal Native Horse with carbines and traditional weapons. They are identified by a white armband and a red puggaree wound around their hats.

Left: Petrus Lafras Uys, Jnr, of the Utrecht District of the Transvaal with his four sons, all dressed and armed in typical fashion for Boers on commando. Note the *agterryers* on the right.

Above: Mounted Infantry of Colonel Wood's personal escort, recruited from the 90th Light Infantry.

Left: The Zulu chest attacking Wood's fortified laager at Koppie Allein on 20 March 1879.

Lieutenant-Colonel Buller leading his mounted men in pursuit of the retreating amaZulu at the battle of Koppie Allein.

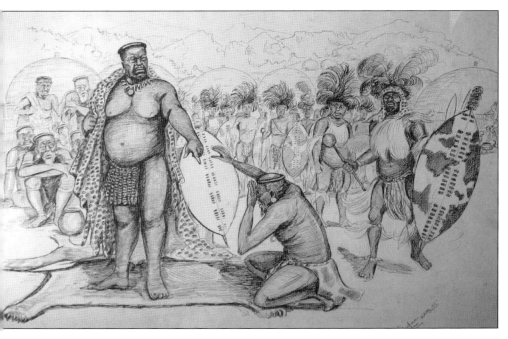

King Cetshwayo berating *Inkosi* Mnyamana for his defeat at the battle of Koppie Allein and threatening his execution.

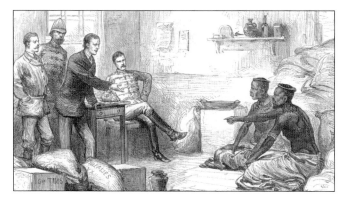

King Cetshwayo's two emissaries, Mfunzi and Nkisimana, detained in Fort Buckingham in late March 1879, being interrogated by British officials.

The Zulu delegation accepting the British peace terms on 17 April 1879.

Henry Francis Fynn, Jnr, the Resident Magistrate of the Umsinga Division since 1876 and in 1879 the first British Resident in Zululand, photographed with members of his Border Guard during the Anglo-Zulu War.

Joubert's very measured tones when he met the high commissioner – were nevertheless seriously contemplating 'active hostility'. Secondly, Frere had received 'official information' only an hour before his meeting with Joubert that:

> Messengers had been intercepted on their way from the Zulu King to Mr. P. Kruger and others, bearing the tidings of the disaster to our troops, pointing out that this was a favourable opportunity for the Boers to rise against the British Government, and begging them in any case to sit still.[8]

Did this intelligence mean that the Boers and the amaZulu were about to put aside their long-standing differences and take up a common position against the British, thus opening up an entirely new front? Certainly, for the disaffected Transvalers, the twin disasters of Isandlwana and Rorke's Drift only confirmed that the poor British military performance in their aborted campaign against the Bapedi in 1878 was no aberration. When that dismal record was taken into account, would it really be so difficult to overthrow British rule by force of arms? And, for the Boers, there was a further consideration. The major reason they had acquiesced, even for a moment, in the imposition of British rule, was that the British had promised not only to relieve them of the menace posed by the Bapedi, but to use their military muscle to prise the Disputed Territory out of Zulu hands and award it to the Transvaal. It now seemed apparent that they could deliver on neither undertaking. What possible advantage, therefore, was to be gained by remaining under British rule?

Chapter 14

Securing the Thukela Frontier against Invasion

—❧—

While Frere fretted, deliberating how best to head off a likely rebellion in the Transvaal by diplomatic means, Chelmsford addressed himself to the more immediately pressing matter of securing the frontiers of Natal against a Zulu invasion. By the end of January the troops under the command of Rowlands, Wood and Glyn held the line north–south between Luneburg and Fort Bengough by way of Koppie Allein and Helpmekaar, thus guarding the Ncome and Mzinyathi river frontier. That still left the Thukela River frontier to be secured. The river itself, with its many oxbows, meandered south-eastwards for some 200 miles through deeply incised and wooded countryside until it flowed into the Indian Ocean. Consequently, that rugged stretch of the border was poorly suited to major military operations, while the Thukela itself, still flowing strongly from the summer rains, continued to act as an effective barrier. All things considered, therefore, Chelmsford believed that the 'Middle Border' (as he termed it) could be adequately defended by the Natal government's Border and River Guards stationed in Colonial Defensive Districts Nos VII and VI, and by the two remaining NNC battalions of No. 2 Column. The latter were encamped on the high escarpment near Kranskop, a great rocky spur of the Drakensberg that drops precipitously down to the Thukela valley below. No. 2 Column's position was well chosen because it commanded the winding track over Middle Drift that was the only conceivably practicable invasion route across that stretch of the Thukela, and for that reason was known to colonists as the 'Gates of Natal'.

Durnford, when he departed on 21 January with the ill-fated reinforcements for No. 3 Column at Isandlwana, left the bulk of the 1st and 3rd Battalions, 1st Regiment NNC behind at Kranskop under the command of Captain Geoffrey Barton, his staff officer. The two battalions were not up to strength and numbered only about 900 men and 130 white officers and NCOs, and to make matters worse there were some desertions after the news of Isandlwana and Rorke's Drift filtered through on 23 January. Nevertheless, the officers regained control of their men and restored discipline by flogging all those deserters they managed to round up. They then set the two battalions and No. 3 Company, Natal Native Pioneer Corps, to building a large, impregnable earthwork redoubt with a parapet 350 metres in length. Named Fort Cherry after the affable, but sickly Captain C. E. Le M. Cherry, the senior officer present, it effectively blocked the route the amaZulu must take into the Natal midlands should they attempt to invade. (On 12 February Chelmsford formally dissolved No. 2 Column, and in his reorganisation of the NNC, the 1/1st NNC became the 1st Battalion NNC, and the 3/1st NNC the 3rd Battalion NNC. The 2/1st NNC at Fort Bengough, formerly part of No. 2 Column, became the 2nd Battalion NNC.[1])

If Chelmsford believed the Middle Border could be left to look after itself, it was quite another matter when it came to the rolling Natal coastal plain with its prosperous farms and thriving villages that stretched south from the mouth of the Thukela to Durban seventy miles away. North of the Thukela, in the Zulu kingdom, the countryside with its hills, numerous streams and coastal bush was very similar, although far less cultivated. That meant the terrain on either side of the Lower Thukela afforded an ideal invasion route, whether for the British or the amaZulu. Precisely for this reason, and to block the path of the amaZulu to Durban, Chelmsford had planned for No. 1 Column under Colonel Pearson to invade Zululand from that point and to draw its supplies through the village of Stanger from Durban.

On 12 January No. 1 Column began to cross into Zululand on ponts drawn over the Thukela at the Lower Drift. The crossing was commanded from the high bluff on the Natal bank by Fort Pearson, a strong, leaf-shaped earthwork thrown up in November 1878 following the contours of the ground and held by two companies of the 2/3rd

Regiment.[2] Once across the river, during 13–17 January the troops set about building Fort Tenedos, named in honour of the Naval Brigade. It was sited 600 metres from the river bank directly opposite Fort Pearson and was intended as a depot for the distribution of stores and provisions to No. 1 Column during its advance deeper into Zululand.

The design and construction of Fort Tenedos were under the eye of Major Warren R. C. Wynne, RE, a meticulous, enthusiastic officer with a keen eye for detail (and with an impressive, drooping blond moustache under his big nose). The 75 by 33-metre earthwork redoubt (the technical term for a closed work of square or polygonal shape) possessed eight faces of different lengths like a flattened hexagon. It had a small bastion on the north-east side, and the entrance facing the river was designed with a dog-leg parapet. The barbettes (gun platforms) at three of its six salient angles and the infantry banquettes were of earth, as was the parapet itself. In his need to complete the work as quickly as possible, Wynne used sandbags instead of sods for some of the revetments holding the earth ramparts in place. A ditch was dug around the fort (from which the earth for the construction of the parapet was collected) and was surrounded by wire entanglements and *trous de loup* (inverted conical holes with stakes at the bottom).[3] However, when he first saw Fort Tenedos on 11 February, Lt.-Col. Crealock was far from impressed. In its embellishments such as 'useless wire entanglements' he found nothing but the pointless 'dandyism of a course at Chatham'. Even worse in his eyes was the fort's site, 'completely open to the fire of a long, strong, stony hill 300 yards off!!'[4]

Apparently unaware of these defects, on 18 January the column, escorting 130 wagons, began its advance in two mutually supporting divisions, leaving behind a garrison of one company of the 99th Regiment to garrison Fort Tenedos. It objective was the Norwegian mission station at Eshowe, some thirty miles away, which the missionaries had abandoned in 1878 for fear of being attacked by Cetshwayo. Pearson intended to use the deserted church and other buildings as a depot for the column's further advance on oNdini. On 21 January a patrol sent out from the column burned the undefended kwaGingindlovu *ikhanda* on its right flank, and on 22 January (the same day as the battles of Isandlwana and Rorke's Drift) the column continued its advance across the Nyezane stream.[5]

Meanwhile, the Zulu *impi* under Godide that had detached itself from the main Zulu army on 17 January had set off in a south-easterly direction to contest Pearson's advance. It bivouacked that same night at kwaMagwaza. Because many of his men came down with dysentery, Godide only resumed the march on 20 January, when the *impi* reached Cetshwayo's first oNdini *ikhanda* (built in 1855) on the southern bank of the lower Mhlathuze River. On 21 January Godide's force, which had swelled to about 6,000 with reinforcements of small elements of *amabutho* clustered at the coastal *amakhanda* that had not proceeded to oNdini, as well as numbers of local irregulars, reached the burnt-out kwaGingindlovu. Deciding against a night attack on the British camp, Godide moved his army back north across the Nyezane with the intention of ambushing Pearson's column when it advanced up the range of hills north of the Nyezane.[6]

The leading 1st Division of the British column was escorting a straggling convoy of fifty wagons, while the 2nd Division was some way to its rear. As the 1st Division began to ascend the steep, hillside track along a long spur with the ground falling away sharply on either side to narrow valleys covered in bush before rising again to high spurs that commanded the route, the amaZulu attacked.[7] Godide's plan was to engage the front of the column in classic attack formation with his chest while the two horns enveloped it. When, at about 08.00, the British observed some amaZulu moving on Wombane, the eastern of the two hills flanking the track, Pearson ordered a company of the 1/2nd NNC to move forward and disperse them. This movement dislocated Zulu plans, for their left horn was provoked into a premature attack before the chest and right horn were ready to commit themselves.

The Zulu left horn routed the company of NNC and rushed down Wombane in extended order and engaged the British who hastily deployed to repel them in a skirmishing line. Pearson sent forward the troops at the head of the column with the two 7-pounders, a Gatling gun and a 24-pounder rocket tube to take up position on a knoll higher up the spur in order to rake the Zulu position with fire. Meanwhile, the convoy closed up and halted and the Zulu left horn made an orderly withdrawal before the advancing British skirmishing line. Those attempting to retire across the Nyezane were intercepted by elements of the 2nd Division now coming up, bringing the total British forces engaged to 73 officers and 2,047 men, of whom 860 were African levies. After the retreat of their left horn, the Zulu right horn began a belated and tentative advance supported by the chest, but was pinned down by the British fire. The British then counter-attacked, seizing the heights before them and taking the dominant crest of Wombane to their right.

With the loss of the key to their position, the amaZulu dispersed in fairly good order under British artillery fire that broke up their attempts to re-form. The last shots died away at about 09.30. Zulu non-combatants who had been watching the battle from the surrounding hills, anticipating a Zulu victory, fled in dismay, but the majority of the defeated Zulu force gathered on a flat-topped hill four miles from the battlefield. They remained there, shouting, singing and dancing while the British attended to their casualties, and only finally dispersed when, at noon, Pearson resumed his advance on Eshowe burning all the *imizi* along the route in retaliation for being attacked.

Nyezane had been an unusual battle. There was little hand-to-hand fighting in what was essentially a running fire-fight. What made the difference was that the British had the discipline to control the situation, while the amaZulu lacked it and failed to co-ordinate their attack. And not only had the British out-manoeuvred the amaZulu, but they had severely out-gunned them too. While the rockets and other artillery cause consternation in the Zulu ranks, it was the steady Martini-Henry volley fire that did the most damage, and the inferior range of the mainly antiquated Zulu firearms meant they could not fire back effectively. What was even more shocking for Godide and the Zulu leadership was that all the advantages of a carefully picked position, surprise and enemy lack of preparations had come to naught. Casualties too were out of all proportion, for while the British had lost only three men of the 2/3rd Regiment and two officers and six NCOs and men of the NNC (with one officer and fourteen men wounded), the Zulu dead numbered 300 or more. All in all, Nyezane was a severe blow to Zulu morale in the coastal country.

Pearson did not advance far on the afternoon following the battle, and halted for the night on a defensible ridge about four miles beyond the Nyezane. Early on the morning of 23 January – as yet quite oblivious of the disaster that had befallen No. 3 Column – No. 1

Column advanced without incident to Eshowe. On arrival, Wynne immediately set in motion his plans to make the place defensible by sending out large work parties to clear the ground preparatory to the erection of an earthwork redoubt with a perimeter of 400 metres (very much on the same lines as Fort Tenedos) around the mission buildings. The necessity of taking in these structures meant that the site of the fort was unavoidably commanded by high ground on its northern and southern sides.[8]

Pearson did not plan to tarry any longer in Eshowe than was necessary to make his depot there defensible. In preparation for resuming his advance – and still entirely ignorant of the movements of the other invading columns – on 25 January he sent back forty-eight empty wagons from Eshowe for the Lower Thukela escorted by two companies each of the 2/3rd and 99th Regiments. The convoy and its escort arrived without interference by the amaZulu at Fort Tenedos on 27 January.[9]

In Eshowe, meanwhile, on the three successive nights of 23–25 January the nervous British garrison was awakened by false alarms. Then, on Sunday 26 January, news finally arrived of the progress of the campaign elsewhere. Sent by Sir Bartle Frere, it came by African runner from Fort Pearson which was connected to Pietermaritzburg by telegraph. Frere's message was superbly misleading. He wrote that Durnford had been killed on 22 January and No. 2 Column forced to retreat, but that Chelmsford had gained a great victory. This message was barely digested than it was followed by a second, the runner bearing word that Fort Tenedos had come under heavy, if ineffective fire on the night of 25 January, but that the amaZulu had vanished back into the dark after an hour's shooting. Unsettled by these messages, on 27 January Wynne redoubled his efforts to make Fort Eshowe defensible.[10]

Then, at about 10.00 on the morning of 28 January, Pearson received by runner a telegram Chelmsford had sent from Pietermaritzburg on 27 January that filled him with 'ill forebodings':

> Consider all my instructions as cancelled, and act in whatever manner you think most desirable in the interests of the column under your command. Should you consider the garrison

of Ekowe as too far advanced to be fed with safety, you can withdraw it.

Hold, however, if possible, the post on the Zulu side of Lower Tugela. You must be prepared to have the whole Zulu force down upon you.[11]

Chelmsford's message, although alarming in the extreme, was nevertheless lacking in vital, specific detail. Not knowing from its contents what had actually befallen the other columns, Pearson called a council of war of his senior officers. This was by no means a usual procedure in Victorian colonial campaigning, but it was forced on Pearson by the necessity to come to a crucial operational decision based on inadequate intelligence. The assembled officers at first almost all counselled retiring at once to the Lower Thukela. However, Wynne and Pearson's two senior staff officers (Brevet Colonel Forestier Walker and Captain H. G. MacGregor) succeeded in persuading them otherwise, arguing that a retreat would be extremely hazardous and that work on Fort Eshowe was already sufficiently well advanced for the place to be held. Still, that brought up the question of whether the garrison would have sufficient ammunition and supplies to hold out for any length of time. After some further discussion it was therefore resolved to send all the mounted troops and nearly all of the two battalions of the 2nd Regiment NNC back to the border immediately. These units began their march that very afternoon at 14.00. The mounted men under Major Percy Barrow pushed on ahead and reached Fort Tenedos at 23.30 that same night; but the NNC, feeling abandoned and vulnerable, especially after night fell, lost discipline and cohesion, breaking up into small, panicking groups along the way. If the amaZulu had attacked them, they would have been massacred, but fortunately for them, they did not. The first parties of NNC came into Fort Tenedos during the following morning, 29 January, but it was late afternoon before the last stragglers made it to the Thukela. Taking their extreme disarray into account, over the next few days Chelmsford and Bulwer agreed to disband the now reduced and severely demoralised 2nd NNC.[12]

Where were the amaZulu that these disorganised and vulnerable troops should have made it safely back unchallenged to Fort Tenedos? After the battle of Nyezane the amaZulu *impi* did not at first disperse as was customary for ritual purification. Expecting Pearson to continue his march north-westwards to oNdini, Godide's forces concentrated in the thorny valley of the Mhlathuze valley with the somewhat desperate intention of again ambushing him. It was to their relief, therefore, when Pearson halted at Eshowe and they had the opportunity to be purified of the evil and contagious influences of homicide. For four days those who had killed were separated from their companions and were treated with ritual medicines to ward off *umnyama* and to gain occult ascendancy over their vengeful victims whose spilt blood formed a dangerous bridge between the living and the dead. Once ritually clean, they could return home or rejoin their comrades for further military operations. Accordingly, it was not until the end of January – by which time the mounted men and NNC of No. 1 Column had made it back to Fort Tenedos – that numerous groups of between forty and fifty men began keeping close watch on Fort Tenedos and Fort Eshowe and on the road between them. Ultimately, the Zulu intention was that the men of the *amabutho* living in the coast country, augmented by local irregulars, would be sufficiently numerous and organised to concentrate and attack Pearson if he attempted a sortie from Fort Eshowe. However, these forces were still too scattered and their morale too depressed by their recent defeat even to consider trying conclusions again with the British.[13]

At 18.30 on the evening of the same day that the mounted men and NNC departed for Fort Tenedos, the garrison of Fort Eshowe was greatly relieved by the arrival of a convoy of provisions in sixty-six wagons escorted by two companies of the 2/3rd Regiment and three of the 99th.[14] The problem then arose concerning what to do with the large number of draught animals now milling about Fort Eshowe since there was not sufficient pasturage available for them in the vicinity. Concluding there was no alternative, on 30 January Pearson decided to send the beasts back to Fort Tenedos in the charge of their unescorted African wagon drivers and leaders. About 1,000 head of oxen and twenty-eight mules duly set out, presenting an astonishingly easy prize for the Zulu patrols that were returning to action. They fell upon the livestock and chased their unarmed drivers and leaders into the bush. Exulting, the amaZulu drove off some 900 head, while the poor remainder and their terrified drivers made it back to the fort.[15]

The fate of the draught animals gave Pearson due notice that the amaZulu were beginning to draw a net around Fort Eshowe, confirmed by the increasing number of alarms sentries raised on account of Zulu activities nearby. Work was consequently hurried on to strengthen the fort, but a new concern arose when some men (including Wynne) began to go down with dysentery. Then, on 2 February, runners arrived from the Lower Thukela with telegrams and letters at last giving the grim particulars of the joint disasters at Isandlwana and Rorke's Drift to Pearson and his assembled officers. Aghast at just how dire the situation really was, Pearson wrote back the same day to Chelmsford requesting to be reinforced by seven companies. But Colonel William Bellairs, the Deputy Adjutant-General and Quartermaster-General on Chelmsford's headquarters staff, responded by telegram from Pietermaritzburg on 4 February advising Pearson that all the other troops in Natal were required for the defence of the colony. In this communication, and in further despatches from Chelmsford himself that reached Fort Eshowe by messenger on 7 and 11 February, the recommendation (but not the order) was for a rapid withdrawal to the Thukela without wheeled transport by half the garrison and all the sick. Behind this recommendation was Chelmsford's desire for the return of the Naval Brigade and its artillery to strengthen the defences of the Lower Thukela, and his preference that Pearson and his staff should be there to take command. As for the remaining half of the garrison, Chelmsford suggested that it should hold on in Fort Eshowe in a reduced entrenchment; however, at the same time he warned that no convoy of supplies would be able to start for Eshowe for at least six weeks.[16]

Altogether, it is clear he was lukewarm about Pearson long remaining cooped up in Eshowe, admitting to Wood that in that regard it was 'a mistake to move in farther than you can get back from easily', especially as it would require 'a bush fight' every time supplies were sent in to the reduced garrison.[17] Nevertheless, it was symptomatic of Chelmsford's uncertainly about what best to do, and an indication of his mental state in the days following Isandlwana and Rorke's Drift, that he gave Pearson no firm instructions. Instead, he cast the decision on whether or not to hold fast in Eshowe – perhaps with a reduced garrison – squarely on Pearson's shoulders.

On receipt of Chelmsford's message of 11 February, Pearson again held a council of war with his senior officers. This time, there was little need for discussion. All agreed that it would be foolhardy to follow Chelmsford's recommendation to abandon half the garrison deep in Zulu territory. Rather, in the light of the extremely adverse strategic situation following the two Zulu victories at Isandlwana and Rorke's Drift, it made far better sense to withdraw the entire column to the Lower Thukela. For fear of being ambushed on the way by the resurgent amaZulu, it was resolved that if the whole garrison sallied out it must march as rapidly as possible to avoid vulnerable halts, and therefore (as Chelmsford had advised) the wagons must be left behind and ammunition that could not be carried away should be buried 'under the floors of some of the rooms' at the mission station.[18] Pearson accordingly sent a messenger advising the general, who had arrived at Fort Pearson from Durban on 11 February, that he would march out at midnight on 16 February. But this vital message never reached the Lower Thukela. The amaZulu had indeed recovered sufficiently to keep a close watch on the fort in large numbers, and their patrols were successful in intercepting and killing all runners attempting to convey messages between Pearson and Chelmsford.[19] So, when no word arrived from Chelmsford either approving or forbidding his plan to withdraw, it was left to Pearson to decide whether or not to proceed.

Pearson knew he was putting the lives of his men at risk if he marched as planned, and what complicated the decision even further was Chelmsford's earlier instruction to concert such a movement with the garrison at the Lower Thukela 'to make your retirement secure'.[20] To that end, Chelmsford had been beefing up the garrison there, so that by 14 February it consisted of five companies of the 99th Regiment, two companies of the 2/3rd Regiment, the Naval Brigade from the *Tenedos* and Barrow's mounted men who had withdrawn from Fort Eshowe on 28 January, namely No. 2 Squadron, Mounted Infantry, and five units of Natal Mounted Volunteers.[21]

This strengthening of the Lower Thukela line had been made possible by the recent arrival of reinforcements from elsewhere in southern Africa. Five companies of the 2/4th Regiment (sent out by the British government with the 99th Regiment in November 1878) had landed at Durban in mid-January; four of the companies had moved up to reinforce Glyn at Helpmekaar and one had been left behind in garrison at Greytown on No. 3 Column's line of supply to Pietermaritzburg. The last three companies of the battalion had remained in Cape Town to form part of the garrison of Cape Colony. But then, on receiving word of Isandlwana and Rorke's Drift, the Cape government had 'behaved with great spirit' (as Chelmsford expressed it) and immediately despatched them to Natal, so that by 2 February they were in Pietermaritzburg.[22] In addition, the Cape government nobly parted with four companies of the 88th Regiment quartered at King William's Town on the Cape's recently pacified eastern frontier, and they arrived in Durban by sea on 8 February. One company went to Pietermaritzburg, two to Stanger (where they relieved the two companies of the 99th Regiment that then moved forward to Fort Pearson), and one remained in Durban. The deployment of these companies sent by the Cape meant that all the major urban centres in Natal conceivably in danger of a Zulu raid were now adequately garrisoned. On the negative side, this deployment left Cape Colony dangerously short of British troops to guard it. Now it would have to rely for its security on under 2,000 white Volunteers and Mounted Yeomanry in conjunction with the Cape Mounted Rifles, the only Cape colonial unit on a permanent footing.[23]

At the Lower Thukela, Chelmsford was anxiously waiting to learn from Pearson whether and when he intended to attempt a breakout from Eshowe. But with no messengers any longer getting though the Zulu lines, and fresh ones sensibly declining to risk their lives, Chelmsford had to concede that he remained 'ignorant' of Pearson's plans and consequently was in no position to 'send any force out to meet him' should he make the attempt. Nevertheless, after Pearson's resounding success at Nyezane, he felt reasonably confident that even without support from the forces at the Lower Thukela Pearson would be able (as he told Wood) 'to get out quite easily'.[24] So Chelmsford continued to wait at the Lower Thukela for Pearson to make his move, correctly anticipating that 'without hearing from me again, he will take steps to withdraw'.[25]

Chapter 15

Stalemate along the Borders

Chelmsford's confidence in Pearson's ability to withdrawal successfully from Fort Eshowe was fuelled by the remarkable inactivity of the amaZulu since their stunning victories at Isandlwana and Rorke's Drift, only partially tarnished by their repulse at Nyezane. On 28 January he had warned Wood to 'be prepared to have the whole Zulu force on top of you some of these days',[1] yet by mid-February the amaZulu still had made no move. There had been no Zulu invasion of British territory despite the firm expectation there would be among the military and colonial authorities and the widespread panic of the settlers. Instead, as Chelmsford reported to Cambridge on 1 February and reiterated to Stanley on 8 February, the amaZulu had been 'perfectly quiet since the 22nd January, and report says they have felt very much the heavy loss inflicted on them', and that, despite their great victories, they had consequently been 'much disheartened'.[2]

For once, Chelmsford's intelligence was close to the mark. After a victory, as at Isandlwana and Rorke's Drift, it was customary for the Zulu army to return in triumph to the king to report and share out the spoils. If beaten, as at Nyezane, it was normal (as we have seen) for the army to scatter and make for home, there to perform the post-combat purification rituals. Victorious *amabutho* had also to be purified over four days of the evil and contagious influences of homicide and to ornament themselves correctly before reporting to the king. Those who had killed in battle presented themselves with their weapons in the great cattle enclosure before their monarch. With the king seated in their midst the *amabutho* exchanged accounts of the fighting and renewed the ritual challenges they had made before setting out for war. The king then rewarded those who had distinguished themselves on campaign with cattle, and publicly humiliated those accused of cowardice.[3]

Yet despite the reports of victory and the great ceremonies at oNdini, Cetshwayo was not pleased. He gave neither Ntshingwayo nor Mavumengwana credit for Isandlwana because it was reported that they had lost control of their men who had not complied with their orders.[4] He was particularly angered with Dabulamanzi, despite his success in taking Rorke's Drift – and even though he was his favourite brother – because he had specifically forbidden any forays into Natal. Moreover, he was highly displeased that his commanders had been unable to prevent the bulk of his army from dispersing home instead of reporting to him, and that they had carried away the bulk of the plunder they had won – especially the 800 or so Martini-Henry rifles – rather than bringing it to him for the customary distribution. Above all, he was deeply shocked at the casualties his armies had sustained – even when victorious – at the hands of numerically inferior British forces. The defeat at Nyezane especially concerned him, as did the heroic (if futile) stands by the British at Isandlwana and Rorke's Drift, for this boded ill for Zulu military successes in the future.[5]

All in all, their two victories notwithstanding, Cetshwayo and his people were left discouraged rather than elated. True, there had been a moment of exhilaration when the news was shouted from hilltop to hilltop that the white soldiers had been killed at Isandlwana and Rorke's Drift, and that they had been driven off Zulu soil, never to return. But as word spread of Godide's defeat at the coast, and as the wounded struggled home, with appalling bone-splitting injuries caused by Martini-Henry bullets beyond Zulu medical art to cure, reality began to set in. The returning *amabutho* also brought word of how many of their comrades they had left dead on the field of battle. Cornelius Vijn, a trader caught in Zululand by the war, described Zulu mourners who 'kept on wailing in front of the kraals, rolling themselves on the ground and never quieting down; nay, in the night they wailed so as to cut through the heart of anyone. And this wailing went on, day and night, for a fortnight.'[6] Cetshwayo soberly ordered those *amabutho* who had reported to him at oNdini to go home, recuperate, and fix new hafts to their spears since he feared the

British would come again and they must be prepared to resist them once more.[7]

What indeed were Cetshwayo's options as January gave way to February? The victories of Isandlwana and Rorke's Drift had certainly brought the British invasion to a halt, and the aggressors had been thrown decidedly onto the defensive. Neither their success at Nyezane, nor their occupation of Eshowe had much modified this strategic reality. Consequently, the conditions had apparently been created for Cetshwayo to exploit his current military advantage to compel the British to negotiate and reach a peace settlement. That certainly was the advice of Mnyamana who feared the dire consequences should full-scale hostilities resume, and was in any case Cetshwayo's own declared policy.[8] Yet, to negotiate effectively from an obvious position of strength, Cetshwayo had to keep the pressure on the British and aggressively menace the frontiers of Natal. Not only that, he knew that the British would have to be brought to the table before reinforcements reached them and reversed the military balance.[9]

Unfortunately for Cetshwayo, two related and insurmountable obstacles stood in the way of his pursuing this initiative. Firstly, despite their defeats, the British were not yet so despondent that they were willing to negotiate, and Chelmsford believed that he could successfully hold the defensive line until reinforcements arrived to turn the tables. Backed up by Frere, who was fiercely unprepared to countenance any Zulu peace feelers or to reach any compromise settlement, Chelmsford stuck rigidly to the order he had sent out to his officers on 17 January 1879. This stressed that no overture by Cetshwayo could even be considered that was not 'preceded by . . . the unconditional acceptance' of all the demands laid down in the ultimatum of 11 December 1878[10] – a stipulation entirely unacceptable to the Zulu king and one that shut down any negotiations before they could begin.

Secondly, despite the two glorious Zulu victories, Cetshwayo was frustrated that the army which had achieved them was disheartened by its casualties, and simply would not take the field to exert the necessary pressure on the frontier, and required at least a month before it would reassemble.[11] There were other factors too. His *ibandla* objected to further military operations until the mealie crop was ripe and there was more food available to feed the *amabutho*; and it was also argued that the rivers along the border were too unpredictably liable to flooding at that time of year to risk an incursion. Consequently, despite all the British fears of imminent invasion after Isandlwana and Rorke's Drift, there was never any possibility of the Zulu marching triumphantly into Natal while 'the white people were tired'.[12]

Instead, Cetshwayo had to be content with minor military activity along the border to demonstrate that the amaZulu were still in the field. Dabulamanzi, who was in quasi-disgrace after Rorke's Drift, had returned home to his eZuluwini *umuzi* near Ntumeni, some ten miles west of Fort Eshowe. Having made his point, Cetshwayo quickly forgave him, and put him in command of the forces slowly reassembling around Eshowe and beginning to show their teeth.[13] Upstream along the Thukela, opposite Colonial Defensive District VII, the two Ntuli *amakhosi*, Mavumengwana and Godide, whom Cetshwayo had banished home in semi-disgrace, initiated some very minor probes into Natal (they barely merited the word 'raid'). So too did the Magwaza *inkosi*, Manqondo kaZwane, and the Cube *inkosi*, Sigananda kaSokufa.[14] The amaZulu across the Mzinyathi were more aggressive, and the abaSithole under Matshana kaMondisa, the Mchunu people under Matshana kaSitshakuza, and especially Sihayo kaXongo's amaQungebe under the enterprising leadership of his son, Mehlokazulu, made a regular practice of raiding the plain between the river and the Helpmekaar heights.

Glyn's forces responded with limited counter-raids.[15] The burnt-out shell of Rorke's Drift, unoccupied by either side, stood mute watch over the low-intensity but endemic military activity in that sector. The bodies of the Zulu dead continued to lie horribly decomposing where Dabulamanzi's men had left them on 23 January, but within a few weeks of the battle those of the British had been buried. On 11 February Glyn himself had led down the two companies of the 1/24th at Helpmekaar and three of the 2/24th to bury as many as they could of the British who had perished in the battle. While they were busy with their grisly task mounted patrols kept watch, but no amaZulu disturbed them. The putrefying British dead lay in and around the post and along the path of their flight to the river. Many were badly charred, others were unidentifiable and not all could be found. Ultimately, eighty-eight of the ninety-six believed to have perished were collected up on stretchers and interred reverently side by side in a large pit close to the stone cattle kraal. Stones were then placed over it and piled up to form a cairn. As was the practice with officers, Bromhead's and Dalton's corpses were buried separately from their men in a single grave next to them.[16]

However, the Rorke's Drift garrison did not attempt to bury the British dead at Isandlwana despite the distress and anger of their families and comrades in Natal and Britain. During February and March Major Wilsone Black of the 2/24th conducted several fleeting reconnaissances of the battlefield when he was overcome by the 'very sickening' stench. His reports convinced Chelmsford to give up 'the idea of burying the poor fellows at Insandlwana [*sic*] until after our campaign is over – It must be a very long business as the skeletons will be spread over a large extent of country.'[17]

Further north, along the line of the Ncome River, the amaQungebe also fronted Wood at Koppie Allein. To their north were the Mdlalose people of *inkosi* Sekethwayo kaNhlaka who had borne the brunt of Wood's initial advance to Fort Tinta. Further north yet were the abaQulusi and the followers of Manyonyoba and Mbilini who threatened the Luneburg garrison. However, Wood's dynamic presence in that sector had them very much on the defensive.

Characteristically, the proactive Wood at Koppie Allein had taken full advantage of the arrival of reinforcements in late January and early February and the consequent redeployments to request that two of the four companies of the 2/4th at Helpmekaar be sent to garrison his and No. 5 Column's supply depot at Utrecht. They duly took possession of the earthwork fort there and iron commissariat sheds were erected within its perimeter.[18] Wood also ensured that a third company of the 2/4th should go to Newcastle in northern Natal which was made into a commissariat and advance depot for supplies being drawn from the Transvaal.[19] This company took up position in the rudimentary Fort Amiel that had been built by the 80th Regiment in 1877 overlooking the village and which consisted of some mud buildings enclosed by a rampart and stone wall surrounded by a ditch.[20]

Even more than infantry, though, Wood required mounted men. The strategy he and Buller proposed to adopt required constant mounted patrolling of the Ncome border between Koppie Allein and Luneburg to the north and Helpmekaar to the south, enlivened by periodic raids into Zulu territory to keep the enemy facing him off balance. He also counted on his mounted scouts giving him good prior warning should the Zulu advance in force on Koppie Allein.[21] Besides Buller's Frontier Light Horse with No. 4 Column, Wood also had the Transvaal Burgher Force. On the eve of the invasion of Zululand Wood had attempted to recruit Transvaal Boers to his column but, resentful of British annexation, almost all were unwilling to serve. The only exception were some forty Boers of the Wakkerstroom and Utrecht Districts along the Zulu border where their long-standing fear of their Zulu neighbours combined with the prospect of plunder to bring them together in a commando under a prominent farmer, Petrus (Piet) Lafras Uys Jnr. These men in their civilian clothes were hardened by years of commando operations, and Wood put much reliance on Uys's advice and experience.[22] Nevertheless, along with the 170 men of the Frontier Light Horse this made for only 200 or so mounted men, inadequate for the role Wood intended them to play. More had to be found, and Wood was the man to acquire them.

Accordingly, Wood pried loose from Glyn's command those members of the 1st Squadron, Mounted Infantry, who had survived Isandlwana. On 14 February they duly marched from Helpmekaar to join No. 4 Column.[23] Wood also laid his hands on the two troops of the Natal Native Mounted Contingent that had survived Isandlwana and on 20 February 1879 had been reorganised at Helpmekaar as the Natal Native Horse under Captain W. F. D. Cochrane. These were the Edendale Horse, an excellent, a well-disciplined force of African Christians raised from the Wesleyan mission community outside Pietermaritzburg, and Hlubi's Troop (or Mounted Basutos) led by Hlubi kaMota Molife, *inkosi* of the Batlokwa. The latter were battle-hardened veterans, having previously served during the Langalibalele Rebellion in 1873.[24] Wood also used his effective authority over Rowlands to detach a number of units from No. 5 Column in order to augment the mounted troops of No. 4 Column under Buller's immediate command. They comprised the erratically uniformed Raaff's Transvaal Rangers which Commandant Pieter Raaff had raised from the tough diggers of the Kimberley diamond fields, and Weatherley's Border Horse which Lieutenant-Colonel Frederick Weatherley – a former soldier and failed speculator – had recruited in the Transvaal and kitted out in corduroy with a red sash and white hat. Wood also brought the Kaffrarian Rifles (which had been in garrison at Luneburg) back to Koppie Allein where they were mounted on horses.[25] Final, late reinforcements to the mounted men under Buller's command were Baker's Horse in their yellow corduroy uniforms, raised in the eastern Cape by Commandant Francis Baker.[26] These additions brought the mounted troops of No. 4 Column up to about 760 troopers, a sufficiently formidable weapon for Wood's purposes.

In their marauding expeditions Buller's mounted men would be supported by about 500 foot-soldiers of Wood's Irregulars, useful for mopping up and taking charge of captured cattle. These were the two battalions of African levies, many of them of Swazi origin, who were labour tenants on white farms pressed into service by the *landdroste* of the Wakkerstroom and Utrecht Districts of the Transvaal. Wood incorporated Fairlie's Swazi, a small force of levies serving initially with No. 5 Column, into their ranks. Many of Wood's Irregulars, who carried spears and shields (although a few antiquated firearms were issued to them), wore full Swazi war panoply and retained their elaborate headdresses into combat. All wore a strip of coloured cloth around the head or upper arm to distinguish them from the amaZulu: red and white for the Wakkerstroom men; and blue and white for the Utrecht contingent.[27]

The situation in mid-February along the Zulu–British border was therefore one of stalemate with neither side able or prepared to take the offensive except for the occasional localised raid. From Cetshwayo's perspective, the course of the war had gone more successfully than he and his advisers had dared hope. The only British troops actually on Zulu soil were Pearson's at Eshowe and the garrison at Fort Tenedos, and the position of the former was tenuous. Moreover, Zulu military successes had led to important consequences that eased Cetshwayo's situation considerably.

Mbandzeni, the Swazi king, while still reluctant to commit himself openly to Cetshwayo's cause and content to stand on the defensive behind his own borders, nevertheless was more averse than ever to offering his support to the British, and Chelmsford reluctantly accepted that he had to 'look upon the Swazies as out of the game.'[28] Cetshwayo, on the other hand, could now be reasonably confident that he would not be attacked in the rear by the amaSwazi. He was heartened by Swazi readiness to take care of some 5,000 Zulu cattle driven over their border for safety, and opened negotiations with Mbandzeni which, if not yielding immediate results, at least were not rebuffed.[29]

Even more important than Mbandzeni's benign neutrality was the positive effect the Zulu victories and the British retreat had had on waverers within the Zulu kingdom. As we have seen, the British initially pinned considerable hope on their military success provoking widespread Zulu defections that would fatally undermine Cetshwayo's ability to survive. At first, this strategy seemed to work well. On 31 December 1878, less than two weeks before their ultimatum expired, John Dunn, Cetshwayo's influential 'white chief' in south-eastern Zululand (and into whose territory No. 1 Column would advance), believing that Britain must surely win the coming war, crossed into Natal with 2,000 adherents and 3,000 cattle.[30] This defection had shaken the Zulu ruling establishment, and caused grave concern that others would follow. The aggressive advance of Wood's No. 4 Column into poorly defended north-western Zululand confirmed these apprehensions. The highly influential Mdlalose *inkosi*, Sekethwayo, the *induna* of the kwaNodwengu *ikhanda*, was old and infirm and inclined to temporise. On 11 January he sent word to Wood of his desire to accept the British terms for surrender. His defection would have been of the same magnitude as Dunn's, and Cetshwayo could not permit it. On 15 January a small *impi*, despatched from oNdini, entered Sekethwayo's territory and brought him smartly back into line. Foiled of this great prize, Wood had to be content with the surrender on 20 January of Thinta, Sekethwayo's uncle, and with that of various old men, women and children directly along his line of advance.

These small successes certainly did not herald the breakup of the Zulu kingdom, and Wood had his sights on Hamu, Cetshwayo's powerful and disaffected brother who (as we have seen) had treasonably opened negotiations with Wood concerning the terms of his surrender even before hostilities had begun.[31] But when the news of Isandlwana and Rorke's Drift reached Wood where he was operating in Qulusi territory and he had to withdraw, Hamu's Ngenetsheni chiefdom was still far to the east and the treacherous prince had not yet made his move. With Wood's retirement to Koppie Allein Hamu's opportunity for his planned defection disappeared. Hamu grumpily returned to oNdini from kwaMfemfe, his great place, and was reported to be engaged in regular, spiteful quarrels with Cetshwayo over the responsibility for the war and the best way of prosecuting it.[32]

Hamu's was doubtless a most unpleasant presence at oNdini, but Cetshwayo knew it meant he was relieved of the possibility of being undermined by the defection of any more of his leading subjects. And with a Swazi invasion now most unlikely, Cetshwayo could turn his attention to Eshowe. He was extremely indignant that Pearson had the effrontery to settle himself down deep in Zulu territory, and Dabulamanzi's forces slowly gathering around Eshowe were, in mid-February, the largest actually then in the field. But they were certainly not strong enough to dare attack Fort Eshowe itself – the casualties suffered at Rorke's Drift and the difficulty in capturing the post were evidence of the suicidal futility of any such attempt. So Cetshwayo ordered Dabulamanzi to keep up as best he could a loose blockade of Fort Eshowe, and to attack Pearson if he made a sortie.[33]

When, as planned, at midnight on 16 February Pearson made his breakout and evacuated Fort Eshowe, the inability of Dabulamanzi's forces seriously to impede him was revealed. It was not as if Pearson's 1,500 men were going to have an easy time of it, though. True, this time the track wound downhill for some thirteen miles until the Nyezane stream was crossed, but most of this difficult stretch had to be traversed in the hours of night. Ahead still lay seventeen miles across the rolling hills with intermittent patches of thick bush. The Msunduzi and Nyoni streams were not difficult to ford at their drifts, but the deep, fast-flowing Matigulu River was a more challenging proposition. During the initial march to Eshowe, on 20 January, work parties had improved the approaches to the drift,[34] and Pearson had to trust that the river would still be fordable. On its outward march No. 1 Column had taken five days (and a battle) to reach Eshowe. This time, Pearson was banking on his column reaching Fort Tenedos in 15–20 hours, or by late afternoon at best. When it originally advanced the column had been escorting 130 wagons, which often became bogged down in the sandy, wet soil; now there were none, although the four essential pieces of wheeled artillery still had to be drawn by horses.[35] On its forward advance the column had proceeded very deliberately in its two divisions with the mounted men fanning out ahead and on its flanks, and with three companies of British infantry and twelve of the NNC, all in skirmishing order, also out on its flanks.[36] But there were no mounted men for scouting and protecting the flanks during the retirement, nor any NNC to perform that task. The column would consequently have to be far more compact than previously, and march in one division with several of the British companies deployed as skirmishers on its flanks and scouting ahead. Aware of their vulnerability on the march, and determined not to halt overnight, all of Pearson's troops were resolved to make what speed they could, and not to permit exhaustion to overcome them.[37]

The march began well, and order was maintained. The moon was in its last quarter and the night dark, but by dawn the column was approaching the Nyezane down the hillside where the battle had been fought on 22 January. It was then that the amaZulu, who had responded to word that the British were on the move, began to skirmish along the British flanks. Dabulamanzi himself, mounted on a black horse, was seen directing their fire. But his forces probably numbered no more than 500 or so, their marksmanship proved distinctly inferior, and, in any case, they were kept out of effective range by the modern rifles of the flanking British skirmishing lines. Undeterred, the amaZulu continued to harass the British column as closely as they could across the undulating countryside, making life very uncomfortable for Pearson's men. At the drift across the Matigulu River the artillery halted to cover the crossing and fired shrapnel in the direction of the pursuing amaZulu, although likely with little effect. Once the British were across the Matigulu, Dabulamanzi gave up any serious pursuit, and although a few amaZulu hung on to the column's flanks as far as the Nyoni River, Pearson was effectively clear. Only three of his men had been lightly wounded by Zulu fire, but the soldiers were utterly exhausted and the column's progress was slowing down to a crawl.

It was late morning and Pearson was still about a dozen miles from Fort Tenedos. Fortunately for him, over the past few days Chelmsford had been sending out strong mounted patrols under Captain Barrow to make contact if the Eshowe garrison did indeed withdraw. Barrow's men fell in with the column just south of the Nyoni River and were able to supply effective flanking support. Barrow immediately sent word back to Fort Tenedos, and in the early afternoon four companies of infantry marched out to give support to Pearson's column as it painfully made its way over the last few miles.[38] It had been a nerve-wracking and debilitating forced march, but the Eshowe garrison was safely back at the Lower Thukela, and the concentration of troops at Fort Tenedos and Fort Pearson was powerful enough to deter any possible Zulu attack at that point.

PART V

Revolts and Reinforcements

Chapter 16

Fresh Threats to British Security

While in Durban on 20 February 1879, Chelmsford composed a comprehensive memorandum in which, with a reasonable degree of confidence, he detailed the state of his defensive arrangements along the borders with the Zulu kingdom.[1] What he did not dilate upon was the extreme demoralisation of the survivors of No. 3 Column at Helpmekaar, wracked by the terrible memories and nightmares of Isandlwana and Rorke's Drift. Most had lost all interest in their work and groundless scares and alarms were frequent. Inactivity and boredom, which quickly afflicted any fresh reinforcements, spawned a nasty atmosphere of rumour-mongering and back-biting. All was made worse by the drenching thunderstorms and chilling fogs of late summer, and by the lack of proper shelter. At night soldiers slept on the damp ground under inadequate tarpaulins inside the newly erected earthwork fort that had quickly replaced the improvised laager, and by day huddled close around its outer walls and ditch. The wet, crowded and unsanitary conditions under which the men lived, surrounded by decomposing sacks of grain and mealies, led to an outbreak of enteric fever (or typhoid) on top of the ubiquitous Natal sores (a bacterial skin infection) and diarrhoea. The ineffectual field hospital, and then the adjoining cemetery, began to fill up with victims.[2]

Chelmsford expected morale to improve once he resumed the offensive, but this depended upon the arrival of reinforcements, and he knew that those he had requested from the War Office on 27 January would take at least six weeks from the receipt of his telegram to arrive. Nevertheless, he was encouraged that some reinforcements were already on their way. The news of Isandlwana and Rorke's Drift had reached

St Helena on 6 February, and the garrison of the remote, mid-Atlantic island – No. 8 Battery, 7th Brigade, RA, and a company of the 88th Regiment (Connaught Rangers) – were embarked on 12 February on HMS *Shah*, then in port. The *Shah* had been on its way back to Britain from the Pacific station, but in this emergency Captain R. Bradshaw turned the frigate around and steamed for Simon's Town, which was reached on 23 February. Bradshaw expected to anchor in Durban during the first week of March when, besides disembarking the St Helena garrison, he also planned to land a Naval Brigade of 400 men.[3] Chelmsford, meanwhile, acutely aware that even with reinforcements he could attempt no forward operations until he had made good all the wagons, carts and draught animals Nos 1 and 3 Columns had lost, set about the expensive and frustrating task of assembling new supply trains from colonists determined to make a commercial killing out of military disaster.[4]

Then, just while Chelmsford was methodically and more optimistically consolidating his border defences against Zulu invasion and was contemplating how to take the offensive once reinforcements arrived and transport was collected, developments elsewhere in British-ruled South Africa suddenly threatened to disrupt his military arrangements and to cast Frere's plans for confederation to the winds.

We have already seen that in 1871 Britain had passed the administration of Basutoland on to Cape Colony. The Sotho chiefs remained uneasy, however, with how Charles Duncan Griffith, the governor's agent attached to Letsie I (the paramount Sotho chief who in 1870 had succeeded his father, Moshoeshoe, the founder of the Sotho state) exercised Cape rule. Griffith attempted to secure the loyalty of the Sotho chiefs through patronage and tact. Nevertheless, by the end of 1878 serious dissatisfaction and suspicion were growing over the Cape government's apparent determination to set about disarming the Basotho and depriving them of the firearms their young men had acquired as migrant labourers at the diamond fields, and which they prized above all things. In early February 1879, the diminutive but truculent Chief Moorosi of the Baphuthi in southern Basutoland,[5] who had a record of disaffection with Cape rule, broke into open revolt over the arms issue and over the payment of taxes, and drove John Austen, the resident magistrate, out of the Quthing District. Griffith immediately responded by invading Moorosi's territory with about a thousand reluctant Sotho levies raised by Letsie, along with 200 Cape militiamen and a contingent of 100 Cape Mounted Rifles. But Moorosi and several hundred well-armed followers took up position on the precipitously-sided 'Moorosi's Mountain' where for years the chief had been preparing well-positioned defensive stone walls and trenches against just such an eventuality. And there Griffith became tied down for months in a debilitating siege, always conscious that other Sotho chiefs to his rear might join the revolt. At the very least, even if the uprising did not spread, Moorosi's revolt meant that the Cape was now fully stretched militarily. Chelmsford had to accept that he would receive no more aid from that quarter; indeed, the likelihood was that the Cape government would demand that he send back the British troops of the Cape garrison it had despatched with such noble alacrity on learning of Isandlwana and Rorke's Drift.[6]

If Chelmsford and Frere could shrug off Moorosi's inconvenient rebellion as likely to amount to little more than an irritant, then the rapidly deteriorating situation in the Transvaal presented an infinitely more serious threat. On 6 February 1879 the Administrator of the Transvaal, Sir Theophilus Shepstone, reported in alarm: 'The Boers are exhibiting a very disloyal spirit, and evidently think that a chance of enforcing the return of their country to them has been put into their hands by providence. They talk loudly and are supplying themselves with ammunition largely and may, most people think, do what they say they will.'[7] Four days later, on Monday 10 February, Piet Joubert, riding hell for leather, returned to Pretoria after his meeting with Frere in Pietermaritzburg on 4 February to discuss the restoration of Transvaal independence.[8] Joubert reported to his colleagues of the *Volkskomitee* that Frere, although polite and deeply desirous of the Transvaal's aid in the war against the amaZulu, would not be moved. Fervently, Joubert reminded them that 'Our forefathers – the Voortrekkers – emigrants because of oppression, wrested the land from the wilderness and the barbarians in order to live here as a free nation with their own government.'[9] This they would – must – do again. The *Volkskomitee* resolved that the time was ripe for action, that (despite Frere's reported pleas for them not to do so) full advantage must be taken of British military weakness following their devastating defeats at Zulu hands, and that the promised 'assembly of the people' must be summoned to a meeting in ten days' time to decide on the next steps to be taken.

About 5,000 *burgers* (or citizens) proved willing to travel often hundreds of miles to attend the meeting set for 20 February, and encamped at Erasmus's farm on the banks of the Hennopsrivier, some ten miles west of Pretoria. Since the mass gathering was a protest under arms, with reviews and sham fights, it indicated that an armed uprising was on the cards. There was much angry rhetoric and many assertions of willingness to die for the *Vierkleur*, the ex-republic's flag with its red, white and blue horizontal stripes and green perpendicular stripe next to the pole; while the rule of 'strangers' and the Queen's sovereignty were roundly denounced.[10]

Pretoria, even though the seat of the British administration of the Transvaal, was a small town with only about eighty houses, a few public buildings, and some 300, mainly English-speaking inhabitants.[11] One company of the 80th Regiment under Brevet Lieutenant-Colonel C. J. R. Tyler was stationed there.[12] All the other troops of the Transvaal garrison were committed to facing the Zulu border and were far away at Utrecht, Luneburg and Koppie Allein. It clearly would be impossible to hold the town should the Boers attack it. Fully realising this, the moment the *Volkskomitee* had issued its summons to *burgers* to assemble at Hennopsrivier, Shepstone had told Frere by telegram of the danger. Alerted, Frere set off for Hennopsrivier, there to beard the Boer leaders and to try and stem the rebellion that threatened. However, when on 21 February he met the *Volkskomitee* in their camp at Hennopsrivier, he was not allowed to forget that he was in an extremely weak position. The High Commissioner wanly offered self-government within the framework of a watered-down confederation, but the Boers would accept nothing short of independence, and Kruger darkly warned Frere that he could no longer restrain his people from open resistance.[13]

His last-ditch mission a failure, Frere left the Boer camp on the morning of Saturday 22 February for Pretoria, and telegraphed Hicks Beach reporting that he had failed to reconcile the Boers to British rule, and that an uprising seemed unavoidable.[14] Equally humiliating, he recognised that if he dallied in Pretoria, he might be taken as a hostage by the rebellious Boers. So, his abject telegram to the Colonial

Office despatched, on the afternoon of the same day he set off with his small escort of Mounted Infantry for the village of Heidelberg on the road back to Natal, leaving Shepstone in Pretoria to uphold British rule in the Transvaal for as long as he could.[15]

As he rode south, apprehensive that Boer patrols might yet attempt to intercept him, what occupied Frere's mind was his growing conviction – every bit as strong as his belief in the 'black conspiracy' master-minded by Cetshwayo – that he was now facing a dangerous pan-Afrikaner challenge (the term 'Afrikaners' for the Dutch-speaking settlers of southern Africa was already current by the 1870s) to British hegemony. And certainly British expansion during the 1870s into the South African interior and Frere's confederation project had stimulated a Boer sense of common brotherhood under imperial oppression that had not been much evident before 1877. Afrikaners living in the British-ruled Cape and Natal loudly and emphatically empathised with the plight of their bullied 'fellow-countrymen' in the Transvaal, as did the Boers of the Orange Free State who were alarmed at finding their republic surrounded by British-ruled territories.[16]

Frere was therefore confronted by the spectre of a rebellion in the Transvaal triggering a general Afrikaner uprising against British domination the length and breadth of South Africa. But how was he to head this off? Rapid and decisive military action to deter the Transvaal Boers from taking further action was the obvious answer, but Frere knew that he simply did not have the necessary forces at his disposal. The garrison in Pretoria of a single company was entirely inadequate if not rapidly reinforced, but the rest of the British forces in the southern Transvaal and Natal were fully committed to defending the frontiers against the imminent threat of Zulu invasion. The Cape garrison could not be spared because, with Moorosi's revolt, Basutoland seemed on the verge of a general rebellion, and the troops were in any case required to overawe potential rebels in the colony. By the time Frere regained Government House in Pietermaritzburg on 25 February he had reached an unpalatable but inescapable conclusion which was the bitterest of pills for the apostle of confederation to swallow. Because he did not possess the military means of forcing the Boers of the Transvaal to endure British rule, and because their leaders would accept nothing less than independence, he must find the means of letting the Transvaal go before an armed revolt triggered a wider Afrikaner uprising.[17]

Yet no sooner had Frere wearily dismounted, his mind as to future policy reluctantly made up, than he was handed a telegram, sent that same day, disclosing that events had already overtaken him. Shepstone tersely reported that the Transvaal had risen in revolt, and that the luckless administrator had effectively surrendered to the Boer leaders.[18] With bitterness in his heart, knowing that both confederation and his own career were now blighted beyond remedy, Frere telegraphed his superiors in London that the Transvaal Territory was lost. To head off the anticipated wider Afrikaner uprising, Frere urged Hicks Beach to persuade the government to sanction negotiations with the Transvaal leaders with the objective of rescinding the British annexation of the Transvaal and restoring the territory its independence[19]

Chapter 17

The Transvaal Rebellion

Developments in the Transvaal had indeed escaped Frere's control. At the Hennopsrivier the *Volkskomitee* had suspended its deliberations during the Sabbath, 23 February, and had then put its designs to a mass meeting on the 24th. The gathering resolved to reconstitute the old *Volksraad*, and in the absence of former President T. F. Burgers (who had left the Transvaal to live in retirement in the Cape), Paul Kruger resumed his vice-presidency of the South African Republic. Like a latter-day Martin Luther, Kruger addressed the overwrought throng:

> I stand here before your face, chosen by the people; in the voice of the people I hear the word of God, the King of all people, and I am obedient . . . After the annexation [the people] protested, have resisted and suffered, and would have attempted every other peaceful means had not English authority in Pretoria made this impossible. The rights of the people are on our side; and although we are very weak, God is a just God. My friends! May the Lord bless your activities and protect our Fatherland.[1]

At Kruger's urging the reconstituted *Volksraad* elected a triumvirate to lead it consisting of himself, former president Marthinus Wessel Pretorius, and Piet Joubert, who had acted as president in 1875–6. The triumvirate then issued a proclamation announcing the restoration of the ZAR on 24 February 1879 and notifying that it was in a state of siege and under the rule of martial law.[2] The assembled burgers next gathered around a flagpole where the *Vierkleur* was unfurled and emotionally swore loyalty to each other and undertook to fight to the death in the republic's defence.[3]

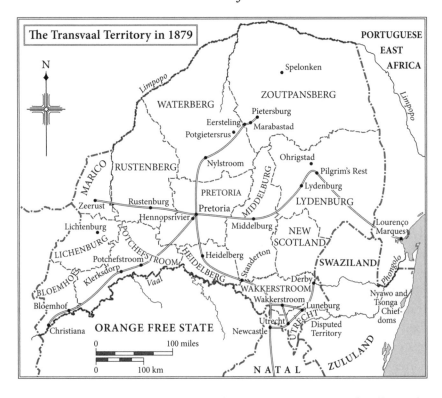

The Transvaal Territory in 1879

To keep such an oath required military organisation. On Kruger's motion the assembled burgers elected Piet Joubert *Kommandant-Generaal* (Commandant-General) even though he protested he was no general and not suited to the job. Nevertheless, he took energetic action and, in terms of the proclaimed martial law immediately sent out far and wide to appoint further military commanders and to mobilise the Boer forces, which consisted all told of approximately 7,000 mounted *burgers*.[4] These *burgers* were not a conventional military force as the British understood it, but a militia, or *kommando* (commando), in which no structured military training or parade-ground drill took place.[5] The outspokenness and informality of the men, even towards their officers, led the British to believe the Boer forces were entirely undisciplined. They scorned them as country bumpkins who did not fight in uniform like proper soldiers but in disreputable civilian clothes, even if these were often specially adapted with ammunition pockets and pouches attached to shirts, waistcoats and jackets. Nevertheless, Boer military structure and style of combat were suited to their particular environment and reflected their notions of a *burger*'s obligations to the community.

With certain exceptions – members of the *Volksraad*, state employees, clergymen and school-teachers – every able-bodied free *burger* between sixteen and sixty was required to serve without pay in time of need as part of his civil responsibility. The selection of Boer officers was by open, popular vote. The most important official in the commando system was the *veldkornet* (or field cornet), invariably elected from a family of local notables. Every *veldkornet* was responsible to the *landdrost*, or magistrate, and through him to the *Krijgsraad*, or state war council. In time of war the *landdroste* mustered *burgers* within forty-eight hours into their district commando under its *kommandant*, or commanding officer, whom the *veldkornette* had previously chosen.

The *burger* on commando was expected to provide himself with a rifle and fifty rounds of ammunition. Requiring his firearm for hunting and defence, the Boer farmer bought the best weapon he could obtain. In 1879 a variety of breech-loading, falling-block or bolt-action rifles and carbines were available for purchase in southern Africa, although the most popular firearm of all was the British-made 1866 pattern Westley Richards rifle – which the Boers personalised as 'Wessel Rykaard' or 'Wessel Riekert' – very accurate up to 600 metres. Along with their rifle, Boer officers often carried an Adams revolver – but never a sword as did their British counterparts. Some Boers still preferred the old muzzle-loading hunting musket, or *roer*, because the slow, round bullet produced more shock to tissue than did the swifter, conical rifle bullet. Besides his weapon, the *burger* was expected to provide his own horse and saddlery. Boer ponies were trained to stand without being held, which allowed every rifle to be put into the firing line. The Boers were easy on their ponies, not usually pushing them more than six miles an hour, and rode light, not carrying much more than a blanket, saddlebag, tin mug and haversack.

On being called out, *burgers* were supposed to carry eight days' rations. After that, they relied on whatever supplies the commando carried in its wagons, or lived off the countryside. They were always accompanied on campaign by their *agterryers* ('after-riders'), black servants on horseback who carried out all the behind-the-line services including driving the wagons and managing the teams of oxen, grooming horses, slaughtering livestock, collecting firewood, cooking, guarding ammunition, digging trenches and emplacements, and helping with the sick and wounded. However, they generally took little part in the actual fighting.

With the proclamation of the restored ZAR on 24 February, *Kommandant-Generaal* Piet Joubert knew he must move swiftly. Small commandos were sent out from Hennopsrivier to carry word of events far and wide, to call every burger to arms, and to secure the main urban centres: Rustenburg, Zeerust and Potchefstroom to the west; Nylstroom and Marabastad to the north; Middelburg and Lydenburg to the east; and Heidelberg, Standerton and Wakkerstroom to the south. Luneburg and Utrecht were both in the territory of the ZAR, but the former was the strongly held headquarters of the British No. 5 Column and the latter (which was Wood's supply base) was garrisoned by a company of the 2/4th Regiment. For the time being, therefore, Joubert decided it was prudent to make no move in the direction of the Zulu border and the British forces stationed there. Instead, on 25 February he advanced on Pretoria with about 3,000 burgers.[6]

Outnumbered and cut off, Shepstone made no attempt to defend the town, but rode out under flag of truce to parley with Joubert. The *Kommandant-Generaal* was only too keen to avoid bloodshed if at all possible, and an armistice was quickly concluded between the two parties. By its terms the company of the 80th Regiment under Lt.-Col. Tyler was to march out of Pretoria with honours of war and without any delay to make for Newcastle in the north of Natal, just over 200 miles away.[7] Shepstone, his staff, and British officials in Pretoria were to accompany it under safe conduct, and British officials in other villages were to be given the option of leaving the ZAR unmolested.[8] Accordingly, the following day (Wednesday 26 February) Shepstone and the British garrison quit Pretoria and ten days later reached Newcastle, which was garrisoned by a company of the 2/4th Regiment stationed in Fort Amiel. The British were barely out of town before Joubert led his jubilant men into Pretoria where the remaining 'English' residents gave them a very cool reception. The other two members of the triumvirate accompanied Joubert, and assisted by an Executive Council immediately seized the reins of government.

That very same afternoon the restored republican government met in emergency session to decide how best to deal with the British should they – despite their full military commitment along the frontiers with Zululand – nevertheless determine to regain the ZAR by force of arms. Joubert persuaded his colleagues that it made best strategic sense to establish a large camp, consisting of three wagon laagers, close by Standerton, a treeless village of some fifty one-storey houses of stone and corrugated iron on the north bank of the Vaal River. From that base mounted patrols could closely monitor the British forces and provide Joubert's commando with ample warning of any advance the British might make, whether it be from Newcastle, Utrecht or Luneburg.

However, *Veld Kommandant-Generaal* Nicolaas Smit, a veteran of the wars against the Bapedi and a proven commander with considerable dash and energy, forcefully put to the meeting that it was essential to adopt a more offensive stance than the one Joubert had advocated. Without contesting the strategic value of forming the main Boer camp at Standerton, he argued that a commando of about 250 men should be sent forward to seize and hold Wakkerstroom. A small village that consisted of a well-built church, a courthouse, a store or two and a few dozen houses, Wakkerstroom stood strategically at the crossroads of the tracks going east to Luneburg, south to Utrecht, west to Newcastle and north to Standerton. To hold it in strength would threaten Wood's lines of supply through Utrecht, and would put unwelcome pressure on his rear while he continued to face the amaZulu to the east. Convinced, the meeting agreed that Joubert must detach Smit and a commando to seize Wakkerstroom while he formed his camp at Standerton.

Although finally agreeing on what military precautions to adopt, the Boer leaders were far from desiring a bruising clash of arms with the British. Rather, they much preferred the alternative of securing British recognition of the ZAR's independence through peaceful consultation. With this objective in view, the meeting went on to debate whether a British attack against the resuscitated ZAR was in fact even likely so long as the amaZulu remained in arms and menaced Natal. Deciding that the odds were against it and that the chances were good for securing a diplomatic solution, the meeting entrusted the experienced and statesmanlike Marthinus Pretorius with making contact with the British government through Frere in order to bring it to the negotiating table.[9]

On 28 February Pretorius telegraphed Frere in Pietermaritzburg indicating the ZAR's desire to treat. Frere, who had feared the worst, was delighted. On 3 March Frere forwarded this offer to London in a long telegram with his strong recommendation that the government respond favourably. In doing so, he added a number of cogent points. Until reinforcements arrived in late March or early April, the British forces along the Zulu border were fully committed to that sector and were unavailable to intervene militarily in the ZAR. And even when reinforcements landed, it would take close to three weeks to march them to Utrecht or Newcastle. Moreover, should the Boers advance and take Utrecht, Wood's depot, his forces at Koppie Allein and Luneburg would be cut off from their supplies. As it was, they were no longer being provisioned from the Transvaal. And, seeing collusion and conspiracy everywhere, Frere drew the government's attention to the likelihood of the Boers and amaZulu forging a dangerous anti-British alliance. Not only that, there was a real danger that if the revolt in the Transvaal were allowed to simmer without resolution, then anti-British Afrikaner sentiment in the Cape and the Orange Free State might be brought to a boil. And, on top of these concerns, Frere reported that during a meeting at Government House on Sunday 2 March Bulwer had made it abundantly clear that Natal was simply not prepared, either financially or militarily, to accept the sacrifice of supporting yet another war. Natal backing for the Zululand campaign had been grudging, and its inhabitants had been thrown into panic and disarray by military disaster and the threat of imminent Zulu invasion. In these circumstances, the prospect of a new front opening up in northern Natal against the Boers – entailing as it would unacceptable economic burdens and an additional menace to lives and property – could not be contemplated. The situation had been reached, Frere informed Hicks Beach that, to salvage the British position in Natal and defeat the Zulu, the Transvaal had to be let go.[10]

Chapter 18

Anxious to Conclude an Honourable Peace

—————

Meanwhile, the government in London had so far had absolutely no inkling that the Transvaal had risen in revolt. It was already well apprised of the joint defeats of Isandlwana and Rorke's Drift, however, since the telegram Chelmsford had sent on 27 January had reached Colonel Stanley, the Secretary of State for War, early on 11 February.[1] The government and the country at large were dismayed, although reaction in the press generally followed political party lines.[2] As Viscount Sidmouth expressed it in the House of Lords, 'The disaster which had befallen our troops . . . had created a profound impression in the country.'[3] *The Times* (or 'The Thunderer' as it was satirically known), whose measured and knowledgeable editorials had a profound influence on informed opinion, declared:

> The extreme gravity, from every point of view, of the recent news from the seat of war in Zululand must not for a moment be denied or deprecated. The defeat, and still more the retreat, of the British forces before the army of the Zulu KING involves consequences which it is important that the country should fully and instantly understand. The war has been changed at once from an offensive to a defensive war, and until the reinforcements ordered to be despatched for service against the Zulus have reached Natal we cannot be sure that either that colony or any other of the South African colonies is secure against a native invasion or insurrection . . . With the increase of difficulty in reducing the Zulus to submission there must be a corresponding

increase in cost. The finances of the country . . . will be weighed down by heavy charges.[4]

The Duke of Cambridge, when Colonel Stanley informed him of Chelmsford's telegram reporting his defeats and requesting reinforcement, was appalled by what was to him an inexplicable disaster. 'This has come like a clap of thunder upon us and is very distressing,' he wrote to Frere on 13 February 1879. Nevertheless, he rose stalwartly to meet the crisis, and assured the High Commissioner that, with the government's approval, 'Large reinforcements are at once ordered out to the Cape . . . and three general officers will accompany them.' Cambridge knew, however, that it would be many weeks before they would arrive in South Africa, and admitted to Frere that 'the intermediate suspense is very anxious and distressing.'[5]

In all, thanks to Cambridge's efforts, 387 officers, 8,895 other ranks and 1,866 horses were earmarked to embark in the United Kingdom for their long sea voyages to Cape Town. They consisted of a cavalry brigade of two regiments– the 1st (King's) Dragoon Guards and the 17th (Duke of Cambridge's Own) Lancers – two field batteries (M and N Batteries, 6th Brigade, RA), five battalions of infantry – the 2/21st Regiment (Royal Scots Fusiliers), the 58th (Rutlandshire) Regiment, the 3/60th (King's Royal Rifle Corps), the 91st (Princess Louise's Argyllshire Highlanders), and the 94th – a company of Royal Engineers, three companies of the Army Service Corps and personnel of the Army Hospital Corps and Army Medical Department. All of these troops embarked at various British ports between 20 and 28 February with drafts scheduled to follow over the succeeding weeks. In addition, the 57th (West Middlesex) Regiment of 809 officers and men, which had been in garrison in Ceylon and was about to be relieved, was ordered by telegraph (there was a direct link with London) to proceed on HMS *Tamar* for Natal, embarking on 22 February. No. 10 Battery (half battery), 7th Brigade, RA, and a company of the 88th Regiment set off from Mauritius on 12 March for Durban. On top of that, HMS *Boadicea*, an iron-built corvette, undertook to furnish a Naval Brigade of 200 men when it landed in Durban in mid-March.[6] The government drew the line, however, at sending any troops from India to South Africa on account of the continuing operations in Afghanistan.[7]

With a considerable degree of satisfaction Cambridge wrote to Frere on 27 February: 'I hope you will admit that the reinforcements have been rapidly prepared', and reported that he had visited many of the troops when they embarked on their 'truly splendid vessels' and found that they were 'all animated with the most admirable spirit and zeal'.[8] Yet things were not quite as they seemed in Cambridge's upbeat letter. *The Times* gravely pointed out that 'Those who know the quality of our unseasoned short-service soldiers will not be certain that their "moral" will not be unaffected by the victory of the Zulus.'[9]

The problem was that the professional Victorian army was small, and its manpower and capabilities overstretched by a multiplicity of commitments across the globe.[10] In January 1879 Cambridge had pressed the government to authorise an increase in the size of the army, but the government had refused despite the concurrent wars in Afghanistan and Zululand.[11] To make matters worse, in Cambridge's eyes – and in those of many other conservative or sceptical senior officers – the reforms recently carried out by Edward Cardwell, the Liberal Secretary of State for War (1868–74), with the objective of modernising the army, had in fact weakened it. Their greatest concern was the introduction of short service in 1870, whereby recruits spent six years in the regular army and six in the reserve, and the creation in 1872 of linked battalions. The intention was that battalions would alternate in recruiting at home and serving abroad, so ensuring that the empire would be guarded only by seasoned troops. The problem in practice was that since the reserve could not be called out except during a national emergency, colonial campaigns could be fought only by draining standing garrisons. And as colonial commitments increased (as they did in 1879) imperfectly trained home-based battalions found themselves serving overseas. Thus, in 1879, eighty-two battalions were serving abroad, and only fifty-nine at home depots. The consequence was that all too many battalions fighting colonial wars consisted of soldiers who were young, physically immature and untried ('mere boys' as Cambridge called them), and that their NCOs were inexperienced.[12]

Besides his concerns about the dubious quality of the troops he was sending out to South Africa, Cambridge was obviously worried about Chelmsford's capacity after his recent defeats and consequent loss of nerve (which was presumed to be only temporary) to lead them effectively. The Duke loyally continued to proclaim his confidence in him but, as he admitted to Frere on 6 March, Chelmsford's inadequate and obfuscatory reports of what had transpired at Isandlwana and Rorke' Drift 'have left us in much perplexity'. And, as Cambridge added, 'This is most unfortunate . . . for the public excitement is very great.'[13] By then Cambridge was beginning to regret that the major-generals he had sent out with the reinforcements (and whom he had increased in number from the original three to four) were all junior in rank to Chelmsford. That left Chelmsford in command, but as his despatches continued to avoid explaining the reasons for his defeat, Cambridge's confidence in his capacity as a commander began seriously to wane.[14]

Then, while the reinforcements (and generals) bound for South Africa were still on the high seas, and while the Liberal opposition in Parliament was girding itself for the scheduled debate on the bungled prosecution of the war in Zululand, two new bombshells exploded in the Cabinet Office one after another on 9 and 11 March. These were Frere's two telegrams of 22 and 25 February informing the government of the Transvaal rebellion and of the ignominious withdrawal of the British garrison and administration from that territory, and urging that the Transvaal be given back its independence. Coming on top of the disastrous Zulu campaign, this latest development was catastrophic for the Tory government and grist to the Oppositions' parliamentary mill. The Liberals' long-held conviction that the empire should be consolidated and its running costs reduced was diametrically opposed to the 'forward policy' Lord Beaconsfield's administration had been pursuing in India and South Africa. Liberals, moreover, were by inclination more sensitive than the government to the rights and liberties of foreign peoples – whether Boer or Zulu – being run over roughshod in the interests of empire.[15]

Cabinet met on 12 March to discuss Frere's Transvaal telegrams. No decision was reached about what ought to be done.[16] Nevertheless, the Transvaal issue added greatly to Conservative disarray and defensiveness when the parliamentary debate began in the House of Commons on 14 March, was taken up in the House of Lords on 25 March, and resumed in the Commons on 27, 28 and 31 March. Predictably in the circumstances, the tone of the debate was harsh and unforgiving. The Opposition excoriated Frere for wilfully and misguidedly starting the unfortunate Zulu war in the first place, Shepstone for woefully misreading the temper of the rebellious Boers of the Transvaal, Chelmsford for his culpable incapacity as a commander and for his failure to bury the dead at Isandlwana, and 'the Royal Person' (Cambridge) and the Horse Guards for corruptly shielding his incompetence.[17]

Frere's telegram of 3 March, pressing that the government accept the ZAR's offer to negotiate its independence, arrived on 18 March. Lord Beaconsfield called an emergency Cabinet meeting for the following day, 19 March. Again, no final agreement was reached, although Britain's thoroughly overstretched military commitments world-wide were discussed, as well as the financial strain of conducting so many campaigns simultaneously. Indeed, no British government of that era, whether Tory or Liberal, was prepared to shrug off the economic implications of a military entanglement. Nor could it ignore the pressure of the press and public opinion.[18] Beaconsfield's cabinet colleagues were all too aware of rising public dismay over the unfortunate course of events in South Africa, as well as of the virulent criticism both inside and outside parliament of the government's handling of the situation. With these considerations in mind, Cabinet met once more on 20 March to hammer out its interrelated policy regarding the Zulu campaign, the Transvaal rebellion, rising Afrikaner anti-British agitation and Natalian disaffection.

Whatever military commanders in the field (such as Chelmsford) might consider the objective of a campaign to be, it was only the politicians in London who had the power to authorise the terms of a negotiated peace settlement. Recognising their responsibility, the Cabinet finally agreed that Frere be instructed to negotiate with Pretorius to hammer out terms for the retrocession of the Transvaal while saving as much British face as he could. Meanwhile, the war against the amaZulu must continue since it was inconceivable to make peace with an African king without a previous demonstration of Britain's superior military might. Once a victory – even a partial one – had been gained, then it would be up to Bulwer (who was believed to be regarded in a less antagonistic light by the amaZulu than Frere) to arrange a ceasefire. The original, implacable demands of Frere's ultimatum would no longer have to be adhered to, but the final peace terms would have to be such that they proclaimed Britain's effective victory in the war. Otherwise, British prestige would be fatally compromised in the eyes of other African leaders.[19]

It was for Hicks Beach to relay the Cabinet's decision to Frere and Bulwer, his subordinates, and to formulate their precise instructions. He wasted no time and did so promptly by telegraph on 21 March,[20] but not before he had telegraphed separately to Frere on 20 March sharply censuring him for embarking on his war with Cetshwayo without the clear sanction of the government. However, not willing to change horses in the midst of 'the present crisis of affairs' in South Africa, and still retaining some residual faith in the proconsul's many capabilities, the Colonial Secretary did not recall Frere or require his resignation, only his future obedience to the government's instructions in bringing 'our difficulties in South Africa to a successful termination.'[21] Like Chelmsford, he was presumed to have learned by his mistakes.

When the debate on South Africa took place in the House of Lords on 25 March, Viscount Cranbrook, the Secretary of State for India and previously the Secretary of State for War, rose to state his government's position on negotiating with the Zulu. 'That Ultimatum,' he declared, 'not having been accepted by Her Majesty's Government to which it had not been submitted, we are no longer bound by the exact terms of it, and in any of our future relations with these people we are not bound to act according to the Ultimatum.'[22] He was followed up by Colonel Stanley in the Commons who unequivocally stated on 27 March: 'The Government have said all along that they were as anxious as any persons in the country could be to conclude this Zulu War at as early a day as was found to be consistent with the safety of our Colonies and the honour of our arms.'[23] During the same debate Hicks Beach rose to outline the government's decision to restore the Transvaal's independence. Both ministers came in for much rough treatment by the Opposition and some disaffection from their own side of the House, but the Liberals were essentially satisfied by the government's change of tack and commitment to seek peace in South Africa; while Conservative members of parliament acquiesced, albeit in surly mood. Hicks Beach nevertheless caught the general feeling of the House when he pronounced: 'For some weeks past, in view of the grave disaster which has occurred, and the serious danger of the moment, there has been I think, but one feeling in the House and in the country – a feeling that everything should be done to help Her Majesty's Government in repairing that disaster.'[24] The government had now done what it could, and it was up to the officials and generals in South Africa itself to ensure that peace – with at least a modicum of honour – could be secured.

PART VI

Battle and Negotiation

Chapter 19

Planning for the Zulu Offensive

———————

On the afternoon of 26 February Colonel Rowlands and his small staff set off as ordered from Luneburg for Pretoria to take military charge of the unsettled Transvaal. As we have seen, his No. 5 Column had been attached to Wood's command, and the attenuated garrison of five companies of the 80th Regiment at Luneburg was left in charge of Major C. Tucker with only a dozen or so Mounted Infantry for patrol work.[1] Rowlands was unaware that the Boers had already thrown off British rule, and that even while he was on the road to Wakkerstroom forty-five miles away, Shepstone and the British garrison were retiring under safe conduct to Newcastle, which they would reach on 8 March. So on 1 March, just as he crossed the Assegai River near Van Rooyen's farm between Wakkerstroom and Standerton, Rowlands was astounded when Boers of Smit's commando *en route* to Wakkerstroom surrounded him and his staff and took them prisoner. Smit carried them with him back to Wakkerstroom where he put them under guard in the courthouse.[2]

Meanwhile, Smit sent out riders to alert the Boers of the Wakkerstroom and Utrecht Districts to the revolt and encourage their adherence to the resuscitated ZAR. At the same time, following the instructions of his government in Pretoria, he despatched a number Wakkerstroom farmers who were personally familiar with leading Zulu of north-western Zululand on a diplomatic mission. The leaders of the deputation were Hendrik Versagie and Conrad Potgieter, and their assignment was to assure Cetshwayo that the ZAR would not intervene on either side in his war against the British. The Boer leadership in Pretoria had been uncertain what their policy towards the amaZulu should be. On the one hand, to ally with Cetshwayo would place Wood's forces at Koppie Allein and Luneburg in an untenable position between two enemy forces and probably compel him to retire behind the Mzinyathi River and to abandon the Utrecht and Wakkerstroom Districts. Desirable as this was, this option entailed allying with an African ruler against fellow whites, and this was repugnant to the Boer leadership. Equally unpalatable was the likelihood that Wood's withdrawal would expose Boer farmers of the two districts to Zulu attack. Moreover, any Zulu success could well give encouragement to the still undefeated Bapedi, and the Boers continued to fear an alliance between the two. To their alarm the withdrawal of Rowlands's former No. 5 Column to Luneburg had already encouraged Sekhukhune to go on the local offensive, striking at chiefdoms that had taken advantage of the First Anglo-Pedi War of 1878 to repudiate their ties with the Maroteng paramountcy.[3] And just how the fence-sitting amaSwazi would respond to that development was also a concern. In these circumstances a position of neutrality in the Anglo-Zulu War seemed the only feasible option for the ZAR.[4]

For his part, during late February 1879 Cetshwayo remained uncertain as how best to act. He still hoped, after the Zulu victories at Isandlwana and Rorke's Drift and Pearson's ignominious withdrawal to the Lower Thukela, to be able to negotiate from strength. But, as we have seen, his initial attempts to do so were cavalierly brushed aside by Frere and Chelmsford who insisted on his accepting the draconian terms of the ultimatum. Cetshwayo was also aware through his spies that British reinforcements were continuing to arrive in ever greater numbers. He had no means of knowing how many more would come, but he had earlier been warned by John Dunn that Britain's resources were bottomless, and he rightly feared Chelmsford's growing strength. Therefore, while he and his *umkhandlu* resolved to attempt to open peace negotiations with the British one more time, they also agreed that they must be prepared if necessary to strike another heavy military blow against the British to force them to treat seriously. Yet if they took that dangerous path it would have to be soon, before Chelmsford's strength was restored and augmented. Consequently, Cetshwayo sent out urgent word to his *amabutho* to reassemble on a war footing at oNdini during the first week of March without their festival finery, and for all the *izikhulu* and other great men of the realm also to attend.[5] At the same time, he ordered his people along the borders facing Wood, Glyn and Pearson to remain in arms and to keep vigilant watch so as to warn the king of any forward movements on Chelmsford's part.[6]

Two Zulu messengers crossed the Thukela on 1 March at Middle Drift and made their way to kwaNtumjambili, the mission station near Kranskop of Bishop Hans Schreuder of the Norwegian Mission Society. Schreuder had remained a long-time friend of Cetshwayo, even though he had withdrawn from Zululand in 1877, and that is why he had been singled out to receive the king's message.[7] The next morning the Zulu emissaries were received by Schreuder on the verandah of his house. Squatting low as suppliants before the sympathetic bishop, they relayed Cetshwayo's message that the war was 'not of his seeking', and that he begged 'the Government' to 'allow negotiations to be resumed with a view to a peaceable settlement'. The emissaries ended with their master's dignified assurance that he did not 'ask to be treated with indulgence, but with fairness and justice'.[8] But Frere, when the telegraphed summary of the meeting at kwaNtumjambili was laid before him, was having none of it. On 3 March (the very same day he telegraphed Hicks Beach that there was no alternative but to allow the Transvaal to resume its independence), he wrote to Chelmsford that there could be peace only if Cetshwayo 'complied unreservedly with all the demands made on him' in the ultimatum.[9] Rebuffed, Cetshwayo's emissaries were sent back across the Thukela with 'long faces' to inform Cetshwayo that to negotiate remained fruitless.[10]

While Cetshwayo and his advisers were digesting their two emissaries' unpalatable report that indicated a resumption of hostilities was inevitable, on 10 March Mahubulwana kaDumisela, the senior *induna* of the abaQulusi in north-western Zululand and a man unswervingly loyal to the king, arrived hotfoot at oNdini. He reported that two days before he had conferred with the two Boer emissaries, Hendrik Versagie and Conrad Potgieter, at ebaQulusini, the Qulusi *ikhanda* nestled below Mashongololo Mountain. The news Mahubulwana brought of the Transvaal rebellion and the assurances of Boer neutrality in the war against Britain were welcomed by Cetshwayo and his *umkhandlu*, and played a crucial part in formulating their strategy for the next stage of the war.[11]

In planning their new offensive, the Zulu leaders could now discount the possibility of a diversionary attack in their rear when they committed their main army to attacking the British forces somewhere along the southern and western borders of Zululand.[12] With the discomfiture of the British, the amaSwazi continued to stay out of the game, and the Boers had just promised to remain neutral. The isolated British garrison at Luneburg was in a defensive posture and could certainly be contained by the local irregular forces under Mbilini, Manyonyoba and the Qulusi *izinduna*.

Of the three concentrations of British troops threatening the Zulu borders, Wood's forces seemed the most vulnerable. His column was the furthest from the coast, so would be the last to be reinforced by troops landing in Durban. Moreover, his fortified camp in the open country at Koppie Allein seemed less formidable than the nexus of daunting forts at the Lower Thukela or the stronghold on the heights at Helpmekaar. Besides, the Zulu could now factor in the threat to Wood's situation posed by the rebelling Boers. At the very least Wood would have to keep an eye over his shoulder for Boer movements that threatened his and the Luneburg garrison's lines of supply to his depot at Utrecht and on to Newcastle in Natal, and the Zulu leaders believed that this would mean that many of his dreaded mounted men would be drawn away to patrol the roads to his rear. Just as the Boer leaders in Pretoria had calculated, they suspected that Wood's exposed position might even compel him to fall back north-west to Utrecht, or south-west to Dundee. Cetshwayo and his military commanders grasped that if Wood did attempt to pull back from the Zulu border it might give the Zulu army the opportunity to catch him strung out on the march and far more vulnerable than behind his defences at Koppie Allein.

The problem was that it might take weeks before Wood finally decided to abandon Koppie Allein, and time was what the amaZulu did not have. More British reinforcements were bound to arrive while the Zulu commanders waited for the ideal opportunity to attack. Besides, the Zulu army was already almost fully mustered at oNdini and could not be provisioned there for many more days. And without the prospect of immediate action the increasingly hungry and frustrated *amabutho* would begin to drift back home. So, left with no viable alternative but to attempt to strike a decisive military blow while they could, on

11 March Cetshwayo and his councillors resolved that soon as it could be 'doctored' the main Zulu army must march against Wood.[13]

So vital was this offensive for the survival of the kingdom that Cetshwayo put Mnyamana, his chief *induna*, in overall command, although Ntshingwayo, the leading general at Isandlwana, would act as his effective chief of staff and direct the *amabutho* during the actual fighting. Dabulamanzi was sent back to the coast to take charge of local irregulars and of regional elements of the *amabutho* still lingering there. His commission was to keep a close eye on Pearson's troops at the Lower Thukela and to hinder them if they took offensive action. However, the king considered this merely a precaution since he was banking on Mnyamana gaining a victory in the west before Pearson could make a forward move of any significance. Similarly, Cetshwayo was confident that the irregulars around Luneburg could be relied upon to mask the British garrison during the coming campaign.

On the other hand, Glyn's troops at Helpmekaar posed a real threat since they were in a position to cross the border at Rorke's Drift and strike Mnyamana's army in the flank when it advanced against Wood. It was resolved, therefore, that when the main Zulu army left oNdini and marched west by way of Nhlazatshe Mountain towards Koppie Allein, that a mixed force of about 3,000 men made up of elements of all the *amabutho* gathered at oNdini would march south-west and take up position on the Nquthu Heights overlooking the Isandlwana battlefield. Under the command of Ndabuko kaMpande (the king's full brother), and Mavumengwana (who had held the joint command at Isandlwana), and supported by local Mchunu, Sithole and Qungebe irregulars, their task was to hold off any aggressive foray Glyn might attempt across the Mzinyathi until the main army had achieved its objective against Wood.[14]

As they had before the previous great offensive in January, between 12 and 14 March the Zulu *amabutho* duly underwent all the required pre-combat rituals of purification and strengthening. This time, though, especial ritual emphasis was placed on their firearms because the 800 or more Martini-Henry rifles looted from the Isandlwana and Rorke's Drift battlefields had augmented the predominantly antiquated firearms already in their hands. Not many Zulu besides those who had been employed by white hunters knew how to use these sophisticated firearms effectively, so supernatural assistance was required. Mpatshana described in detail how an *isangoma* who had obtained his *imithi* from the distant Rain Queen of the Balobedu:

> ... made all those with guns hold their barrels downwards on to, but not actually touching, a sherd containing some smoking substance, i.e. burning drugs, fire being underneath the sherd, in order that smoke might go up the barrel. This was done so that bullets would go straight, and, on hitting any European, kill him.

The *isangoma* also 'made marks on our faces ... and declared that the Europeans' bullets would be weakened ... and not enter'. Unhappily for the *amabutho*, the *isangoma*'s *imithi* would prove to be entirely ineffective.[15]

The *amabutho* being doctored were the victorious veterans of Isandlwana and Rorke's Drift and were brimming with confidence that they would prove their mettle once again. In this regard there was unfinished business to resolve. After Isandlwana there had been a heated dispute between the iNgobamakhosi and uKhandempemvu as to which of them had been first among the British tents. So, before the army marched, Cetshwayo summoned these two crack *amabutho* into the cattle enclosure where they ritually harangued and challenged each other, each swearing to outdo the other in the coming battle and to prove their superior mettle once and for all.[16]

On the morning of 15 March the *amabutho* marched out of oNdini in one great column accompanied by their *izindibi* carrying supplies, and then divided on their separate ways. Ndabuko's much smaller force set off in the direction the army had previously taken in the Isandlwana campaign. Mnyamana led his approximately 17,000 men in the direction of Koppie Allein. All the *amabutho* were represented in Mnyamana's army and they consisted of the cream of the fighting men in each *ibutho* since theirs was the vital mission upon which the fate of the Zulu kingdom hung.[17]

Chapter 20

Wood's Fortified Laager

———»•«———

Cetshwayo and his commanders were correct in believing that the Transvaal rebellion and the presence of Smit and his commando of about 250 men at Wakkerstroom would have a direct effect on Wood's situation. On 4 March Piet Uys, accompanied by his four sons, manfully strode up to Wood's tent and informed him that in the circumstances the men of his Transvaal Burgher Force could no longer serve with the British, and would be returning to their farms. Wood extracted their promise that they would not join Smit's commando, and late that morning 45 Boers rode off unmolested. Seeing them go, a number of men of Weatherley's 53-strong Border Horse decided that their loyalties too lay with the ZAR and not with Britain, and Wood allowed 21 of them to ride off as well. That left Wood with 99 Mounted Infantry, 193 Frontier Light Horse, 143 Raaff's Transvaal Rangers, 108 Baker's Horse, 40 Kaffrarian Rifles, 32 Weatherley's Border Horse, and 74 Natal Native Horse, 689 mounted men in all.[1]

Although Wood was confident that the small garrisons holding his depot at Utrecht and his rear base at Newcastle would be sufficient to hold off any Boer raid, he was acutely aware that he must safeguard the roads connecting them to his fortified camp at Koppie Allein and the garrison at Luneburg. That meant he must cease using his mounted troops to harass the Zulu border lands and redeploy them to his rear. With that in mind, on 5 March he detached the 422 men of Raaff's Transvaal Rangers, Baker's Horse, the Kaffrarian Rifles, the suspect remnants of Weatherley's Border Horse and the Mounted Infantry to patrol his lines of supply and keep them open. He placed them under the dependable command of Captain (local rank) Edward

S. Browne, 1/24th Regiment, who was attached to No. 1 Squadron, Mounted Infantry. Browne had been commanding Mounted Infantry since August 1877, and had seen service in the Ninth Cape Frontier War and with No. 3 Column in Zululand.[2] Wood retained his two most experienced and enterprising mounted units, the 267 men of the Frontier Light Horse and Natal Native Horse with him at Koppie Allein under Buller's command.[3] Their task would be to continue to patrol the eastern bank of the Ncome River to give forewarning of any hostile Zulu movements. They were assisted in their patrolling by the 517 African levies of the two battalions of Wood's Irregulars under the command of Major W. K. Leet, 13th Light Infantry.[4]

Wood suspected that in the light of his vulnerable situation the Zulu might well decide to attack his camp. Nevertheless, he was confident he was strong enough to beat off any Zulu assault. Besides Buller's mounted men and the African levies, he had the 711 British infantry of the eight companies of the 90th Light Infantry under Brevet Lieutenant-Colonel R. M. Rogers, VC, and the 527 men in the seven companies of the 1/13th Light Infantry under Lieutenant-Colonel P. E. V. Gilbert. Crucially, he also had at his disposal No. 11 Battery, 7th Brigade, RA, with its six 7-pounder RML (rifled muzzle-loader) Mark IV steel mountain guns and 110 artillerymen under the command of Brevet Lieutenant-Colonel E. J. Tremlett. Eleven Royal Engineers were also in camp and played their part in erecting its defences.[5] In all, he had just short of 3,000 men at his disposal, of whom a small number were sick.

There had been time enough since Wood had first made camp at Koppie Allein on 26 January to prepare a formidable defensive position. The laager was sited on very gently sloping open grassland in a bend of the sluggish Ncome River, with its high banks, a thousand metres to its east and 400 metres to its south. A shallow watercourse in a wide, deeply incised donga with thick bush at its bottom ran down to the river 300 metres east of the camp. Rocky Koppie Allein, with its thickly wooded southern and western slopes, was 2,000 metres to the north and made an ideal vantage point for the picquet infallibly stationed there. A low, round, wooded hill, Mabeta, was 2,000 metres to the north-west of the camp and commanded the track to Utrecht. A vedette was stationed there. Some 1,500 metres from the camp, a system of dongas starting midway between Koppie Allein and Mabeta ran eastwards into the river. Further dongas starting close by Mabeta incised the veld southwards to the Ncome 1,000 metres west of the laager.

In designing his fortified camp, Wood attempted nothing overly ambitions. His column had forty-one wagons and five carts attached to it for its supplies. Although a wagon could technically carry a load of between 1,350 and 3,600 kg and a cart 900 kg, the inferior tracks they had to traverse and the consequent additional strain on the oxen meant that loads were usually only a third of that weight.[6] Consequently, the column's five carts and five of the wagons had constantly to be on the road to Utrecht to bring up provisions escorted by mounted men of Browne's command, so Wood could count on thirty-six wagons being in camp at one time. These he formed into a wagon laager according to the best principles.

An ox wagon was a ponderous vehicle constructed of wood with four spoked wooden wheels with iron rims, the two at the back being a third larger than those in front. It was long in proportion to its breadth, its dimensions being 5.5 metres by 1.5 metres (which is why Boers called it a *kakebeenwa*, or jawbone wagon). The conductor (or driver) sat in front on a wooden chest and plied his long whip to urge on the span of 10–18 oxen drawing the wagon. The two most powerful oxen were yoked on either side of the *disselboom*, or shaft, and the rest were yoked in pairs to a *trektou*, a long chain or leather rope attached to the *disselboom*. A young African *voorlooper* led the front pair of oxen by a thong attached to their yoke, and the rest obediently followed.[7] Wood's wagon train was a motley collection of the three types available: tent-wagons in which the whole body was covered by canvas on semi-circular hoops; half-tent wagons in which the rear third of the body was similarly covered; and buck-wagons that had no raised cover.[8]

When constructing a laager of wagons, what had to be taken into account was whether or not it had to be formed in a hurry. The quickest way was to park the wagons side-by-side, or to slant them diagonally with each *disselboom* facing outwards. When there was time and a semi-permanent laager was intended, then the neatest and strongest formation entailed placing the wagons end to end with each *disselboom* threaded under the one in front and lashed fast. Such an enclosure was laborious to construct since it required first outspanning the oxen some distance away and then running in the wagons by hand. But it was ideal for a relatively large force like Wood's with a moderate convoy since it possessed the great advantage of requiring far fewer wagons for the same amount of interior space because wagons parked end-to-end provided three times the defensible length of those parked side-by-side.[9]

With 36 wagons placed end-to-end Wood was able to construct a laager 60 metres square with 9 wagons along each face. That provided an interior space of 3,600 square metres, large enough to accommodate the piles of stacked provisions and a fenced-off group of six hospital tents, and offered sufficient room when under attack to corral the 500 or so draught oxen and spare horses which inevitably stampeded when the firing got hot, along with their 80-odd conductors and *voorloopers*. The African levies could also just squeeze in too until the moment came for them to sally out in a counter-attack.

Following orthodox principles, Wood constructed a defensive bank of earth 20 metres outside the lines of wagons, 100 metres long on each of the four sides and derived from the ditch dug immediately in front of it. The sturdy earthwork parapet was 120 cm high and at least as thick, low enough to fire over but thick enough to give protection from bullets, while the V-shaped ditch was three metres wide and a metre deep. The parapet was faced with revetments of hurdles (portable wooden frames) to prevent it crumbling should it rain. An L-shaped traverse was placed behind each of the two entrances through the north-west and south-east faces of the parapet. A rolling wooden bridge wide enough for a wagon to pass across was run out over the ditch and was pulled back at night or in the event of an attack.

Since the tactical objective was to hamper the enemy when they attacked in order to extend their time in the killing zone before the trench, 40 metres beyond it Wood made sure to add a circuit of wire entanglements 12 metres wide. Rows of stakes were driven into the ground 1.5 metres apart and strong wire wound around them 45 cm from the ground. Paths clear of the entanglements were deliberately left opposite the two entrances to the fortifications to allow for the passage of wagons and the garrison. Wood also followed the usual procedure of clearing the bush and keeping the grass burnt within 125 metres of the laager's line of defences to deny the amaZulu using them as cover,

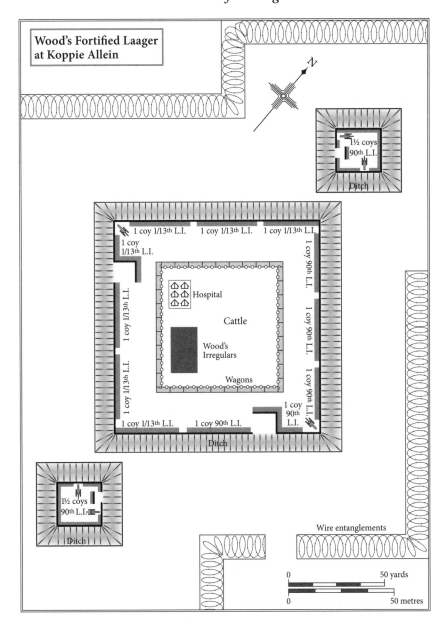

Wood's Fortified Laager at Koppie Allein

and to prevent them from setting the vegetation alight to endanger the camp or in order to advance under the cover of a smoke screen.

The wagon square with its surrounding earthworks was orientated with its four corners north–south and east–west. To enhance its defensibility, two flanking earthwork redoubts were thrown up

15 metres beyond the ditch at its northern and southern corners. These redoubts were each 20 metres square with a formidable parapet and V-shaped ditch directly in front matching the laager's earthworks, and were also surrounded by wire entanglements. The single entrance to each was guarded by a traverse behind it. Two of the 7-pounder guns and their crews were placed on barbettes (platforms a yard below the top of the parapet) in each redoubt so that every side of the laager was enfiladed by their fire. Of the remaining two guns, one reinforced the vulnerable eastern salient angle of the earthwork around the laager and the other the western. Blindages, or screens of sandbags, protected the gunners from enemy fire. When firing shrapnel shells these guns had a maximum range of 3,000 metres, but case-shot, or canister, with its burst of small projectiles like that of a shotgun, could be employed only at ranges of less than 250 metres.[10]

Wood knew that the effect of his men's rifle fire depended on the range and the volume of fire. At close range (100–300 metres) two minutes' fire at six shots per minute would only be 10 per cent effective against a mass attack; at medium range (300–700 metres), effectiveness would decrease considerably to 5 per cent for four minutes' fire at six shots per minute. But at point-blank range (below 100 metres), a wall of fire would be nigh impenetrable for a charging enemy if the troops lining the defences were sufficiently concentrated and maintained the necessary volume of twelve shots a minute.[11] To achieve this, it was Wood's intention to line the earthworks around the laager and the redoubts with two ranks of riflemen, a yard between each man. One-and-a-half companies of the 90th Light Infantry would garrison each of the two redoubts. Three of the remaining five companies of the 90th would hold the east face of the laager as well as the adjacent two-thirds of the south face. One of the seven companies of the 1/13th would man the rest of the south face, and the remaining six would defend the whole length of the west and north faces.[12] This meant that on average 200 men held each side of the laager and there were 120 riflemen in each redoubt. Those dispositions would leave enough men for five marksmen to be stationed along the top of each wagon where the stores would form an impromptu rampart with gaps left open to fire through. Each line of wagons forming the laager served the additional purpose of defilading the earthworks in front of that face from reverse firing coming over the laager – an important consideration because of the well-known Zulu tendency to fire high. To ensure accurate firing from his men, Wood placed whitewashed stones at specific distances paced out from the laager, and these range-markers would guide the officers who were responsible for ordering their men to adjust their sights correctly. Inspecting the defensive preparations he had made at Koppie Allein, Wood could be confident that no enemy without artillery would be able to carry it.[13]

While waiting for the amaZulu to make a move, Wood's British infantry and mounted men pitched their tents between the laager and the earthworks and outside the two redoubts. Wood's Irregulars erected makeshift huts 500 metres away from the south-west side of the laager, close to the river. A number of them were put in charge of herding the oxen when they were driven out of the laager to graze. For fear of fire, all cooking was done beyond the trenches. Water was fetched daily from the river, but because the amaZulu were not expected to be able to keep up a long siege it was unnecessary to have a permanent supply in the fort itself. Even so, Wood ensured that butts full of water were available within the defences to quench his men's thirst during combat.

To make sure that all ran as clockwork when the amaZulu attacked, Wood drilled his men in the procedure to follow when the alarm was sounded. The outlying picquets and vedettes were to fall back to the laager and the companies of British troops and the troops of mounted men were to fall in to the front of their tents. The last man out of each tent was to pull away the pole to collapse the tent onto the ground. Then, on receiving the requisite order, each infantry company was to advance to its designated stretch of the earthworks, the snipers were to take up position on the wagons, and the artillerymen were to man their guns. The mounted men were to saddle up their horses and move inside the laager once a few wagons had been run out to let them in. Wood's Irregulars were to make all speed to take shelter in the laager, and to bring in any cattle still out grazing. As firing commenced officers and staff were to move about in the space between the laager and earthworks to circulate orders and to ensure that ammunition was efficiently distributed. When the order came, the mounted men and Wood's Irregulars were to move out of the laager into the space behind the earthworks preparatory to making a sortie or pursuing the retiring foe.[14]

Chapter 21

The Battle of Koppie Allein

————⋙●⋘————

Mnyamana led out his resolute army from oNdini on 15 March, making first for the looming bulk of Nhlazatshe Mountain in central Zululand (flat-topped as are all the great mountains of that region) with its thickly wooded slopes. By 19 March the *amabutho* were bivouacked along the streams that flowed close by the southern base of Nceceni Mountain where it reared up in daunting cliffs to Bhobomzana, the rocky peak of its south-eastern spur. Koppie Allein was some five-and-half miles due west of the Zulu bivouac. The army needed to rest because it had advanced by forced marches of about twenty miles a day, covering the broken and difficult ground at the same rate it had in the Isandlwana campaign. This time, though, it was better supplied than it had been then because, with the advance of the season and the bringing in of the harvest, food was more plentiful for an army that, ever since it had left Nhlazatshe and its *izindibi* behind, had been compelled to live off the land. In consequence, although footsore, the army was in good shape and its morale was very high.[1]

While the army rested, scouts went forward to gain an idea of Wood's dispositions. They reported back late that afternoon to Mnyamana, Ntshingwayo and their war council of the commanders of the *amabutho*. Wood's camp was described as being surprisingly compact, but heavily fortified. Tents and troops were everywhere, and the scouts had seen a number of mounted patrols, and almost been cut off by one. Their belief was that the British knew of the Zulu army's proximity, and that it did not hold the advantage of surprise. Having digested this intelligence, the war council agreed that there was no alternative (despite the sharp lesson of Rorke's Drift) but to mount a conventional attack with the objective of entirely surrounding Wood's position and storming its defences. The site of the battle of Blood River (Ncome) – just five miles downstream from Wood's camp – was an unwelcome reminder of how impregnable a fortified laager could prove. Nevertheless, the Zulu commanders believed that if they could co-ordinate their attack – which their predecessors at the battle of Ncome had failed to do – then their courage and numbers could still carry them through. So they set about making their dispositions for the following day.[2]

The Zulu scouts were not mistaken in suspecting that Wood knew of the proximity of the Zulu army. According to his instructions his mounted men, backed up by groups of Wood's Irregulars, were patrolling the eastern banks of the Ncome, only venturing a few miles into Zulu territory. It was while they were scouting eastwards of Wood's camp in the direction of Nceceni Mountain that men of Hlubi's Troop, led by the Tlokwa chief himself, saw distant smoke rising from the southern flanks of the mountain. They rode closer to investigate, and caught sight of Zulu scouts scampering through the tall grass. They pursued them for a space, and came close enough to the Zulu bivouac to grasp that the smoke came from the cooking fires of a great host. That was sufficient for Hlubi, who turned his men around and rode as fast as he could back to Koppie Allein to raise the alarm.[3]

Since it was already late in the day, Wood believed the amaZulu would not risk a night attack. His Principal Staff Officer, Captain the Hon. Ronald Campbell, agreed with him that they must expect the enemy to attack the following morning. When consulted, Buller concurred. That gave Wood time to address his men in cheery and encouraging tones about the coming battle, and to make sure that all his defensive arrangements were in place and properly understood. He called in all his mounted patrols so that at very first light they would form an effective screen between the camp and the Zulu army, giving early warning of any forward movement. He also sent out mounted messengers to find Captain Browne, to warn him of the Zulu advance, and to order him to concentrate as many of the mounted men under his command as he could. He was to bring them back into the vicinity of Koppie Allein so that they could hover disruptively on the Zulu flanks and join in the pursuit once the Zulu were repulsed.[4]

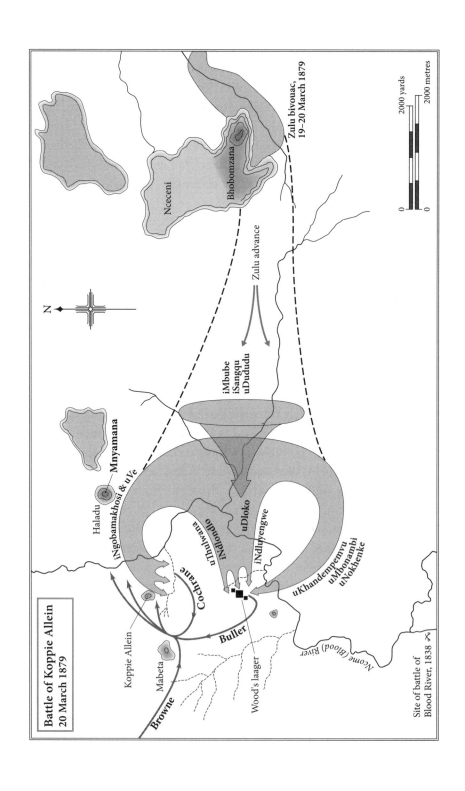

Battle of Koppie Allein
20 March 1879

Ncaceni

Bhobomzana

Zulu bivouac,
19–20 March 1879

N

Zulu advance

Mnyamana

Haladu

iNgobamakhosi & uVe

iMbube
iSangqu
uDududu

uThulwana

iNdlondlo

uDloko

iNdluyengwe

uKhandempemvu
uMbonambi
uNokhenke

Cochrane

Buller

Koppie Allein

Mabeta

Browne

Wood's laager

Ncome (Blood) River

Site of battle of
Blood River, 1838

2000 yards

2000 metres

0

0

When the eastern horizon brightened on the fine, clear morning of Thursday 20 March, and the fine wisps of autumn mist melted away, the Zulu army began its preparations for the day of battle. They made a sketchy meal, and then formed up in several great circles for the war doctors who had accompanied the army to sprinkle them with *izintelezi*, the ritual medicines intended to counteract both the sorcery of their enemies and the evil effects of *umnyama* attendant on the shedding of human blood. Once the *amabutho* had been ritually fortified, Mnyamana fervently addressed them, exhorting them to be worthy of their ancestors and of the trust their king had placed in them, and to go forth and 'eat up' the despicable white men who had dared to invade their land. The *amabutho* excitedly responded with a great stamping of feet and a rattling of spears on shields, accompanied by a deep bellowing of '*uSuthu!*' the national battle cry. Satisfied that he had succeeded in stirring up his army, Mnyamana turned and led them deployed in five great columns towards Koppie Allein.[5]

At about 09.00 the Zulu columns halted some 3,000 metres short of Wood's camp, just out of the furthest range of the British artillery, and began to deploy north and south into a great arc about 5,000 metres long. In earnest of the celebrated rivalry between the iNgobamakhosi and uKhandempemvu, Mnyamana placed the former, the largest *ibutho* in the army and Cetshwayo's favourite, in a place of honour on the right horn, along with the younger uVe which had been incorporated into it. Its commander was Sigcwelegcwele kaMhlekehleke, *inkosi* of the Ngadini people, self-assured, tall and broad-shouldered, with a reputation as an aggressive warrior.[6] To even up the strength of the two horns, Mnyamana bolstered the less numerous uKhandempemvu of the left with the uMbonambi and uNokhenke *amabutho*, both of which had distinguished themselves at Isandlwana. The centre was made up of the victors of Rorke's Drift: the uThulwana, iNdlondlo, uDloko and iNdluyengwe. Just behind them were the loins, or reserve, consisting of the iMbube, iSangqu and uDududu who had formed the right horn at Isandlwana.

The right horn under Sigcwelegcwele spread out towards Haladu Mountain north-east of Koppie Allein where Mnyamana himself took up position on its rocky peak with a number of his staff, while the left horn manoeuvred towards the south of Wood's camp. Ntshingwayo stayed with the Zulu chest, directly to the east of the laager, from where he would closely direct the fighting, as Dabulamanzi had at Rorke's Drift.[7]

Buller's mounted scouts had been out before dawn monitoring the movements of the Zulu army and reporting back regularly to Wood.[8] Alerted when the Zulu army began its advance at about 07.30 from Nceceni, Wood sent out the word to Wood's Irregulars in their huts to the south-west to come into the laager and to drive in any oxen still grazing outside. He then ordered the garrison to have their breakfast in preparation for a long day without any further chance to eat. While the men were finishing their meal the Zulu columns came into distant sight, and it was daunting to see them beginning to deploy in great swarms along the horizon, their two horns beginning to curve in menacingly towards the north and south of the camp. By then the garrison was drawn up in front of their tents, and at about 09.10 Wood gave the order to strike the tents and for the men to take up their battle stations.

Intently watching the Zulu deployment through their field glasses, Wood and his staff quickly noticed that the Zulu right horn was about twice as far away from the laager as the left horn. They grasped with grim eagerness that it if the latter could be induced to attack before the right horn was in position and was repulsed, then the Zulu attack would lose coordination and might be driven off piecemeal. Accordingly, while the Natal Native Horse under Captain Cochrane continued to monitor the Zulu chest and right horn, at about 09.15 Buller led the Frontier Light Horse south across the front of the Zulu left horn that was advancing rapidly preceded by clouds of skirmishers. Buller's men coolly dismounted, fired, remounted, fell back, dismounted and fired again, drawing on the Zulu with complete success. Stung by the impertinence of this puny force of less than 200 men, and smarting at the casualties their accurate firing was inflicting, Vumandaba kaNtati, the *induna* of the uKhandempemvu – a tall, thin old man with grizzled hair and beard who had taken part in the battle of Ncome and was an intimate of Cetshwayo's – took the bait and the other *amabutho* of the left horn followed suit.[9] They surged forward in pursuit as Buller fell back across the river, splashing up to their waists in the slowly running Ncome and scrambling up the opposite bank under daunting fire. When Buller and his men were within about 300 metres of the laager they suddenly swung around and made for the north-western side of the fortifications. There Buller halted the Frontier Light Horse, ready either to retreat into the laager through the entry on that side, or to continue skirmishing with the amaZulu.

Artillery fire by three of the 7-pounders supported Buller's withdrawal and brought the Zulu left horn sharply up short as shrapnel burst among the *amabutho*. Like it or not, the pursing Zulu found that they were now committed to their attack and there was no turning back. So they charged forward at a run directly at the southern redoubt and the earthworks on either side of it. They were already in close range of the rifles that opened up with deadly volleys, while the artillery began to fire canister. Apparently undeterred by the heavy casualties they were taking, the left horn pushed forward into point-blank range of the defenders. Only a few made it as far as the cordon of wire entanglements, the survivors dropping to the ground under the appalling, unremitting weight of fire. Behind them, the ranks of amaZulu wavered, fell face down with their shield over them, or began to crawl or run back to the Ncome to take shelter in the river bed, or among the empty huts of Wood's Irregulars. And there the assault led by Vumandaba and the uKhandempemvu stalled, the ground between them and the laager littered with their dead, and their wounded groaning and screaming piteously. From behind the river banks and huts the survivors kept up something of an ineffective fire on the laager until smartly driven out by some well-placed shells from the artillery. So, at about 09.35 they scrambled even further back until they were about 1,000 metres away from the laager and in relatively ineffective long range of the garrison's rifles.

From his elevated position on Haladu, just outside the laager's artillery range, Mnyamana could just see that the left horn had attacked prematurely, and had been driven back. It was now about 09.45 and the iNgobamakhosi and uVe, who had been advancing rapidly in the wake of the retiring Natal Native Horse, were just beginning to flounder their way across the Ncome to the west of Haladu. The Zulu chest, led on by Ntshingwayo himself, and supported by the loins a few hundred metres to its rear, was coming on at a far more deliberate pace and had reached the eastern bank of the Ncome. Despite the repulse of the left horn, which badly dislocated his intention of surrounding the laager and attacking it simultaneously from every side, Mnyamana could not now check the forward impetus of the right horn and the chest. It was still possible that the iNgobamakhosi and uVe, burning to outdo the uKhandempemvu, might be able to sweep around the western side of the British laager and surround it. So Mnyamana sent an *induna* down from Haladu to urge the right horn forward while the chest commenced a frontal attack on the eastern side of the laager.

At this critical moment Buller, joined by Cochrane's Natal Native Horse as they fell back before the Zulu right horn, decided to remain outside the laager and harry the right flank of the iNgobamakhosi and uVe as they advanced. He reached this decision when a vedette from his post on Mabeta Hill to the north galloped up to him and reported that he had seen Captain Browne approaching with a large body of horsemen. Browne had in fact managed to rally 373 men of his command, representing elements of all units (the remaining forty-nine were too distantly dispersed) and their numbers brought the mounted men under Buller's command up to 640: a formidable force. Buller cantered his men north to meet Browne's, and they all took position on the eastern slopes of Mabeta at about 10.00 just as the Zulu right horn swirled around either side of Koppie Allein and began their leftward turn towards the laager 1,100 metres away. Dismounting, firing and remounting again and again, the manoeuvring troopers severely mauled the right flank of the iNgobamakhosi and uVe, thwarting its turning movement and pushing it back to behind the donga just south of Koppie Allen, 900 metres from the laager. Four of the 7-pounders lobbed shells at them there from the laager. They remained out of effective rifle range of the defenders, but still under constant fire from the mounted men who danced out of their way when they attempted a charge in their direction.

With both horns stalled far short of their objectives and effectively pinned down, at about 10.15 the Zulu chest, first breasting the muddy waters of the Ncome, came on determinedly against the eastern side of the laager. As always in such a situation, overwhelming numbers counted as naught since the attackers had to bunch up against their small objective and their constricted front ranks took terrible punishment from the defenders while those behind impatiently pushed them forward. When the attackers (stooping low to avoid the bullets and shrapnel and moving as fast as they could to minimize their time under fire) reached the deep donga about 230 metres east of the laager, they took cover and gathered their courage for another final push.

Meanwhile, at about 10.20 Vumandaba decided that the left horn must advance in support of the centre and it pushed back again across the river. But coming under heavy fire as before, it faltered and fell back and Vumandaba was unable to rally it. At that moment the chest tried to charge forward from the donga but was mercilessly cut down by close range fire. Unnerved, it pulled back to the partial shelter of the donga. But Ntshingwayo again loudly urged his men forward, reminding them of the glory they had achieved at Isandlwana and of the king's trust in their prowess. His *izinduna* along the ranks repeated his exhortation to their *amabutho* and stirred them up to a fresh assault. This, the chest's third charge of the day, made at about 10.40, was its most determined, and it was reinforced by members of the reserve who moved forward to make up the chest's heavy casualties. Regardless of its losses, and swept at point-blank range by remorseless volleys of rifle fire and riddled by case-shot, the chest pushed forward to reach the circuit of wire entanglements. A few fanatically courageous men survived to make it through the wire to within thirty metres of the ditch, charging the eastern salient of the defences where the British fire was least concentrated. But they were too few and the cross-fire from the two redoubts swept them away. Badly shaken by its terrible losses, at 10.55 the chest retreated once more to the donga.

The commanders on both sides saw this latest repulse as the sure sign that the Zulu attack had failed, and that they had no alternative but to disengage. For his part, Mnyamana knew this was the most hazardous moment for any army, for an effective counter-attack by the foe could transform an orderly withdrawal into a murderous rout. On the other hand, Wood understood that a premature sortie could have dire consequences, and resolved to follow the more prudent course of waiting until the amaZulu began pulling back before going onto the offensive.

The Zulu right horn was closest to Mnyamana on Haladu, and he sent a direct order to Sigcwelegcwele to fall back across the Ncome. This withdrawal would give the signal to the rest of the army. The moment

Buller saw the Zulu right horn begin to turn and retire from the donga south of Koppie Allein he knew the best moment to attack had come, and that he could not afford to wait for Wood's order to do so. Taking responsibility for the crucial decision, he launched his and Browne's mounted men at the iNgobamakhosi and uVe in a furious charge, firing from the saddle into the retreating mass at point-blank range. Those with sabres slashed at the amaZulu who, exhausted they were, tried to break into a run, holding their shields across the backs. Others among the mounted men seized spears from the fleeing amaZulu and used them to kill at close quarters. The victorious mounted men became delirious with slaughter, and Commandant Schermbrucker saw Buller himself acting 'like a tiger drunk with blood'.[10]

Here and there, a few of the more intrepid amaZulu, disgusted with themselves for being herded like panicked cattle by the rampaging horsemen, turned to stand their ground, spear in hand, or took a hasty shot at their pursuers. But the horsemen rode them down, or they lost their nerve and merged again into the bolting throng. As was typical of any mounted pursuit of a thoroughly demoralised and fleeing enemy, the horsemen suffered only minimal casualties. During their relentless pursuit of the amaZulu at the decisive battle of Blood River on 16 December 1838, the only casualties the Boer commando had sustained were three men wounded.[11] Likewise, only a handful of Buller's horsemen were wounded, and none killed. However, the veteran Sergeant Edmund O'Toole of the FLH, a Cape colonist of Irish stock who had fought in the Eighth and Ninth Cape Frontier Wars and in the First Anglo-Pedi War,[12] had the narrowest of escapes. As he rode alongside Buller at the head of their men, a lucky musket shot brought down his wiry little horse and he was heavily thrown. O'Toole, dazed and vulnerable, staggered clumsily to his feet. But before the amaZulu could take advantage of his plight, Buller reined up his over-excited horse and leaped down to help him. The New Zealand-born Lieutenant Cecil D'Arcy of the FLH, a veteran of the Ninth Cape Frontier War and the Pedi campaign of 1878,[13] also dismounted, and between them he and Buller heaved O'Toole up with difficulty onto D'Arcy's plunging horse. D'Arcy remounted, and with O'Toole clasping him around the waist rode to the rear while Buller rejoined the remorseless chase. Wood subsequently almost failed to report this joint act of bravery because Buller proved reluctant to speak of it.[14]

Mnyamana was appalled when he saw the right horn disintegrate under the impact of Buller's charge, but understood there was no possibility of rallying it. He himself was now in imminent danger and made haste to decamp from Haladu and make his way eastwards towards Nceceni.

Buller's men pursued the fleeing Zulu right horn east across the Ncome, cutting many down as they struggled through the stream, and then swung south to take the Zulu chest in its right flank. Wood responded to Buller's perfectly timed charge by ordering three companies of the 90th forward over the earthworks and across the ditch with bayonets fixed to pour volleys into the Zulu sheltering in the donga and to drive them out. To cover this sortie, two companies of the 1/13th were redeployed at the double from the unthreatened westerly defences to take their place behind the ramparts. Faced by the advancing British to his right and front, Ntshingwayo attempted to pull back, but the morale of his men was shattered and they too began to scatter and run. The mounted men cut many off as they attempted to cross the river, and the advancing companies of the 90th fired into their backs as they huddled under the eastern banks. No more able than Mnyamana to rally his fragmenting *amabutho*, Ntshingwayo made off to the south-east where the Zulu left horn, seeing the rout of the rest of the army, was pulling back more or less intact. Buller and Wood let them go. This was the moment, though, to let loose Wood's Irregulars from the protection of the laager. At about 11.15 they gleefully emerged to scour the killing fields around the laager and to probe the dongas and river to kill the Zulu wounded and flush out those who were attempting to lie low. They were supported by the British infantry who gave them cover as they went cheerfully about their merciless work. Across the Ncome Buller's mounted men fanned out to finish off more distant amaZulu taking cover or too badly wounded to escape.

It had taken Wood's men about two hours to inflict a catastrophic defeat on the amaZulu. Mnyamana and Ntshingwayo made it back to Cetshwayo on 25 March with about a third of their army intact. The rest of the survivors, seeing themselves thoroughly beaten, simply dispersed to their homes without reporting back to the king as custom required. Zulu losses had been unacceptably high, as high if not higher than those suffered at Isandlwana and Rorke's Drift combined. As in both those battles many of the desperately wounded carried away by their comrades never made it back home. Thus, in addition to the nearly 2,000 Zulu dead that littered the field at Koppie Allein, there must have been at least another thousand who died of their bone-shattering, untreatable bullet wounds. The number of prisoners the British took alive was negligible, for they had been actuated by a grim determination to avenge Isandlwana and Rorke's Drift. British casualties were extremely light by comparison: 3 officers and 14 NCOs and men killed; 5 officers and 32 NCOs and men wounded; and 19 horses killed. A high proportion of wounds had been inflicted by fire from the captured Martini-Henry rifles in Zulu hands, and it was fortunate for the British (especially their horsemen manoeuvring in the open) that so few of the amaZulu knew how to use them effectively. As it was, Mnyamana's army had never seriously threatened Wood's fortified camp, and his victory was a comprehensive one.

Chapter 22

The Transvaal Regains its Independence

—————⟫•⟪—————

In late January terrible sounds of lamentation had been heard across Zululand, and again in the last days of March cries of grief day and night chilled the blood. It was the flower of the Zulu army that had died, the strong young men of the crack *amabutho*, the future fathers of the nation. Among the dead were a great many *izinduna*, many more than at Isandlwana or Rorke's Drift for, as Cetshwayo later commented, they had 'exposed themselves a great deal, attempting to lead on their men'.[1] Among the dead were men of the highest status, including cousins of the king himself, and sons of other important chiefs and royal councillors, not least two of Mnyamana's own. As for Mnyamana and Ntshingwayo, Cetshwayo was understandably furious with his commanders for the shattering defeat and partial dispersal of his army. The king's first enraged reaction was to order the execution of the two commanders and the *izinduna* who had so signally failed him,[2] but he quickly recovered his usual composure and rescinded that command. When he took stock, he noted that a third of Mnyamana's army was still intact, that Ndabuko's small army had not been engaged or even threatened by Glyn's forces at Helpmekaar, and that Dabulamanzi had not been challenged at the coast either. Yet, as always with Zulu armies, it would be difficult to keep them in the field for lack of supplies, and the survivors of Koppie Allein had to disperse to go through their post-combat purification rituals. Consequently, Cetshwayo was wretchedly aware that his military position was now considerably weaker than it had been before the battle of Koppie Allein. To make matters worse, his spies kept him informed of the stream of British reinforcements arriving in Durban. Only a negotiated peace, it seemed to him, could now prevent the inexorable advance of the British juggernaut. So, despite the repeated rebuffs his messengers had suffered previously when they attempted to parley on his behalf, he resolved to try again.[3]

Accordingly, three royal messengers approached the ferry at Middle Drift on 28 March. They were fired upon by the Border Police, but under an improvised white flag they were allowed to cross the Thukela and were sent under guard to Fort Cherry on the heights above the river. There they spent the night with their hands tied painfully behind their backs before being interrogated the next morning by John Eustace Fannin, the local Natal Border Agent. The royal messengers so roughly handled as likely spies were Johannes, a Christian convert from Bishop Schreuder's eNtjumeni mission, and Mfunzi and Nkisimana. The last two were elderly and dignified emissaries who in the past Cetshwayo had regularly sent on important missions to the Natal government, and were well known to Natal officials. Despite their shock and resentment at their churlish reception, they maintained their dignity when delivering Cetshwayo's simple and straightforward message to Fannin. The king, they declared, saw no reason for the war being waged against him, and requested the government 'to appoint a place at which a conference could be held with a view to the conclusion of peace'. A highly sceptical Fannin passed on what he clearly considered the spurious message to the Natal authorities for their consideration, and until he heard back from them detained the messengers in the semi-derelict Fort Buckingham close by.[4]

Chelmsford's response to Bulwer's telegram of 30 March telling him of Cetshwayo's latest peace initiative was curt: 'All communications from the King should be addressed to me at my camp,' which then happened to be at Fort Pearson.[5] Bulwer, already aware of Wood's victory at Koppie Allein and anxious for an end to the war, was frustrated by Chelmsford's inflexibility, and on 3 April proposed to Frere that 'to avoid possible difficulties and delays' any peace feelers from Cetshwayo should be accepted wherever his messengers might bring them.[6] The problem, as Bulwer appreciated, was not merely that Chelmsford desired to keep everything pertaining to the conduct of the war out of civilian hands; nor was it only that the general was determined to force Cetshwayo to accede in full to the onerous British terms as laid down in the ultimatum. Behind Chelmsford's evident reluctance to treat with Cetshwayo was his patent determination to bring the war to a conclusion with a glorious victory of his own that would wipe away the disgrace of Isandlwana and Rorke's Drift. Wood's triumph at Koppie Allein threatened to steal his thunder, and Chelmsford's reaction to the outcome of the battle was (to say the least) decidedly grudging. 'One line', he wrote Wood, 'to congratulate you upon your successful repulse of the [Zulu] attack . . . I am up to my ears in work & cannot say as much as I could wish.'[7]

The 'work' that was so engrossing Chelmsford was his preparation for a major advance of his own up the coast from Fort Pearson towards oNdini. The 'Coastal Column', as he dubbed the force that was concentrating at the Lower Thukela, was already made up of approximately 1,500 British infantry and 300 mounted men of the original No. 1 Column, reinforced (as we have seen) by contingents that had arrived in the course of March from St Helena, Ceylon and Mauritius. These totalled 1,020 infantry, along with one-and-half batteries of 7-pounder guns (nine in total). Chelmsford also had the naval brigades from HMS *Shah* and *Boadicea* numbering 600 men. To this tally of 3,120 white soldiers and sailors were added 2,000 African levies. During the reorganisation in February 1879 of the NNC, the former 1/3rd and 2/3rd NNC became the 4th and 5th Battalions of the new NNC under Captain G. Barton and Commandant W. Nettleton, respectively. The 4th Battalion was issued with Martini-Henry rifles and the 5th Battalion with Martini-Henrys or Sniders. Both battalions were outfitted with red tunics and trousers (although many discarded the latter).[8] Wood's victory at Koppie Allein had conclusively demonstrated that if a commander could take up an all-round defensive position in a laager, and had the capacity to make an effective counter-attack, then the largest army the Zulu could muster would be defeated. Wood had had about 3,000 men in all, so Chelmsford's 5,000 men of the Coastal Column were already sufficient for the task. But what was Chelmsford then to do with the reinforcements Cambridge had rushed out to him from Britain? To add them to the Coastal Column would prove a logistical nightmare and clog his ability to manoeuvre.

But by the end of March the first of these reinforcements had already landed in Durban: a full battery of 7-pounder guns and another of 9-pounders and 2,750 British infantry of the 2/21st, 3/60th, and 91st

Highlanders. The 1st Dragoon Guards and the 17th Lancers, which were expected in Durban by the second week of April, numbered close to 1,200 men with an equal number of cavalry chargers. A company of Royal Engineers, and a further 1,860 infantry of the 58th and 94th Regiments were anticipated during the same period, as were the four major-generals in command of these troops.[9] For Chelmsford, already sufficiently burdened, a singularly unwelcome arrival on 1 April would be that of Louis Napoleon, the exiled Prince Imperial of France and pretender to the Bonapartist throne, who took up residence in the luxurious house near Durban Bay of the agent of the Union Navigation Company.[10] The eager but flighty prince came armed with a letter of 25 February 1879 from Cambridge to Chelmsford requesting that the general take him on as an unofficial member of his staff.[11] It was perhaps fortunate for all the individuals involved and for the future of the Bonapartist cause that the Prince Imperial's mettle was destined never to be tested in the field in Zululand.

In a lengthy letter to Frere written on 25 March following news of Wood's great victory, Chelmsford informed the High Commissioner that he planned to attach the recently arrived battery of 7-pounders to the Coastal Column during its imminent advance into Zululand, as well as the 17th Lancers since the column was short of mounted men. The troops under Wood and Glyn already stationed along the Zulu border were sufficient, he added, to deter a Zulu invasion of British territory while probably distracting part of the Zulu army from opposing the Coastal Column's advance. But what, Chelmsford went on rhetorically to enquire, was he then to do with the remaining regiment of cavalry, the 9-pounders and the five battalions of infantry – along with their four major-generals? The answer to him was self-evident. He conceded that Frere had undertaken to allow the Transvaal its independence, but (he argued) Wood's victory had drastically altered the strategic situation in the general's favour and it was now feasible to confront the rebellious Boers militarily. He therefore put to Frere that the reinforcements arriving in Durban must march inland and concentrate at Newcastle to form a 5,000-strong 'Natal Field Force'. There it must halt and face down the Boers until he had finished off the Zulu in the decisive battle he was seeking. With the amaZulu out of the war, all the troops currently engaged in the Zulu campaign would be freed up to join the Natal Field Force in retaking the Transvaal from the rebels.[12]

Precisely that scenario had also occurred to the Boers. Intelligence of the British military build-up had succeeded in making their leaders extremely nervous, and at Standerton Joubert was compelled to begin discussing with his commanders where and how best to make a stand against a likely invasion from Natal.[13] Likewise, Frere's thinking had been developing along precisely the same lines as Chelmsford's, and he was beginning to see the way forward to retrieving the situation in both Zululand and the Transvaal – along with his tattered reputation. But the circumstances that made a revised policy feasible had seemed unimaginable less than a month before, and he now had cause bitterly to regret his panicked telegrams to London urging the retrocession of the Transvaal.[14] They could not be undone, and before acceding to Chelmsford's recommendation to form a Natal Field Force, Frere had to hear back from his superiors.

He did not have long to wait. On Friday 4 April 1879 three telegrams arrived simultaneously at Government House in Pietermaritzburg. The first was the one Hicks Beach had sent Frere on 20 March censuring him and requiring him to obey his government's instructions in future. The other two were those he had wired on 21 March to Frere and Bulwer with the government's orders to negotiate the retrocession of the Transvaal and to make peace with the amaZulu (provided Britain's military might had been conclusively asserted). Frere was utterly mortified by Hicks Beach's stern personal admonition, and crushed by the government's orders which humiliatingly undid all his plans for confederation. Yet in the circumstances he was in absolutely no position to protest or put forward Chelmsford's plans for the reconquest of the Transvaal. All he could do was to obey. Bulwer, by contrast, was not at all dismayed since he had long hoped for a way out of the war with the Zulu kingdom and desired at all costs to avoid a war with the Transvaal. Diametrically opposed as their reactions were, the High Commissioner and the Lieutenant-Governor nevertheless spent the rest of the day closeted together as obedient public servants deciding on how best to proceed in obeying their categorical instructions.[15]

Early the next morning Frere telegraphed Chelmsford at Fort Pearson commanding him not to move the recently arrived reinforcements up-country from their camps in the cool hills above Durban (the 94th had landed on 2 April and the 58th on 4 April) and to desist from any offensive action against the amaZulu.[16] Chelmsford, who had believed himself on the brink of bringing the Zulu campaign to a victorious conclusion and of initiating a successful Transvaal one, was distraught. Having issued the orders required of him, he spent the day agonising about how best to salvage his honour now that all possibility of retrieving his military reputation had been snatched away.[17]

The next day was Sunday 6 April, and Chelmsford received a telegram from Durban announcing that Major-General the Hon. Sir Henry Clifford, VC, KCMG, had disembarked from the *England*. With him were Major-General Sir Frederick Marshall, who was in command of the cavalry brigade that was expected to land on 9 April, along with the remaining two major-generals, Edward Newdigate and Henry Crealock (Lt.-Col. Crealock's elder brother).[18] The aristocratic and handsome Clifford, whom Cambridge had characterised as 'an officer of great knowledge and experience in former Cape wars [the Eighth Cape Frontier War], and moreover a most agreeable and satisfactory man to deal with',[19] was the senior of the four.

Chelmsford decided that same day (6 April) to resign his command to Clifford with immediate effect, and to return to England with no delay. In high dudgeon he telegraphed his decision to both Frere and Colonel Stanley, informing them that he was thereby extricating himself 'from a false position'.[20] The next morning he called his troops together, and to their astonishment bitterly announced that at the very moment a final victory was in their grasp the government had called a halt to the war and that he had resigned his command in consequence. To the troops' resounding cheers he then set off for Durban where the following day, 8 April, he sought out General Clifford and formally handed over his command.[21] Understandably, the French journalist who saw him at this time described 'the gloomy and preoccupied air natural to him' being more accentuated than ever.[22] Chelmsford then travelled by train and post-cart to Pietermaritzburg where he took his official and heartfelt farewell from Frere. The two men had worked well together, but both had seen their plans upended and their careers blighted. Chelmsford's parting from Bulwer was polite, as good manners required, but neither was sorry to see the other's back. After a short stay in Durban in awkward semi-seclusion, Chelmsford, accompanied by a subdued Lt.-Col. Crealock, finally took ship for Britain on 14 April, there to face his many vociferous critics. He had let the Duke of Cambridge down badly, and would never again hold a command in the field.[23]

Meanwhile, on 5 April, besides telegraphing Chelmsford, Frere had also telegraphed Kruger in Pretoria and *Kommandant-Generaal* Piet Joubert in Standerton requesting an armistice and proposing that the two sides meet to discuss an honourable peace.[24] On 7 April (the previous day had been the Sabbath) Kruger conferred on Joubert full authority to negotiate. After a further flurry of telegrams, the two parties agreed to meet on 11 April at Gibson's farm on the Sandspruit River in the Transvaal, midway between Newcastle and Standerton. The farmhouse where the parley took place was single-storied with a thatched roof. A deep, shady verandah ran along its front. Inside, the room where the meeting took place was low, dark and cramped with rudimentary tables and chairs. Frere, dapper as always and concealing his deep humiliation, arrived with Sir Theophilus Shepstone, whom he had picked up *en route* in Newcastle, and who was maintaining his habitual poker face. They were accompanied by a small staff and escorted by 100 Frontier Light Horse under Buller's command whom Wood had despatched from Koppie Allein to match the small Boer commando guarding Joubert and a number of his senior commanders.

Frere's one concern as he faced the heavily bearded Boers in their simple, rumpled civilian clothes was to whitewash the debacle as far as he could to protect Britain's reputation in southern Africa; the Boers simply wanted their independence recognised. Joubert was also anxious to disband his commando, idly kicking its heels in Standerton and Wakkerstroom. Boers on commando had the disconcerting habit of yoking up their wagons and setting off for home if affairs were not going to their liking, and numbers had already trekked off. While the talks were tough, they were also rapidly concluded and on 12 May Joubert accepted Frere's terms. The British acknowledged the right of the Transvaal people to complete independence subject to British suzerain rights, the nature of which had still to be negotiated. The question of the Maroteng Paramountcy and Pedi independence would be left to the ZAR to solve, and Britain would play no further part in that matter. Pending a final treaty to be hammered out in Pretoria over the coming months, Joubert agreed to disperse his commando.

Blinking in the sunlight the members of the two negotiating teams emerged from their dark meeting-room to be photographed for posterity standing amicably in front of Gibson's modest house. When he received the news from Joubert that all was settled, Kruger gave public thanks to 'God the Lord who has helped us – the God of our fathers, to whom we have addressed our prayers and supplications. He has done great things to us, and hearkened to our prayers.'[25] The Transvaal rebellion was over (if only to the satisfaction of the Boers), and British forces still facing the amaZulu no longer had to fear a Boer attack against their rear.

Chapter 23

Making Peace with the Zulu Kingdom

It still remained for the British to settle with Cetshwayo. On 5 April, when Frere was busy contacting Chelmsford and the Transvaal Boers, Bulwer sent urgently to Fannin to release the Zulu emissaries, who were still languishing in Fort Buckingham pending further instructions. Fannin was to send them back post-haste to Cetshwayo to relay the message he enclosed, but not before the Border Agent was satisfied that they understood it perfectly.[1] Surprised but elated, the three emissaries sped back to their king as fast as their elderly legs could carry them. Arrived at oNdini, they faithfully repeated the gist of Bulwer's message, to wit, that the government agreed to the Zulu king's request for a conference to achieve a lasting peace; that the conference must convene on 16 April and be held on the Natal bank of the Thukela precisely where the British ultimatum had been delivered the previous December; and that the Lieutenant-Governor would consent to negotiate only with high Zulu chiefs who had the king's authority to speak for him and to come to terms, and not with mere messengers.[2]

Cetshwayo and his *umkhandlu*, who were bracing themselves for Chelmsford's renewed invasion, were astounded to receive Bulwer's message, and simply could not understand why the British should wish to negotiate just when they seemed to have won the war. Nevertheless, they eagerly grasped the quite unexpected opportunity to bring hostilities to an end since they were finding it difficult to reassemble the *amabutho* for further fighting and had realistically abandoned any hope of pursuing the war to military victory.[3] Accordingly, the now weary and footsore Mfunzi and Nkisimana appeared outside Fort

Tenedos on 12 April under a white flag of truce. Under armed escort they crossed the Thukela on the pont plying between the two banks and were taken to General Clifford in Fort Pearson. To Clifford's great satisfaction the two emissaries assured him that high-ranking Zulu dignitaries would arrive to discuss peace terms on the date and at the place Bulwer had specified.[4]

Early on the morning of Wednesday 16 April the Zulu deputation of twenty members approached Fort Tenedos accompanied by some fifty attendants.[5] The garrison, made up of two companies of the 2/3rd Regiment (The Buffs), were expecting them. They detained the Zulu attendants under guard on their side of the river while an armed detachment escorted the deputation across the Thukela to the Natal bank. There another company of the Buffs was drawn up with bayonets fixed to receive them. On 11 December the previous year when John Shepstone had delivered the ultimatum his military escort had been unarmed, but this time there was to be no mistaking British armed might. The Zulu deputation was ushered into the shade of an awning erected under a large Natal fig tree commanded by Fort Person looming above them on its hilltop – the very selfsame spot where the ultimatum had been presented. A table and four chairs were set out for the British delegation: Bulwer and John Shepstone (the Acting Secretary for Native Affairs) representing the Natal government; General Clifford, representing the British Army; and Captain Henry Hallam Parr, Frere's Military Secretary, representing the High Commissioner.

The eminence of the members of the Zulu delegation, who sat on the ground in a semi-circle in front of the four British delegates, was testimony to Cetshwayo's genuine commitment to the talks. No less a personage than Mnyamana himself led the envoys, and he was flanked by Ziwedu kaMpande, Cetshwayo's favourite brother, who stood high in status among the Zulu princes and was a man of talent and good sense. Various *izikhulu* were also present, including Godide kaNdlela, the aged and spindly *inkosi* of the Ntuli and *induna* of the uMxhapho *ibutho* who had been defeated at the battle of Nyezane. With them were trusted officers of state who had been part of the delegation that had received the ultimatum before the war. They included Vumandaba, who as Cetshwayo's *inceku* and royal messenger (besides being *induna* of the uKhandempemvu) had led the Zulu deputation in December

1878 and had commanded the right wing at Koppie Allein; Gebula, an *induna* of the kwaGqikazi *ikhanda* and once a favoured messenger of King Mpande's; and Mabilwana kaMhlanganisa, *induna* of the kwaGingindlovu *ikhanda*. These men would be in a position to judge to what extent the terms now being offered them were an amelioration of those laid down the previous December.

Bulwer, whose words were translated into Zulu by Frederick B. Fynney, the local Natal Border Agent, was polite and conciliatory in his greeting, and plied the Zulu delegation with meat and sugared water (much relished by them) before settling down to business. Knowing that he was no longer obliged to adhere strictly to the terms of the ultimatum which he had officially approved on 4 December 1878, Bulwer began by waiving its minor demands for Cetshwayo to make compensation in cattle for border incidents in 1878 and to surrender the perpetrators for trial in Natal. Cetshwayo had been fixated on this issue, especially since it affected the sons of his favourite, Sihayo, and the Zulu delegation heard Bulwer with unfeigned relief. Bulwer then reiterated the stipulation that missionaries must be readmitted to Zululand and be ensured of Cetshwayo's protection, a matter close to Frere's evangelical heart. The Zulu delegates did not demur. Nor did they object when Bulwer required safe conduct for troops to bury the British dead at Isandlwana without any delay.[6]

That was the easy part. The ultimatum had required that Cetshwayo effectively abolish the Zulu military system: an impossible demand for Cetshwayo to accept. Before the meeting on 16 April Bulwer and Frere had carefully discussed this issue. While they would greatly have preferred to have seen the Zulu army disbanded and the institution of *amabutho* abandoned, they feared that to require this would scupper any hope for an agreement. They consequently came to the reluctant conclusion that it would be enough for the security of Natal to deprive Zulu warriors of all their firearms. Bulwer therefore informed the delegates that as a first step the amaZulu must not only give up the hundreds of Martini-Henry rifles and the two 7-pounders they had captured in the war, but that they must also surrender the many thousands of other firearms in Zulu hands. The Zulu delegation had been anticipating this demand for they knew that the disarmament of potentially hostile African societies had been a central platform of

British policy in southern Africa for some time. They argued only that it would take time to gather and deliver the rifles and other firearms to the specified collection points along the Natal border, and that likely resistance by many *amabutho* would have to be overcome. Bulwer did not see this proviso as unreasonable, and gave the Zulu two months in which to comply.

In their prior discussions about diminishing the Zulu military threat to Natal, Frere and Bulwer had decided that besides depriving the *amabutho* of their firearms, they would have to rely on political checks to Cetshwayo's power rapidly undermining his command over the military potential of his subjects.[7] So, having secured the Zulu delegates' agreement to relinquish all their guns, Bulwer proceeded to his political stipulations. First, though, he declared that the British government no longer required the abolition of the *ibutho* system, and a ripple of approval and relief ran through the assembled Zulu dignitaries because they too had seen this issue an immovable obstacle. But this welcome concession was only the sweetener. For Bulwer went on to reiterate one of the central stipulations of the original ultimatum: a British Resident must be stationed permanently in Zululand. His commission would not only be to ensure that any agreements the British and Zulu might reach were carried out in full. It was also to be his responsibility to advise Cetshwayo on the effective and humane government of his kingdom. Nor did his remit stop there. Cetshwayo was to undertake to follow his counsel in all his external relations with other states, and never to go to war without his express consent. Consternation rippled through the semi-circle of Zulu delegates when Bulwer's words were translated for them.

Bulwer had not finished, however, and he went on to modify what he had said. He explained that by accepting a British Resident Cetshwayo would not be agreeing to the British annexation of the Zulu kingdom. What he would be doing would be to place himself under British protection as an ally of Queen Victoria's, and this meant security from any external enemy. In making this final assurance, Bulwer and Frere had been looking to precedent elsewhere in the British Empire. Britain ruled half the enormous landmass of India through allied and dependent princely states in precisely the fashion Bulwer was proposing for the Zulu kingdom, a practice with which

Frere, with his extensive administrative experience in India, was entirely familiar. By following the Indian precedent and offering positive British protection to Cetshwayo as an ally, Bulwer was of course going a considerable step beyond the terms of the previous year's ultimatum that had stopped well short of such a commitment. Both he and Frere were well aware that in making this undertaking they were tying their government far more closely to the future integrity of the Zulu kingdom than it might wish, but it seemed necessary to do so in order sweeten the pill for the amaZulu.[8] So when Mnyamana began to protest against the imposition of a Resident and characterised it as an intolerable affront to Cetshwayo's sovereign authority, Bulwer retorting by hammering home the advantages of accepting guaranteed British protection. In particular, he reminded Mnyamana that now that the ZAR had regained its independence it was likely to resurrect its claims to the Disputed Territory, and British support would be essential in thwarting them.

The day was now drawing in, and Bulwer proposed that the delegation go back across the river to discuss his terms, and return the following morning with their answer. Discussion that night in the Zulu camp was long and urgent. The leading notables of the delegation were in favour of accepting Bulwer's terms as the very best they could hope for, but most of them feared Cetshwayo's response if they did so. The wisdom of including Ziwedu in the delegation now became apparent. He counselled acceptance, and as a prominent member of the royal house could speak for the king and his royal kin, and was sufficiently intimate with Cetshwayo to mollify him if it proved necessary.

Their fateful decision taken, the members of the delegation snatched a few hours' sleep before crossing the river once again and reappearing before Bulwer and his associates under the Ultimatum Tree. Mnyamana announced their acceptance of the British terms, and business was rapidly concluded with a minimum of fuss. The four British representatives all signed the prepared document specifying the terms of the treaty. Then, with Fynney guiding their hands, Ziwedu, Mnyamana and Godide made their crosses on the paper. At 10.00 on Thursday 17 April 1879 the day's business concluded with the escort of the Buffs crashing to the salute. The Zulu delegates – in mingled relief, regret, bemusement and trepidation – began their journey home to oNdini to tell Cetshwayo what they had agreed to in his name.

General Clifford, in consultation with Bulwer and Frere (who was back in Pietermaritzburg), resolved that until the Zulu king had complied with all the terms of the treaty his representatives had assented to that British forces must remain stationed along the Zulu borders. Their presence would maintain the pressure not only on Cetshwayo and his advisers, but on those *amabutho* – especially the younger and feistier ones – that might be contemplating further resistance. However, there were far too many troops in Natal for that purpose, especially now that an armistice had been concluded with the ZAR.[9] Accordingly, arrangements were immediately set in train to return the several naval contingents to their ships and to send back the bulk of the British troops that had arrived from St Helena, Mauritius, Ceylon and England, along with the batteries of artillery. The five battalions of the NNC and the Natal Native Horse were rapidly disbanded. Only two battalions of infantry were retained for the time being to reinforce those Chelmsford had commanded at the beginning of the war, namely the 3/60th Rifles and the 94th. Because it would be difficult to keep all the units of colonial mounted volunteers in the field for much longer, Clifford decided to retain the Dragoon Guards when the 17th Lancers sailed for Britain. The three supernumerary major-generals would also leave for home.[10]

All in all, the rushing out to South Africa of all those unnecessary reinforcements represented a heavy and undesirable charge on the exchequer that would give Gladstone's Liberal opposition in parliament effective ammunition for months to come. So too would the terms of the Pretoria Convention, finally signed on 18 June 1879 after considerable wrangling between the Boer and British commissioners.[11] Its convoluted articles conceded the ZAR the substance of independence while appearing to retain ultimate British control with the placing of a British Resident in Pretoria to represent the Queen's nebulous 'suzerainty'. With good reason, the Liberals saw in this arrangement future grounds for acrimonious squabbling over the precise meaning of 'suzerainty' that must bedevil relations between the ZAR and Britain. What the Liberals could not foresee was the discovery in 1886 of gold in huge paying quantities on the Witwatersrand. This gold would rapidly present the ZAR with unanticipated economic and political clout in the affairs of South Africa. To counteract this threat to British hegemony in the region, a Tory government of the future would revive the confederation agenda that had foundered in disaster in 1879. In its redoubled determination to achieve South African confederation, in 1899 it would tip the whole region into a devastating war to carry its policy through by force of arms.[12]

If the Liberals criticised the Pretoria Convention as potentially divisive and unsatisfactory, then they positively lambasted the treaty of 17 April 1879 with the amaZulu as unworkable and the likely source of fresh armed conflict. As anticipated, in the matter of handing over all Zulu firearms Cetshwayo encountered much opposition from his younger *amabutho*, from influential members of the royal house such as the bellicose Dabulamanzi, and from leading *izikhulu* and commanders such as Ntshingwayo.[13] The difficulties were made greater by the dispersal of the army and the reluctance of the *amabutho* to report to their *amakhanda*. It consequently took three months, rather longer than the stipulated two, before the British eventually declared themselves satisfied that the firearms had been surrendered as required – not because they believed this to be the case, but because they did not wish to jeopardise Cetshwayo's authority further. In any event, the way was now clear to implement the next stage in the treaty.

Accordingly, on 2 July 1879 the British Resident in Zululand finally took up his post close by the Norwegian mission station in the hills four miles north of oNdini. He was Henry Francis Fynn, Jnr, the son of one of the original hunter-traders at Port Natal during King Shaka's reign, and a long-standing Natal official. Bulwer had selected him because he was fluent in Zulu, possessed an extensive and sympathetic knowledge of Zulu customs and institutions, and was liked and respected in turn by the Zulu people. Moreover, Fynn had known Cetshwayo for many years and the two men enjoyed a close and cordial friendship.[14]

With Fynn finally established as British Resident in Zululand, Clifford believed his mission had been accomplished, and all British forces other than the regular South African peacetime garrison began their march to Durban for embarkation. By 19 July 1879 they were all gone, and Clifford's replacement as General Officer Commanding in South Africa, Lieutenant-General the Hon. Sir Leicester Smyth,

KCMG, was on his way out from England. Frere was not far behind Clifford in leaving South Africa. His harassed and disappointed government recalled him on 1 August 1879 and replaced him as High Commissioner with Sir Hercules Robinson, GCMG, who had enjoyed a long and successful career as a colonial governor.[15] Frere, grim and disappointed, sailed from Cape Town with his wife and four daughters on 17 September 1879. He would never again hold public office.[16] As for Beaconsfield's embattled Tory administration, it would not long survive the fallout from its disastrous showing in Zululand and the Transvaal. In the general election of 21 April 1880 the Liberals handily defeated the Tories and Gladstone became prime minister for the second time.

As the Liberals had predicted, Fynn's sympathetic presence at Cetshwayo's side would not be enough to prevent the many chronically discontented and ambitious individuals among the Zulu elite from immediately hatching plots against their king, whose prestige and authority had been fatally compromised by the war of 1879. After a period of localised revolts and assassination attempts, outright civil war finally erupted in 1883. The centralised *ibutho* system unravelled as the king's authority faltered and powerful warlords such as Hamu and Zibhebhu raised their own regional armies. Cetshwayo died of poison in February 1884 and Dinuzulu, his teenage son and successor, was not able to muster sufficient support to prevail over his enemies in the continuing civil war. None of this mattered much to the authorities in Natal so long as the fighting in Zululand did not compromise the colony's security unduly. Indeed, they could not regard the self-destruction of the Zulu kingdom but with grim self-satisfaction.

However, it became another matter when freebooting Boers from the ZAR intervened actively in the conflict and began to stake out farms in the old Disputed Territory and the lands beyond. The Tories, back in power since 25 July 1886 and determined to put a brake on the ZAR's territorial ambitions, decided to invoke the treaty of 17 April 1879 and to come to Zululand's protection. British troops entered Zululand in April 1887 and the Boer freebooters, under pressure from a ZAR government that was unwilling to risk an open confrontation with Britain, withdrew from Zulu territory. But the British did not. The ZAR was not alone in showing an interest in Zulu territory.

The Germans, late-comers to colonial empire but seeking their own 'place in the sun', were also paying unwelcome attention to Zululand. To forestall them, and to prevent a disintegrating Zululand from destabilising the entire region, Lord Salisbury's government decided it must annex the unravelling kingdom. So utterly ruined was Zululand by years of civil war, and so feeble the residual power of the royal house, that the proclamation of the annexation of Zululand on 14 May 1887 was welcomed rather than resisted. Dinuzulu was deposed as king and reduced to the status of one chief among many in the new colony, and the rule of the House of Shaka was at an end.[17]

Thus, the Zulu kingdom fell, only eight years after the great Zulu victories at Isandlwana and Rorke's Drift and the negotiated peace that had ended the Anglo-Zulu War. It was not brought down by its great war with Britain, but by the civil strife unleashed by the internal consequences of that campaign, and by the destabilisation brought about by the unrelenting advance of colonialism in southern Africa during the last decades of the nineteenth century.

Afterword

This alternate history of the Anglo-Zulu War diverged from the true path of events on 22 January 1879. It did so, not with the Zulu victory at Isandlwana, nor with the British success at Nyezane the same day, but with the Zulu capture of Rorke's Drift. The putative consequences that flowed from that event have been the subject of this book. However, for the record, the real course of the war and longer-term consequences that followed on the successful British defence of Rorke's Drift were very different.

With the failure of his first invasion of Zululand Lord Chelmsford fell back in late January 1879 to Natal to regroup, the British government rushed out reinforcements, and by May he had built up a total force of nearly 17,000 troops (7,000 of whom were African) and raised over 8,000 African levies to defend the borders of Natal.[1] Meanwhile, Colonel Pearson and No. 1 Column did not retire to Natal (as they did in this alternate history) but remained blockaded by the amaZulu in Fort Eshowe where their presence proved ineffectual because the lack of mounted men diminished their ability to raid the surrounding countryside. Colonel Wood and No. 4 Column did not fall back south-west from Fort Tinta to Koppie Allein in the Transvaal as described in this alternate history, but instead retired on 1 February to a fortified camp at Khambula in north-western Zululand. From there (in contrast to the lacklustre No. 1 Column) the mounted troops under the dynamic leadership of Lieutenant-Colonel Buller made the British presence sorely felt as far north as Luneburg through constant raids against the local Zulu population. On 26 February No. 5 Column was attached to Wood's command.

— *Afterword* —

The inadequacy of Zulu logistics and the requirement for ritual purification after battle meant that after the Zulu victory at Isandlwana King Cetshwayo was unable to press his temporary military advantage. He reopened negotiations with the British, presuming that their disaster at Isandlwana would persuade them to seek a way out of the war, not grasping that their military humiliation and the damage done to their standing in South Africa would impel them to fight on until complete victory was attained.

The amaZulu were ready for a second round of hostilities by March and their main army under Mnyamana's command marched against Wood's bothersome forces at Khambula. On the way, on 28 March, the amaZulu overwhelmed a large British raiding force on Hlobane Mountain. Wood was saved from censure for this defeat by his victory the following day (29 March) when the Zulu attacked the fort and laager at Khambula. In this, the most hard-fought and decisive battle of war, the Zulu army was routed and its morale permanently shattered. To compound this Zulu defeat, on 2 April Chelmsford's Eshowe Relief Column, secure in its wagon laager at Gingindlovu, broke a smaller Zulu army under Somopho kaZikhala and evacuated the Eshowe garrison (which was close to running out of supplies) to the Thukela. These British successes ensured that the threatened Boer revolt in the Transvaal was staved off for the time being.

Reinforced and with his forces consolidated, by May Chelmsford was in a position to launch his second invasion of Zululand. While the 1st Division, South African Field Force, under Major-General Henry Crealock moved cumbrously up the coast plain from Fort Tenedos enforcing Zulu submissions, the 2nd Division under Major-General Edward Newdigate (accompanied by Chelmsford and his staff) advanced east into the Zulu heartland from its depot at Dundee. By following this line of advance the 2nd Division avoided the disastrous route past Isandlwana where the British dead lay unburied until patrols commenced their interment on 21 May. Wood's force, renamed the Flying Column, advanced southwards on 5 May from Khambula to effect a junction with the 2nd Division on 3 June. The joint columns devastated the Zulu countryside along their line of march towards oNdini in order to break the Zulu spirit of resistance, and many amaZulu were persuaded to surrender rather than face the loss of their homes and livestock. The war sprang momentarily into the international news when Prince Louis Napoleon, the Bonapartist claimant to the French throne and an observer on Chelmsford's staff, was killed in a minor skirmish on 1 June at the Tshotshosi River.

On 26 May the British government, having finally lost faith in Chelmsford's abilities as a general, appointed General Sir Garnet Wolseley to replace him and bring the unacceptably expensive and prolonged war to a speedy conclusion. It took Wolseley six weeks to reach the theatre of operations, however, and Chelmsford, who learned of his supersession only on 16 June, was spurred on to win a conclusive victory before his rival could arrive and steal his thunder. Determined to fight, he consequently dismissed all of Cetshwayo's increasingly desperate attempts to parley. With a final battle unavoidable, Cetshwayo summoned his army to assemble for a last time at oNdini to confront Chelmsford, thereby abandoning the coastal districts to the sluggish 1st Division. On 4 July Chelmsford's joint force, drawn up in an impenetrable infantry square, conclusively routed the Zulu army under Ziwedu kaMpande at the battle of Ulundi. Thoroughly beaten, the Zulu army dispersed, never again to reassemble, and Cetshwayo fled north towards the remote Ngome forest.

Victory achieved, Chelmsford resigned his command on 5 July. He would never hold another command in the field. A disgruntled Wolseley was left with the unglamorous task of concluding the pacification of Zululand. To that end, during July he broke up the two British divisions, retaining only enough men in the field to form two flying columns. The coastal chiefs formally surrendered on 19 July, and during the course of August those of central and northern Zululand followed suit. By 8 September Baker Russell's Column had subdued the last Zulu resistance in north-western Zululand. Likewise, Clarke's Column secured the submission of the southern part of the country by 21 September. Meanwhile, any possibility of organised resistance ended with the capture of the fugitive Cetshwayo on 28 August. The former king was sent as a prisoner to exile in the Cape, and other Zulu leaders formally surrendered to Wolseley on 1 September. They accepted the terms Wolseley imposed on them whereby the Zulu monarchy and military system were abolished, and the kingdom broken into thirteen independent and militarily feeble chiefdoms under appointed chiefs.

The last British troops evacuated Zululand by the end of September 1879, but the unfortunate country's travails were only just beginning in earnest. Wolseley's settlement rapidly broke down as strife erupted between the thirteen appointed chiefs and was compounded by their deliberate victimisation of the royalist party – known as the uSuthu. The Liberal government in Britain that had come to power in 1880 began to rethink the Zululand settlement it had inherited from the Tories, not least because the situation in South Africa had changed drastically since the end of the Anglo-Zulu War. The threat posed by Sekhukhune had been removed by the swift and successful Second Anglo-Pedi War of late 1879, and Moorosi's revolt in Basutoland had also been suppressed.[2] But in September 1880 the Basotho broke into a full-scale rebellion, known as the Gun War, forcing the Cape forces to agree to a ceasefire in February 1881 that marked the first steps towards the dismantling of colonial rule in Basutoland.[3] However, if the Gun War shook the edifice of confederation, the First Anglo-Boer War of 1880–1 (the Transvaal Rebellion) demolished it. By the Pretoria Convention of 3 August 1881 the British ceded the Transvaal the substance of independence and thereby abandoned the confederation project for the foreseeable future.[4]

It was in this context that the Liberal government allowed the exiled Cetshwayo to travel to Britain in August 1882 to negotiate his restoration to his kingdom.[5] He was treated decorously and lionised by the public, and Queen Victoria granted him a brief audience. But the terms of his restoration, which he agreed to on 11 December 1882, fell far short of his expectations. He was to be returned only to the central portion of his former kingdom, hemmed in to the south by British-controlled territory and to the north by Zibhebhu, the only one of the former thirteen chiefs to be granted an independent territory, and a proven collaborator who could be relied upon to oppose Cetshwayo's aspirations. Predictably, Cetshwayo was soon at war with Zibhebhu and his allies, who conclusively defeated him on 21 July 1883. Cetshwayo, a fugitive once more, fled to British territory where he died on 4 February 1884. Fighting continued desperately after his death between his heir, the teenage Dinuzulu, and Zibhebhu. Land-grabbing Boers opportunistically intervened on Dinuzulu's side and helped him defeat Zibhebhu decisively on 5 June 1884. In return, they exacted a vast grant of land in north-western Zululand that encompassed a full third of the former kingdom. The British recognised this territory on 22 October 1886 as the independent New Republic (it was subsequently incorporated into the ZAR on 20 July 1888) but, alarmed by Boer and German aspirations, annexed the rump of Zululand on 19 May 1887. Dinuzulu rebelled against colonial rule in 1888, was defeated and exiled to St Helena. On 30 December 1897 the Colony of Zululand was annexed to the Colony of Natal, which in turn became a province of the Union of South Africa on 31 May 1910. Meanwhile, on 31 January 1906 the best agricultural and grazing land in Zululand was thrown open to white occupation, and the amaZulu became labour tenants on white-owned farms or were restricted to inadequate reserves set aside for them in the country that had once been their own.

Notes

Invented 'alternate' sources are marked with an asterisk.

Chapter 1: **Priming the Engine of War**

1. Lt.-Col. J. N. Crealock to Maj.-Gen. Sir Arthur Alison, 9 January 1879, in Clarke, *Zululand at War, p. 68.*
2. Lord Chelmsford to Sir Theophilus Shepstone, 7 December 1879, in Laband (ed.), *Chelmsford*, p. 37.
3. To avoid confusion, the General will be referred to as 'Chelmsford', even before he succeeded to the title. For a full account of his life and career, see Laband, 'Lord Chelmsford', pp. 92–126.
4. Crealock to Alison, 14 January 1879, in Clarke, *Zululand at War*, p. 74.
5. *British Parliamentary Papers* [henceforth *BPP*] (C. 2719): *Report of the Committee of General and Other Officers of the Army on Army Reorganisation* (1881), Q. 4699.
6. Preston (ed.), *Wolseley's Journal*, p. 39: 21 June 1879.
7. Molyneux, *Campaigning*, p. 32.
8. Laband, *Zulu Warriors*, pp. 166–82.
9. Benyon, 'Frere, Sir (Henry) Bartle Edward'; Benyon, *Proconsul*, pp. 144–8; Benyon, 'Isandlwana', p. 38.
10. *BPP* (C. 2222), no. 5: Frere to Hicks Beach, 10 December 1878.
11. Frere to Sir T. Shepstone, 20 November 1878, in Laband, *Kingdom in Crisis*, p. 12.
12. See Cope, *Ploughshare of War*, chaps 7–9; Laband, *Kingdom in Crisis*, pp. 10–14.
13. Hallam Parr, *Wars*, p. 101.
14. Cartoon by 'Ape', *Vanity Fair*, 22 August 1874. The reference is to Hicks Beach's perfect classical features, like the replicated bust of a Greek god.
15. Pugh, 'Beach, Michael Edward Hicks'.
16. O'Connor, 'Causes of the Anglo-Zulu War', pp. 31–5; Robson, *Road to Kabul*, *passim*; Beckett, 'Road from Kandahar, *passim*.
17. For a résumé of this correspondence, see O'Connor, *Frere*, pp. 149–51.
18. The standard language of the telegraph was Morse's code using sounding keys. Duplex and quadruplex systems allowed the simultaneous transmission of several messages in both directions, and the galvanometer made possible the transmission of messages over a long distance with a low voltage current.
19. Webb, 'Lines of Power', p. 31; Thompson, 'Great Britain and the Afrikaner Republics', pp. 289–90.

20. Chelmsford to Frere, 1 January 1879, in Laband (ed.), *Chelmsford*, p. 52.

Chapter 2: Mustering the Troops

1. War Office, *Field Exercise*, pp. 53–4.
2. Gon, *Road to Isandlwana*, pp. 134–40, 145–6.
3. Fynney, *The Zulu Army and Zulu Headmen*.
4. Clery to Alison, 13 April 1879, in Clarke, *Zululand at War*, p. 126.
5. Laband, *Historical Dictionary*, pp. 70–1,163.
6. For troop movements, see War Office, *Narrative* [henceforth *Narrative*], pp. 5, 8, 12 –13.
7. See Dominy, *Last Outpost, passim*. The transfer of troops on special duties from one area to another, the complex system of reliefs, and the detachment of units on special expeditions into the interior makes it very difficult to be absolutely precise about Fort Napier's garrison strength at any particular date.
8. The British recognised the ZAR by the Sand River Convention of 17 January 1852, and the Orange Free State by the Bloemfontein Convention of 22 February 1854.
9. For the Boer–Pedi War and confederation, see Laband, *Zulu Warriors*, pp. 42–5, 59–72.
10. Greaves and Knight, *Who's Who*, vol. I, pp. 161–2.
11. Laband, *Zulu Warriors*, pp. 189–94.
12. Thesiger [Chelmsford] to Col. F. A. Stanley, 14 September 1878, in Laband (ed.), *Chelmsford*, pp. 9–11.
13. In April 1893 Col. Stanley succeeded his elder brother as the 16th Earl of Derby.
14. *Hansard:* 3rd series, vol. 244 c. 2070: House of Commons, 28 March 1879: Colonel Stanley.
15. *Colonial Office Confidential Print*: CO 879/14, African, No. 164: Memorandum on the Zulu Question, p. 54: Hicks Beach to Frere, 21 November 1878.
16. *Narrative*, pp. 14, 18–19.
17. *Narrative*, pp. 14, 19.
18. Laband, *Historical Dictionary*, pp. 71, 72.
19. The fullest treatment of the NNC is to be found in Thompson, *Black Soldiers of the Queen*. See pp. 5–36 for the enrolment and organisation of the NNC.
20. Chelmsford to Stanley, 25 November 1878, in Laband (ed.), *Chelmsford*, p. 34.
21. Laband, *Historical Dictionary*, pp. 71,163. A squadron of Mounted Infantry consisted nominally of three officers and 110 men.
22. Callwell, *Small Wars*, pp. 57–9, 64, 66.
23. See *Narrative*, pp. 171–2: 'Transport in South Africa'; War Office, *Précis*, p. 58; Lt.-Col. Bennett, *Eyewitness in Zululand*, pp. 43–5, 49–54; Mathews, 'Chelmsford and Problems of Transport', pp. 1–9, 42–3.
24. Brookes and Webb, *Natal*, pp. 54, 75.
25. Chelmsford to Frere, 11 September 1878, in French, *Chelmsford*, p. 48.
26. Clery to Alison, 22 October 1878, in Clarke, *Zululand at War*, p. 59.
27. Clery to Alison, 22 October 1878 (very confidential), in Clarke, *Zululand at War*, p. 59.
28. Preston (ed.), *Wolseley's Journal*, p. 48: 30 June 1879.
29. Crealock to Alison, 2 March 1879, in Clarke, *Invasion of Zululand*, p. 98.

30. Sir H. Bulwer to E. Bulwer, 8 December 1878, in Clarke, *Invasion of Zululand*, pp. 213–14.

31. Preston (ed.), *Wolseley's Journal*, p. 48: 30 June 1879.

32. 'Assistant' referred to the rank of Crealock's military appointment as Chelmsford had no other secretary. The originals of his watercolours are in the Sherwood Foresters Museum in Nottingham, England, and a selection has been published in Brown (ed.), *Road to Ulundi*.

33. In contrast, that thrusting, progressive and very professional soldier, Sir Garnet Wolseley, favoured the College's graduates in his staff appointments, and habitually assembled his 'ring' from officers chosen for their proven gallantry and efficiency rather than for their seniority. See Spiers, *Late Victorian Army*, pp. 67–9, 109–11, 157.

34. Officers in the British Army held substantive rank based on their seniority in their regiments, but between the ranks of captain and lieutenant-colonel could concurrently hold a higher rank in the Army as a reward for distinguished service in the field, when serving in a staff appointment, or when it became necessary on campaign to hold a more senior command.

35. Crealock to Alison, 26 August 1878, in Clarke, *Zululand at War*, p. 53.

36. Clery to Alison, 6 December 1878, in Clarke, *Zululand at War*, p. 52.

37. Gon, *Road to Isandlwana*, p. 147; Laband, 'Crealock, John North'.

38. H. Bulwer to E. Bulwer, 8 December 1878, in Clarke, *Invasion of Zululand*, pp. 212–14.

39. Clery to Alison, 1 February and 18 March 1879, in Clarke, *Zululand at War*, pp. 81, 124.

40. Crealock to Alison, 9 December 1878, in Clark, *Zululand at War*, p. 66.

Chapter 3: **Planning the Invasion**

1. Harness, 'Zulu War', pp. 478–9.

2. For laagering procedure as laid down by Chelmsford, see Lieutenant-General Commanding, *Special Instructions*, pp. 10–11: items 15 –26.

3. See Anon., *Regulations for Field Forces in South Africa 1878*, p. 3: item 19.

4. Laband and Thompson, *Anglo-Zulu War*, pp. 68–9.

5. Memorandum by Chelmsford on the military requirements of the Natal Colony with regard to its north-eastern border should offensive or defensive measures against Zululand be considered necessary, 23 October 1878, in Laband (ed.), *Chelmsford*, pp. 19–22; Laband, 'Bulwer, Chelmsford and the Border Levies', pp. 150–3; Laband and Thompson, *Anglo-Zulu War*, pp. 35–9, 68–9.

6. H. Bulwer to E. Bulwer, 19 January 1879, in Clarke (ed.), *Invasion of Zululand*, p. 215.

7. Frere to Hicks Beach, 30 September 1878, in Martineau, *Frere*, vol. II, p. 238.

8. Hallam Parr, *Wars*, pp. 170–1; Laband, *Kingdom in Crisis*, pp. 12–14; Williams, *Running the Show*, pp. 157–8.

9. *Narrative*, pp. 18–19, 141–6.

10. While an improvement over earlier maps such as Lt.-Col. A. W. Durnford's *Sketch of Zululand &c. Compiled from Original Sources and from Personal Observation & Information* of September 1878, even the Intelligence Branch of the Quartermaster-General's Department of the War Office's *Military Map of*

Zulu Land Compiled from Most Recent Information, and published in March 1879, was still far from accurate.

11. Ashe and Wyatt-Edgell, *Story of the Zulu Campaign*, p. 189.
12. See Bonner, *Swazi State*, pp. 109–44, 155–7; Maylam, *African People*, pp. 92–5. In 2018 Swaziland was renamed Eswatini.
13. Laband, *Kingdom in Crisis*, pp. 59–60.
14. In sunny conditions the flashes sent from a Mance pattern heliograph could be seen up to fifty miles away with a telescope.
15. Memorandum by Chelmsford, 5 November 1878; Chelmsford to Col. Glyn, 17 December 1878, in Laband (ed.), *Chelmsford*, pp. 26 and 47.
16. Chelmsford to Wood, 4 January 1879, in Laband (ed.), *Chelmsford*, p. 53. Realistically, a horse could not go further than 30 miles a day over the difficult terrain.
17. For a selection of anxious letter addressed by Chelmsford to his commanders on the eve of the invasion, see Laband (ed.), *Chelmsford*, documents 13, 23, 24, 26, 28.
18. H. Bulwer to E. Bulwer, 8 December 1878, in Clarke, *Invasion of Zululand*, p. 213.
19. Preston (ed.), *Wolseley's Journal*, p. 48: 30 June 1879.
20. Preston (ed), *Wolseley Journal*, p. 40: 21 June 1879.

Chapter 4: **Resolving to Resist**

1. For the Zulu handling of the ultimatum crisis, see Laband, *Rope of Sand*, pp. 196–205.
2. The major axis of oNdini is 640 metres and the minor 507 metres.
3. Dlamini, *Two Kings*, pp. 43–6.
4. Laband, *Eight Zulu Kings*, pp. 171–2.
5. Vijn, *Cetshwayo's Dutchman*, p. 15: 24 November 1878.
6. N. L. G. Cope, 'Defection of Hamu', pp. 43–4.
7. Laband, 'Cohesion of the Zulu Polity', pp. 6–7.
8. Webb & Wright (eds), *James Stuart Archive* [hereafter *JSA*] 4, p 344: Ndukwana.
9. Guy, *Destruction of the Zulu Kingdom*, pp. 17, 37–8.

Chapter 5: **The Zulu Way of War**

1. *JSA* 5, p. 57: Ngidi.
2. For detailed descriptions of the Zulu military system, see Knight, *Zulu Army*, pp. 46–90; and Laband and Thompson, *Anglo-Zulu War*, pp. 9–19.
3. The following discussion is based on Laband, 'War-Readiness', pp. 37–41.
4. Iliffe, *Honour*, p. 142.
5. For a discussion on Zulu battle tactics, see Laband, *Rope of Sand*, pp. 39–41; Knight, *Zulu Army*, pp. 192–223.
6. Knight, *Companion to the Anglo-Zulu War*, p. 96. See also Guy, 'Imperial Appropriations', pp. 193–7.
7. For the campaign of 1838, see Laband, *Rope of Sand*, pp. 89–105.
8. The ensuing discussion on the Zulu import of firearms in the 1870s is based on the research of Guy in 'Firearms', pp. 559–60.
9. In February 1878 the British pressured the Portuguese to halt the sale of guns and ammunition to Africans through Delagoa Bay, although it took until August that year to make the ban effective.

10. Ballard, *John Dunn*, pp. 112–22.
11. See Guy, 'Firearms', p. 560; Storey, *Guns*, pp. 270–2; Knight, *Zulu Army*, pp. 167–9.
12. *JSA* 3, p. 305: Mpatshana.
13. Peers, *African Wars*, pp. 10–13; Laband and Thompson, *Anglo-Zulu War*, pp. 14–15; Laband, *Historical Dictionary*, p. 86.
14. *JSA* 2, p. 144: Mahungane. See also Pridmore, 'Introduction', pp. vii–x.

Chapter 6: Mustering for a Defensive Campaign

1. Webb and Wright (eds), *Zulu King*, p. 30.
2. Laband, *Kingdom in Crisis*, p. 54.
3. Laband, 'Zulu Options', pp. 5–7.
4. The amaMpondo would be annexed by the Cape in 1884.
5. Monteith, 'Cetshwayo and Sekhukhune', pp. 173–6; Delius, *Pedi Polity*, pp. 236, 238.
6. Vijn, *Cetshwayo's Dutchman*, p. 31.
7. Laband, 'Zulu Civilians', p. 65; Laband, 'Zulu Options', p. 5.
8. For Cetshwayo's strategic calculations, see Webb and Wright (eds), *Zulu King*, pp. 30–2, 55.
9. Norbury, *Naval Brigade*, p. 219.
10. Laband, *Kingdom in Crisis*, pp. 59–60.
11. Laband, 'Zulu Options', p. 8.
12. Kumbeka Gwabe, 'Supplement', *Natal Mercury*, 22 January 1929.
13. See Laband, 'Zulu War Rituals', pp. 1824–5.
14. *JSA* 3, p. 324: Matshana.
15. Laband, 'Fighting Stick of Thunder', pp. 240–1.
16. *JSA* 3, p. 306: Mpatshana.
17. Vijn, *Cetshwayo's Dutchman*, p. 39.
18. Nzuzi, 'Supplement', *Natal Mercury*, 22 January 1929.
19. Laband, 'Zulu Civilians' p. 64.
20. Nzuzi, 'Supplement', *Natal Mercury*, 22 January 1929.

Chapter 7: The Enemy Has Taken Our Camp

1. For a critical bibliography of works published on the Anglo-Zulu War, see Laband, 'Zulu Wars'.
2. Hallam Parr, *Wars*, p. 183.
3. Greaves and Knight, *Who's Who*, vol. II, pp. 211–13; Laband, *Historical Dictionary*, p. 256.
4. Child (ed.), *Harford*, pp. 18–21.
5. Clery to Alison, 13 April 1879, in Clarke (ed.), *Zululand at War*, p. 126.
6. Laband, 'Lord Chelmsford', pp. 105–6.
7. Knight, *Zulu Rising*, p. 431.
8. Greaves and Knight, *Who's Who*, vol. II, pp. 199–201; Laband, *Historical Dictionary*, pp. 204–5.
9. Greaves and Knight, *Who's Who*, vol. II, pp. 165–6; Laband, *Historical Dictionary*, pp. 152–3.
10. Greaves and Knight, *Who's Who*, vol. II, pp. 143–5; Laband, *Historical Dictionary*, p. 105.

11. Greaves and Knight, *Who's Who*, vol. II, pp. 57–8.
12. There is are excellent and informed discussions of the Isandlwana campaign in Beckett, *Isandlwana 1879*, pp. 47–91, and in Beckett, *Rorke's Drift and Isandlwana*, pp. 37–61. A detailed and authoritative narrative is to be found in Knight, *Zulu Rising*, pp. 233–473. See also Laband and Thompson, *Anglo-Zulu War*, pp. 99–108 for a succinct account.
13. Greaves and Knight, *Who's Who*, vol. II, pp. 172–5; Laband, *Historical Dictionary*, pp. 157–8.
14. Thompson, *Black Soldiers*, pp. 41–3.
15. Clery to Harman, 17 February 1878 [*should read* 1879], Clarke (ed.) *Zululand at War*, p. 84.
16. Child (ed.), *Harford*, p. 23.
17. Henry Curling to his mother, 2 February 1879, in Greaves and Best (eds), *Curling Letters*, p. 92.
18. Clery to Harman, 17 February [1879], in Clarke (ed.), *Zululand at War*, p. 84.
19. Clery to Alison, 18 March 1879, in Clarke (ed.), *Zululand at War*, p. 122.
20. Captain Matthew Gossett, in Knight, *Zulu War*, p. 111.
21. Clery to Harman, 17 February [1879], in Clarke (ed.), *Zululand at War*, p. 85.
22. 'Letter from an Abergavenny Man,' *Abergavenny Chronicle*, 29 March 1879, in Spiers, *Victorian Soldier*, p. 42.
23. Clery to Harman, 17 February [1879], in Clarke (ed.), *Zululand at War*, p. 85.
24. See War Office, *Field Exercise*, pp. 224–6: 'Advance by a Battalion in Fighting Formation'.
25. Arthur Harness to Co., 25 January 1879, in Clarke, *Invasion*, pp. 70–1.

Chapter 8: **Camped among the Bodies**

1. *JSA* 3, p. 301: Mpatshana ka Sodondo.
2. 'Zulu Deserter', in Laband, *Fight Us in the Open*, p. 14.
3. *JSA* 3, p. 304: Mpatshana ka Sodondo.
4. *JSA* 3, p. 304: Mpatshana ka Sodondo.
5. Swinny, *A Zulu Boy's Recollections*, p. 11.
6. 'Warrior of the uMbonambi', in Mitford, *Zulu Country*, p. 91.
7. Thompson, *Black Soldiers*, pp. 53–8. ; Laband, 'Lord Chelmsford', p. 111.
8. Mehlokazulu kaSihayo's account, in Norris-Newman, *In Zululand*, p. 81.
9. Nzuzi, 'Supplement', *Natal Mercury*, 22 January 1929.
10. *JSA* 3, p. 301: Mpatshana ka Sodondo.
11. Laband, *Kingdom in Crisis*, pp. 88, 109.
12. Laband, 'War Rituals', p. 1825.
13. The eclipse reached its greatest phase at 14.29.
14. *JSA* 3, p. 318: Mpatshana ka Sodondo.
15. Clery to Col. Harman, 17 February 1879, in Clarke, *Zululand at War*, p. 86.
16. Chelmsford to Frere, 23 January 1879, in Laband (ed.), *Chelmsford*, p. 77.
17. *Narrative*, p. 44.
18. Norris-Newman, *In Zululand*, pp. 62–3.
19. Sergeant W. E. Warren, RA, *The Bristol Observer*, 29 March 1879, in Emery, *Red Soldier*, p. 94.
20. Child (ed.), *Harford*, pp. 34–5.
21. Hamilton-Browne, *Lost Legionary*, p. 138.

22. Thompson, *Black Soldiers*, p. 69.
23. Child (ed.), *Harford*, p. 33.
24. Knight, *Zulu Rising*, pp. 161–3.
25. Hamilton-Browne, *Lost Legionary*, pp. 138–9.

Chapter 9: **We Seemed Very Few**

1. Clery to Alison, 16 May 1879, in Clarke (ed.), *Zululand at War*, p. 131.
2. Greaves and Knight, *Who's Who*, vol. I, pp. 35 –6.
3. Thompson, *Black Soldiers*, p. 65.
4. Knight, *Nothing Remains*, pp. 34–5.
5. Greaves and Knight, *Who's Who*, vol. I, pp. 159–60.
6. Pvt. Henry Hook, *The Royal Magazine*, February 1905, in Emery, *Red Soldier*, p. 126.
7. Captain Walter Parke Jones, RE, in Emery, *Red Soldier*, p. 241. See also Greaves and Knight, *Who's Who*, vol. I, pp. 50–4; Knight, *Nothing Remains*, pp. 45–6; Knight, *Zulu Rising*, p. 486.
8. Chard's 'simple, soldier-like' handwritten report on Rorke's Drift, dated January 1880, was forwarded by Captain Edwards to Queen Victoria on 21 February 1880 (Royal Archives VIC/0 46). A facsimile is reproduced in Laband and Knight (eds), *Archives of Zululand*, vol. 2, pp. 139–88 [henceforth Chard's Report]. Chard submitted a first, less developed official report on 25 January 1879. For its text and a facsimile, see Greaves, *Rorke's Drift*, pp. 353–66.
9. For comprehensive biographies of the defenders of Rorke's Drift, see Greaves, *Rorke's Drift*, pp. 230–84.
10. For a discussion on the situation at Rorke's Drift up to the Zulu attack, see Beckett, *Rorke's Drift* and *Isandlwana*, pp. 61–6.
11. Harry Lugg, *The New Devon Herald*, 24 April 1879, in Emery, *Red Soldier*, p. 131.
12. Knight, *Nothing Remains*, pp. 50–3.
13. Greaves and Knight, *Who's Who*, vol. I, pp. 72–4; Greaves, *Rorke's Drift*, pp. 106–7.
14. Laband, *Zulu Warriors*, pp. 116–18.
15. Pvt. Henry Hook, *The Royal Magazine*, February 1905, in Emery, *Red Soldier*, pp. 126–7.
16. Knight, *Zulu Rising*, pp. 488–9.
17. Laband, *Historical Dictionary*, pp. 12, 151.
18. Thompson, *Black Soldiers*, p. 65.
19. Eye-Witness, *Rorke's Drift*, p. 4.
20. Laband, 'Fight at Jim's', p. 112.
21. Greaves and Knight, *Who's Who*, vol. II, pp. 137–40; Laband, 'Fight at Jim's', pp. 112–13.
22. Laband, 'Fight at Jim's', p. 113.
23. Ludlow, *Zululand and Cetywayo*, p. 61.
24. Laband, *Kingdom in Crisis*, pp. 98–9.
25. Swinny, *Zulu Boy's Recollections*, p. 10.
26. Knight, *Zulu Rising*, p. 482–5; Laband, 'Fight at Jim's', p. 111.
27. Knight, *Zulu Rising*, p. 480.
28. Laband, 'Fight at Jim's', p. 115–16.
29. Eye-Witness, *Rorke's Drift*, p. 7.

30. Thompson, *Black Soldiers*, p. 65; Knight, *Nothing Remains*, p. 56.
31. Chard's Report, p. 156.
32. Laband and Thompson, *Anglo-Zulu War*, p. 109. The precise number of patients in the hospital remains in some doubt, and only about nine were so ill they could not be moved or take some part in the defence of the post.
33. Pvt. Frederick Hitch, *The Cambrian*, 13 June 1879, in Emery, *Red Soldier*, p. 136; Knight, *Nothing Remains*, pp. 53, 56, 71, 72; Greaves and Knight, *Who's Who*, vol. I, p. 128.
34. Laband, 'Fight at Jim's', p. 116–17; Knight, *Zulu Rising*, pp. 493–4.
35. Eye-Witness, *Rorke's Drift*, p. 3.
36. Laband, 'Fight at Jim's', pp. 117, 119.
37. Chard's Report, pp. 157–8; Knight, *Nothing Remains*, p. 78.
38. Eye-Witness, *Rorke's Drift*, p.8; Knight, *Nothing Remains*, p. 80; Knight, *Zulu Rising*, p. 507.
39. Dabulamanzi's interview, *Natal Examiner*, 16 May 1880.*
40. Swinny, *Zulu Boy's Recollections*, p. 10.
41. Laband, 'Fight at Jim's', p. 119.
42. Chard's Report, p. 161.
43. Chard's Report, p. 162; Eye-Witness, *Rorke's Drift*, pp. 8–9.
44. Chard's Report, p. 166.
45. Knight, *Nothing Remains*, pp. 80–4; Knight, *Zulu Rising*, pp. 497–8; Yorke, *Rorke's Drift*, pp. 98, 100, 102.
46. Chard's Report, p. 162.
47. Surgeon Reynolds' report in the British Medical Association *Yearbook 1878–9*, in Greaves, *Rorke's Drift*, pp. 402–3; Yorke, *Rorke's Drift*, pp. 103–8.
48. Chard's Report, p. 171.
49. Knight, *Nothing Remains*, p. 80.
50. Knight, *Nothing Remains*, pp. 38, 73, 78; Greaves and Knight, *Who's Who*, vol. I, p. 34.
51. The plan for the British garrison's withdrawal from Rorke's Drift and its execution is based on *BPP* (C. 2260), enc. 1 in no. 10: Lt. Chard to Col. Glyn, 29 January 1879: Report on the Retirement from Rorke's Drift. [Henceforth, Retirement from Rorke's Drift.]*
52. Yorke, *Rorke's Drift*, pp. 98, 100; Knight, *Zulu Rising*, pp. 508–9; Knight, *Nothing Remains*, pp. 84–6; Knight, *Rorke's Drift*, p. 55.
53. *JSA* 3, p. 304: Mpatshana.
54. Pvt. Frederick Hitch, *The Cambrian*, 13 June 1879, in Emery, *Red Soldier*, p. 137; Knight, *Nothing Remains*, pp. 85–6.
55. Elliott, *Victoria Cross*, p. 98; Greaves and Knight, *Who's Who*, vol. I, pp. 160–1.
56. Yorke, *Rorke's Drift*, pp. 105–7; Knight, *Nothing Remains*, pp. 94, 96; Knight, *Zulu Rising*, pp. 504–6.
57. Eye-Witness, *Rorke's Drift*, pp. 13–14.
58. Dabulamanzi's interview, *Natal Examiner*, 16 May 1880.*
59. Laband, 'Fight at Jim's', pp. 120, 122; Laband and Thompson, *Buffalo Border*, p. 97; Knight, *Nothing Remains*, p. 86.
60. War Office, *Field Exercise*, pp. 174–8: 'Deployments'; and pp. 90–96: 'Extended Order'.

61. *BPP* (C. 2252), enc. 2 in no. 13: copy of Major Spalding's report, n.d.
62. Laband and Thompson, *Buffalo Border*, pp. 46, 97.
63. Dabulamanzi's interview, *Natal Examiner*, 16 May 1880.*
64. Retirement from Rorke's Drift.*
65. Retirement from Rorke's Drift.*
66. Ntshelele kaMatshobana's testimony in Marriott, *Travels in Zululand*, pp. 181–2.*
67. Retirement from Rorke's Drift.*

Chapter 10: **Falling Back to Natal**

1. Quoted in Knight, *Zulu Rising*, p. 518.
2. Hamilton-Browne, *Lost Legionary*, pp. 141–2.
3. Child (ed.), *Harford*, pp. 35–6.
4. Clery to Col. Harman, 17 February [1879], in Clarke, *Invasion of Zululand*, p. 88.
5. Chelmsford to Stanley, 26 January 1879, in Laband (ed.), *Defending the Borders*, p. 5.*
6. Quoted in Knight, *Zulu Rising*, p. 519.
7. Chelmsford to Col. Stanley, 26 January 1879, in Laband (ed.), *Defending the Borders*, pp. 5–6.*
8. Dabulamanzi's interview, *Natal Examiner*, 16 May 1880.*
9. Chelmsford to Col Stanley, 26 January 1879, in Laband (ed.), *Defending the Borders*, p. 6.*
10. Laband and Thompson, *Buffalo Border*, pp. 102–4.
11. Laband and Thompson, *Buffalo Border*, pp. 95–6.
12. Capt. William Smith's interview, *Natal Post*, 27 February 1879.*
13. Sergeant Edward Daly to Mrs McCaffery, 5 February 1879, in Emery, *Red Soldier*, p. 103.
14. Retirement from Rorke's Drift.*
15. Chelmsford to Col. Stanley, 26 January 1879, in Laband (ed.), *Defending the Borders*, p. 7.*
16. Thompson, *Black Soldiers*, p. 74.
17. Laband and Thompson, *Buffalo Border*, p. 42 and Appendix IV.
18. Capt. William Smith's interview, *Natal Post*, 27 February 1879.*

Chapter 11: **Thrown Open to Zulu Invasion**

1. *BPP* (C. 2252), enc. 2 in no. 12: statement by Captain Alan Gardner, 26 January 1879; Greaves and Knight, *Who's Who*, vol. I, pp. 102–3.
2. Clery to Lady Alison, 16 May 1879, in Clarke, *Invasion of Zululand*, p. 132; see also p. 137, nn. 32, 37.
3. Chelmsford to Frere, 23 January 1879, in Laband, *Chelmsford*, p. 76.
4. *BPP* (C. 2260), enc. 1 in no. 10: Chelmsford to Glyn, 24 January 1879.*
5. Laband, 'Lord Chelmsford', pp. 110–12.
6. https://en.wikipedia.org/wiki/Victoria_Cross [accessed 13 August 2018].
7. Johnson, *Rorke's Drift*, pp. 29–31.
8. Best, 'Zulu War Victoria Cross Holders'; Mitchell, 'Medals of the Zulu War'.
9. Greaves and Knight, *Who's Who*, vol. I, pp. 34, 53, 80, 161.
10. *Supplement to the London Gazette*, 2 May 1879, p. 3178: Memorandum.
11. *Supplement to the London Gazette*, 2 May 1879, pp. 3177–8.

12. Thompson, *Black Soldiers*, p. 75; Laband and Thompson, *Buffalo Border*, pp. 100–1. For a diagram of Fort Bengough, see Laband and Thompson, *Anglo-Zulu War*, p. 92.
13. Thompson, 'Defence of Pietermaritzburg', pp. 273–84; Laband and Thompson, *Anglo-Zulu War*, pp. 184–7.
14. For an overview of the response of settlers across Natal to the invasion panic, see Thompson, 'Town and Country', pp. 234–40.
15. For an exhaustive account of Durban's defensive arrangements, see Thompson, 'Defence of Durban', pp. 295–325. See also Laband and Thompson, *Anglo-Zulu War*, pp. 188–90.
16. Laband and Thompson, *War Comes to Umvoti*, p. 38.
17. Thompson, 'Defence of Pietermaritzburg', p. 284.
18. Laband and Thompson, 'Reduction of Zululand', p. 194.
19. Laband and Thompson, *Anglo-Zulu War*, p. 38.
20. Crealock to Alison, 9 February 1879, in Clarke, *Zululand at War*, p. 94.
21. Chelmsford to Stanley, telegram, 27 January 1879, in Laband (ed.), *Chelmsford*, pp. 81–2.
22. Chelmsford to Cambridge, 1 February 1879, in Laband (ed.), *Chelmsford*, pp. 86, 88.
23. Chelmsford to Stanley, 9 February 1879, in Laband (ed.), *Chelmsford*, p. 102.
24. Harness to Co, 28 January 1879, in Clarke, *Invasion of Zululand*, p. 76; Crealock to Alison, 2 February 1879 and Clery to Harman, 17 February 1879, in Clarke, *Zululand at War*, pp. 88 and 93.
25. Crealock to Alison, 2 February 1879, in Clarke, *Zululand at War*, p. 93.
26. Chelmsford to Wood, 28 January 1879, in Laband (ed.), *Chelmsford*, p. 82.
27. According to *Narrative*, pp. 156–7, 166 white colonists were killed at Isandlwana.
28. For an excellent contemporary summary of the adverse public reaction in Natal by one predisposed to defend Chelmsford, see Crealock to Maj.-Gen. Henry Crealock, 2 March 1879, in Clarke, *Zululand at War*, pp. 98–9. For typical critical reactions in the colonial Natal press, see the *Natal Colonist*, 15 February 1879 and the *Natal Witness*, 27 February 1879.
29. Henry Bulwer to Edward Bulwer, 27 January 1878, in Clarke, *Invasion of Zululand*, p. 218.

Chapter 12: **Securing the Ncome Border against Invasion**

1. Crealock to Alison, 9 February 1879, in Clarke, *Zululand at War*, p. 93.
2. Chelmsford to Wood, 29 January and 3 February 1879, in Laband, *Chelmsford*, pp. 86, 90.
3. Manning, 'Evelyn Wood', pp. 30–7; Greaves and Knight, *Who's Who*, vol. I, pp. 184–6. See Crealock's sketch in Brown (ed.), *Road to Ulundi*, no. 42.
4. Greaves and Knight, *Who's Who*, vol. I, pp. 39–40; Laband, *Historical Dictionary*, pp. 21–2, 100. See Crealock's sketch in Brown (ed.), *Road to Ulundi*, no. 43. While on campaign officers were permitted to adopt their own preferred style of dress, and this often comprised a strange assortment of jackets and headgear.
5. Laband, *Historical Dictionary*, pp. 135, 144, 153, 224–5. For a succinct description of the local inhabitants and political developments before the Anglo-Zulu War, see Laband, 'Phongolo River Frontier', pp. 181–93. For a minutely detailed account, see Jones, *The Boiling Cauldron*, pp. 1–191.

6. Laband, *Historical Dictionary*, pp. 64–5.
7. Laband, *Historical Dictionary*, p. 129.
8. For descriptions and diagrams of these fortifications, see Laband and Thompson, *Anglo-Zulu War*, pp. 133–4.
9. For Wood's opening operations, see Laband, *Kingdom in Crisis*, pp. 124–8; *Narrative*, pp. 50–2.
10. For a descriptions and diagram of Fort Tinta, see Laband and Thompson, *Anglo-Zulu War*, p. 175.
11. Chelmsford to Wood, 28 January 1879, in Laband, *Chelmsford*, pp. 82–3.
12. Laband and Thompson, *Anglo-Zulu War*, p. 137.
13. Chelmsford to Wood, 3 February 1879, in Laband, *Chelmsford*, pp. 91–2.
14. Harness, 'Zulu War', pp. 479–80.
15. Banting, *Evelyn Wood*, pp. 94–9.*
16. Chelmsford to Wood, 29 January 1879, in Laband, *Chelmsford*, p. 85.
17. *Narrative*, p. 68.
18. Chelmsford to Wood, 16 February 1879, in Laband, *Chelmsford*, p. 106; *Narrative*, p. 68.

Chapter 13: Agitation in the Transvaal against British Rule

1. See War Office, *Transvaal Territory*, pp. 50–3. *BPP* (C. 2950), Appendix II: Sketch Map of the Transvaal Territory, published in March 1880 by the British Intelligence Branch of the Quartermaster-General's Department, gives the unrealistically precise population figures of 33,739 'Dutch', 5,316 'Non-Dutch' and 774,930 'Kaffirs'.
2. Laband, *Transvaal Rebellion*, pp. 37–8, 49. For an unflattering description of the Boers and their way of life by Henry Rider Haggard, who had first entered the territory in April 1877 on the staff of Sir Theophilus Shepstone, see Haggard, *Last Boer War*, pp. 10–14.
3. For an assessment of Shepstone's lacklustre administration of the Transvaal, see Theron, 'Shepstone and the Transvaal Colony', pp. 104–27.
4. Davenport, 'Kruger'.
5. Nöthling, 'Military Commanders', p. 78.
6. Laband, *Transvaal Rebellion*, pp. 20–1. See *BPP* (C. 2260), no. 11: minutes of the meetings of the Joint Committees of Pretoria and Potchefstroom at Rietvallei, 10, 11, and 13 January 1879.
7. For Frere's despatch concerning the meeting, and for the official report of his interview with the Transvaal delegate, see *BPP* (C. 2260), no. 11: Frere to Hicks Beach, 10 February 1879; official report, 4 February 1879.
8. *BPP* (C. 2260), no. 11: official report of meeting, 4 February 1879.

Chapter 14: Securing the Thukela Frontier against Invasion

1. Thompson, *Black Soldiers*, pp. 24–25, 105–6; Laband and Thompson, *War Comes to Umvoti*, pp. 108–11; Laband, *Historical Dictionary*, pp. 177–80.
2. *Narrative*, p. 22. For Fort Pearson, see Laband and Thompson, *Anglo-Zulu War*, p. 77.
3. Whitehouse (ed.), 'Widow-Making War', pp. 15–21, 53–63: Wynne's diary, 14–17 January 1879. For the pattern and construction of British fieldworks such as Fort Tenedos, see Laband, 'British Fieldworks', pp. 68–77.

4. Crealock to Alison, 14 February 1879, in Clarke, *Zululand at War*, p. 140.
5. *Narrative*, p. 23.
6. Laband, *Kingdom in Crisis*, pp. 114–16.
7. For the battle of Nyezane, see *Narrative*, pp. 23–4, 155; Laband and Thompson, *Anglo-Zulu War*, pp. 82–5; Laband, *Kingdom in Crisis*, pp. 116–21; Knight, *Fearful Hard Times*, pp. 49–73; Thompson, *Black Soldiers*, pp. 79–80.
8. Whitehouse (ed.), '*Widow-Making War*', pp. 83–5: Wynne's diary, 23–25 January 1879.
9. *Narrative*, p. 53.
10. Whitehouse (ed.), '*Widow-Making War*', pp. 84 –6: Wynne's diary, 24–27 January 1879.
11. *BPP* (C. 2260), enc. A in enc. in no. 3: Chelmsford to Pearson, 27 January 1879.
12. Whitehouse (ed.), '*Widow-Making War*', pp. 86, 90 –1: Wynne's diary, 28 January 1879; *Narrative*, pp. 53–4; Thompson, *Black Soldiers*, pp. 82–3.
13. Laband, *Kingdom in Crisis*, pp. 109, 121, 138.
14. Six wagons broke down and had to be abandoned on the road.
15. *Narrative*, p. 54; Knight, *Fearful Hard Times*, p. 85.
16. *Narrative*, pp. 54–5; Knight *Fearful Hard Times*, pp. 89–91.
17. Chelmsford to Wood, 3 February 1879, in Laband (ed.), *Chelmsford*, pp. 90, 92.
18. Chelmsford to Pearson, 2 February 1879, in Laband (ed.), *Chelmsford*, p. 89. *BPP* (C. 2308), enc. 1 in no. 16: Pearson to Chelmsford, 19 February 1879.*
19. *Narrative*, p. 55.
20. Chelmsford to Pearson, 2 February 1879, in Laband (ed.), *Chelmsford*, p. 89.
21. *Narrative*, pp. 61, 142. The colonial mounted units were the Natal Hussars, Durban Mounted Rifles, Alexandra Mounted Rifles, Stanger Mounted Rifles and Victoria Mounted Rifles.
22. Chelmsford to Cambridge, 1 February 1879, in Laband (ed.), *Chelmsford*, p. 87.
23. *BPP* (C. 2260), enc. 4 in no. 2: telegram, Colonial Secretary to High Commissioner, 28 January 1879.
24. Chelmsford to Wood, Private, 13 February 1879, in Laband (ed.), *Chelmsford*, p. 103.
25. Chelmsford to Wood, 13 February 1879, in Laband (ed.), *Chelmsford*, p. 104.

Chapter 15: **Stalemate along the Borders**

1. Chelmsford to Wood, 28 January 1879, in Laband (ed.), *Chelmsford*, p. 82.
2. Chelmsford to Cambridge, 1 February 1879; Chelmsford to Stanley, 8 February 1879, in Laband (ed.), *Chelmsford*, pp. 87–8, 102.
3. Laband, *Kingdom in Crisis*, pp. 109–10.
4. *JSA* 4, p. 147: Mtshayankomo; Gibson, *Story of the Zulus*, p. 188.
5. Webb & Wright, *Zulu King Speaks*, p. 32; Vijn, *Cetshwayo's Dutchman*, pp. 30–1; Mehlokazulu's account, *Natal Witness*, 2 October 1879.
6. Vijn, *Cetshwayo's Dutchman*, pp. 28–9. See also *BPP* (C. 2260), no. 10: statement of Ucadjana, 3 February 1879.
7. *JSA* 3, p. 317: Mpatshana; *JSA* 4, p. 148: Mtshayankomo.
8. Laband, *Kingdom in Crisis*, pp. 111, 132.
9. Laband, 'Humbugging the General', p. 49.
10. *BPP* (C. 2252), no. 20: Chelmsford's Order, 17 January 1879.
11. Webb & Wright, *Zulu King Speaks*, pp. 31, 57.

12. Laband, *Kingdom in Crisis*, pp. 132, 133.
13. Dabulamanzi's interview, *Natal Examiner*, 16 May 1880;* Greaves and Knight, *Who's Who*, vol. II, p. 140.
14. Laband and Thompson, *War Comes to Umvoti*, pp. 23–4, 35–41.
15. Laband and Thompson, *Buffalo Border*, pp. 58–61.
16. *Natal Examiner*, 14 February 1879;* Stoughton, *War with the Zulus*, pp. 101–3.*
17. Chelmsford to Wood, 17 March 1879, in Laband (ed.), *Chelmsford*, p. 127.
18. Laband and Thompson, *Anglo-Zulu War*, p. 137.
19. Chelmsford to Wood, 3 February 1879, in Laband (ed.), *Chelmsford*, p. 91.
20. Laband and Thompson, *Buffalo Border*, pp. 88–9; Laband and Thompson, *Anglo-Zulu War*, pp. 144–5.
21. Banting, *Evelyn Wood*, pp. 99–100.*
22. Laband, *Historical Dictionary*, pp. 288–9; Greaves and Knight, *Who's Who*, vol. II, pp. 112–13.
23. *Narrative*, pp. 59–61.
24. Laband, *Historical Dictionary*, pp. 80, 118, 180.
25. *Narrative*, p. 72; Laband, *Historical Dictionary*, pp. 129, 226–7, 303.
26. Laband, *Historical Dictionary*, p. 180.
27. Laband, *Historical Dictionary*, pp. 84, 309–10.
28. Chelmsford to Wood, 3 February 1879, in Laband (ed.), *Chelmsford*, p. 91.
29. Laband, *Kingdom in Crisis*, p. 133.
30. Laband, 'Cohesion of the Zulu Polity', pp. 4–5.
31. Laband, 'Cohesion of the Zulu Polity', pp. 7, 9.
32. Laband, *Kingdom in Crisis*, p. 141.
33. Webb & Wright, *Zulu King Speaks*, p. 33; *Laband, Kingdom in Crisis*, p. 138.
34. *Narrative*, p. 23.
35. Two 7-pounders, a Gatling gun and a 24-pounder rocket tube.
36. *BPP* (C. 2260), enc. A in no. 3: Letter of Proceedings by Capt. H. F. Campbell, RN, 24 January 1879.
37. *BPP* (C. 2308), enc. 1 in no. 16: Pearson to Chelmsford, 19 February 1879.*
38. *BPP* (C. 2308), enc. 1 in no. 16: Pearson to Chelmsford, 19 February 1879.*

Chapter 16: **Fresh Threats to British Security**

1. Memorandum by Chelmsford, 20 February 1879, in Laband (ed.), *Chelmsford*, pp. 107–12.
2. Clarke, *Invasion of Zululand*, pp. 86–7; Laband and Thompson, *Buffalo Border*, pp. 98–9. For diagrams and photographs of the fort at Helpmekaar, see Laband and Thompson, *Anglo-Zulu War*, p. 96.
3. *BPP* (C. 2260), no. 12: Governor H. R. Janisch of St Helena to Hicks Beach, 14 February 1879; *Narrative*, p. 61.
4. Mathews, 'Transport and Supply', pp. 92–3.
5. The Baphuthi, who thought of themselves as distinct from their Sotho and Xhosa neighbours and spoke their own language akin to siSwazi, had become Moshoeshoe's vassals in the 1820s.
6. Storey, *Guns, Race, and Power*, pp. 257, 262, 264–5, 268–9, 274.
7. Quoted in Knight, *Zulu War*, p. 177.

8. Pietermaritzburg by way of Newcastle was 360 miles from Pretoria. Joubert would not have travelled on the Sabbath, 9 February 1879. See War Office, *Transvaal Territory*, p. 14.
9. Quoted in Van Jaarsveld, *Afrikaner Nationalism*, p. 161.
10. Van Tonder, *Boereweerstand*, pp. 124–5.*
11. War Office, *Transvaal Territory*, pp. 24–5.
12. Mackinnon and Shadbolt, *South African Campaign*, pp. 348–9.
13. Stephenson, *Frere*, pp. 217.*
14. *BPP* (C. 2308), enc. 1 in no. 18: telegram, Frere to Hicks Beach, 22 February 1879.*
15. Stephenson, *Frere*, p. 219.*
16. Le May, *Afrikaners*, pp. 78–82; Van Jaarsveld, *Afrikaner Nationalism*, p. 159; Templin, *Ideology on a Frontier*, pp. 167–70.
17. Stephenson, *Frere*, pp. 221–2.
18. *BPP* (C. 2308), enc. 3 in no. 18: telegram, Shepstone to Frere, 25 February 1879.*
19. *BPP* (C. 2308), enc. 4 in no. 18: telegram, Frere to Hicks Beach, 25 February 1879.*

Chapter 17: **The Transvaal Rebellion**

1. Quoted in Templin, *Ideology on a Frontier*, p. 173.
2. *BPP* (C. 2308), enc. 2 in no. 18: Proclamation, South African Republic, 24 February 1879.*
3. Van Tonder, *Boereweerstand*, p. 136.*
4. Van Tonder, *Boereweerstand*, pp. 138–9.*
5. For the Boer military system, see Laband, *Majuba*, pp. 37, 39–41.
6. Van Tonder, *Boereweerstand*, p. 140.*
7. War Office, *Transvaal Territory: Appendix to Précis*, pp. 22–3.
8. *BPP* (C. 2308), no. 19: Shepstone to Frere, 7 March 1879; enc. 1 in no. 19: Terms of armistice between Shepstone and Joubert, 25 February 1879.*
9. For the proceedings of the meeting of the restored ZAR government on 26 February 1879, see Van Tonder, *Boereweerstand*, pp. 140–3.*
10. *BPP* (C. 2308), no. 18: Frere to Hicks Beach, telegram, 3 March 1879; enc. 1 in no. 18: Marthinus Pretorius to Frere, telegram, 28 February 1879.*

Chapter 18: **Anxious to Conclude an Honourable Peace**

1. War Office, *Narrative*, p. 61.
2. For press reaction to disaster in Zululand, see Beckett, *Isandlwana and Rorke's Drift*, pp. 89–97.
3. *Hansard:* 3rd series, vol. 243, c. 1502: House of Lords, 20 February 1879: Viscount Sidmouth.
4. *The Times*, 13 February 1879.
5. Cambridge to Frere, private, 13 February 1879, in Clarke, *Zululand at War*, pp. 109–10.
6. War Office, *Narrative*, p. 62; and Appendix B: Despatch of Troops to Natal.
7. Cambridge to Frere, 6 March 1879, in Clarke, *Zululand at War*, p. 112.
8. Cambridge to Frere, 27 February 1879, in Clarke, *Zululand at War*, p. 110. For Cambridge's indefatigable inspections of the departing troops, see St Aubyn, *Royal George*, pp. 191–2.
9. *The Times*, 13 February 1879.

10. Burroughs, 'Imperial Defence', pp. 58, 66, 72.
11. St Aubyn, *Royal George*, p. 191.
12. Laband and Thompson, *Anglo-Zulu War*, pp. 21–2.
13. Cambridge to Frere, 6 March 1879, in Clarke, *Zululand at War*, p. 112.
14. Cambridge to Frere, 13 February 1879, in Clarke, *Zululand at War*, p. 109.
    The major generals were the Hon. Sir Henry H. Clifford, Henry H. Crealock,
    Frederick Marshall (who commanded the cavalry brigade) and Edward
    Newdigate.
15. Hughendon, *Disraeli*, pp. 257–8.*
16. Hughendon, *Disraeli*, pp. 260.*
17. See *Hansard*: 3rd Series, vol. 244 cc. 907–24; cc. 1865–1950; cc.1991–2090; vol. 245,
    cc. 20–127: House of Commons: Questions and Debate, 14, 27, 28 and 31 March,
    1879; and vol. 244 cc. 1605–1697: House of Lords: Debate, 25 March 1879.
18. For the political and financial constraints on governments at war in the Victorian
    era, see Collins, 'Defining Victory', *passim*; and Beckett, 'How Wars End',
    passim.
19. Hughendon, *Disraeli*, pp. 261–4.*
20. *BPP* (C. 2316), no. 26: Hicks Beach to Frere, telegram, 21 March 1879; no. 27:
    Hicks Beach to Bulwer, telegram, 21 March 1879.*
21. *Colonial Office Confidential Print*: CO 879/14, African, No. 164, pp. 57–8: Hicks
    Beach to Frere, 20 March 1879.
22. *Hansard: 3rd Series, vol. 244* c. 1626: House of Lords, 25 March 1879:
    Viscount Cranbrook.
23. *Hansard: 3rd Series, vol. 244* c. 1626: House of Lords, 25 March 1879:
    Viscount Cranbrook.
24. *Hansard: 3rd Series, vol. 244* c. 1916: House of Commons, 27 March 1879:
    Sir Michael Hicks Beach.

Chapter 19: **Planning for the Zulu Offensive**

1. *Narrative*, pp. 68, 143–4.
2. Van Tonder, *Boereweerstand*, pp. 146–7.*
3. Laband, *Zulu Warriors*, p. 265.
4. Van Tonder, *Boereweerstand*, pp. 149–51.*
5. *BPP* (C. 2318), sub-enc. 4 in enc. 2 in no. 10: minute, J. E. Fannin, Border Agent
   of Umvoti to Colonial Secretary (Natal), 22 March 1879.
6. Hughes, *Conversations with Cetywayo*, p. 14.*
7. Laband and Thompson, *Umvoti*, pp. 29–30.
8. *BPP* (C. 2318), enc. 2 in no. 9: Fannin to Colonial Secretary (Natal), 2 March
   1879.
9. *BPP* (C. 2318), enc. 2 in no. 9: Frere to Chelmsford, 3 March 1879.
10. Laband, 'Peace Overtures', p. 50.
11. Hughes, *Conversations with Cetywayo*, p. 16.*
12. For Cetshwayo's strategic options in March 1879, see Hughes, *Conversations with
    Cetywayo*, pp. 16–18.*
13. Hughes, *Conversations with Cetywayo*, p. 18.*
14. Hughes, *Conversations with Cetywayo*, p. 18–20.*
15. *JSA* 3, pp 296–7, 312–13: Mpatshana.
16. Laband, *Rope of Sand*, pp. 23, 271.

17. Hughes, *Conversations with Cetywayo*, pp. 20–21.*

Chapter 20: **Wood's Fortified Laager**

1. Banting, *Evelyn Wood*, pp. 102–4;* *Narrative*, pp. 159–61; 168–9; Van Tonder, *Boereweerstand*, p. 153.*
2. Mackinnon and Shadbolt, *South African Campaign*, p. 340; Gon, *Road to Isandlwana*, pp. 171, 172, 175, 206, 215, 216.
3. Banting, *Evelyn Wood*, p. 104.*
4. Mackinnon and Shadbolt, *South African Campaign*, p. 336; *Narrative*, p. 159.
5. Mackinnon and Shadbolt, *South African Campaign*, pp. 326–7, 336, 352; *Narrative*, p. 161.
6. *Narrative*, pp. 145, 171; Laband and Thompson, *Anglo-Zulu War*, p. 29.
7. The maximum distance a wagon could cover was about twelve miles a day, and draught oxen could not be kept in the yoke for more than three or four hours at a time.
8. *Narrative*, p. 171; Molyneux, 'Hasty Defences', p. 809; Laband, *Historical Dictionary*, p. 212.
9. For the accepted contemporary guidelines for the construction of defensive works such as Wood constructed at Koppie Allein, see *BPP* (C. 2505), sub-enc. C in enc. 2 of Appendix: Report on work performed by Corps of Royal Engineers, by Capt. B. Blood, R.E., 18 July 1879; Molyneux, 'Hasty Defences', pp. 807–8, 810–12, 814; Plé, *Les Laagers*, pp. 7–8, 10, 13. See also Laband, 'British Fieldworks', pp. 70–7.
10. Laband, *Historical Dictionary*, pp. 8–9.
11. Laband, *Historical Dictionary*, p. 151.
12. *BPP* (C. 2367), enc. 1 in no. 8: Wood to Chelmsford, 21 March 1879;* Banting, *Evelyn Wood*, p. 106.*
13. Banting, *Evelyn Wood*, p. 106.*
14. Banting, *Evelyn Wood*, p. 106–7.*

Chapter 21: **The Battle of Koppie Allein**

1. Hughes, *Conversations with Cetywayo*, p. 22.*
2. Hughes, *Conversations with Cetywayo*, pp. 22–3.*
3. *BPP* (C. 2367), enc. 1 in no. 8: Wood to Chelmsford, 21 March 1879; enc. 2 in no. 8: Buller to Chelmsford, 22 March 1879;* Banting, *Evelyn Wood*, pp. 107–8.*
4. *BPP* (C. 2367), enc. 1 in no. 7: Wood to Chelmsford, 21 March 1879;* enc. 2 in no. 8: Buller to Chelmsford, 22 March 1879;* Banting, *Evelyn Wood*, p. 108.*
5. Hughes, *Conversations with Cetywayo*, pp. 23–4.*
6. Greaves and Knight, *Who's Who*, vol. II, pp. 207–8.
7. Hughes, *Conversations with Cetywayo*, pp. 24–5.*
8. For the course of the battle of Koppie Allein, see *BPP* (C. 2367), enc. 1 in no. 7: Wood to Chelmsford, 21 March 1879;* enc. 2 in no. 8: Buller to Chelmsford, 22 March 1879;* Hughes, *Conversations with Cetywayo*, pp. 24–6;* Banting, *Evelyn Wood*, p. 108–13;* Randall, 'Koppie Allein', pp. 37–44.*
9. Greaves and Knight, *Who's Who*, vol. II, pp. 228–9.
10. Letter by F. Schermbrucker in *The Friend of the Free State and Bloemfontein Gazette*, 1 May 1879, in Emery, *Marching over Africa*, p. 65.

11. Laband, *Rope of Sand*, p. 101.
12. Greaves and Knight, *Who's Who*, vol. II, p. 79.
13. Greaves and Knight, *Who's Who*, vol. II, pp. 20 –1.
14. *BPP* (C. 2367), enc. 1 in no. 7: Wood to Chelmsford, 21 March 1879;* Miller, 'Buller', p. 55.

Chapter 22: **The Transvaal Regains its Independence**

1. Webb & Wright, *Zulu King Speaks*, p. 37.
2. Vijn, *Cetshwayo's Dutchman*, p. 115: Mehlokazulu's statement.
3. Hughes, *Conversations with Cetywayo*, pp. 26–7.*
4. *BPP* (C. 2318), enc. 1 in No. 10: minute, J. E. Fannin to the Colonial Secretary (Natal), 28 March 1879. Fort Buckingham, close by Kranskop, had been built in 1861 and abandoned in 1868. During the Anglo-Zulu War it was used as British outpost
5. *BPP* (C. 2318), enc. 1 in No. 10: telegram, Col. Hopton to F. S. Haden, Private Secretary, Government House, Pietermaritzburg, Monday morning [31 March 1879].
6. *BPP* (C. 2318), enc. 1 in No. 10: Bulwer to Frere, 3 April 1879.
7. Laband (ed.), *Chelmsford*, pp. 150–1: Chelmsford to Wood, [?] April 1879.
8. *Narrative*, p. 170; Thompson, *Black Soldiers*, pp. 88–9; Laband, *Historical Dictionary*, p. 178.
9. *Narrative*, Appendix B: Despatch of Troops to Natal.
10. Deléage, *End of a Dynasty*, p. 37
11. Knight, *Face to the Foe*, p. 145.
12. *BPP* (C. 2316), enc. 1 in no. 18: Chelmsford to Frere, 25 March 1879.*
13. Van Tonder, *Boereweerstand*, pp. 156.*
14. Stephenson, *Frere*, pp. 232–3*.
15. Stephenson, *Frere*, pp. 233–4*.
16. *BPP* (C. 2316), enc. 3 in no. 18: Frere to Chelmsford, 5 April 1879.*
17. Crawford, 'Lord Chelmsford's Resignation', pp. 428–9.*
18. *Narrative*, Appendix B.
19. Cambridge to Frere, 27 February 1879, in Clarke, *Zululand at War*
20. *BPP* (C. 2316), enc. 4 in no. 18: Chelmsford to Stanley, 6 April 1879, enc. 5 in no. 18: Chelmsford to Frere, 6 April 1879.*
21. Crawford, 'Lord Chelmsford's Resignation', p. 432.*
22. Deléage, *End of a Dynasty*, p. 55.
23. Crawford, 'Lord Chelmsford's Resignation', pp. 432–9.*
24. For the negotiations at Gibson's farm, see Van Tonder, *Boereweerstand*, pp. 157–64;* Stephenson, *Frere*, pp. 239–44*.
25. Laband, *Transvaal Rebellion*, p. 211.

Chapter 23: **Making Peace with the Zulu Kingdom**

1. *BPP* (C. 2316), enc. 2 in no. 19: Bulwer to Fannin, 5 April 1879.*
2. Hughes, *Conversations with Cetywayo*, p. 29.*
3. Hughes, *Conversations with Cetywayo*, pp. 29–30.*
4. *BPP* (C. 2316), enc. 3 in no. 19: Clifford to Frere, 12 April 1879.

5. For the two days of Anglo-Zulu negotiations, see *BPP* (C. 2316), enc. 1 in no. 21: Bulwer to Frere, 17 April 1879;* enc. 2 in no. 21: Clifford to Stanley, 17 April 1879;* *Durban Despatch*, 18 April 1879;* *Natal Examiner*, 18 April.*

6. Over five days, beginning on 25 April, Major Black and the garrison at Helpmekaar buried the British dead at Isandlwana without any Zulu interference.

7. Stephenson, *Frere*, p. 236.*

8. Stephenson, *Frere*, pp. 236–7.*

9. *BPP* (C. 2367), no. 58: Clifford to Stanley, 20 April 1879.*

10. *BPP* (C. 2367), no. 61: Clifford to Stanley, 22 April 1879.*

11. *BPP* (C. 2374), enc. 1 in no. 42: Pretoria Convention, 18 June 1879.*

12. McKnight, *South Africa*, pp. 158–80.*

13. For the situation in Zululand between April 1879 and May 1887, see Fellowes, *Fall of the Zulu Kingdom*, pp. 41–182.*

14. Laband, *Rope of Sand*, pp. 356–7.

15. Robinson had been successively governor of Hong Kong, Ceylon, New South Wales, Fiji and New Zealand.

16. Stephenson, *Frere*, p. 259–83.*

17. For a photograph of the proclamation of annexation, see Laband, *Atlas of the Later Zulu Wars*, p. 84.

Afterword

1. For a concise account of subsequent field operations in the Anglo-Zulu War, see Laband and Thompson, *Anglo-Zulu War*, pp. 51–65.

2. Laband, *Zulu Warriors*, pp. 265–77; Atmore, 'Moorosi Rebellion', pp. 2–35.

3. Storey, *Guns*, pp. 287–318. In 1884 the Crown Colony of Basutoland became the first of the South African High Commission Territories with considerable internal autonomy under its own chiefs.

4. See Laband, *Transvaal Rebellion*, *passim*. Britain revived the confederation scheme late in the nineteenth century and brought on the terrible Second Anglo-Boer War of 1899–1902 with its over 100,000 casualties.

5. For events in Zululand between Wolseley's settlement and 1910, see Laband, *Later Zulu Wars, passim; Rope of Sand*, pp. 325–440; *Eight Zulu Kings*, pp. 242–303.

Select Bibliography

The following sources are referred to in the footnotes.
Invented 'alternate' sources are marked with an asterisk.

Anon., *Regulations for Field Forces in South Africa 1878* (Pietermaritzburg: 1878)

Ashe, Major, and Captain E. V. Wyatt-Edgell, *The Story of the Zulu Campaign* (London: Sampson Low, Marston, Searle, & Rivington, 1880)

Atmore, Anthony, 'The Moorosi Rebellion: Lesotho, 1879', in Robert I. Rotberg and Ali A. Mazrui (eds), *Protest and Power in Black Africa* (New York: OUP, 1970)

Ballard, Charles, *John Dunn: The White Chief of Zululand* (Craighall: Ad. Donker, 1985)

* Banting, Herbert S., *Sir Evelyn Wood: Victorian General and Military Reformer* (Barnsley: Pen & Sword Military, 2011)

Beckett, Ian F. W. *Battles in Focus: Isandlwana 1879* (London: Brassey's, 2003)

——, 'The Road from Kandahar: The Politics of Retention and Withdrawal in Afghanistan, 1880–81', *Journal of Military History*, 78, 2 (Oct. 2014), pp. 1263–94

——, 'How Wars End: Victorian Colonial Conflicts', *Journal of Military History*, 82, 1 (January 2018), pp. 29–44

——, *A British Profession of Arms: The Politics of Command in the Late Victorian Army* (Norman: Univ. of Oklahoma Press, 2018)

——, *Rorke's Drift and Isandlwana* (Oxford: OUP, 2019)

Bennett, Lt.-Col. I. H. W, *Eyewitness in Zululand: The Campaign Reminiscences of Colonel W. W. Dunne, CB, South Africa, 1877–1881* (London: Greenhill, 1989)

Benyon, John, 'Isandlwana and Passing of a Proconsul', *Natalia*, 8 (December 1978), pp. 38–45

——, *Proconsul and Paramountcy in South Africa: The High Commission, British Supremacy and the Sub-Continent 1806–1910* (Pietermaritzburg: Univ. of Natal Press, 1980)

——, 'Frere, Sir (Henry) Bartle Edward, first baronet (1815–1884)', *Oxford Dictionary of National Biography* (Oxford: OUP, 2004)

Best, Brian, 'Zulu War Victoria Cross Holders', *Journal of the Anglo Zulu War Historical Society*, 1 (June 1992), https://www. anglozuluwar. com/journal [accessed 13 August 2018]

Bonner, Philip, *Kings, Commoners and Concessionaires: The Evolution and Dissolution of the Nineteenth-Century Swazi State* (Johannesburg: Ravan Press, 1983)

British Parliamentary Papers [cited as *BPP*], (C. 2222), (C. 2252), (C. 2260), (C. 2308), (C. 2316), (C. 2318), (C. 2367), (C. 2374), (C. 2505), (C. 2719), (C. 2950)

Brookes, Edgar H., and Colin C. de B. Webb, *A History of Natal* (Pietermaritzburg: Univ. of Natal Press, 1965)

Brown, R. A. (ed.), *The Road to Ulundi: The Water Colour Drawings of John North Crealock (the Zulu War of 1879)* (Pietermaritzburg: Univ. of Natal Press, 1969)

Burroughs, Peter, 'Imperial Defence and the Victorian Army', *Journal of Imperial and Commonwealth History*, XV, 1 (October 1986), pp. 55–72.

Callwell, Col. Charles E., *Small Wars: Their Principles and Practice*, 3rd edn (London: HMSO, 1906)

Castle, Ian, illustrated by Raffaele Ruggeri, *Zulu War: Volunteers, Irregulars & Auxiliaries* (Oxford: Osprey, 2003)

Chard, Lt. John R. M., 'Report on Rorke's Drift, January 1880, Sent to Queen Victoria, 21 February 1880', in Laband and Knight (eds), *Archives of Zululand*, vol. 2, pp. 139–88 [cited as Chard's report]

Child, Daphne (ed.), *The Zulu War Journal of Colonel Henry Harford, C.B.* (Pietermaritzburg: Shuter & Shooter, 1978)

Clarke, Sonia, *Invasion of Zululand 1879: Anglo-Zulu War Experiences of Arthur Harness; John Jervis, 4th Viscount St Vincent; and Sir Henry Bulwer* (Houghton: Brenthurst Press, 1979)

——, *Zululand at War: The Conduct of the Anglo-Zulu War* (Houghton: Brenthurst Press, 1984)

Collins, Bruce, 'Defining Victory in Victorian Warfare, 1860–82', *Journal of Military History*, 77, 3 (July 2013), pp. 895–929

Colonial Office Confidential Print: CO 879/14 (African)

Cope, Nicholas L. G., 'The Defection of Hamu' (unpublished B.A. Hons thesis, Univ. of Natal, 1980)

Cope, Richard, *Ploughshare of War. The Origins of the Anglo-Zulu War of 1879* (Pietermaritzburg: Univ. of Natal Press, 1999)

Corvi, Steven J., and Ian F. W. Beckett (eds), *Victoria's Generals* (Barnsley: Pen & Sword Military, 2009)

*Crawford, Benjamin. 'Extrication from a False Position: Lord Chelmsford's Resignation in April 1879', *The Society for Army Historical Research*, 81, 328 (Winter 2003): pp. 420–39

Davenport, T. R. H., 'Kruger, Stephanus Johannes Paulus [Paul] (1825–1904)', *Oxford Dictionary of National Biography* (Oxford: OUP, 2004)

Deléage, Paul, trans. Fleur Webb, ed. Bill Guest, *End of a Dynasty: The Last Days of the Prince Imperial, Zululand 1879*, (Pietermaritzburg: Univ. of KwaZulu-Natal Press, 2008)

Delius, Peter, *The Land Belongs to Us: The Pedi Polity, the Boers and the British in the Nineteenth-Century Transvaal* (Berkeley: Univ. of California Press, 1984)

Dlamini, Paulina, compiled by H. Filter, ed. and trans. S. Bourquin, *Servant of Two Kings* (Durban: Killie Campbell African Library; Pietermaritzburg: Univ. of Natal Press, 1986)

Dominy, Graham, *Last Outpost on the Zulu Frontiers: Fort Napier and the British Imperial Garrison* (Urbana, Chicago & Springfield: Univ. of Illinois Press, 2016)

Elliott, Maj. W. J., *The Victoria Cross in Zululand and South Africa: Isandhlwana and Rorke's Drift*, vol. I (London: Dean & Son, 1882)

Emery, Frank, *The Red Soldier: Letters from the Zulu War, 1879* (London: Hodder & Stoughton, 1977)

——, *Marching over Africa: Letters from Victorian Soldiers* (London: Hodder & Stoughton, 1986)

An Eye-Witness, *Defence of Rorke's Drift, January 22, 1879* (Durban: 'Natal Mercury' Press, n. d.)

* Fellowes, Gordon G., *The Fall of the Zulu Kingdom, 1879–1887* (London: Longman, 1980)

French, Maj. the Hon. Gerald, *Lord Chelmsford and the Zulu War* (London: John Lane at the Bodley Head, 1939)

Fynney, F., *The Zulu Army and Zulu Headmen. Compiled from Information Obtained from the Most Reliable Sources, and Published by Direction of the Lieut.-General Commanding for the Information of Those under His Command*, 2nd rev. edn (Pietermaritzburg: 1879)

Gibson, J. Y., *The Story of the Zulus* (London: Longman, Green, 1911)

Gon, Philip, *The Road to Isandlwana: The Years of an Imperial Battalion* (Johannesburg: Ad. Donker, 1979)

Greaves, Adrian, *Rorke's Drift* (London: Cassell, 2002)

Greaves, Adrian, and Brian Best (eds), *The Curling Letters of the Zulu War. 'There Was Awful Slaughter'* (Barnsley: Leo Cooper, 2001)

Greaves, Adrian, and Ian Knight, *Who's Who in the Zulu War. vol. I: The British;* vol. II: *Colonials and Zulus* (Barnsley: Pen & Sword Military, 2006, 2007)

Guy, Jeff, 'A Note on Firearms in the Zulu Kingdom with Special Reference to the Anglo-Zulu War, 1879', *Journal of African History*, 12, 4 (1971), pp. 557–70

——, *The Destruction of the Zulu Kingdom: The Civil War in Zululand, 1879–1884* (London: Longman, 1979)

——, 'Imperial Appropriations: Baden-Powell, the Wood Badge and the Zulu *Iziqu*', in Benedict Carton, John Laband and Jabulani Sithole (eds), *Zulu Identities: Being Zulu, Past and Present* (New York: Columbia Univ.Press, 2009)

Haggard, Sir H. Rider, *The Last Boer War* (London: Kegan Paul, Trench, Trübner, 1900)

Hallam Parr, Captain Henry, *A Sketch of the Kaffir and Zulu Wars. Guadana to Isandhlwana* (London: C. Kegan Paul, 1880)

Hamilton-Browne, Col. G., *A Lost Legionary in South Africa* (London: T. Werner Laurie, 1912)

Hansard's Parliamentary Debates (3rd Series): vol. 243 (1878); vol. 244 (1879)

Harness, Lt.-Col. Arthur, 'The Zulu War from a Military Point of View', *Fraser's Magazine*, new series XXI, 21 (April 1880): pp. 477–88.

* Hughendon, Robert, *Disraeli's Second Administration, 1874–1880* (Oxford: OUP, 1993)

* Hughes, Percival, *Conversations with Cetywayo in Zululand* (London: C. Kegan Paul, 1881)

Iliffe, John, *Honour in African History* (Cambridge: CUP, 2005)

Johnson, Barry C., *Rorke's Drift and the British Museum: The Life of Henry Hook, V.C.* (London: British Museum, 1986)

Jones, Huw M., *The Boiling Cauldron: Utrecht District and the Anglo-Zulu War, 1879* (Bisley: Shermershill Press, 2006)

Knight, Ian, *Nothing Remains but to Fight: The Defence of Rorke's Drift, 1879* (London: Greenhill, 1993)

——, *Fearful Hard Times: The Siege and Relief of Eshowe, 1879* (London: Greenhill, 1994)

——, *The Anatomy of the Zulu Army from Shaka to Cetshwayo 1818–1879* (London: Greenhill, 1995)

——, *Go to Your God like a Soldier. The British Soldier Fighting for Empire, 1837–1902* (London: Greenhill, 1996)

——, *Rorke's Drift: 'Pinned Like Rats in a Hole'* (Great Britain: Osprey Military, 1996)

——, *With his Face to the Foe. The Life and Death of Louis Napoleon, the Prince Imperial* (Staplehurst: Spellmount, 2001)

——, *The National Army Museum Book of the Zulu War* (London: Sidgwick & Jackson in association with the National Army Museum, 2003)

——, illus. Adam Hook, *British Fortifications in Zululand 1879* (Oxford: Osprey, 2005)

——, *A Companion to the Anglo-Zulu War* (Barnsley: Pen & Sword Military, 2008)

——, *Zulu Rising: The Epic Story of Isandlwana and Rorke's Drift* (London: Macmillan, 2010)

Laband, John, *Fight Us in the Open: The Anglo-Zulu War through Zulu Eyes* (Pietermaritzburg: Shuter & Shooter; Ulundi: KwaZulu Monuments Council, 1985)

——, 'British Fieldworks of the Zulu Campaign of 1879 with Special Reference to Fort Eshowe', in Laband and Thompson, *Kingdom and Colony* (1990)

——, 'Bulwer, Chelmsford and the Border Levies: The Dispute over the Defence of Natal, 1879', in Laband and Thompson, *Kingdom and Colony* (1990)

——, '"O! Let's Go and Have a Fight at Jim's!" The Zulu at the Battle of Rorke's Drift', in Laband and Thompson, *Kingdom and Colony* (1990)

——, 'The Cohesion of the Zulu Polity under the Impact of the Anglo-Zulu War: A Reassessment', in Laband and Thompson, *Kingdom and Colony* (1990)

——, 'Humbugging the General? Cetshwayo's Peace Overtures during the Anglo-Zulu War', in Laband and Thompson, *Kingdom and Colony* (1990)

——, 'Mbilini, Manyonyoba and the Phongolo River Frontier: A Neglected Sector of the Anglo-Zulu War of 1879', in Laband and Thompson, *Kingdom and Colony* (1990)

—— (ed.), *Lord Chelmsford's Zululand Campaign 1878–1879* (Stroud: Alan Sutton Publishing for the Army Records Society, 1994)

——, *Rope of Sand: The Rise and Fall of the Zulu Kingdom in the Nineteenth Century* (Johannesburg: Jonathan Ball, 1995)

——, 'Zulu Strategic and Tactical Options in the Face of the British Invasion of January 1879', *Scientia Militaria: South African Journal of Military Studies*, 28, 1 (1998), pp. 1–15

*——, (ed.), *Defending the Borders of Natal: Lord Chelmsford's Further Correspondence from the Anglo-Zulu War, 1879* (Stroud: Alan Sutton, 1999)

——, *The Atlas of the Later Zulu Wars 1883–1888* (Pietermaritzburg: Univ. of Natal Press, 2001)

——, 'Crealock, John North (1836–1895)', *Oxford Dictionary of National Biography* (Oxford: OUP, 2005)

——, *The Transvaal Rebellion: The First Boer War 1880–1881* (London: Pearson Longman, 2005)

——, 'Zulu (amaZulu) War Rituals', in Bron R. Taylor and Jeffrey Kaplan (eds), *The Encyclopedia of Religion and Nature* (London and New York: Thoemmes Continuum, 2005), pp. 1824–5

——, *Kingdom in Crisis: The Zulu Response to the British Invasion of 1879* (Barnsley: Pen & Sword, 2007)

——, 'Zulu Civilians during the Rise and Fall of the Zulu Kingdom, *c.* 1817–1879', in John Laband (ed.), *Daily Lives of Civilians in Wartime Africa from Slavery days to Rwandan Genocide* (Westport: Greenwood Press, 2007)

——, *Historical Dictionary of the Zulu Wars* (Lanham: The Scarecrow Press, 2009)

——, 'Lord Chelmsford', in Corvi and Beckett (eds), *Victoria's Generals*

——, 'The War-Readiness and Military Effectiveness of the Zulu Forces in the 1879 Anglo-Zulu War', *Natalia*, 39 (December 2009), pp. 37–46

——, 'Zulu Wars', in Dennis Showalter (ed.), *Oxford Bibliographies Online: Military History*, New York: OUP, 2012

——, '"Fighting Stick of Thunder": Firearms and the Zulu Kingdom: The Cultural Ambiguities of Transferring Weapons Technology', *War & Society*, 33, 4 (October 2014), pp. 229–43

——, *Zulu Warriors: The Battle for the South African Frontier* (New Haven and London: Yale UP, 2014)

——, *The Battle of Majuba Hill: The Transvaal Campaign, 1880–1881* (Solihull: Helion, 2017)

——, *The Eight Zulu Kings* (Johannesburg and Cape Town: Jonathan Ball, 2018)

——, and Ian Knight, *The War Correspondent: The Anglo-Zulu War* (Stroud: Sutton Publishing, 1996)

—— (series ed.), and Ian Knight (volume ed.), *Archives of Zululand: The Anglo-Zulu War 1879*, 6 vols (London: Archival Publications International, 2000)

——, and Paul Thompson, *War Comes to Umvoti: The Natal–Zululand Border 1878–79* (Durban: Department of History, University of Natal, Research Monograph No. 5, 1980)

——, and Paul Thompson, *Kingdom and Colony at War: Sixteen Studies on the Anglo-Zulu War of 1879* (Pietermaritzburg: Univ. of Natal Press; Cape Town: N & S Press, 1990)

——, and Paul Thompson, *The Illustrated Guide to the Anglo-Zulu War* (Pietermaritzburg: Univ. of Natal Press, 2000)

——, and Paul Thompson, with Sheila Henderson, *The Buffalo Border 1879: The Anglo-Zulu War in Northern Natal* (Durban: Department of History, Univ. of Natal, Research Monograph No. 6, 1983)

Le May, G. H. L. *The Afrikaners: An Historical Interpretation* (Oxford: Blackwell, 1995)

Lieutenant-General Commanding, *Special Instructions Regarding the Management of Ox Transport on the Line of March, and for Conducting the Line of March when Troops March with Ox Wagon Transport, and for Forming Wagon Laagers* (Durban: 'Mercury' Press, n.d.)

The London Gazette, 1879

Ludlow, Capt. W. R., *Zululand and Cetywayo* (London: Simpkin, Marshall, 1882)

Mackinnon, J. P., and S. H. Shadbolt, *The South African Campaign of 1879* (London: Sampson Low, Marston, Searle, and Rivington, 1880)

* McKnight, William R., *South Africa Comes of Age* (Harlow: Pearson Education, 2010)

Manning, Stephen, 'Evelyn Wood', in Corvi and Beckett (eds), *Victoria's Generals*

* Marriott, Bernard St J., *Travels in Zululand* (London: Kegan Paul, Trench, 1882)

Martineau, J., *The Life and Correspondence of the Right Hon. Sir Bartle Frere*, vol. II (London: John Murray, 1895)

Mathews, Jeffrey, 'Lord Chelmsford and Problems of Transport and Supply during the Anglo-Zulu War of 1879' (unpublished MA thesis, Univ. of Natal, 1979)

Maylam, Paul, *A History of the African People of Southern Africa: From the Early Iron Age to the 1970s* (London: Croom Helm, 1986)

Mitchell, Capt. F. K., 'The Medals of the Zulu War, 11th January to 1st September, 1879', *Military History Journal*, 4, 4 (December 1978), samilitaryhistory.org/journal. html [accessed 13 August 2018]

Miller, Stephen M., 'Redvers Buller', in Corvi and Beckett (eds), *Victoria's Generals*

Mitford, Bertram, *Through the Zulu Country: Its Battlefields and Its People* (London: Kegan, Paul Trench, 1883)

Molyneux, Maj. W. C. F., 'Notes on Hasty Defences as Practised in South Africa', *Journal of the Royal United Service Institution*, vol. XXIV (1881), pp. 806–14

——, *Campaigning in South Africa and Egypt* (London: Macmillan, 1896)

Monteith, Mary, 'Cetshwayo and Sekhukhune 1875–1879' (unpublished MA thesis, Univ. of the Witwatersrand, 1978)

Morris, Donald R., *The Washing of the Spears: A History of the Rise of the Zulu Nation under Shaka and Its Fall in the Zulu War of 1879* (London: Jonathan Cape, 1966)

Natal Colonist 1879

* *Natal Examiner*, 1879, 1880

Natal Mercury, 1929

* *Natal Post*, 1879

Natal Witness, 1879

Norbury, Fleet Surgeon Henry F., *The Naval Brigade in South Africa during the Years 1877–78–79* (London: Sampson Low, Marston, Searle & Rivington, 1880)

Norris-Newman, Charles, *In Zululand with the British* (London: W. H. Allen, 1880)

Nöthling, Cmdt C. J., 'Military Commanders of the War (1880–1881)', *Scientia Militaria: South African Journal of Military Studies*, 11: 1 (1981), pp. 76–80

O'Connor, Damian P., *The Zulu and the Raj: The Life of Sir Bartle Frere* (Knebworth: Able Publishing, 2002)

——, 'The Causes of the Anglo-Zulu War of 1879', *Natalia*, 39 (December 2009), pp. 28–36

Peers, Chris, *The African Wars: Warriors and Soldiers of the Colonial Campaigns* (Barnsley: Pen & Sword Military, 2010)

Plé, James, *Les Laagers dans la Guerre des Zoulous* (Paris: Libraire Militaire de J. Dumanine, L. Baudoin, 1882)

Preston, Adrian (ed.), *The South African Journal of Sir Garnet Wolseley 1879–1880* (Cape Town: A. A. Balkema, 1973)

Pridmore, Julie, 'Introduction', *The Journal of William Clayton Humphreys . . . Trader and Hunter in the Zulu Country during the Months July–October 1851*, No. 6, Colin Webb Natal and Zululand Series (Durban: Killie Campbell Africana Library; Pietermaritzburg: Univ. of Natal Press, 1993)

Pugh, Martin, 'Michael Edward Hicks Beach, first Earl St Aldwyn (1837–1916)', *Oxford Dictionary of National Biography* (Oxford: OUP, 2004)

* Randall, Sidney, 'The Battle of Koppie Allein', *Military History Journal*, 6, 1 (June 1983), pp. 37–44

Robson, Brian, *The Road to Kabul: The Second Afghan war 1878–1881* (Stroud: Spellmount, 2003)

St Aubyn, Giles, *The Royal George 1819–1904: The Life of HRH Prince George Duke of Cambridge* (New York: Alfred A. Knopf, 1964)

Snook, Lt.-Col. Mike, *Like Wolves on the Fold: The Defence of Rorke's Drift* (Barnsley: Frontline Books, rev. edn, 2010)

——, *How Can Man Die Better: The Secrets of Isandlwana Revealed* (Barnsley: Frontline Books, rev. edn, 2018)

Spiers, Edward M., *The Late Victorian Army 1868–1902* (Manchester: Manchester UP, 1992)

——, *The Victorian Soldier in Africa* (Manchester and New York: Manchester UP, 2004)

* Stephenson, Conrad H., *Sir Bartle Frere: Proconsul of Empire* (London: Hutchinson, 1934)

Storey, William Kelleher, *Guns, Race and Power in Colonial South Africa* (Cambridge: CUP, 2008)

* Stoughton, Frederick, *The War with the Zulus* (London: Sampson Low, Marston, Searle & Rivington, 1880)

Swinny, G. H., ed. C. de B. Webb, 'A Zulu Boy's Recollections of the Zulu War', *Natalia* 8 (December 1878), pp. 8–21

Templin J. Alton, *Ideology on a Frontier: The Theological Foundation of Afrikaner Nationalism, 1652–1910* (Westport and London: ABC-CLIO, 1984)

The Times, 1879

Theron, Bridget, 'Theophilus Shepstone and the Transvaal Colony, 1877–1879', *Kleio*, 34 (2002), pp. 104–27

Thompson, Leonard, 'Great Britain and the Afrikaner Republics, 1879–1899', in Wilson and Thompson (eds), *Oxford History of the British Empire*, vol. 2, *South Africa 1870–1966* (Oxford: Clarendon Press, 1971)

Thompson, Paul S., 'The Defence of Durban', in Laband and Thompson, *Kingdom and Colony* (1990)

——, 'Town and Country and the Zulu Threat, 1878–9: The Natal Government's Arrangements for the Protection of Settlers', in Laband and Thompson, *Kingdom and Colony* (1990)

——, '"The Zulus Are Coming!" The Defence of Pietermaritzburg, 1879', in Laband and Thompson, *Kingdom and Colony* (1990)

——, *Black Soldiers of the Queen: The Natal Native Contingent in the Anglo-Zulu War* (Tuscaloosa: Univ. of Alabama Press, 2006)

Van Jaarsveld, Floris A., *The Awakening of Afrikaner Nationalism 1868–1884* (Cape Town: Human and Rousseau, 1961)

* Van Tonder, Brig. Christoffel Anton, *Boereweerstand teen Britse Regering in Transvaal, 1877–1879* (Pretoria: Tafelberg, 1982)

Vijn, Cornelius, ed. Bishop J. W. Colenso, *Cetshwayo's Dutchman: Being the Private Journal of a White Trader in Zululand during the British Invasion*, (London, Longmans, Green, 1880)

War Office, *Field Exercise and Evolutions of Infantry* (London: HMSO, pocket edition, 1877)

——, Intelligence Department, *Précis of Information concerning South Africa: The Transvaal Territory* (London: HMSO, 1878)

——, Intelligence Division, *Narrative of the Field Operations Connected with the Zulu War of 1879* (London: HMSO, 1881)

——, Intelligence Division, *Précis of Information Concerning Zululand, Corrected to December 1894* (London: HMSO, 1895)

Webb, Colin de B., 'Lines of Power: The High Commissioner, the Telegraph and the War of 1879', *Natalia*, 8 (December 1978), pp, 31–7

——, and John Wright (eds), *The James Stuart Archive of Recorded Oral Evidence Relating to the History of the Zulu and Neighbouring Peoples*, 6 vols (Pietermaritzburg: Univ. of Natal Press; Durban: Killie Campbell Africana Library, 1976, 1979, 1982, 1986, 2001, 2014) [cited as *JSA*]

—— (eds), *A Zulu King Speaks: Statements Made by Cetshwayo kaMpande on the History and Customs of His People* (Pietermaritzburg: Univ. of Natal Press; Durban: Killie Campbell Africana Library, 1978)

Whitehouse, Howard (ed.), *'A Widow-Making War': The Life and Death of a British Officer in Zululand* (Nuneaton: Paddy Griffith Associates, 1995)

Williams, Stephanie, *Running the Show: The Extraordinary Stories of the Men Who Governed the British Empire* (London: Penguin Books, 2012)

Yorke, Edmund, *Rorke's Drift 1879: Anatomy of an Epic Zulu War Siege* (Stroud: Tempus, 2001)

Acknowledgements

This book would never have been attempted had not Michael Leventhal, the publisher of Greenhill Books, suggested that I consider writing an alternate history of the Anglo-Zulu War. From the moment when I decided to run with the idea, he has closely and enthusiastically supported and encouraged me every inch of the way, and it has been the greatest pleasure to work with him.

The writing of alternate history has been a new and invigorating venture for me, and I am extremely grateful for the helpful and informed comments by the publisher's anonymous readers of the manuscript, by Adrian Greaves and, above all, by Ian Knight (my old comrade-in-arms) who also wrote the stimulating Foreword. They all have given me valuable pointers and suggestions and have saved me from any number of inconsistencies and plain mistakes. Donald Sommerville, my hawk-eyed editor, has continued that process and has furthermore purged the manuscript of textual infelicities. Nevertheless, this alternate history in its final form is my responsibility alone, and those who commented on the manuscript or made corrections cannot be held accountable for any errors or implausibilities that still linger in the finished book.

I also owe a real debt to Peter Wilkinson who, with practised cartographical skill and infinite patience, turned my maladroit sketches into clear and elegant maps. Ian Knight stepped to the fore by providing the bulk of the illustrations from his enviable private collection. In this regard my thanks go also to Ron Sheeley for the use of material from his collection, as well as to the repositories that permitted the reproduction of images under their curatorship.

Fenella has succoured me throughout the gestation and writing of yet another book. I am not sure, though, that I was entirely successful in dispelling her misgivings about what I have found to be the fascinating and exacting genre of alternate history.

Index

*Words from Nguni languages are entered
under the root rather than under the prefix.*

Allen, Cpl. W. 81
Afrikaner nationalism 143–4
Anderson, Cpl. W. 72
Anglo-Boer War, First 205
Anglo-Afghan War, Second 10, 16, 17
Anglo-Pedi War, First 16, 66, 105, 162,
    182
Anglo-Pedi War, Second 205
Assegai River 106, 161

Baker, Cmdt. F. 131
Balte Spruit 106
Bapedi 9, 15, 16, 23, 27, 41, 42, 45, 108, 113,
    149, 162
Barrow, Maj. P. H. S. 120, 123, 134
Barton, Capt. G. 115, 187
Basotho 8, 41, 42, 45, 140, 205
Batshe River 70, 71, 85
Bellairs, Col. W. 122
Bemba's Kop 27, 28, 106, 107
Bengough, Maj. H. M. 98–9
Black, Maj. W. F. 129
Blood River, *see* Ncome River
Blood River, battle of, *see* Ncome, battle of
Boer military system, *see* Transvaal
    commandos
Boer–Pedi War 15
amaButho, see Zulu *amabutho*
Bourne, Clr.-Sgt. F. 78, 83, 98
Bradshaw, Capt. R. 140
British African mounted units

Natal Native Horse 130, 167, 168, 178,
    179, 180, 198; Edendale Troop 130;
    Mounted Basutos (Hlubi's Troop) 69,
    130, 175
Natal Native Mounted Contingent 18,
    57, 69, 70, 72, 130
British African infantry units
    Border Guard 25, 101
    Border Guard Reserves 25, 101
    Fairlie's Swazi 131
    Natal Native Contingent 18, 26, 60,
        85, 90, 91, 103; 1st Battalion 115, 198;
        2nd Battalion 115, 198; 3rd Battalion
        115, 198; 4th Battalion 187, 198; 5th
        Battalion 187, 198; 1st Regiment 27, 99,
        102, 115; 2nd Regiment 117, 118, 120,
        121, 134; 3rd Regiment 56–7, 62–3, 65,
        66, 72, 86, 91, 99, 102, 187
    Natal Native Pioneer Corps 18, 57, 115
    River Guards 114
    Special Border Police 25
    Wood's Irregulars 131, 168, 173, 175, 178,
        179, 183
British Army Hospital Corps 152; Army
    Medical Department 67, 152
British Army Service Corps 152
British Royal Artillery 14
    N Battery, 5th Brigade 15, 16
    M Battery, 6th Brigade 152
    N Battery, 6th Brigade 152
    No. 8 Battery, 7th Brigade 140
    No. 10 Battery, 7th Brigade 152
    No. 11 Battery, 7th Brigade 15, 16, 57,
        168, 172, 179, 180

Royal Marine Artillery 17, 122
British campaign formations
Baker Russell's Column 204
Clarke's Column 204
Coastal Column 187, 188
Eshowe Relief Column 203
Flying Column 203, 204
Natal Field Force 188–9
No. 1 (Right) Column 26, 27, 28, 55, 115–20, 121–3, 124, 131, 133–5, 140, 165, 187, 202
No. 2 Column 26, 27, 57, 69, 98–9, 114–15
No. 3 (Centre) Column 3, 26, 27, 28, 47, 53, 55–65, 66, 67, 85–6, 88–92, 96, 128–9, 139, 140
No. 4 Column 26, 27, 28, 35, 95, 105, 106, 107–9, 129–30, 132, 164, 167–9, 170, 172–3, 175, 178–9, 180, 181–4
No. 5 Column 26, 27, 45, 106, 108–9, 129, 148, 161, 162, 202
South African Field Force: 1st Division 203; 2nd Division 203, 204
British cavalry 18, 102
1st (King's) Dragoon Guards 152, 188, 198
17th (Duke of Cambridge's Own) Lancers 152, 188, 198
British Commissariat and Transport Department 19
British infantry 13, 14
2/3rd Regt. (East Kent, The Buffs) 15, 118, 121, 123, 194
2/4th (King's Own Royal Regt) 17, 123–4, 129, 148
1/13th (1st Somersetshire) Prince Albert's Lt. Inf. 15, 16, 26, 106, 168, 172, 183
2/21st Regt. (Royal Scots Fusiliers) 152, 187
1/24th (2nd Warwickshire) Regt. 15, 16, 26, 40, 57, 67, 82, 83, 128
2/24th (2nd Warwickshire) Regt. 15, 16, 26, 40, 57, 64, 66, 75, 86, 90, 91, 99, 128
57th (West Middlesex) Regt. 152
58th (Rutlandshire) Regt. 152, 188, 190
3/60th Regt. (King's Royal Rifle Corps) 152, 187, 198

80th Regt. (Staffordshire Volunteers) 15, 16, 26, 97, 107, 129, 142, 148, 161
88th Regt. (Connaught Rangers) 15, 124, 140, 152
90th Regt. (Perthshire Volunteers Lt. Inf.) 15–16, 26, 106, 168, 172, 183
91st Regt. (Princess Louise's Argyllshire Highlanders) 152, 187–88
94th Regt. 152, 188, 190, 198
99th (Duke of Edinburgh's Lanarkshire) Regt. 17, 26, 116, 119, 121, 123, 124
British Mounted Infantry 18, 57, 85, 92, 123, 130, 143, 161, 167, 168
British Naval Brigade 17, 122
HMS *Active* 17
HMS *Boadicea* 152, 187
HMS *Shah* 140, 187
HMS *Tenedos* 17, 116, 123
Royal Marine Light Infantry 17, 18
British Resident in Pretoria 198
British Resident in Zululand 36, 196, 197, 199
British Royal Engineers 14, 15, 17, 152, 168, 188
British settler infantry units
City Guard, Pietermaritzburg 99
Rifle Associations 24
British settler mounted units
Baker's Horse 131, 167
Cape Mounted Rifles 124, 167
Frontier Light Horse (FLH) 16, 18, 105, 106, 130, 167, 178, 179, 191
Kaffrarian Rifles 106, 131, 167
Mounted Burghers 24
Natal Mounted Police 18, 24, 56, 85, 89, 103
Natal Mounted Volunteer Corps 18, 24, 56, 86, 103, 123
Raaff's Transvaal Rangers 130, 167
Transvaal Burgher Force 130, 167
Weatherley's Border Horse 130–1, 167
Bromhead, Lt. G. 66, 68, 73, 78, 79, 80, 81, 98, 129
Browne, Capt. E. S. 167–8, 169, 175, 180, 182
Buffalo River, *see* Mzinyathi River
Buller, Capt. E. 21

Buller, Lt.-Col. R. H. 105, 106, 107, 108, 129, 130, 131, 168, 175, 178, 179, 180, 181, 182–3, 191, 202

Bulwer, Sir H. E. G. 19–20, 24, 25–6, 28, 101, 103, 104, 120, 150, 155, 156, 186, 189, 190–1, 193, 194, 195, 196–7, 198, 199

Byrne, L. A. 81

Cambridge, HRH Field Marshal Duke of 20, 97, 102, 125, 152, 153–4, 155, 187, 188, 190, 191

Cape Colony 8, 15, 16, 42, 111, 124, 131, 140–1, 143, 150, 152, 204

Cape Frontier War, Eighth 68, 182, 190

Cape Frontier War, Ninth 3, 6, 8, 9, 13, 14, 16, 21, 28, 40, 53, 56, 57, 60, 66, 67, 69, 73, 103, 105, 106, 168, 182

Cardwell, E. 153

Carnarvon, Earl of 111, 112

Cetshwayo kaMpande, Zulu King 9, 10, 12, 16, 20, 23, 31, 32, 33–6, 40, 42–7, 48–9, 50, 54–5, 56, 63, 70, 105, 106, 108, 116, 117, 126, 127–8, 131–2, 143, 156, 161 63, 164, 165, 166, 167, 177, 178, 183, 185–7, 193, 194, 195, 196, 197, 198, 199, 200, 203–4, 205

Chard, Lt. J. R. M. 26, 67, 68, 69, 72, 76, 77, 78, 79, 80, 81, 83, 84, 90, 91, 98

Chelmsford, Lt.-Gen. Sir F. A. Thesiger, Baron 3, 6–7, 9, 11, 12, 13–16, 18–19, 20–7, 28, 31, 35, 46, 47, 53–9, 62, 64, 65, 71, 85–6, 88–92, 95, 96–7, 98, 99, 101, 102–3, 104, 105, 107, 108, 109, 114, 115, 119–20, 122 23, 124–5, 127, 129, 130–31, 134, 139–40, 141, 151, 152, 153–4, 155, 156, 162–3, 186–91, 193, 198, 202, 203, 204

Cherry, Capt. C. E. Le M. 115

Clery, Maj. C. F. 14, 21, 53, 57, 58, 59, 64, 85, 95

Clifford, Maj.-Gen. Hon. Sir H. 190, 194, 198, 199

Cochrane, Capt. W. F. D. 130, 178

Coghill, Lt. N. J. A. 98

Colonial Defensive Districts 24, 101
  No. I 25
  No. VI 25, 114
  No. VII 25, 114, 128
  Sub-District of Durban 24

Sub-District of Pietermaritzburg 24, 99

Confederation of South Africa 7–9, 11, 15, 28, 96, 112, 140, 142, 143–4, 189, 199, 200

Conference Hill 107

Connolly, Pvt. J. 81

Conservative Party 7, 17, 154, 155, 199, 200, 205

Court of Enquiry into Isandlwana 62, 96, 98

Cranbrook, Viscount 156

Crealock, Maj.-Gen. H. H. 190, 203

Crealock, Lt.-Col. J. N. 20–2, 23, 53, 59, 86, 92, 99, 102, 103, 104, 116, 191

Curling, Lt. H. 57

Dabulamanzi kaMpande, *Umntwana* 70–1, 75, 76, 83, 88, 126, 128, 133, 134, 165, 178, 185, 199

Dalton, Act. Assist.-Comm. J. 68, 76, 81, 98, 129

D'Arcy, Cmdt. C. D. 182

Dartnell, Maj. J. G. 56, 58, 86, 89

Delagoa Bay 42, 44, 45, 46

Derby 27, 106, 108, 109

Dingane kaSenzangakhona, Zulu King, 31, 108

Dinuzulu kaCetshwayo, Zulu King 200, 201

Disputed Territory 106, 113, 197, 200

Distinguished Conduct Medal (DCM) 97, 98

Doornberg 108

Dunbar, Pvt. J. 75

Dundee 95, 108, 164, 203

Dunn, J. 42, 43, 132, 162

Dunne, Assist.-Comm. W. 66, 78, 98

Durban 11, 17, 24, 46, 67, 100, 115, 123, 124, 139, 140, 152, 164, 185, 187, 188, 190, 191, 199

Durban defences 100

Durnford, Col. A. W. 26, 27, 57, 60, 62, 69, 96, 99, 115, 119

Edwards, Pvt. G. 75

Eshowe mission station 116, 118, 119, 121

Fannin, J. E. 186, 193

firearms, Zulu use of 40, 41, 42–3, 48, 64,

68, 73, 76, 118, 126, 165–6, 184, 195–6, 199.
See also, Zulu military system
Fort Amiel 129, 148
Fort Bengough 99, 114, 115
Fort Buckingham 186, 193
Fort Cherry 115, 186
Fort Clery 106, 109
Fort Eshowe 119, 120, 121, 122, 123, 125, 128, 133, 202
Fort Napier 15, 19, 100
Fort Pearson 114, 116, 119, 123, 124, 135, 186, 187, 189, 194
Fort Pine 89, 92, 100
Fort Tinta 107, 129, 202
Fort Tenedos 116, 119, 120, 121, 131, 133, 134, 135, 194, 203
Frere, Sir H. B. E. 7, 8, 9, 10–12, 13, 15, 17, 19, 25–6, 28, 31, 36, 44, 64, 96, 99, 102, 103, 104, 107, 112–13, 114, 119, 127, 140, 141, 142–4, 145, 150, 152, 153, 154, 155–6, 162, 163, 186, 188, 189–90, 191, 193, 194, 195, 199–7, 198, 200
Fugitives' Drift, *see* Sothondose's Drift
Fynn, H. F., Jnr. 199, 200
Fynney, F. B. 195, 197

Gardner, Capt. A. 58, 95, 107
Gebula, *Induna* 195
Gibson's farm 191–2
Gilbert, Lt.-Col. P. E. V. 168
Gingindlovu, battle of 203
kwaGingindlovu *ikhanda* 116, 117, 195
Glyn, Col. R. T. 26, 27, 53, 57, 58, 86, 88, 92, 95, 96, 114, 124, 128, 130, 163, 165, 185, 188
Godide kaNdlela, *Inkosi* 55, 117, 118, 121, 126, 128, 194, 197
Gossett, Maj. M. W. E. 21
Greytown 24, 67, 99, 100, 124
Greytown Laager 100–1
Griqualand West 8, 9, 41
Gun War 205

Haladu Mountain 177, 179, 180, 181, 183
Hallam Parr, Capt. H. 9, 53, 194
Hamilton-Browne, Cmdt. G. 65
Hamu kaNzibe, *Umntwana* 35, 36, 132–3, 200

Harford, Lt. H. 57, 65
Harness, Lt.-Col. A. 60, 86
Heidelberg 143, 148
Helpmekaar Heights 67, 71, 81, 82, 99, 128, 164
Helpmekaar Laager 67, 68, 72, 79, 82, 83, 84, 89, 91, 92, 95–6, 99, 107, 108, 114, 124, 128–9, 130, 139, 164, 165, 185
Henderson, Lt. A. F. 69, 72
Hennopsrivier meeting 142, 145, 148
Hicks Beach, Sir M. 10, 12, 17, 112, 142, 144, 150, 156–7, 163, 189
Hitch, Pvt. F. 73, 80, 84, 98
Hlobane, battle of 203
Hlobane Mountain 105, 107
Hlubi kaMota Molife, *Inkosi* 130, 175
Hook, Pvt. H. 98
Howard, Gnr A. 81
Huskisson, Maj. J. W. 100

Ibeka, battle of 68
Isandlwana, battle of 46, 58, 61–4, 71, 72, 77, 88, 95, 96, 97, 98, 99, 102, 103, 113, 116, 122, 123, 124, 125, 126, 127, 128, 130, 132, 139, 141, 151, 154, 162, 165, 166, 177, 181, 184, 185, 187, 201, 202, 203
Isandlwana, burial of British dead 128–9, 155, 195
Isandlwana campaign 55–60, 64–5, 66, 67–8, 69–70, 82, 83, 85–92, 115, 174

Johannes, Zulu envoy 186
Jones, Pvt. R. 98
Jones, Pvt. W. 98
Joubert, *Kmdt-Gen* P. 112 13, 141, 145, 146, 148–9, 189, 191–2

Khambula, battle of 203
Khambula Laager 202, 203
Koppie Allein, battle of 177–84, 186, 187, 195
Koppie Allein Hill 108, 168, 202
Koppie Allein Laager 108, 114, 129, 130, 131, 132, 142, 150, 162, 164, 165, 167, 168–73, 191
Kranskop 114, 115, 163
Kruger, Vice-President S. J. 111, 113, 142, 145–6, 191–2

amaKubheka 46, 106

Ladysmith 24, 67, 99
Laffnie's Drift 108
Landman's Drift 108
Leet, Maj. W. K. 168
Letsie I, Sotho Paramount 140, 141
Liberal Party 154, 155, 156, 198, 199, 200, 205
Lonsdale, Capt. R. de la T. 56, 57, 59, 91
Louis Napoleon, Prince Imperial of France 188, 204
Luneburg 105, 106, 109, 114, 129, 131, 142, 148, 149, 150 161, 162, 164, 165, 167, 202
Luneburg Laager 106
Lyons, Cpl. J. 81
Lytton, Baron 10

Mabeta Hill 168, 169, 180
Mabhudu-Tsonga 45, 46
Mabilwana kaMhlanganisa, *Induna* 195
MacGregor, Capt. H. G. 120
Mahlabathini plain 31, 32, 39, 47
Mahubulwana kaDumisela, *Induna* 163
Manqondo kaZwane, *Inkosi* 128
Manyonyoba ka Maqondo, *Inkosi* 106, 109, 129, 164
Marshall, Maj.-Gen F. 190
Martini-Henry rifle 13, 64, 69, 118, 126, 165, 184, 187, 195
Matigulu River 55, 133, 134
Matshana kaMondisa, *Inkosi* 55, 56, 128
Matshana kaSitshakuza, *Inkosi* 128
Mavumengwana kaNdlela, *Inkosi* 55, 126, 128, 165
Mbandzeni waMswati, Swazi King 27, 44 5, 46, 131, 132
Mbilini waMswati 105–6, 107, 109, 129, 164
Mehlokazulu kaSihayo 56, 62, 128
Melvill, Lt. T. 98
Mfunzi, Zulu envoy 186, 193–4
Mhlathuze River 117, 121
Michell, Lt.-Col. C. B. H. 99
Middle Border 99, 114, 115
Middle Drift 27, 114, 163, 186
Milne, Lt. A. Berkley 21, 58
Mnyamana ka Ngqengelele, *Inkosi* 33,

34–5, 54–5, 127, 165, 166, 174, 177, 179–80, 182–4, 185, 194, 197, 203
Moorosi's Revolt 140 1, 143, 205
Mpande kaSenzangakhona, Zulu King 31, 32, 33, 35, 40, 54, 55, 105, 195
amaMpondo 8, 45
Msebe kaMadaka, *Induna* 107
Mswati II, Swazi King 27
Mzimvubu River 8, 16
Mzinyathi River 25, 53, 63, 65, 66, 67, 70, 71, 72, 85, 88, 89, 96, 98, 108, 114, 128, 162, 165

Natal Border Agent 25, 186, 193, 195
Natal, Colony of 8, 9, 15, 16, 17, 19, 20, 21, 23, 24, 25, 26, 36, 42, 44, 45, 56, 65, 66, 70, 71, 82, 85, 88–9, 91, 92, 96, 100, 101–2, 107, 110, 114, 115, 122, 124, 126, 127, 128, 129, 132, 143, 148, 149, 150, 151, 152, 155, 186, 189, 194, 195,196, 198, 200, 202, 206
Ncenceni Mountain 174, 175, 178, 183
Ncome, battle of 108, 175, 178, 182
Ncome River 27, 89, 106, 107, 108, 114, 129, 168, 169, 175, 178, 179, 180, 181, 183
Ndabuko kaMpande, *Umntwana* 165, 166, 185
oNdini *ikhanda* 23, 31, 32–3, 36, 42, 47, 54, 116, 117, 121, 126, 132, 133, 162, 163, 164, 165, 166, 175, 187, 193, 198, 199, 203, 204
Ndondakusuka, battle of 40
Newcastle 24, 106, 129, 148, 149, 150, 161, 164, 167, 188, 191
Newdigate, Maj.-Gen. E. 190, 203
New Republic 205–6
Nhlazatshe Mountain 165, 174
Nkisimana, Zulu envoy 186, 193 4
Norris-Newman, C. 64, 99
Northern Border War 8
Nquthu Heights 165
Ntshingwayo kaMahole, *Inkosi* 54–5, 126, 165, 174, 177–8, 181, 183, 185, 199
kwaNtumjambili mission 163
Nyezane, battle of 117–18, 120 1, 124, 125, 126, 127, 194, 202
Nyezane River 116, 117, 118, 133, 134
Nyoni Hills 54, 56, 62
Nyoni River 133, 134